Apocalypse

Now-ish

Mellisa Amelia

Published by

**MELROSE
BOOKS**

An Imprint of Melrose Press Limited
St Thomas Place, Ely
Cambridgeshire
CB7 4GG, UK
www.melrosebooks.com

FIRST EDITION

Copyright © Mellisa Amelia 2011

The Author asserts her moral right to
be identified as the author of this work

Cover designed by Jeremy Kay

ISBN 978 1 907732 43 0

Printed and bound in Great Britain by:
CLE Digital Solutions. St Ives, Cambridgeshire

FSC
www.fsc.org
MIX
From responsible
sources
FSC® C019549

In memory of my Gran, Dorothy Black. A woman I could only ever aspire to be. A woman who was so much more than the quoted knitting skills.

Preface

Once upon a time in a land far, far away and a time long forgotten...
No. Please. I'm a writer, that line just never worked and this is a long
way from the world of fairy tales. Hm, once upon a time, right here,
in a time denied and dismissed, apparently, monsters walked with
humans. The Egyptians painted them in gold lacquer on dusty walls,
the Chinese built charms to repel the glistening serpents that flew
through the air, and the Greeks desperately scribbled them in the
equivalent of best-sellers of the eighth century.

Anyone see a pattern? People are stubborn. We wrote, we painted,
so that the next generation and then the generation after that couldn't
forget. And we didn't, we just denied them. Called the people who
invented pulleys and paint ignorant because that's what kids do; we
don't actually respect our elders. We placed them in myth and story;
we certainly didn't place them in Tesco. We, I, never thought there'd
be monsters on the six o'clock news; I never thought I'd be able to
give a name to a monster, or laugh with a monster, or cry with one,
kiss one or die by one.

I thought the biggest things I'd ever have to worry about would
be cigarettes prematurely ageing me (though on the brighter side
to Armageddon, anti-ageing products will hopefully have hit a
record bottom). I was wrong: we all were. We separated science from

religion, we got caught up in our own little lives speeding by so fast that every step and second was taken for granted. I really wish I had something a bit more enlightening to say, some amazing revelation that would bring us back to our feet, bring us back our fight. We expected a meteorite or massive tornadoes. Frankly we weren't the least prepared for a four-headed dog. And now we're all going to pay for studying chemistry at school rather than Dr Who re-runs and Harry Potter's potions classes.

And at this very moment, watching the world fall apart, I'd really give a lot for one... last... freaking... fag.

Chapter One

I could still see my little, woolly-gloved hand stretched out in front of me, but in a flicker, as instant as a light switch, the rows of cereal on the supermarket shelves blinked away, leaving only dead space and dull light. I withdrew my hand quickly, stumbling back in the new, dank room, the bright yellow lights and muggy warmness of Sainsbury gone too quickly to process, and replaced with a white-grey light and the icy, winter-day wind.

"Where am I? Mrs Corrie?" My shout was high-pitched, young and childlike and so unfamiliar it scared me more than how the world around me had just disappeared and been replaced empty and cold. I could feel my heart trembling, the dull thud of it hitting my ribs, speeding up and filling my ears. I was suddenly very alone, that kind of alone where you could literally HEAR the silence, my chattering teeth, the wind pushing fallen leaves and debris across the flagstone floor...

The kitchen where I now stood, shocked and trembling, looked lost, abandoned... like me. French doors leading outside to the courtyard had blown open, lodging in place by mud and rain and flooding the room with enough sludge and dirt that outside and inside weren't very distinguishable any more. There was something familiar about this place. I swallowed, running my fingertips across the splintered, wooden work-tops as if I could still smell the sage and rosemary, as if they were fresh and hadn't dried, crumbled and scattered, as if I still expected to find a bowl of pastry mix. There wasn't

1

anything sweet left here; everything was left grey and bitter.

I hit the counter as I backed up, a shockingly frigid wind carrying leaves and wet specks of snow howling through the open door and lashing them against my face. I put my arms up to protect myself, eyes locked onto something lying on the snow-covered ground. Without thinking, I started forward, dragging my feet as I walked against the wind to get to the black and silver mass lying twitching, shaking – with what I couldn't tell – in a pool of water within the snow.

The closer I got, the warmer the fierce wind became, the crisp new snow slushy, heat radiating like fire from where the wolf lay, its head thrown back, howling so softly the sound was lost in the wind. Sparks glistened in the air above it, tiny blue flames dancing and falling to the ground, sizzling the snow where they landed and sending streams of steam upwards. I stopped dead. Eyes wide and every muscle tense. The wolf's body lurched, its bristly, black-furred chest heaved upwards unnaturally, sounds like ripping fabric filling the air as lumps of fur fell away. The skin underneath split, exposing a new, much paler layer streaked with blood and fluid. Something else was breaking through from inside the animal's body.

I gasped, ducking closer to the ground on all fours, transfixed. Paralysed with horror. As the wolf's body ripped away in front of my eyes, a full-grown, naked man, too large to have fitted inside the poor creature in the first place, flopped moaning in the snow where the wolf had lain moments ago. Lines of blood and strips of torn flesh rolled off his shoulders as he pulled himself up onto all fours, his head rising slowly, gaze locking with my own. Those eyes.

Is my head damp? I blinked, pushing myself off the icy window pane and running one sleeve-covered hand over my now slightly sticky forehead. A quick glance around the nearly empty coach told me by the way the few passengers left kept shooting me bewildered side glances. I may have moaned slightly in that little doze. You see, the "do-we-ask-or-go-direct-and-get-the-straitjacket?" looks are why I have stringently trained myself not to fall asleep on planes... Now to turn my attention to buses.

I shot a few courteous smiles back, trying not to roll my eyes, and straightened myself in the threadbare coach seat. I didn't try to remember the dream; in fact I'd also had practice trying to erase them completely from my mind. It was just a shame the post-mental-breakdown shudders weren't under my conscious control. A sharp glance at the quickly darkening streets outside told me I'd either missed or was close to my stop. Either way, very soon I was going to have to get my very numb arse out of this seat. My name's Khyle, Khyle Exeter, and yes, that's a name. You try going through life called Kahlillyne and we'll see how many beatings you take before you change it. I'm nineteen, a foster child, and as of today I'm officially a resident of the UK's equivalent of the Bronx – if the Bronx were in Oxfordshire, and if Peckham didn't already hold that particular position... And moving swiftly on. Blackleigh was an almost-charming, rather run down town lost somewhere in the Cotswolds between Swindon and Oxford. In fact, you could meld those two together, throw in some half decent graffiti, *et voilà*, Blackleigh.

The coach started to brake as I crouched over to grab my battered green suede suitcase (hand-me-down; few people under middle age actually own green suede as far as I'm willing to believe). It had grown dark enough outside that the lights illuminated the inside of the bus, turning the alley windows to mirrors; I caught a glimpse of myself, sighed and started toward the doors.

Do you know what it's like to have the personality of a vapid narcissist, the face of a china doll, the ironing board chest of an eight-year-old boy, and the thighs of a sumo wrestler? Well, I can sum it up: Ouch! I'm five foot six, petite, kind of plump or round where

3

no woman wants to be, and utterly padding-deprived in the places where you're not meant to be (my chest is so flat you can count the ribs). My foster mother was the one who coined my face as being that of a china doll, big hazelnut shell-shaped eyes, small plump pout, and pale freckle-dusted skin.

A very small percentage of women truly love the way they look, but to feel your appearance is almost totally disrespectful to your character is almost weirdly painful. People look at me expecting sweet, meek and mild, and get an acid-tongued cynic instead. If I could have chosen, I would have been as tall as any man, all hard edges and high cheekbones, and painfully serious. Of course, the twenty-first century has plastic surgery so what am I complaining about? Publish a few articles, maybe a couple of books, win the lottery, and I may just be able to indulge my vanity. There are two aspects I can safely say I do like about myself: wavy mousy-brown hair that feels tousled and perpetually messy a few inches below my shoulders, and mahogany-brown eyes. No blonde, no red, no auburn, no highlights; no blue eyes, no hazel eyes, no green eyes. Brown is honest, it's earth, down-to-earth, and it's strong, just like me.

I had to practically throw my luggage out onto the street. I didn't pack light, and yet when I did pack, I'd been surprised by how much I actually did have. I know to most that would sound a bit obnoxious, but being a foster child for as long as I could remember, I'd learnt to keep things to the minimum: no decorating bedroom walls, no photos, just clothes, utensils and, in my case, a spare Red Bull just in case. After three years of barely spending more than a month with the same *happy* family, I'd been sent to live with the Corries, with about seven others, and I'd found a home, sort of. It appeared with that home I'd also accumulated enough to make my luggage very heavy: dog-eared books, endless pairs of socks, actual make-up, hair things...

The bedroom walls stayed defensively bare though.

Outside in the typical British drizzle stood the most prized possession I'd ever accumulated from any foster home, towering over the rest of the world and slightly damp: Zean "no-second-name" as he always told me. Whether that was a denial of any past he might remember I didn't know, but either way my best friend had never given me or anyone else, as far as I knew, any connection to a heritage. What on earth he would put on any potential CV was an argument I'd lost countless times. I'd met Zean when I moved to the Corries when I was nine; he was fourteen and one of the seven. As a nine-year-old who wouldn't talk to a soul for a smile, a cookie or a good hiding, he'd seen a challenge, and before anyone knew it, we were sneaking out to the park and seeing who could swing the highest. Then a little later on we were sneaking beer bottles and packs of fags down to the same park, and laughing about bizarrely unfunny things that at the time seemed to crack us up. He'd been my first and last kiss, and as far as I was emotionally concerned my only family.

He waved at me, grabbing my bag out of the gutter before it had time to soak through. "Blimin' 'ell, girl, what you pack... the fridge?" he grunted, peeking out from his slightly greasy mane of sand-and-straw hair. To me Zean was Zean, but to other girls, for a guy who wasn't particularly good-looking, he seemed to have a weird charm. He was almost six foot five, and usually had a couple of bruises hidden at his hairline to prove it; lean, but broad enough that most of his clothes gripped his shoulders and then hung from them like a coat hanger. I bought him a shaver for his seventeenth birthday; he gave it back six months later, suggesting I learn to shave my legs, and now walked around with at least a good half inch of beard, and he now had a stud speared through his eyebrow. The best I could put it down to was that he had a knack for choosing girls with poor eyesight.

"Oh, hello, I'm brilliant, the journey was glorious, not sticky, smelly, and you see that indentation on my forehead from sleeping on one too many windows? No idea where that came from. How are you? And yes, the fridge and the TV; I left them a few bucks on the dining table as compensation," I returned, giving him my best fake-perky smile.

He scoffed, throwing an arm around me in a bear hug.

"Well, the indentation suits you. I'm okay, I guess. Glad you got off at the right stop for a change. You ready?" He pointed down the street and started dragging my suitcase down the paving.

I raised an eyebrow. "We're walking? It's raining, what happened to your car?" I sighed, pulling my parka closer around my shoulders.

He rolled his eyes. "It's barely five minutes. Any idea how much petrol that short a drive would take up? Hardly any. That hardly any would cost about seventeen point six three one nine p, seventeen point six three one nine p that could pay for one more Sainsbury's own Red Bull in the fridge, but then they've got an offer on all their own-brand products boosting that net total up roughly to one Red Bull and one sixth another Re—"

I cut him dead.

"I get it, thanks. I get wet, hypothermic; have to stick my clothes on the radiator. Can we pick up the pace, please? My sneakers are starting to sponge."

Zean is a mathematical genius who tries not to be, a talent our foster father had been delighted to invest into the stock market, and which had allowed an extension to be built. He'd sat his A-level maths at eight, apparently, and, I guessed, for that reason never seemed to be short of cash. Imaginably the constant bombardment of incomprehensible numbers and equations gets pretty odd so you learn not to bring up anything that could involve a number in front of him if you want to spare half an hour. That lump sum was the reason why, when he turned twenty, he'd packed his bag and left to come to his house here in Blackleigh, and for six years I'd been confined to seeing him only through a webcam or when I could rustle up the cash to get down here. He never once came back to the Corries; 'never look back'S seemed to be his unsaid motto for life. Now I was nineteen, I wanted a life, my life, and he'd offered up an affordable room in his place. How could I say no to the only family I'd ever had? Why would I want to? Uni? Well, Oxford and Cambridge took one look at my Bs, Cs and one A and burst out cackling; Warwick and York probably did the same but with a hint less sarcasm. Bristol took pity and offered me a place with an interview, but it was pointless anyway: no money, or at least not enough, rather cut out the possibility full stop, and as much as I did in fact love learning, the idea of any potential grandchildren paying off my student loans was less appealing.

I could feel Zean's eyes on me. "What? Oh, I'm sorry, I didn't mean to snap. Look see–" I held up one unfortunate-looking Nike, "they've already gone to sneaker heaven, it's fine."

From what I could make out behind the beard, he smiled. "Nah, not your bitchiness. Just wondering whether you're okay. You look different, tired. It's a big step I'd get if you wanted to, eh, lean… on a… shoulder."

Given that he was trying to be sweet, I repressed any laughter. He was awful at anything resembling tenderness, and it looked a lot like someone was tightening a chastity belt on him. "It's a three-and-a-half-hour journey, it's eight-thirty, and I'm running on a bagel and a diet Coke. Yeah, I'm tired, I'm not worried. Really it's you who should be worried: you're gonna have to learn all over again how to live with me," I laughed.

The man of many words shrugged. "Mmm, heaven, speaking of food and the preceding cost of buying food" – aye, here we go – "you got a job."

Hmm, not the route I thought we were gonna take. My heart suddenly leapt with hope. "The local rag? They liked what I sent them? You heard back from them?"

He looked away; was he cringing? I felt my heart fall to play with my kidneys. "Er, yeah, they were here," he said.

I glanced away for a second feeling my heart go to play a little further down with Mr Intestine. We had walked about a block away from the edge-of-town bus stop, and now were standing at the end of a row of interlocked, greying, exposed-brick houses. Fine. These houses had a good dose of colourful graffiti, very little charm or front lawns (some had boarded windows), but they weren't turquoise, unlike the corner house I was now standing in front of, gaping; and Zean was now inserting a key into the flaky pink-painted front door. For almost a full second I actually forgot about my potential loss in the job department.

"Did I miss something? Are you auditioning for the next male *Legally Blonde*?" I asked as he pushed the door open and lugged my bag into a dark front hall.

He glanced over his shoulder. "Huh?"

I'd forgotten how good with words men are. "The colour!" I didn't mean to screech that.

He stuck his head out of the front door by which I was still standing and gaping up at this tiny rainbow-coloured wreck. "Oh right. No, I haven't had time to redecorate. Besides, the whole front's about twenty-five squared, assuming three coats and buying a five litre—"

I sighed. "Oh, shut up, I get it. What were you saying about a job? And trying to avoid saying about the pieces I sent to the *Blackleigh Weekly*?" I muttered, pushing past him.

Inside was less painful, though I guessed that the occasional patch of exposed brick wasn't a fashion statement. The front door, with its many sliding bolts and locks, opened up into a narrow hallway, white plus brick wall, washed-out wooden floors, and not an ounce of anything resembling decorating. There was a set of painted white stairs straight ahead, a lounge to my left, complete with baby-blue walls, a couple of low couches with moth-eaten throw rugs arranged snugly around a stained coffee table with the remnants of beer bottles and salted pretzels spread over it. Tucked into the room's corners were about a dozen book shelves, a chipped flowery-tiled fireplace, and I despair at how a TV could possibly look battered, especially in a boy's place. To my right was an orange bead curtain which, I could just make out, had a tiny kitchen diner crammed behind it.

I smiled. I already loved it. Zean pushed past, flicking on a couple of lights, kicking the door closed behind him, and through the beaded curtain. I left my suitcase in the hall looking strangely like it belonged. There was, in fact, a kitchen big enough for some wooden counters; also a fridge, green stove, an oak table, two chairs, and red and green tiling on the wall. Note to self: to protect self-respect, redecorate!

I lowered myself into a chair. "Zean, come on. I already know the answer. They didn't go for my stuff, did they?"

Zean was lighting the stove in an attempt at coffee.

"I haven't heard anything," he said, "but you know that doesn't mean anything. All you need is a story they want, and before you know it you'll be published in *The Times*, with your own column dealing with some load of something having nothing to do with finance because your maths sucks." In Zean's world that may have been an attempt to encourage me. "Until then, rather than writing them, you can spend your time cleaning and sorting them. You've got a job at a bookstore in town." He placed a cup of tea (what is it with us English and tea?) – black, one sugar – down on the already ringed table top. Note two: coasters are good.

I nodded, digesting.

"Mm, hm! What kind of bookstore and why are you saying I've got a job? I know nothing about this; you really had so little faith in me, and so much fear for your fridge, that you went searching for a job for me?"

Zean could tell a tantrum might just be brewing and gave me his best matter-of-fact face.

"It's actually a pretty cool place; it's a physics and philosophy place, and the guy who runs it is a pretty sought-after professor, Professor Jackson." I shrugged. "Well, he does lectures there, at the Town Hall, and even Oxford and stuff. He owes me a few favours; heard you were coming into town; asked whether you'd like to make some cash, okay? I have every faith in my next li'l J.K. Rowling; just not your ability to fill the fridge."

We both laughed at that. Zean was right; a few spare pennies would help at the moment and my dreams of being a journalist could wait; at least until, as he put it, I found a story they were dying for, and could bribe my way to a pay check.

* * *

Two cheesy stuffed-crust-and-sausage pizzas and half a bottle of vodka later, and about three hours of talking about absolutely nothing; a few relative snippets about Zean's working at an IT place near Oxford decoding and recoding software; and having to leave the shower running for three minutes before stepping in unless I wanted to turn blue in five seconds flat; and Zean had gone down to the pub to meet up with some girl I wasn't allowed to know the name of. I'd resigned from going down for three reasons: I didn't need to see Zean's bad flirting techniques at eleven thirty at night; my bag wouldn't get upstairs to my bedroom on its own; and given the amount of vodka in my system at that moment, I feared neither would I.

After about five minutes standing beside my suitcase, and looking from the now very steep-looking stairs to my green suede monster, I gave up dreaming and plodded into the living room, almost falling down onto the padded-yet-deflated plaid sofa. I placed one cool palm to my forehead. People weren't supposed to drink these days, we weren't supposed to smoke, or eat stuffed cheese pizzas. At least, that's what we were told, and we lay back and took it. The United Kingdom, a tiny country which gave birth to the English language, conquered the Germans, set discussing the weather as the axis around which small talk revolved, had learnt to roll over and play robot. That's why I wanted to become a journalist: I wanted to throw out a few opinions to turn the accepted ones into turmoil. I turned over on my side looking at the blank TV screen opposite me. What I would give to bring Britain off its knees.

I picked myself up, slightly perching on the side of the couch, and reached for almost-yesterday's newspaper which was lying open at the finance section on the coffee table. I'd lifted it barely three inches when a shock of static discharge leapt from the black and white type to my finger. I let out a yelp and let it fall to the floor with a slight flump. Before I could reach down for it, the once-dim room burst into a flickering light. I glanced up. The TV was on, fuzzed black and white lines running across the screen.

I frowned, glancing around for the remote. A screeching sound suddenly filled the room. "What the hell?" I whispered, clapping my hands to my ears and looking frantically around the table. "Help!"

My head shot up, and I felt my heart kick into terror mode. The TV screen was distorting: a face, a woman's face; white static still running across the screen, as if she were on the other side and the screen was a sheet of fabric; as if she were gasping desperately for breath behind it. She was staring at me. Right at me. I could feel her eyes even though they were empty spaces of black and white. Her screaming filling the room, or was that mine? I stumbled, the back of my leg hitting the couch arm, making me tip off balance, my head colliding with the edge of the coffee table.

For a second I thought the blow had knocked me out as everything faded back to darkness, with only the sound of the occasional car gliding past outside; but, of course, it was unlikely my head would feel like someone had axed it if I was out cold. I'd never been so scared. I couldn't move, but sitting curled up on the floor I honestly didn't believe I'd ever move again. I didn't want to, for fear that I was walking around in one of my nightmares where anything could happen; David Hasselhoff could attack me any second! It was probably hysteria, but at that thought I actually let out a shaky laugh, and managed to make myself move as far as the light switch.

The room looked the same, except that the coffee table had been pushed out a few inches from where I'd fallen over. The remote was lying on the couch, peeking out at me under one of the throw rugs that in the hysteria had slid to the floor. Tentatively I picked it up, turning to face the TV and pressing the 'on' button. The 12 p.m. news flicked up; some very well-groomed man talking about yet more financial cuts in coming Bills. I swallowed so hard, I heard the muscles in my throat contort. Channel Two, global warming documentary; Channel Three, bad free porn. I flicked the 'off' button, slumping back down onto the couch, my heart still throbbing. Then something caught my eye. A black and white face was staring at me again. I leant down to pick up the newspaper, which had fallen open to display a snapshot of a young girl about my age – maybe a year or two younger – with the words **Missing: Delia Bronzebard** headlining her in bold print. I glanced at the date: September 14th It was almost a month old. I spared half a second to despair at Zean's housekeeping.

* * *

Delia Bronzebard, age 17, daughter of James and Eliza Bronzebard from Oxfordshire, has now been missing for three weeks at the date on which this was published. Delia was last reported seen returning from Reading town centre with friend Catharine Sollowmine at nine o'clock, September 1st 2012. Catharine and Delia were driving a red Ford Focus which was found abandoned between Reading and Swindon. Sadly, according to recent police reports, Catharine's body has been found a mile from the site at which the car was discovered, maimed, badly beaten and with severe blood loss.

Police are yet to comment on any potential suspects and the search for Delia is ongoing. James and Eliza Bronzebard made a plea on national news on September the 6th begging for anyone with any news of where their daughter may be or any potential sightings. Her parents describe her as a sweet, artistic and, perhaps to her now disadvantage, naive girl. There is potential speculation within our own sources that this may be in connection with other equally brutal killings spanning the last ten years, though police have yet to confirm. If you have any information on Delia's whereabouts, please call…

* * *

What's ironic was that the scariest thing about the whole of that story was how badly written it was. I mean, seriously, it's like reporters have a template for the same kind of stories and just edit in the right names. A computer could incite more passion and sympathy than that. And they had yet to return the pieces I sent them. Bad taste.

My eyes wandered back up to Delia's photo. She looked just like any other seventeen-year-old, a bit hippy-ish maybe. She had quite a square jaw, doughy eyes, shoulder-length hair pulled back into several intertwined braids. I'd place money that if the photo was more than a head shot, at least one thing she was wearing when this was taken was either tie-dyed or eco-friendly. My stomach started to churn. Delia was genuinely smiling but that awful screaming was still running through my mind. She'd asked me to help her… I let the newspaper slide back to the floor, and buried my head in my hands, trying to neither shake nor cry because in my opinion both of those things would be demeaning. There was really only one option: I was going mad. Just like Mum.

Chapter Two

Mocha, mocha Chocó, mocha Chocó with a shot, latte, vanilla latte, skinny latte, skinny vanilla latte… jeez, you need a translation guide to order a coffee these days. Seriously, people; coffee, water, dilute – it really is that simple. This small local coffee shop was about three stores down from Starbucks, explaining why their prices were practically half that of anywhere else. Cuppa barely seemed larger than Zean's living room, and yet they'd managed to pack about a dozen knobbly round table and chairs, oversized worn brown leather sofas and bizarre abstracts of things pretending to be coffee cups hung on soft beige walls. There was also a coffee and deli counter oozing the smells of just-baked seed buns, butterscotch icing, almond sugar croissants flaking in tissue paper nests, ham, cheese, cooking bacon, wholewheat buns, and a few smells I couldn't even place. At the moment I was standing in the line, staring up at today's specials written in multi-coloured chalks on three imposing blackboards behind the counter, trying to decipher the twenty-first century equivalent of black coffee.

It was 8.30. Despite a night of *The Ring*-esque dreams, I'd actually slept pretty well (vodka), and woken up slumped on the couch with a yellow sticky label slicked onto my forehead reading: *Sleeping beauty, gone to work. Unless you want to get fired before you start, good idea if you do too. Directions on fridge, that's all that's on or in fridge, go to supermarket, you're cooking tonight, regretting be my roomy yet? Luck Z.* After stumbling to the fridge I'd found that I was meant to start at nine, and had just enough time to change, brush my teeth and hair, and curse Zean like mad. The place I was looking for was called GUTs and Co. (I'm not even going to bother questioning it), and was actually found in the upper crust area of Blackleigh town central, so about a twenty-minute run from Zean's as I recently discovered.

The blonde behind the counter was tapping her tacky French manicure on the counter, her eyes half-lidded and resting lazily on me. "Erm, sorry, yeah, can I have a, eh, large Americano and a smoked salmon and cream cheese roll, please?" I asked. The girl pushed lazily away from the counter. You'd think nowadays people would be happy to have ANY job. I started to fish in my massive red and black tartan shoulder bag for my purse.

"I hope you have an umbrella in there, too."

I glanced up in the direction of the soft voice, and felt the wind being knocked from me. I try not to be a superficial person. I fail, but I do try very hard, and at that particular moment I suddenly felt myself physically deflate. A six-foot goddess was smiling absently at me from beside the counter. If Morticia from the Addams family had worn a soft pastel summer dress and had been about three times as beautiful, she'd be this woman… girl? The more I looked at her, the younger she looked; in fact, I was so busy staring at her silvery-white skin and waist-length wispy black-blue hair that I entirely missed what she said.

"Huh?" was the best I could muster as I absently spilled a few pounds onto the counter and let the blonde deal with them. She smiled almost too warmly at me, her pale pink lips stretching wide over marble-like cheekbones to encompass it, and nodded slightly to something behind me. I glanced around. There was a slick flat screen snugly placed in the corner. A red headline was gliding across the screen with extreme weather warnings for all of England: heavy storms, thunder and lightning expected. My glance darted over to the windows. It was so cold and dreary outside that the inside of the coffee store windows seemed to have steamed up, and a steady misty rain had already begun to fall.

I groaned, collecting my coffee and roll and looking around for sugar. The girl pointed to a counter next to her where sachets of sweeteners, brown and white sugar, spoons, salt and pepper were laid out. "Thanks," I replied, pouring sweetener into my coffee, "and no, no umbrella. Left in a rush this morning. Weird for late October, huh? England just can't wait to return to its miserable self." I was starting to fear that if my thighs grew any larger, they'd start to chafe when I walked.

The girl laughed airily.

"Tut-tut! You shouldn't blame your mother country. Besides, it's everywhere. Heavy storms all over the world. It's making headline news: weather, the Englishman's favourite topic. I wonder whether we've always been this boring."

I laughed, forgetting for a moment how jealous of this girl I was.

"I know, right. My name's Khyle."

She looked away for a second, pinning something to a cork board in front of her. "Ka (Cu)-Hi-Yl? Pretty. Short for something? You're new here, right? I'm fairly sure I've identified most of the cute girls around here so I'd know you for sure. I'm Loraline; it's nice to meet you."

I vaguely registered what she'd said, and that it wasn't common practice to say that one had "identified all the cute girls in the local area" when that one was female, but my eyes had been caught by two, recently familiar, words on the flyer she'd pinned. Eliza Bronzebard. I quickly scanned it, my pulse already quickening; from fear or panic I couldn't tell. It was a flyer for a local fair a week away organized by the Fairstar *Coven*. Oooookay, Blair Witch project? The fair came complete with apple bobbing, toss the coconut, a baking fund-raiser by the local primary, face-painting, Tarot and fortune-telling by *Eliza Bronzebard,* and for those who wished to stay to midnight, a *coven circle.*

Okay, so my impression of Delia being a hippy extended to her mother, but, well, witches?

Loraline glanced at the flyer. "We raise funds for our local charities, plus it helps community spirit and everything. You should come along and help out; give you a chance to meet everybody. Do you practise?"

I absently took a bite of my roll, trying to avoid eye contact, not entirely sure WHAT to think. "I didn't say I was new here. Practise what?" I said between chews. I didn't have to look at her to see she was a little startled

"You don't have to; I know you are and, you know… the Craft?"

"Mmm, yep, I have a flying vacuum and all."

To my surprise she actually laughed. "Well, absolutely, I'd much rather fly on one than use one," she said, handing me a flyer and turning to go.

I couldn't help myself. Normal people put psychotic episodes out of their mind; they don't further encourage them. I'm abnormal. "Excuse me, that… that, eh, lady doing the Tarot, Eliza Bronzebard? Is that… that girl Delia's Mum?"

She hesitated, mental clockwork clearly ticking away in moments. Her eyes flittered up past my shoulder for a split second.

"It's ten to nine."

I frowned, bewildered. "W-what?" I stuttered, glancing over my shoulder and sloshing coffee over the brim of my cup onto my fingers. "Shyat," I muttered as my fingers started to sting. I then glanced up to the clock over my shoulder: 8.50. "shyat hoot," I muttered again, slightly more loudly. When I looked back I wasn't very surprised to see that the girl had gone, but I was worried enough that my stomach knotted that bit more as I rushed out of the door and into the drizzle. I walked briskly, glancing at street names whilst trying to scoff down a roll and a lukewarm coffee. Kings Street. Kings Street. Was I going steadily loopy? How the hell did she know I needed to be somewhere at nine o'clock? Lucky guess? I mean, it's obviously the most universally common time to start work, but witches? I don't think so. Just because you look like you belong in the Addams family... Hold on! Pastel summer dress? No coat? It's freaking freezing out here. I'm wearing three jumpers.

I groaned, throwing the rest of my sandwich and coffee down my throat just as I came across a sign nailed to the side of one red brick building. King Street.

King Street was long and wide enough for two cars to have passed side by side. It seemed rather devoid of shops with the exception of one for Macmillan Cancer Support and what looked like an entrance to the main shopping centre. GUTs and Co. was the first shop down and probably the least distinctive; a worn, old-fashioned, and rather formal black and gold sign bearing the name almost fading into the red brick wall it hung from. Two side-by-side panelled windows looked into a dark and cluttered store filled floor to ceiling with shelves of books. I discreetly left my coffee cup on the window sill and went inside.

A bell clattered as I entered the total silence. It smelled musky, but I'd been wrong. From the outside, the shop had looked puny: it was actually rather large, with an iron ladder leading to a makeshift second storey. It was just very, very overstocked. I had to resist the urge to call out "hello". Frankly, the last twenty-four hours had been freaky enough without Freddie Krueger jumping out at me and putting an end to my already frayed nerves. There was a sudden crashing as books fell to the floor from a nearby step-ladder. I had to reach for the cash counter, thinking I might faint as I reached breaking point, and then a pair of thick wire-rimmed glasses and magnified blue eyes peeked out from the mess.

"Ah, you startled me, obviously," he said in such a crisp BBC English accent that I had a sudden flashback to a 30s radio programme that I'd had to study endlessly for English Lang. last year. I gave who I guessed was Professor Jackson a shaky grin, and walked over to help collect the fallen books.

"No, no, please don't. May I help you with anything? If you're here for the lecture, it's not until ten."

I handed over a copy of Einstein's *Theory of Special and General Relativity*.

"Erm, no, I'm not. My name's Khyle Exeter. My friend Zean said you offered me a job here… " doing something as yet unspecified.

Recognition fluttered behind those half-moon lenses. "Ah, yes, of course. Wonderful, you're early. In that case, carry on." He sprang to his feet, leaving me to pick up the rest of the books.

Beggars can't be choosers. I piled the books onto the step-ladder, and glanced round to give my new employer a quick once-over, just to check he wasn't going to sprout a horn and announce himself the Devil incarnate. With my luck lately… He looked early-mid sixties, though he still had a complete head of thick, stark white, perfectly slicked and parted hair, and still reached a good height. Deep ridges had dug around his eyes and forehead, and probably around his mouth too, though a tamed and groomed grey moustache stopped any confirmation. He reminded me of an old oak, dressed in an informal tweed suit, tall and sturdy but weathered with age. When he smiled at me, though, I felt a few knots in my stomach untwist.

"I'm glad you found your way here alright. If I know Zean, he was probably as accurate with his directions as a satellite navigation system. Do you know if he'll be dropping by later? There are a few things I could do with discussing with him?"

I shook my head. "Sorry, I haven't seen him yet today, but he left instructions for dinner so I'm guessing he's not expecting to see me until then," I offered.

"Very well, shall we get started?" he said.

I smiled, but was at a loss. "Absolutely. Get started with what?" Even to me that sounded intellectually despairing.

He obviously suppressed a smirk. "Do you know much about physics, Khyle?"

I blinked. "I have an A-level in it."

At that he seemed a little too delighted, and this time the knots came back for a totally different reason. "Well then, fresh blood for enlightenment. If you took an A-level in physics, I'm guessing you know your alphabet." He didn't wait for an answer. "Indexing, looking after the shop while I'm not here, handling the phone, maybe after a while helping out when I do a presentation in the back... You're my assistant. It's incredibly simple: you assist."

I giggled. "Check, check. I'll assist away."

★　★　★

Quantum Phenomena And The Unexplained Made Explainable; was that Q or P, was there a P and three quarters? I sighed, placing it on the bottom shelf of the Ps. GUTs was actually a pretty cool place, all dark corners and display cabinets filled with atomic structure models through the centuries, but indexing was tiresome, and after four hours and getting nowhere I was starting to think a rule should be made against men owning either houses or shops due to the states they ended up in.

"Professor? May I ask what GUTs actually means?" I called over the banister. I was on the second floor, and the professor had been out of his seminar for about an hour. He didn't even look up from the book he was looking through.

"If you ever become a student of mine, professor is fine. Until that day, Jackson, please, Khyle. And of course you may. GUTs: Grand Unified Theories. I and many others like me search for a way to link quantum and mechanical physics. Put it this way: if Newton and Einstein could conceive, a GUT would be the result. What makes my opinions and research different is that I seek to unite science with religion, or aspects of religion, believing that the two are not intertwined. Do you understand?"

I found myself staring a little dreamily out of one of the small oval windows that were up on this storey, watching as rain streamed down them like a kid stuck in a carwash.

"So you search for God in science? Or do you search for God with science? I mean, like, are you trying to find a new theory of God in physics or whatever, or are you using science to back up religion, and I mean, if you are, which religion exactly are you trying to prove or disprove?" I stopped rambling to get an answer, but there was a small silence until I finally pulled my attention away from the window to glance over the railings. Jackson was looking up at me almost bewildered.

"Did you take theology?"

"No, I just think way too much," I replied, returning to the indexing. I heard him laugh from downstairs.

"In that case, both, a convergence of the two. I'll give you one of my papers to read; you may find it fairly interesting. Oh, and incidentally I said aspects of religion. All religion has a few underlining truths, truths that hold steady within science, you know."

Right; so far, deadly TVs, missing women, witches and Newton/God Messiah. Progress: flipping awful. I wasn't willing to go any further with this today.

"Cool name by the way, GUTs," I called down, instead, as I inspected *The Atom of Noetics* (A or N?).

"Isn't it? I'm afraid I can't be given credit for it, though. You'll find out that, of all the sciences, physicists have the greatest sense of humour. No one could try and understand the world and be too serious about it; one would go mad. Khyle, if you would excuse me a moment, I'm just going to go and get some lunch. May I get you something?"

Wouldn't getting lunch be my job? "Eh, okay, anything's great, go wild, no quiche."

I heard his throaty laugh as the bell rang and the shop fell into silence.

Or rather fell into Donny Osmond's *I'll Never Fall In Love Again*. I'd been humming it to myself, which was weird; not because, hello, more of a Marina and The Diamonds girl, but because I didn't actually know the song, and I wasn't humming any more. It had been in the background all afternoon. Professor Jackson listened to 70s American chick-trash. I'd let it rest at that, except now that Jackson had gone, I had the strangest prickling at the nape of my neck, like being watched, eyes burning there.

I very gently placed the thin modern copy of *Astronomy and Modern Physics* down onto the floorboards. If I turned around and found a werewolf or banshee behind me, I was packing my bag tonight and investing in the best psychiatrist my savings would get me. I turned, but rather than seeing a drooling, four-eyed creature of the beyond, sitting about eight foot away, peeking out from behind a bookcase, was an angel, an angel about four foot high and wearing frayed pink jeans. I mean, of course, she wasn't an angel; she just had that quality that most little girls have that make them look like cherubs, plump rosy cheeks and fine blonde hair curled so tightly it twisted into a tight halo around her head. Eight? Ten? What was a kid doing in a place like this? Jackson was too old to have a daughter that young, surely?

"Hey, are you, are you lost? Did your parents leave you here or something?" I asked tentatively, walking over to her.

The kid seemed to lose interest and glanced away. The closer I got, the weirder the feeling I got; no kid that age sat quietly for so long, and she must have been up here the whole time I had been. Behind the shelf was a low desk and table with the CD dishing out Donny Osmond perched at the corner along with notepads and broken colouring pencils. She was staring out of a window at the street behind. I came over to her.

"What you up to? Drawing?" I reached down to pick up one of the notebooks, getting a quick glimpse of an almost perfect blue and yellow sphinx, but one pudgy fist suddenly clamped it shut. I was startled, surprised so much force could come from something so small.

"Why does she want you so badly? Did you hurt her?"

When kids speak, they do the bay talk thing; any kid under twelve will drop or blend a few syllables *somewhere*. She didn't. Her voice was high, and definitely pretending to be innocent, but her accent was so crisp and her words so well defined, they may as well have come from someone my age, if not older. I walked over behind her to look out of the window. The rain was hitting the glass so hard, I could barely make out the darkening street below, and pelting down on the alley's cobblestones and bouncing back upwards. My stomach flipped; someone was standing down in the alley below, their head bent straight back to stare right up at us. Rain hit that now familiar square, familiar if devoid of the smile it held in her newspaper photos; her cheeks were sallow, and her eyes black holes burning pinpricks right into me. Her loose-fitting boxy white dress wasn't the least bit affected by the rain, which was sliding away from an invisible aura around Delia, as if the rain itself was too intimidated to hit her.

I jumped back, grabbing one of the bookcase's shelves and sending a few to-be-indexed books onto the floor. I wanted to fall to the floor, curl up in a ball and burst into tears, but instead I jumped back to the window pressing my nose to the glass. I knew, before I even looked, she wouldn't be there. It was less that my pulse had unreasonably returned back to normal, or that the creeps I'd been getting just a second ago had disappeared, than it was that the girl was now looking at me as if I'd gone mad. The incredulous look on her angelic-like features turned to concern and, to my utter shock (and a little hysterical panic), she got up and hugged me around the waist.

"Don't be scared. I'm here, I'll protect you."

Now that sounded like an eight-year-old. "You'll protect me? I'm sorry, have I been knocked unconscious and am living a nightmare like *The Exorcist*? …Wait! You'll protect me from what? You saw that? So I'm not mad?" I'd never heard myself sound so unbalanced before.

She giggled. "You sound a bit crazy, you look really crazy, but I saw the girl in the street. She wants you bad."

I crouched, leant against the window still, staring down into the street.

"You're the new girl, right?" she continued. "Zean told me you'd be coming here. Do you like the books? They smell awful like socks."

I glanced at her. She was looking up at me, her chin resting on my

25

stomach and her baby sea-blue eyes sparkling. I started to feel more calm. "You know Zean?" I breathed.

"Uh huh. Khyle's a weird name, by the way."

I ignored that. "Is she like a ghost?" Why was I asking her?

"If she were dead, that would make her a ghost, and I'd think she'd have more important things on her mind than bothering you," she said as if I'd asked the most obvious question in the world. "What are you, like eight?"

"That's a bit too much sarcasm from an eight-year-old, surely. Ah, I'm going mad…" I moaned as she unwound herself, obviously very put out by how preoccupied I was that a non-ghost was scaring me half to death any chance she could get, and not discussing how weird my name was or how this place reeked of twenty-year-old wool socks!

"Maybe you should believe what you see and not what you've been taught to see," she shrugged, picking up a pencil to examine like an insect.

"Khyle, I see you've meet Jazmine, my granddaughter… Dear God, girl, are you alright? I've seen ice with more colour than you."

I glanced up. Jackson was standing by one of the shelves, holding two brown paper bags with the Starbucks logo printed on the front, and a cup holder with two steaming green coffee cups. Alright, so take away a deadly TV, witches, ghosts, and terrifying eight-to-ten-year olds. What I should probably be the most freaked out about is that a sixty-something physics professor, who can't alphabetize a single book in his shop, buys his lunch at Starbucks.

Ghosts or not, I definitely had a potential story, and if Delia wasn't going to leave me alone, I may as well make the upcoming heart failure worth it.

Chapter Three

A week had passed and, almost to my surprise, I had survived minus any encounters of the third kind. I'd even got as far as moving my suitcase, which for the first three days had been left spilling clothes onto the hallway floor, up to the six-by-ten spare room that Zean had kindly removed his junk from. I'd almost made a dent in the indexing at GUTs, and was even getting used to the permanently skulking Jazmine (she didn't seem to be going to school at any point) playing bad chick-trash music from decades past, and providing me with a constant array of drawings of Delia, asking whether she should make her hair pink or orange. All in all I'd managed to conjure up a safe routine of sleep, eat, work, and avoiding all TVs, newspapers, alleys, and science fiction films at any costs. Life was peachy.

Now I was standing in a damp field trying not to let my nose get frostbitten. Zean had apparently been very upset with my social skills after I'd refused five times straight to go down to the pub with him and meet people accusing me of potentially being labelled the Blackleigh hermit, and had got me up this morning by throwing my parka at me, handing me a cup of coffee, and declaring we were going to the Blackleigh Fair or he was taking my key and locking me outside in the eight-degree weather in my underwear.

Needless to say, if I'd had to choose between the Loraline witch projects and having my greying boy shorts displayed to the world, I would happily have changed into something a little more feminine and stood outside Zean's front door turning my extremities blue. But there was the chance of meeting Eliza, and so far what I'd been able to find out about Delia's disappearance had been so sparse I was surprised the guy who had written that article had had as much to say as he did. I'd asked at a few places whether anyone knew Delia or Catharine. Catharine had been the most known, but not in a good way. A lot of people described her as the local whore who wasn't all that local. Others just shrugged and said she was "that age". That age, my arse! When I was that age, the most outrageous I'd got was heavy eye-liner, vodka, and an extremely productive gambling issue, not sleeping with the majority of the males in this area, raves, drugs, and numerous hospital admissions. Delia – from the impression people gave me, not the impression I got from our own personal encounters – was a lot more humble. I was thinking it might be something to do with drug money, or even a seriously pissed-off girlfriend, but really I needed to know what Delia had been up to before she'd gone missing.

Zean came back holding two napkin-wrapped sausage sandwiches. I almost snatched mine, biting into the crispy, meaty goodness for any source of warmth. You may have noticed I'm about as good with cold as the Titanic was with icebergs.

"What you looking so glum 'bout? Look, I'll introduce you to loads of people. I come every year, I'm a coconut smashing genius, you know," he said, sausage rolling around in his mouth as he did.

I grimaced. "Prehistoric man was good at smashing things, Zean. No one calls the Neanderthal a genius, and did it occur to you maybe I want to get there in my own time? Settle into things first?"

Zean grabbed my arm as we waded through the crowd. "Nope. Right, that Brian Lukins" – he pointed over at a bullish man inspecting the meat pie stall with extreme concentration – "he owns the 24-hour place down the road. He's cool. I dated his daughter for a while. She broke up with me, thank God, so I still get a discount on a six-pack. Eh, let's see, that's Adam. If you'd come down yesterday I was going to introduce you. He's been looking for a girlfriend for ages, and you need to lose it soon or you'll rust shut."

I'd stopped hitting Zean in the ribs for the virginity jokes about four days after I'd arrived. They occurred just about every ten minutes, and after a while my elbow became sore. Zean being my first and last KISS was my first and last everything else. It wasn't that guys hadn't tried; it was more that I thought most guys were Cro-Magnons not worth bothering with, and as a consequence (or possibly reward) I'd never fallen into bed with one of them. I'd never even wanted to; when it came to sex I was as physically responsive as a lump of clay. Zean had once asked me whether I was waiting to get married as, with him being the biggest man-whore imaginable, he couldn't understand it at all. I'd responded that when it comes to marriage, in my opinion it would be a lot cheaper just to check myself into the local prison, and on the bright side, that way I would keep my last name and still be able to make fifty percent of my own decisions; so no, it was nothing to do with marriage. Looking over at Adam now I got the same stomach-sinking feeling as always. He was okay-looking (coming from a girl who would describe Brad Pitt as alright), but the look in his eyes as he spotted me with Zean, smiled, and moved away from the apple bobbing to get to us, was enough to make me wish I'd stayed at home with frostbite.

"Oh yeah, and that hottie is Loraline. Nice… huh? Blimey, she just waved."

My heart sped up. Sure enough, standing just across the field was a familiar tall silhouette clad in distressed jeans and a peasant top that made her perfectly perked-up cleavage look like they were trying to escape. Jeez, the things some girls do for fashion; she must have been frozen. I had gloves, a scarf, and a soft black wool coat wrapped around me and I still couldn't feel my toes. She met my eyes, that same burning warmth emanating pools of onyx-coloured fire. Her eyes slid from me to my right where chav Adam had just emerged, clapping Zean on the shoulder.

"Ad, yeah, this is my lil sis, Khyle. Remember I told you she was living with me now?"

Adam's acne-scarred face stretched into something meant to be charming: he looked like a shark at the dentist.

"Yeah, right, the elusive Khyle. How you feel 'bout apple bobbing, gorgeous?"

I rolled my eyes. "One way trip to a chipped tooth," I said bluntly. If you had to choose between a witch and a weasel, which would it be? Witch it was. "Sorry, gentlemen, the elusive Khyle is once again becoming elusive."

Loraline was arranging iced cakes and buns on a table, a smug smile playing on her pale lips. She really must have been cold. "Didn't like the looks of Adam?" she asked quietly, licking her finger of icing.

"I don't have much patience for guys who hit on me," I muttered.

"Mm, would you guess, me neither? I'm not actually in luck, am I?" I knew she was teasing, but I still felt my cheeks burn.

"Hey, I'm kidding. I know I'm not that lucky. I didn't mean to—"

I cut her off. This wasn't a conversation I liked to have, and had had one too many times. Yes, I'm unresponsive to men; no, I wasn't a lesbian.

"It's fine," she went on. "Men are pointless. I only wish I was as lucky as you that I could like women instead, not that I understand women any better. So how's the fair going?" she beamed. "Ha, take my advice. Don't try to understand people, just enjoy them. Yeah, it's okay. It's usually a pretty big thing, Blackleigh. Blackleigh isn't very eventful, if you know what I mean. If it wasn't because you were so desperate for my body, why'd you decide to come?"

I laughed. "My friend Zean dragged me down here with accusations of potential hermit-ism. Oh, and by the way, if you ever decide to bat the other way, he's into you bad time."

She laughed musically. "Oh, I'll keep that in mind. He works at GUTs sometimes, right? He's quite a genius, incredibly, really. Shame about the penis."

It was my turn to laugh. She was actually looking at him longingly. Poor Zean, if only he knew what he was missing. "You know GUTs? I'm working there at the moment."

She nodded. "Yeah, of course. I'm Jazmine's aunt. I live with her and Jackson at the edge of town. Didn't he tell you?"

I don't know why I was shocked. Creepy and beautiful were obviously two alleles inherited together. A witch, a physicist, and an angel living together. Someone should write a play. I guess it just wasn't a question I'd think to ask my employer. Go figure. I couldn't really think of anything to say so I blurted out exactly what was on my mind.

"Is, eh, Eliza here? I wanted to have my tarot done."

The look she gave me was so terrifying, I would rather have been trapped in an alley with six TVs.

"You'll make a brilliant journalist, Khyle: story first, people later." Her tone was more melancholic than angry, but her eyes were still burning at me. I wasn't going to shrink back and swallow my words. How did she know about my journalistic needs anyway? Maybe Zean had said something.

"That isn't fair. I would never say anything to hurt her further, and maybe I'm actually trying to help rather than just get a story."

The moment the words left my mouth, I immediately wondered whether they were true. I remembered that forlorn feeling that had filled me when I had first seen Delia's face. "And besides, why are you being so defensive anyway?" I hissed under my breath.

Loraline seemed to think twice, the anger visibly slipping away.

"Khyle, look at you. You're pretty breakable. You shouldn't get yourself into something that could get you hurt." She sighed.

I frowned. "Do you know something?" All anger had slipped from my voice, too, replaced with ripe curiosity.

Loraline groaned, rubbing her forehead, and turned on her heel gesturing for me to follow. I had to resist the urge to pull out a notepad and pen and starting writing down comments. "I know how common it is for people to go missing… Lately, that's all I know that's any help to anyone at the moment."

I bit my lip. "Well, what does that mean, Lora? Innocent people could be, are, getting hurt!" I practically screeched.

"We on a nickname level now?" she laughed, pushing everything we had just said aside as if it were nothing. She turned. "Eliza, this is Khyle… erm?"

I raised my eyebrows. "Oh, finally something you *don't* know? Exeter," I supplied.

Loraline turned back to the woman sitting behind the low ink-and green-cloth-covered table, suppressing a grin. "Exeter. She'd like a tarot reading if you feel up for it. Please feel free to tell her she has a long future of skanky prostitution and a job at MI6." She stuck her tongue out at me as she passed, walking off to the face-painting area. I smiled to myself. In spite of everything, I really did like Loraline, regardless of whatever it was she wasn't telling me.

Eliza was an image of Delia, if Delia had spontaneously aged thirty years. Same square jaw, almond eyes, curly mane of brown hair, except her skin had been weathered and wrinkled with time, and at this particular moment dark shadows and red blotches marred her complexion. I had an intense inkling that they were new additions to her. I lowered myself down into the knobbly wooden chair, feeling it sink several inches into the damp ground. Eliza smiled at me, but seemed so absent and withdrawn, lost in her little world of worry, and already mourning a mother's loss that I started to feel unsure about what I was about to do. Loraline was right. This woman seemed so fragile, what right did I really have to rake up what was already so clearly looming in her mind? But if I found Delia, either way, story or no story, maybe that would help, the finally knowing. I feared maybe what had been a simple self-gain situation from a series of paranormal encounters might be becoming more. With every passing second I was becoming attached, and I hurt for Eliza, if not for Delia.

"Are you new here, Khyle? Or is this just your first time to the fair?" Her voice was willowy but warm. How was I going to play this?

"No, I'm new here, I've only been here a week, actually."

She took my hand across the table. I thought this was tarot.

"Where are you from originally?" Her fingers very lightly brushed my hands, her eyelids lowering, veiling her eyes from me.

"Eh, nowhere really, at least it feels like that most of the time. I'm a foster child. Zean who I'm now living here with is my only family. I owe him a lot, I guess, for rescuing a little lost girl from a world of strangers."

Something was making me open up; I just felt calm sitting in the midst of buzzing crowds, in the middle of a damp field, with a woman I'd never met holding my hands while she pretended to be going into a trance. Go figure. I could feel the world moving in slow motion around me, every heartbeat pumping out a chaotic clash of drumming as each thumped to its own internal rhythm, each soft absent thought rolling around in their minds, humming energies flowing through and around them, connecting...

"You know how to take what you can from life. If only everyone thought like that. You remind... "She broke off as her voice grew smaller.

"I expect a lot of things remind you of Delia these days."

It just escaped. I was so busy winding down into a trance of my own, it slipped from my mind to my tongue. I saw her eyes flicker slightly, glancing up and meeting my eyes for a split second, her fingers trembling. "I'm sorry, I didn't mean to, I... " I was so overwhelmed with guilt and the instant pain I'd ignited in this damaged woman that I did the only thing I could think of. I lied. "I, I knew Delia, she was a friend of a friend. I was terribly sorry to hear about what happened when I read it in the newspaper... I just wanted to give my sympathies... "

I trailed off slightly, but Eliza seemed to have regained her composure, giving me a warm, if worn, smile. "Thank you. I've fallen to pieces so many times in the last month I just can't cry any more. When did you last meet my daughter?" She asked it absently, but as she lowered her eyes to brush her fingertips against my hands again, I could hear the hint of urgency in her tone.

I'd dug my hole; now I had to *lie* in it. What was I going to say? Parties? I thought of how I imagined Delia when I wasn't recalling *The Exorcist*. "I used to part-time at some charity shops down in Swindon. She liked a bargain, I think, because she was always hopping from one to the other."

Well it was worth a try! And it paid off too. Eliza smiled absently, her finger tracing a line in the middle of my palm.

"You have a good heart, Khyle; good intentions, too, even when you don't believe it. A strong life energy."

I nodded, trying to think where to go with this.

"Do you mind me asking what you think happened? Was it… I mean, I knew Catharine too… " I was starting to think if I wanted to do this for a living I was going to have to try a little harder at my interrogating.

"Catharine wasn't as bad as people say. There's nothing wrong with a healthy sexual appetite. I mean, I always encouraged Delia to be out there with other men, but she was only interested in the covens, she wanted to be high priestess one day, her school work was terrible." She laughed, dropping my hands. She reached for a velvet package, unwrapping it to reveal a crisp set of tarot cards face down.

"I never knew Delia was…" – into hocus pocus – "a Craft practitioner. What's a high priestess?" I asked.

There was a flicker of surprise behind her eyes as she watched me from across the table. By the way she was looking at me, I was starting to feel as if the cards (so to speak) had been reversed, and I was now the one being interrogated. "You aren't a witch. That's fascinating; you must trust your instincts incredibly to have such highly attuned senses."

I couldn't think what to say so the inevitable seemed best. "Huh? I think I understand." *I wonder whether you can take interrogation 101 at the local college.*

"Close your eyes, Khyle. Do it. I promise I won't turn you into a cat once your guard's down," she joked warily.

"That's a shame. I always wanted to be a cat; no time of the month issue," I said, trying to lighten her a little. I didn't know why, but a protective instinct seemed to roll around in me for Eliza.

Hesitantly, I let my eyes slide closed. Eliza began.

"Just breathe… feel the world around you… people passing by… the ground… the breeze… each individual strand of grass… it's all connected. And it's all pressing in on you every second; you just have to let those energies in."

I was trying not to giggle, trying to take it seriously, but I guess like every other atheist out there I'd trained my brain to mock anything that could come close to a religion. Obediently, all the same, I let myself *feel* the world around me. It was easy to feel people's presence pressing in on you, melding in with everything around you, everything you take for granted, tuning out just to be able to hear yourself think every second, but I didn't feel anything new or divine, just life. Maybe that's what was divine. My own heartbeat was loud in my ears; I could feel it thumping against my chest; da dum, da dum, da da dum dum. I frowned, concentrating on keeping my eyes closed. I could feel it: feathery-like wings against my own heart, but not there. I could hear it, feel its warmth, but there was no physical ache as it hit my ribs like my own. A second heartbeat, not quite in rhythm with my own but my own was trying to match it constantly, as if the moment the two individual drumbeats came into rhythm an empty void would be filled. I could feel it, the way I felt it every night, every time I fell asleep, quietened myself enough to be able to feel, hear how empty I wa—

"I think it was when Delia started to go to that place, where Catharine worked some nights. Do you know it? The police went there to question people; I only found out she'd been there through them… She would never have lied to me, but I don't know any more."

Something deep in my totally spaced-out mind, desperately trying to hold onto this feeling, registered that something Eliza had just said was important, relevant; and that was it, that's all it took, and I came hurtling back to reality so fast it was like being slapped. Immediately, the strange silence and focus I had had a moment ago was intruded upon by voices and smells and hustle and bustle, and I had a sudden urge to take up meditation.

"No, I'm sorry, I don't know. Club?"

Eliza was looking at the table. Her brow furrowed as she examined the cards she'd drawn.

"Oh, yes; Casper's. Somewhere in Swindon, I think. I'd never even heard of it, but I'm told that's where they were coming back from. I thought someone connected to that place had my baby—" She broke off for a second, swallowing, her eyes drawing closed. "I'd burn the place to the ground." She suddenly looked up at me, her gaze sharp, as if she'd heard a thought that I hadn't had.

"Don't!" I said. "I understand you want to find her, goddess. I do too, but one life has already been torn from us. She doesn't need to be sent company from those same demons."

I couldn't help but wonder, having been through what I had recently, whether she meant the term literally.

"You say one death. So you believe Delia's still alive?" Eliza placed her hands on the table in front of her, smiling so sadly my whole chest constricted. "Call it a mother's hope, maybe, a mother's faith."

I shook my head, feeling tears sting my eyes. "Being a mother has nothing to do with it. I believe with everything I have she is, too," I said, taking her hand.

Eliza brushed back a tear that had slipped down her sunken cheek, and then shook her head to clear it, and examined the cards which I now glanced down at. If I didn't believe in any religion other than nicotine, then I had very little regard for tarot cards, but I was fully capable of understanding and believing other people's care for it, and the intense look of both bafflement and worry in Eliza's eyes was enough to make the breath release from my lungs in a short burst. Eliza ran her fingers again over three cards spread out over the cheerful lavender-scented table cloth. One even *I* knew; two people stretched towards each other with angelic wings spread almost regally over them, connecting them in the metaphorical shape of a heart: The Lovers. Either side of this card were the two others, the first of which was The Moon, showing two dogs separated by a river and barking up at the moon, and a scorpion in the foreground; and the other showed a man and a woman, each holding a cup, and a lion's head with wings hovering, spread wide over them: The Two of Cups. All looked like crude drawings, their colours bright and the lines blurred. They should have looked innocent, harmless like one of Jazmine's pictures, but they didn't. They looked foreboding.

"What do they mean?" I asked Eliza tentatively, brushing stray strands of hair out of my face as the wind caught up.

"Great love, unconditional, almost unnatural, everlasting… " I was about to ask why she was looking so confused, unless she really believed I was to be that devoid of anything resembling a relationship the *whole* of my life, when she continued. "And the greatest of betrayals, from the moment it begins."

I shouldn't really have felt unsettled. I wasn't in love with anyone solid, just an image, a fantasy, and a nightmare. It didn't exist, and what didn't exist couldn't cause me harm.

Eliza glanced up suddenly as if someone had called her name; I followed her gaze to Loraline who was making her way over, holding two slices of fruit cake. A sudden gust of wind knocked a few cards loose, scattering them. Eliza immediately started to gather them, a few others stopping and passing them over. One skimmed me, floating away on the breeze. I shook myself out of my dazed state and jumped up, rushing after it. It kept popping out of reach until I was horribly aware of how ridiculous I must look to anyone watching. Thankfully it eventually fluttered to rest a foot from me.

I reached down, but a hand in a black cotton glove with the fingers cut off, touched it before I did, picking it up and leaving me crouching by the place where it had landed.

A flood of heat blazed under my skin almost painfully, the blood rushing from my head leaving me dizzy and disorientated. I was sure I was going to faint – I'd always suffered from low blood pressure and I'd clearly crouched down too fast – when an unimaginably strong grip grabbed my elbow, so tightly it was almost painful, and brought me slowly to my feet. I placed my palm to my forehead feeling feverish and wondering whether I was going to be seeing that sandwich again. "Thanks," I mumbled, slightly breathlessly. Glancing up, I had to almost crane my neck right back to see who had caught me. Two frosty grey eyes were staring at me with an intensity that almost knocked me away all over again. He was taller even than Zean, maybe six foot five? A little under, but almost twice the width, making me feel uncomfortably similar to a mouse crouching in front of a wolf.

I pulled out of his grip, taking a step back so I didn't look like quite such an idiot craning my neck back. He was looking down at the card he held in his bulky hand, one bushy brown eyebrow raised slightly. He was all hard angles, his face wide but sharp, razor-like cheekbones and square jaw covered with a thick bristly flourish of stubble. Washed-out skin, deep-set eyes and heavy brow, he looked a bit like he'd stepped out of a film of Dracula meets the Godfather, clad in dark jeans and jacket and a scarf that looked more there to hide rather than heat. His hair looked like he'd gone to a hairdresser intent on making each client a cookie monster representative, sticking out at haphazard angles and alternating between a rich black and a rusty gold. I couldn't help but stare for a second before I was able to shake myself back to myself. Clearly, the tarot card thing had my already dangerously overactive imagination going wild. This was not the man who haunted my dreams; he was just a... a... well, even I wasn't that good with words. This was just a rather fortunate, okay handsome-looking guy. Did I actually just call him handsome? I thought he was cute... No more tarot, girl! Ever! Still, he reminded me so strongly, queasily, of someone; someone who'd been haunting every dreaming moment I could remember. Aside from the fact that the guy I knew didn't have an inch of hair on his body, hell, this guy was overgrowing. Best of all, he had yet to try to kill anyone; more specifically, me

"Death. Rather self-explanatory in its meaning. Mind you, how you interpret death isn't as easy." His eyes shot fast and steadily to my face, and then something cocky pulled the corner of his thin lips up. "For your sake, I hope this card was meant for me. We wouldn't want something so fragile to have such a bad fortune."

He flipped the card over to show me the cloaked, skeletal smile painted there and the word beneath it, big, black, and as foreboding as that word ever is to people.

I plucked it from his fingers, unable to take my eyes from his. I wanted to say "You have to have a beginning to have an end, and there aren't many of those for me, so I think it's safe to say it's yours." Thankfully I resisted the urge.

Something about that wolf grin, that hidden joke, seemed to piss me off. As if he knew it would piss me off he only laughed, throwing his head back a little, his eyes never once leaving mine. I could feel myself glaring. Mockery was not something I accepted from anyone. He must have seen me running after the card. Great.

"I'm not fragile." I sounded like a six-year-old about to have a tantrum.

"Okay," he practically drawled. If sarcasm were visible, this guy would be smothered from vision.

"I'm not." Well so far, at least, I hadn't stamped my foot.

"I said okay." He was enjoying this way too much; his eyes had gone from frosty to a wicked heated silver.

"No, but it's the way you said it," I sighed, feeling sillier by the second.

He nodded, trying barely convincingly not to smile again.

"Fine. How about you are a butch bear of a woman who could not be crushed by any man, let alone a six-inch-long piece of cardboard with an ugly picture drawn on it?"

He crossed his arms, raising one eyebrow, ready for me to burst. I swallowed it, nodding curtly, lips pursed and fists clenched. Good God, could anyone be more annoying? Too right. This guy wasn't the guy from my dreams who terrified the hell out of me every night; he was a whole new type of bloodcurdling.

"Marcus." Loraline appeared next to me with Eliza, who I passed the card to instantly; just the touch of it was like acid. "Interesting to see you here. Are you enjoying the fair? I wasn't expecting to see you at all."

Loraline sounded charming, but there was something hostile in her eyes, something animal almost, shouting *my territory*. Marcus's eyes rose from me to Loraline as if the strain of doing so was that bit too much of a bother.

"Just passing through, Lora. No danger to any tree huggers, I swear," he said, irony biting at every word. His eyes danced over me for one split moment before he stalked off, disappearing into the crowd. I couldn't help but watch him as he went, unable to look away until he had gone totally from view.

"That man is weird." The emphasis Loraline put on *weird* made me feel uneasy.

"He's done no harm. We shouldn't judge before we have reason to. You should know that, Loraline." Eliza's reprimand was tinged with uncertainty.

"Who is he exactly?" I asked carefully, watching their expressions.

Loraline semi-rolled her eyes, looking younger than she usually did, less mature. I preferred her that way.

"He moved here about two years ago. He mostly keeps to himself; I think he likes to think of himself as a bachelor. Men," she said, taking a huge bite of fruit cake as if to avoid more questions.

I frowned. "Okay, so he's male and a sarky shit. What's the actual issue here?"

Eliza put her arm around my waist like the mother I like to think I never really had. "We think he breeds wolves." She looked at my expression. "No no, in the forests at the edge of town; there's been an increase in some rare breeds since the very day he moved here, and there's been attacks."

I glanced over towards where Marcus had disappeared. I didn't want to be, but I was intrigued.

There was shouting from a few feet away, and all three of us looked up. Four boys, including Zean, had fallen into the apple bobbing tank and pushed it over. "Men," we muttered in unison and then laughed. Normality had returned. For now. From my experiences so far I was going to savour every last second of it.

Chapter Four

I was once told that a question is only as important as it is relative to that moment, so the big "Are we the only ones in the universe?" may be pretty important in the big picture, but has very little relevance to, say, whether to buy free-range or what A-levels to take. The big question at this very moment? Whether Weetabix could actually go off to the point of being lethally poisonous. I stared down into the packet, which was a year past its sell-by date, not really thinking about possible death-by-cereal consequences.

My head felt horribly heavy having been sleep-deprived for most of the night (Zean's mysterious girlfriend was, as of yet, faceless, but assuming it had been her last night in his room, she sure as hell had a pair of vocal cords). I finally shrugged and gave up, dishing out two into a bowl and fishing in the fridge for low-fat Greek yogurt (milk never a safe bet) and something still resembling fruit. In all fairness to Zean, even without the gorilla impressions I would probably have gone sleepless anyway; every time I closed my eyes, I either saw Eliza's eyes staring at me pleadingly, a death card etched on the inside of my eyelids, or a horribly, nerve-racking familiar wolfish grin. I couldn't help but find it awfully ironic that I could be haunted by a girl I'd never met, and the thing that would keep me up all night would be a guy. Turns out I must be female, an illogical female.

There was a rapid cascade of thumping as someone hurtled down the stairs two at the time, and then Zean, with his best gorilla impression, swung around the door frame looking very awake for someone who'd had less than an hour's sleep.

"Morning, Zombie," he chimed, reaching straight for the milk carton (brave man). I grunted, taking my bowl over to the table and grabbing a Red Bull as I went. Caffeine, sweet mother caffeine.

"Good night?" I asked, not intending to hide the sarcasm.

He smiled, leaning against the fridge. "Why? You have a bad one?"

I dug into my cereal, ignoring him. I'd been the oldest after Zean in foster care, I'd never taken a boy up to my room, never spent a night around someone's house. I knew about everything because I wasn't mentally and socially retarded, but it didn't make me any more comfortable with the fact that I was nineteen and physically unresponsive to all other living beings.

Something seemed to change in Zean. As his face fell from cheeky to kind, he flopped down next to me at the table, taking my spoon from me.

"Look, Khyle, you're beautiful. You don't realize it, but you're kind and generous and funny; you don't realize it, but you ain't got nothin' to be ashamed of. If anythin', you should be proud, coz when he gets you he'll almost deserve you. Besides, you're my girl. No one's gonna dare touch you without my approval so you might as well get used to being the celibate roomy." He ruffled my hair and dug into my cereal, looking at me like I was an annoying kid sister. I felt myself blush. That was the thing about Zean: just when you thought he was only a testosterone-pumped primate, he surprised you with something borderline empathetic.

I hid my smile from him and snatched back my spoon.

"Thanks, but that was not what was on my mind. Unlike certain people, sex is not a twenty-four-seven circulating thought of mine. Remember, I'm a girl. Actually, I was wondering whether you knew 'bout a place called Casper's?"

Zean looked like he was thinking, which for Zean, if it had nothing to do with maths, always looked like work. "Yeah, think so actually, down Swindon way. If I'm right. and I'm simply never wrong, then it'd be like a gothic tramp place, all spirit, no beer." Suspicion crept in. "Why?"

I shrugged. "No reason. Just wondering whether you'd been or, er, wanted to go."

"What part of 'all spirit, no beer' did you miss? And you're not going either. You just got here. I don't need your body turning up on the six o'clock news. 'Vampiric killing of local: Khyle Exeter sacrificed alive for demonic fun'." He raised his hands as if to picture the headline running across the TV screen I still couldn't bring myself to look at.

"Okay. One: if that headline ever caught on, I'd need to choose a new job inspiration; two: that's not in the least funny; and three: what part of 'nineteen and self-sufficient' did you not get?" I joked, trying to keep hold of my spoon as he tugged to pull it out of my grasp for another bite.

There was a small cough and we both looked up, our smiles frozen on our faces like guilty school kids. The girl from the coffee store stood in the doorway wearing Zean's WWE T-shirt and a no more interested expression than she had the last time we'd met. I was horribly aware for a moment how awkward this looked. Zean dropped the spoon.

"Hey-y-y, babe. Breakfast?"

She shrugged, tucking one stray strand of fine blonde hair behind her ear. Christ, he was screwing the deaf and dumb. I got up, awkwardly fiddling with the back pockets of my khaki trousers. "Hi, I'm Khyle, it's nice to finally meet you." I got a pursed smile and a nod.

"Jessica. Nice jumper."

That smile was too sweet… I glanced down at the long-sleeved, black and pink Minnie Mouse jumper I'd thrown on that morning, feeling the sudden urge to burn it while it was still on. There was a thud from the hallway as a rustle of falling papers hit the wood-panelled floor. Post. Thank you, God. An escape.

"I'll get it. You guys'll probably need some time deciding the lifelong question of what to feed an anorexic for breakfast." I dodged out to the hallway just as yesterday's newspaper hit the space on the wall my head had been directly in front of. Notice how Zean didn't say a word, though.

I gathered the pile of letters and catalogues on the floor. Zean seemed to subscribe to every 'man magazine' and scientific journal imaginable. The familiar question: where did all his money *come* from? Popped up, I starting chucking the maggies on the corner table, then bills, junk mail, charity appeal, thick white envelope… I stopped, my hand hovering mid-air. I drew in a heavy breath, running my thumb over the familiar velvety expensive white exterior, four even-more-familiar words written in mock gothic type: 'St Matthew's Psychiatric Care Home.'

Zean's head flung around the corner. "Anything good?" he asked, clearly looking for escape; talking was obviously not a pivotal part of their relationship. His eyes slid over to the envelope in my hands. My heart jumped. Almost instinctively, I crumpled the letter (not easy considering its thickness) and shoved it into my back pocket.

"No, junk. Listen, I'm going out: long day's research. Those directions for the library are good, yeah?" I asked, already reaching for my black wool coat and scarf. I hadn't even had time to brush my hair yet, and it stuck out in a wild mess of waves that I knew from experience could only be tamed with a good bristle brush. No time. I wanted this letter and all its baggage as far from my little shred of life as possible.

Zean shook his head, his eyes mock-wide as he waved one hand over his throat. "Don't leave me," he mouthed.

I almost giggled, walking into the kitchen just enough to grab my unfinished breakfast off the table. Never leave food behind; it's a jungle out there. I leant into Zean for a split second whispering in his ear, "First came alcohol, then came sex, then came the ability to make actual conversation. Good luck." I didn't duck fast enough to avoid the quick swipe over my head.

* * *

3:48 blinked in iridescent green numbers from the screen of my little red Nokia E63 (the closest thing my savings would ever take me to a Blackberry). I pulled back from the microfiche, the hard pine chair rocking on its back legs as I stretched and suppressed a yawn. Five hours and forty-eight minutes after searching through newspapers dating back to the eighties, searching the Internet until my eyes watered, and flicking through book after book (thick leather-bound Bibles to slim vinyl-covered modern history books on witchcraft, metaphysical theory, religion, folklore, haunting; hell, I even read a chapter or two of *The Ghost and Mrs Muir*), what had I learnt? You can knock ten years off your vision by not looking up once from pages of information for that long.

Blackleigh Library was in the best part of town next to the Blackleigh Private Girls School, set in well-manicured lawns and parks and rows of tall, arrogant Edwardian houses. Considering it was a five-minute walk down from city central, which decreased the further down you went until you were finally in the real Blackleigh, it was like another planet – though why Blackleigh had public and private primary schools and no secondary school was beyond me. Set over three storeys of the snug moss-covered outhouses which were once part of the complex the school had been built in, it was almost cosy, unlike any other library I'd been in, which from experience were large and airy and painfully silent. The lower and middle storeys were devoted to rows and rows of books of all ages with separate archiving rooms. The third storey, where I sat now near to the bolted, misty window, was devoted entirely to electronic information, with computers, Internet connection, microfiche, archived photos, pictures, birth certificates, newspapers, and an individual study area of only four small tables, art deco green lamps pulsating fluorescent light over the oak surfaces.

It was lovely, and held a lot in a small space. In fact, now that me and the TV had had our little falling-out I could make it a second home; not musky or too dark like GUTs, but still quiet and devoid of people, and a brilliant view over the school grounds, or at least there had been until the rain had decided to see if it could drown a few ten-year-olds during P.E. and hadn't stopped since.

I shook my head, frustrated beyond belief. Okay, I had found out a hell of a lot more than just how to make my eyes water, but none of it was fitting into place, no connection, not enough to spin a tabloid piece of pulp fiction, let alone actually attempt to *help* Delia. The newspapers hadn't been devoid of information, exactly; in fact, they had been overflowing. There were thousands of disappearances from Oxfordshire alone over the last twenty or so years; some found, some not, some dead, some alive. There was absolutely nothing to connect any of them. They varied in sex, times they were taken, ages from pre-school to care home. There was an effective sea of black and white spread before me and blinking back at me from the microfiche, and I had no idea how to begin to narrow it down. A couple of times I'd considered calling up Zean and asking him to apply some logic to my search, but that would then involve explaining what I was up to, in which case he would either see me as delusional, insane, or a cruel sadist revelling in others' pain, and after what he'd said that morning I'd lost the heart. No one had ever been, or said anything, so sweet. I wasn't going to contradict it yet.

The occult stuff? I wasn't sure whether it was real curiosity or an unconscious reaction created by the unread letter crumpled in my back pocket to try and prove some semblance of sense in my encounters of the third kind but so far… Well, it was all incredibly interesting, and in many ways, as Jackson had said, I too could see a lot of connections between the way this religion worked, the way a lot of religions worked, and the way physics explained the world; but honestly, it was all so jumbled I couldn't decipher fact from folk tale. It melded into a mixture of history, faith and fantasy.

I rested my head on the open copy of *The Metaphysical Realm* in front of me, my eyes sore, and bleeding watery droplets. One hour's sleep wasn't enough for the human body. How did people like Catharine, and I guess maybe Delia, do it and not fall down at any second taken for a breather? My blood sugar was low; my blood nicotine negligible. My eyelids were anvils, the world was getting dark, blurry, grey, swirly, *hot. Tendrils of blistering wind wrapped around my ankles and gently stroked my cheeks, building ribbons of sweat at the back of my neck. I glanced around, my head shooting back and forth to take in my surroundings. Put simply, Toto, we ain't in Blackleigh any more. In fact I could go as far as to say I possibly wasn't in the UK.*

The temple was dark, constructed that way with columns of onyx threaded with sparkling minerals, and floors of grey and green mosaic marble, and left open to its coarse surroundings, allowing the deadly smoky wind to push the light airy green silk curtains so they danced in its current. Exposed sky blinked down at me, abrasive desert peeked back through the temple's circular openings, and twelve blurred, shadowy, hooded figures circled the spot where I stood; but not where I stood, where he did, the same dead look showing from behind those metallic eyes. I had never once seen actual happiness there; everything else, a few things I wish I never had seen in anyone's eyes, but never happiness. He was younger than most of the times we were together, his shoulders leaner and his body more gangly, but scars already dotted the pasty whiteness of his skin, somewhere freshly bleeding. His robes, which flapped violently in the wind, stuck to the inky blood dripping freely to the floor.

My mind seemed to flutter. I could feel everything sinking away until there was only this place; everything else was the dream. Desperation – mine and his – was what life was made of. I followed his and the twelve others' gaze to the centre of the circle.

A boy, his skin peachy and pimply, too normal against the darkness of this place, his short ginger hair too bright. He looked older than me. Seventeen. No, wait! Older?… He moaned as I did, my hand pressed against my temple. He moved weakly, flailing around on the floor. His skin was burning red where the wind touched him; he was so clearly in pain. One of the twelve figures stepped forward, one hand clamping down hard on the man standing next to me, his eyes still staring, emotionless, at the boy flailing about on the floor.

"A reward, my son, a reward for the trials. Soon you are to become a man and begin the transition. I am very proud of you."

For such a dark place the voice was so warm, full of pride and admiration: a father's love. I knew better than to look up, though. I kept my eyes fixed on the spot where the boy lay so helpless.

Tears were rising in my throat and I didn't know why, yet. I never knew. It didn't matter how many times I stood here watching, I didn't know truly until it was too late. He brushed past me, crouching down beside the boy as the robed figure resumed his place, watching, honouring. I couldn't be this far from him; it hurt not to be within inches of where he stood, but something held me back. I didn't want to be close to this. His eyes moved slowly over the boy's torso. I moved just a step closer, bending over him. He was crying, his face crunched up with pain, the sores caused by the wind starting to blister.

I tried to swallow the crying, but a muffled sound like a wounded animal broke through my trembling lips. His eyes, just momentarily, came up from the boy and landed on me. He knew just how to stop me crying; those looks of pure undiluted hatred were enough to make me paralytically scared, to stop any tears or trembling. He only kept my gaze for a second, but his lip drew up in a snarl as he did, and, infuriated, he shot out one hand immediately over the poor boy. Raw energy, which had crackled in the air, sizzled like doused flames as new ones built. Microseconds became slow motion as a path of energy ignited, from the boy's chest to his hand. At once, the boy stopped twitching mindlessly; instead, he screamed in agony, his whole body defying gravity, and arching up to where the hand hovered over him. If I'd had the courage to cry, or scream, or fight for him, I would have been doing all three, but instead I slipped to my knees. One small, childish hand stretched out like he was a wounded animal already lost to its predator.

The figure's eyes closed, his face glowing with something that looked horribly like ecstasy as the boy rose involuntarily to touch his fingertips. Finally, he seemed to lose it. He snapped back, grabbing the now washed-out frame of the boy like a rag doll, and buried his teeth into his lower neck, ripping away flesh and chipped bones, and sloshing blood onto the pristine marble floor as he drank. It seemed to take forever, as I kneeled wishing I could just hold the boy's hand as he went. Finally, screams turned to whimpering, whimpering to feeble shudders. In one last pathetic attempt to help, I finally *found enough slips of courage to whisper, in a voice too young to be mine, "You monster, you nasty, mean, spiteful monster." I was shaking but my voice was steady. The figure dropped the boy to the floor, a very literally empty shell of life. Blood, glowing red with the life force still emanating from it, dripped from the corners of his smirking mouth.*

"You are the monster, you little brat." His voice shook with power now, raw and untamed. His eyes snapped shut, and he threw back his head to the heavens, screaming with what I didn't want to think. Silent tears running down my cheeks, I followed his gaze, wishing that I could consciously resist mimicking his every move, to the night sky above where the moon shone gold; and down on us, its identical silvery shadow, much smaller, about the size of a fist, hovered an inch behind it. The golden moon pulsated, glowing life fire as if approvingly; the little silver one, the one I like to look up to in moments of pure desperation, looked from where I was kneeling like it was shivering, following every tremble of my own body like I had to follow his.

"Dear, wake up, listen to me, wake up." A soft hand was pushing the hair out of my face and shaking me slightly. I opened my eyes, but was still crying so hard I shook from head to toe. I didn't know why, of course; the dream fled from me, my mind shielding me from the pain of it as it always tried its best to do. In fact, the tears, and the stark image of the moon and his eyes were the only indicators it had been one of *those* dreams. The plump, middle-aged library assistant who'd been helping me most of today was bent over me, a look of stark worry and avid care shining from behind her round glasses, which had slipped to the end of her squat little nose. She placed the small stack of newspapers she was carrying carefully on the table, and turned back to me, placing two cool hands against my burning hot face.

"Are you alright? Do you need to talk, sweetie?"

I was expecting to be reprimanded about too much noise so had to drop the defensive remark I had prepared. "Yes I'm fine, thank you, I'm sorry about… " I trailed off, not knowing how to finish. No one had ever seemed to care once I'd woken up from a dream; even Zean had never mentioned them, putting them down to a common occurrence among fosters.

"What on earth are you apologizing for? Can you remember what it was about?" I shook my head, glancing over to the table where a picture of the moon, depicting the lunar cycle every twenty-nine days, twenty-three hours and forty-four minutes, blinked back at me, sending fresh shudders down my body. The woman pulled away a little, still surveying me speculatively. "Hm, I'll make you a cup of tea. You must be working too hard. I was just bringing you a couple of recent newspapers that haven't been put into the microfiche. What did you say you were doing all this for, again?"

I didn't, I thought pointedly as I gave her a weary smile, while she got up and moved over to an adjoining room, knocking a couple of the newspapers onto the floor as she did.

"It's okay, I've got it. Tea sounds nice, thanks." I was surprised at how weak my voice sounded. I bent over, collecting the fallen newspapers and missing persons flyers. I'd read them so many times I could recite them from memory: Lea Blocksmith, June 19th 1998; Charlie Embers May, 20th 1998; Chloe Slower… Wait a damned second! I fumbled, spreading the fallen papers on the earthy brown carpet in front of me. I didn't even hesitate, and reached blindly up to the table, my eyes wide and stuck to the individual dates. I grabbed my mobile.

I ran through my contact list. Zean answered on the fifth ring, chatter buzzing from the background. "Hello," he answered.

"Don't ask why, okay, but I need some maths help right this second," I stumbled, running my fingers over each face.

"Eh-h-h, ri-i-ight, fine, go," Zean drawled from the end of the line.

"June 19th 1998; May 20th 1998; September 11th 1994, 3.15; October 9th 1994, three o'clock; January 11th 2001; March 18th 2000, one o'clock; December 22nd 2001, twelve o'clock; April 16th 2000—"

Zean cut me off. "On average? Twenty-nine days, twenty-three hours, and I think at one point there, forty-four minutes separation of those within the same year. Khyle, what the hell are you on about?"

Just when you think he's useless, you remember he's a genius!

"Cheers, mate, owe you one," I said nonchalantly, ignoring his protests as I thumbed the 'end' button on my phone. I picked the papers up, placing them on the table, and pulled the book closer to me. Yep, twenty-nine days, twenty-three hours and forty-four minutes on average between one full lunar cycle. I jumped up, shuffling through the stacks to find the most recent papers for this year. Nothing. The assistant was yapping from the supply room, going on about a story of an escaped mental person or something in the recent newspapers. I lunged for the pile, flicking through page after page as a flowery printed cup of warm tea was set on a coaster on a bare table next door (no liquids near the books). Then I found it. On the front page of the *Oxfordshire Messenger* a boy blinked up at me: 'Missing – Oliver Connolly, August 2nd 2012.' I wasn't as fast as Zean, but I could do the maths. Roughly.

The assistant was still going on, oblivious to my sudden franticness. I felt a little guilty for not listening since she'd been so kind, but this was important. I cut her off just as she was describing how the nutter had wandered into a cafe in Oxford squealing about the end of the world.

"I'm sorry, but can I have copies of every missing person case reported in these papers, and I'd like to check these books out." I pulled the lunar phase one to me, as well as those on the history of the occult.

She blinked. "Of course. It's fifty pence per copy. Do you mind me asking; you're not with the police, are you?" She seemed a bit bewildered.

"Fifty pence is fine. And eh, no, I'm not with the police, I'm just…" I paused to think for a second. "I'm trying to help some friends."

Chapter Five

Dear Miss K. Exeter,

We are sorry to inform you that over the past six months your mother, Ms Jane B. Exeter, has been showing symptoms of a worsening condition, including increasing time in a state of delirium and a decrease from six to two episodes of lucidity per week. For these reasons she has been transferred to a newly-founded specialist ward at our premises for conditions similar to her own.

The payment is standard, but this transfer has included a change in her current medication dosage as well as additional applied medications. As always, we at St Matthew's encourage any possible visits by you, and any other family members you may have, to suit your own convenience. Your mother speaks of you often, in and out of her moments of lucidity. We do, though, wish to arrange a meeting between you and the Matron, Dr Pauline Thelmen, as these recent changes in your mother's condition are severe, and a change of doctor to monitor her condition is an essential requirement.

This may include a change in the costs of both treatment and rental accommodation. Please feel free to call on the number below or reply by letter via the return address provided.

Sincerely
Lisa Long, secretary.

I read the letter again, then again, and then again, grinding my teeth together harder and harder until I thought I may have reduced my molars to low stumps. I leant back against the pillows of my soft, fluffed-up single bed, at a loss. I'd tried on my way home to throw the thing away without reading it, but the hole it burned in my back pocket had remained until finally I had given in and ripped into the wretched thing. Was it loyalty to my mother that made me read it? No. I spent hours of sleepless nights lying to myself that I had no loyalty to my estranged mother, and nowadays I almost believed it.

My mother, Jane. My mother who wasn't my mother. The mother who I had never had a full conversation with, who had left me to years of foster care with no awareness of the pain she'd put a little girl through, the mother who abandoned me to go and play with the fairies twenty-four-seven, my mother who had never given a name to the man who was meant to be my father, the mother who had denied me a family.

Jane had been diagnosed with acute cases of depersonalization and schizo-affective disorders since before I could remember. Some of my first memories were of the stark cold white of the insides of treatment wards, watching my mother rock back and forth with multiple test tubes and wires stuck to her, in empty one-way-mirrored rooms. I shuddered; I would rather live a thousand of those dreams that forced me to wake up crying in my sleep than totally remember one full memory of my Mum.

As I leant back, the letter crumpling in my clenched fist, the thought that had been playing in the back of my mind since my first night here was staring me point-blank in the face. A face in the TV, ghosts, panic attacks? Was I becoming my mother? I had been around enough psychiatrists to know that what I'd been experiencing could easily be called 'episodes'. If it hadn't been for Jazmine, and seeing the girl in the alley before I even looked, I probably would have gone to see a doctor a couple of days ago.

There was a light tap on the door. I'd got back about an hour before Zean and had locked myself away in my tiny room, which I had yet to do anything with, going through each missing person story and occult book word by word. "Come in," I called weakly.

Zean pushed the door open, taping a cordless phone to his shoulder. "Jackson called, wanted to know if you felt any better and would you be able to make work tomorrow."

I bit my lip. "Yes," I lied.

"I told him you were as fit as a fiddle now, and would be doing extra hours a.s.a.p. to make up for the lost work. Spill!" He seemed almost angry as he came over to the bed, sweeping the room and taking in the piles of photocopies and books, and then the letter clenched in my fist.

I shrugged. "I told you I needed to go to the library, it was important, okay? I'll do as much as Jackson asks. I *am* thankful for the job, I just… " I trailed off, my voice getting smaller and smaller. Zean came over to perch on the side of the bed, prising the letter from my fist and reading it unbearably slowly.

Zean knew, everyone at the foster home had known, about Mum because I'd been obligated to go and see her every holiday. When I was little I had started crying several days before I'd had to go, then once I was a little older I'd run away a couple of times. Zean looked back up, a sympathetic look on his face, but he didn't say anything. Instead, he stood up and started picking through everything I'd gathered from the library. When he was done, he turned slowly and said in a very no-nonsense tone, "I repeat. Spill."

In spite of myself, in spite of my self-dependence and the fact that I was so, so scared that the moment I told him, in days I'd be the one rocking back and forth in a hospital chair, I spilled. Everything, not just what I wanted for the story or what I'd found out, but everything, even the little details about my 'episodes'. By the end I was crying so hard I could barely speak.

Zean put two fingers on my lips to stop me, and made shushing sounds. "Will you just relax 'n' stop beating yourself to a pulp, or you *will* be ready for the nutter." There was something going on behind Zean's eyes, a hidden battle. "Khyle, listen, you are not mad. I believe you, okay? I'm going to help you," he said, slowly emphasizing each word like speaking to a six-year-old.

I shook my head, my hair flopping over my face. "Don't humour me, okay? I'm a big girl; this isn't sane thinking," I mumbled.

Zean shook his head, now annoyed. "Don't talk shit, for Christ's sake. I work with Jackson; metaphysics is a well-accepted science as is noetics, and you are not the only one who has seen things. I'm not saying the TV's ever attacked me but, well, let's just say, past experiences have made the word 'paranormal' irrelevant in my vocabulary." There was a dark look in his eyes as he spoke the last bit. I frowned, opening my mouth to speak, but he cut me off. "No. No, I won't tell you what past experiences means. I have never seen a ghost, I can promise you that." There was silence while I tried to process this, and Zean sat brooding in his dark place.

The whole of this time that I had been convinced that I was mad, some part of me had just known this was going to happen, so even when I'd been looking to help Delia, I'd never really believed that this could be… real?

"Look," Zean said, "I'll help; we'll figure out what's going on together. Small steps, one of which will be plonking you in front of the screen to conquer a new-found fear of the television, but not tonight. Tonight you are coming out of this room. You will not think of psych clinics, or Casper's, or the Wicked Witch of the West; you are coming to the pub with me, you are going to drink, rediscover the miracle of pub food, and even socialize. Right?"

I laughed, tears still in my throat. "I hate socializing. I'm shy," I moaned.

Zean rolled his eyes. "Yes. But you love pub food."

★ ★ ★

The Horse and Mead was in the more broken-down area of town and only a five-minute walk from Zean's. It was a typical English pub: slightly damp musky smell, cottage-like thatch roof and big bulging stone exterior, and beamed interior. Two vodka and diet Cokes, a plate of mushy peas, ale-battered fish and chips later, and a gang of Zean's mates, including Jessica, had materialised, and after only two games of pool I could take no more and had stepped outside for a fag. As I leant against the cool stone, touching the fag to my lips and flicking my English-flag Zippo, praying dear God it worked in the damp night air, I thought about Zean. His almost total acceptance of everything I'd told him; not an ounce of doubt had been more totally worrying than anything else. I mean, yes, it was comforting, but it wasn't the *right* reaction. Did that make sense? I didn't know why, but something in the back of my mind had an irrational feeling that it was something to do with the lost past he never spoke about. I had to suppress images of him being expelled from a Hogwarts look-alike or being the mathematically-minded antichrist.

I giggled while I inhaled the idea of Zean walking around in a robe and wizard's hat, shouting 'wingardiam leviosa'. It was going to haunt me until the day I died. Maybe it was just me. I was the cynical disbeliever, and ironically it was all happening to me. God (if there is one) must have one hell of a sense of humour. I stared across the almost empty car park, surrounded by oaks and pines, as a tiny red spark moved up and down in mid-air. At first I thought it was a reflection of someone's car, or from one of the glowing orange windows of the bar, but then I realized it was getting larger and the sound of footsteps on gravel was coming with it.

Finally, light fell over the painfully familiar huge shape of Marcus walking from the pub; the little red spark turning out to be the glowing tip of his roll-up in the dark. I watched him, hoping from where I stood in the shadows he wouldn't see me staring at him. He looked fairly dishevelled as if he'd been walking in the wind a while; his hair was still messy in the best way possible, and the stubble, though it must have recently been shaved, had grown back. Now that I had time to stare I could notice tiny imperfections that were almost comfortable, making him human, real; he was not a murderer. His nose was slightly crooked and raised in the middle like it had been broken and hadn't quite healed; his left eyebrow had a very thin line right in the corner, leaving a gap in its bushiness as a scar ran down through it and down his hard cheekbone, and his eyes, black pools in this light, were bloodshot, badly. And clearly this over-analysis was totally beyond my control and I would be self-harming over it until the day I died. I leant further into the wall. He didn't look up; his eyes didn't focus on me or even this patch of wall, but he kept walking past the entrance straight towards me until, less than a foot away, he spun round a hundred and eighty degrees and leant on the wall beside me, taking a deep drag from his own fag, his eyes staring out to nowhere.

"Clearly you've never heard it's rude to stare."

His voice was rough, deep and too cold. I was gaping. He hadn't looked at me. How could he even see me, and why was my stomach repeating that fish and chips? I immediately wished I'd skipped the third vodka and Coke: it was going to impair my ability to answer back.

"And that statement wasn't just a little cliché. Good evening to you too, by the way." Of course, I was an expert at answering back so a tiny bit of impairment wasn't going to make much of a difference.

I felt two eyes burning at me. "Forgive me. Good evening, Khyle. How are you finding Blackleigh?" If he could inject as much sarcasm as that into ten words, God knows what he could do with actual conversation. I rolled my eyes, though of course he couldn't see me.

"Oh, it's lovely, the grass is green, everything's wet, the world's filled with witches and axe murders, and I'm missing dessert because, frankly, I'm an unsociable hermit. How 'bout you? Enjoyed your year in the Bronx?"

If the Devil laughed, I was hearing exactly how it would sound. "You give Loraline too much credit. She is not a witch, she's a tree-hugging banshee; and as for axe murders, all I can say is that your two weeks has been a lot more interesting than my year."

I laughed. I couldn't help it. I wanted to because I knew he wasn't being nice or trying to make me laugh. He meant what he said, and said it in such an icy tone that small children would have cried after hearing him say it; but I couldn't do anything about it. I found brutal honesty soothing.

"Not from what I hear," I muttered.

"And what do you hear that you believe?"

He reached in his jacket pocket, pulling out a tin of ready-made roll-ups. I watched him light one lazily as if he had nothing left to do in the world than this one moment. I wanted benignly to mention the dangers of chain-smoking just to see if he'd laugh or attempt to stab one into my eye. "That I believe? I'm not sure what I believe any more. But what I hear is that you're raising a little wolf-cub army and are even more of a hermit than I am."

I felt rather than saw him shrug, but after waiting almost a minute for a response and getting thin air I snapped, "Well, are you going in or not? Or was your whole objective to come and litter the car park with fag ends?" I stamped my own out, walking past him to go inside.

"Khyle." He barely whispered it, but it was like someone had clamped handcuffs on me. I stopped dead. "Would you like to find out?" I turned, one hand poised on the door handle. "I can promise you a dessert you would otherwise have to endure the burden of unwanted company with." He was smiling that wolfish grin again. I pursed my lips.

"You are unwanted company."

He stepped closer to me, throwing light onto his face. Just one look at his face and I was a rabbit caught in headlights. He bent down so I could feel his breath against my cheek.

"Then go in."

It was a moment before I realised my eyes had fluttered closed, and that I was holding my breath in case any sudden movement should set him off. When I opened them, he was already skulking toward the end of the car park. I hesitated, opening the door an inch and then letting it slide back closed. I wasn't going to follow him; that would be both wrong and stupid, neither of which were in my nature. I started off to the end of the car park, taking one glance over my shoulder where I could just make out through the foggy window Zean and the others knocking balls around the table. Yep, neither were in my nature. Not even a little.

As I approached, the inside of a car lit up, igniting a halo of white light around the sleekest car imaginable. I stopped for a second, scanning the woods to see if he'd gone ahead, and then I heard a window being smoothly rolled down and that drawl oozing out.

"Happy admiring the *stunning* view, or are you actually going to get in?"

I turned on my heel, reached for the door handle, and signed my life away as I slid smoothly into the Jaguar XKR's soft charcoal-and-ivory interior, trying to keep the shock and admiration off my face. I knew little about cars, but Zean had been gushing on about this car since it had first hit the market and he had been right: low slung-back ivory leather seats, all smooth black lines on the outside and a multitude of colourful blinking gadgets on the inside, boys' toys and beauty at their best. Somehow I'd more been expecting a broken down Seat, not luxury in car form.

"Do you know what they say about men with great cars?" I asked, taking care not to look him in the eyes as I buckled in.

"They say they're over-compensating for a lack in other male departments," he answered before I could get a word in, then paused. "Of course, those people don't know how to fully appreciate beautiful things." His eyes ran over me as he said it, and I felt my face burn like fire despite the cold. His eyes moved to my face and he burst out laughing again, leaning back and kicking the car into first. It purred just like its name promised it would. I only had a moment to savour how well it ran before I was grabbing onto the door and dashboard all at once.

"Are you mad? This is a thirty road," I seethed through gritted teeth, trying not to screech as he glided over the curb, onto the road, and was turning the corner in under a minute.

"Relax. Why do you think I got the car? She can handle me." He was toxic.

I rolled my eyes. "Where are we going?" He gave me a side glare of pure contempt. "Oh right, so you're kidnapping me! That's exactly what I need to top off my two-week anniversary in hell." I should have been terrified, not only because he was a raving maniac driver, but because he was dangerous. Anyone could tell that by the way he held himself, the way he moved, or looked at you with such a dark expression you wanted to go back to pre-school, but I wasn't scared. Actually, I was kind of comfy, and it wasn't the £75000 seat I was being forced back in. Headlights passed, each time throwing his profile into the light. I stopped staring at him, not because I didn't want him to know I was doing it, but because he kept staring back, totally unfocused on the road.

"How old are you?" I was as surprised as he was; I hadn't even been thinking about it.

"How old do I look?" He sounded somewhere between amused and very bored.

I shrugged. "I dunno. Maybe if you took five minutes in the morning to groom, one may be able to determine a little better. Twenty-seven?" The corners of his lips twitched; he was mocking me again. "More? Less? Come on," I moaned. Jeez, what was wrong with me? My personality had been reduced by five years to a state of hormone-driven female adolescence I hadn't even experienced five years ago.

"More," he said, with great stress.

I frowned. "Really? How much more? Thirty? Thirty-five? More? More?" I asked, chewing my lip.

He laughed. "How old are you?"

"Nineteen."

"You're an infant."

It was my turn to laugh. "Nineteen is old. At twenty I'll be young again."

He rolled his eyes. "Well, at that, I can see you're a very logical person." I sat up in my seat. "You won't even tell me how old you are, and I'll have you know that's perfectly logical. Nineteen! You're an old teenager—"

I cut in. "Infant," I continued as if he hadn't said anything. "At twenty you're a young adult."

"Ever had a craving?" he asked.

No idea precisely how I was supposed to answer that one. Lost in thought, trying to think of a comeback that wasn't too easy to turn back on me, I was startled when the car plunged suddenly forward, swerving to the right into the tightest spot imaginable and forcing me painfully forward into my seatbelt. He jumped out without cutting the engine, the words *stay here* unsaid but mutely implied.

I tried to catch my breath, mad, stupid infant. I had to be to have got in here. He'd pulled into the local grocery store, and I'd expected him to come out holding a six-pack or a bottle of Jack Daniels; instead, as he climbed back into the car, something freezing cold and the size of a fist was thrown, hard enough to knock the wind out of me, into my lap. "Ow!" I glared at him, picking up what he'd thrown at me and holding it close to the light: a huge tub of Ben and Jerry's Chunky Monkey ice cream, banana ice cream, chocolate banana shapes and walnuts. My favourite.

"Sorry, I shouldn't have thrown it so hard. Told you… you were too bloody fragile," he muttered, starting the car again.

"I can't eat all this," I said, peeling back the lid and digging in with a plastic spoon. He laughed, his hand snapping out like a snake and grabbing my wrist. His hand was so large it could have almost wrapped around my wrist twice; but it was the heat – his skin felt like it was on fire. The ice cream on the spoon in an instant softened and bubbled, dripping onto my jeans. He pulled the spoon over to him, taking the huge dollop of ice cream in one.

"Good thing it's not all yours." He smiled, his mouth full of ice cream. I wished for Christ's sake I could stop smiling.

"Chunky Monkey's my favourite too." I was at a loss as to what else to say. My wrist had red rings from where his fingers had been.

"Mine's Phish Food," he said bluntly, reaching blindly for my wrist again and another spoonful. I attempted to hand him the spoon, but he just grabbed my hand, twisting it back on itself so that he could direct it to his mouth. He had a grip like iron to match; I winced.

"Didn't they have it?" I didn't know what I was saying. I was staring at his hand as if it was a lethal scorpion.

"They did. It's your dessert."

I didn't ask how he knew what my favourite was. I didn't want to know. "Your hand's like fire," I breathed.

It was then, in that second, I realized I'd finally become scared. The car pulled to a halt as he cut the ignition. "We're here." His voice had grown dark as he stepped out of the car. He didn't answer my point.

I stepped out too, rubbing my hand against the side of the tub. Even in the murky moonlight I could see it was glowing red and sore. We were on this side of the town's park, surrounded on all sides by woodland. It was a mass of wire fencing, trash, and broken park apparatus. It wasn't the kind of place you wanted to be at *any* hour of the day.

I swallowed, turning to him. "You are going to kill me, aren't you?" I was dead serious. He laughed, walking up to me and looming over me, almost a foot taller. I really did feel like a kid, my heart rhythmically hitting my chest, but unnaturally slowly. I braced, waiting to see the knife and aim a knee in the exact right place, but instead he reached out and snatched the ice cream from my hand, prising my fingers loose one by one, little tingling sensations left over from where his fingertips had brushed me. Scooping out a tennis ball-sized clump of banana and walnuts, he inclined his head to where a cluster of oaks stood, bent double, their branches looming over the ground, heavy with age and leaves, and almost touching the ground.

I frowned. He was bizarre. If he was going to pull a knife on me, I'd made it incredibly easy for him. If he had been anyone with half an ounce of sense, he would have been screwed ages back. The moonlight barely made it through the branches here, leaving a patchwork pattern of silver and black on the thistle-covered ground below.

"What am I—?" I began to shout, but stopped mid-sentence. There, right at the edge, where clearing turned into woods, slowly padding towards me, its muzzle pointed low towards the ground, was the most beautiful grey wolf. Its coat was a banded mixture of greys and blacks and silvers running across the five-foot length of its back, up its head and to the tips of its arrow-pointed ears; its eyes were the colours of honeysuckle

"Beautiful, isn't she?"

I started. Marcus leant on the oak next to me, his eyes for once not on me, but locked on the wolf. His presence seemed to match her own: sultry, deadly, and yes, beautiful. I swallowed, not sure whether to approach or run.

"So you *do* breed wolves," I whispered.

He smiled, shaking his head. "Not really. I have an affinity with them; I take care of them when I have to. I certainly prefer them to humans." His eyes moved slowly to meet my own. Something had changed, darkened in them; something about the way he said "humans".

"What's her name?" I asked.

He tilted his head slightly, considering me. "What makes you think I have the right to give her a name?" The coldness had bitten back into his tone, and I felt my defences spring up; but before I could retaliate, a soft, quivering growl tore through the night. I glanced up. Two yellow-gold eyes were locked on me. Marcus might not have been planning to kill me, but someone definitely had dinner on her mind. I glanced around, ready to back away, but the moment I lifted my foot an inch, another growl came, this one louder, deeper. She started to press forward, lowering further toward the ground, ready to jump if need be. I was trapped, caught between two predators, one armed with incisors the size of my little fingers, the other with a plastic spoon and a half-eaten pot of Ben and Jerry's. I think you'd agree the choice was easy; clearly I'd be throwing myself to the wolf.

I turned, ready to run, but before my foot left the ground I was pinned, my whole body hitting the floor as a huge weight pushed down on me. I choked, the air being squeezed out of my lungs. The muscles in my chest tightened painfully, exploding with tiny spasms of pain, desperate to relieve the pressure, but I couldn't even push air out. She bore down on me, teeth bared as she snarled, breath freaking enough to strip paint off walls, eyes narrowed. I wanted to close my eyes or cry or beg or do something other than stare a gruesome fate right in the eye, but instead all I could do was stare right back. And then I felt the sharpness, if not the weight, of her paws on my chest recede. The growls stopped; her muzzle ducked down. I braced myself for the ripping agony and got... a face load of saliva. What was this, tenderization of meat? Her growls turned to panting as she bent down in a rush to lick me again. I was at a loss; wolves just didn't act like this. Their relationship to man's best friend was close in evolutionary terms but, practically, not *that* close.

I reached up, placing one hand between her ears and smoothing down the silky fuzz of her fur there. In response, her whole head pushed against my hand, her eyes half-closed. I heaved her away; just enough to slip out from beneath her huge weight and kneel on the ground beside her, too terrified to stop petting her frantically. I didn't want to. She was beautiful, and not just because she hadn't torn me to shreds.

"How did you know she wouldn't kill me?" I asked, my voice still shaky from leftover adrenaline, but free of fear.

"I didn't." The words were so cold. I felt my heart stop dead. I looked up. Marcus's eyes were pulsating, his face a blank white mask of hatred and surprise as he looked at me. Terror – like nothing I'd actually felt in real life, not when facing ghosts or other-worldly TVs, or even a wolf ready to make me its supper – kicked in. I jumped back, my eyes not leaving his for less than a heartbeat. The wolf jumped up, her hair standing on end as she stood between us, looking between me and Marcus as if caught in an animalistic battle which even she didn't want to get involved in.

"Who are you, Marcus? Honestly, what is it you want?" I breathed.

He threw the pot aside, pushing himself away from the tree. Every move he made, my body shook. Every move was a reminder of someone else, someone lethal, someone I'd grown up with. "Don't you dare ask me those questions, kid." He took a step forward, and I almost fell back.

"No. No, it's not… it's not… it's not possible," I stuttered desperately. My knees felt like they would go from beneath me any second.

"Do you get ever tired of saying that to yourself? Before you could walk properly you were denying what you faced every day because it didn't fit into your set grid of reasoning and beliefs." He walked forward, fast.

I jumped backwards, until my back hit a tree and I almost tumbled over. "You are not real," I whispered when he was barely inches away. Far away in the background I could hear the wolf whimpering, cowering, as she retreated into the shadows; there was a more danger-ous predator here than herself. The heat coming off him rippled in the cold air. Raw energy. He brushed his fingertips against my cheeks. I closed my eyes tightly, turned my head away like when you're little and you tell yourself that the monster under the bed isn't real, except I could feel the flames where my non-real monster was touching me.

"Will you still say I don't exist when I'm killing you, my love?" he breathed, his face inches from mine. I opened my eyes, looking him straight in those eyes I had been forced to do every night, daring him to do what I knew he was trying to. I was not a weak child, not any more. This wasn't happening.

"What do you want?" I hissed.

He smiled. "You. It's always been you."

He reached closer but I was too quick, gathering every last ounce of courage and strength I could muster. I did the one useful thing Zean had ever showed me. I right-hooked him. The moment my fist had settled, I heard the bones crack and splinter. Not the right bones, though.

I clamped down on my fist, crying out in pain as spasms ran up through my hand and to my brain, telling me I'd just broken it. Marcus looked more surprised than anything else, like I'd hit a brick wall which was wondering who the hell would be so stupid as to hit it in the first place. He stumbled back about an inch, blinking, glancing to my hand, something strange displayed on his face. Worry, maybe? His lips parted slightly, and I half expected him to ask whether I was alright when he recovered. So did I. Sod the pain in my hand; I lurched forward, one knee going straight to where it had planned to. He of course blocked me, pushing me away with what seemed like no effort at all, but enough so that I hurtled four feet away, hitting the ground so hard I thought I might have broken something else. I didn't wait to see. I crawled to my feet, lurching forward again. I knew, I just knew; I could feel the decision in his mind not to follow. In *my* mind.

At the speed I was running, it wouldn't take me long to get to Zean's. I just prayed he'd be there. I had a horrible feeling that if I was alone, Marcus would follow. My hand hurt but I couldn't feel it. I could only process one thing. I had been right: that was the brutal, inhuman abomination from my dreams. It wasn't possible, of course, but nothing else could look at me with that much self-induced hatred. Okay, I was a believer; now let's find out what the fuck was going on.

Chapter Six

"It's three-thirty in the morning!" I cried despairingly, the fluorescent green clock in Zean's beat up, battered, bruised, and just plain abused Citroen blinking as if defiantly backing me up. Zean shot me a glance. His driving was usually as careful as a mum on the school run with police tailing her, but now those little white lines in the middle of the road seemed to be insignificant.

"I don't give a shit. You won't let me go and take you to the hospital, let alone the police. This is the next best thing. I'm gonna show that fucker a piece of my mind when I get my hands on him."

"He'd crush you like a nutshell. A barely-understandable-by-most-logical-human-beings physics professor, and the good witch of Blackleigh is the next best thing? And you will not go near him. You understand? I shouldn't have said anything."

"Khyle, look at your hand. That thing's going to pop off unless we get someone to look at it. And you leave what I do with that shit to me," he growled, turning the car erratically into the front drive of a vine-covered, two-storey grey stone cottage, and jumping out of the car before he'd fully pulled the keys from the ignition.

I hesitated, feeling somewhere between embarrassed and nerve-wrecked. Unfortunately, when I'd finally made it home Zean had been waiting, wondering what had happened (because of course

I couldn't just have been picked up by a guy or anything normal like that). He'd taken one look at my mud-streaked clothes and bowling-ball-sized purple hand and had begun the interrogation. It had been all I could do to stop him from grabbing a kitchen knife and getting himself killed. As it was, I had to knock the phone out of his hand three times when he tried to call the police, and locked myself in the bathroom when he'd tried to drag me out to the car to take me to the hospital. I'd finally agreed to see Jackson, and even then it was just because of the six Ibuprofen coursing through my system. Thanks to that very fact I was now physically numb everywhere. Except where being numb would actually be useful. My hand was in utter agony; purple, black in places, and a couple of fingers stuck out at odd angles, and I couldn't bring myself to touch them.

But now I was here, I was faced with what we were going to tell them. I didn't want to let them know about Marcus. I hadn't even spilled to Zean about how he was the guy who'd been paying visits to my dreams since I could remember. Zean had given me a nice earful of what an idiot I was to have gone with him (like I needed to be told), but all in all Zean was more freaked than I was. In fact, he was having the natural reaction to an assault whereas I felt quite good, actually. I knew I should be shaking or crying, but I just wasn't; I felt calm, together, like something I couldn't put my finger on exactly had slipped into place and left me feeling right. Of course that didn't mean I wanted the world to know about what had happened between me and Marcus; and even less about Delia, not the least because someone could steal my story.

Zean opened my door, all but dragging me up the cobblestone pathway. It was dark and I couldn't make much out. We were on the real outskirts of town where it was more woodland and hedgerows with the occasional cottage dotted in-between. The peculiar thing about Oxfordshire is that one moment you're in a rather gothic-looking town, the next the wilderness. Zean fumbled around for a door-knocker, rapping ten times before the door actually swung open an inch to reveal a hooked nose with a pair of crooked glasses on the tip.

"Zean? What are you...? What time is it?" Jackson fumbled, his voice heavy with sleep. Zean opened his mouth to respond, maybe apologize, but there was a jumble of padded thumping sounds before the door was snatched from Jackson's hand and swung wide to show Loraline wearing a mismatching pair of wool socks, Wonder Woman knickers, pink frilled bra, and a worried expression.

"Khyle, what's wrong?" she said.

Jackson rolled his eyes as if this meant he was certainly up for an early start, and opened the door to let us in. Zean's eyes were transfixed by Loraline as she grabbed my arm and towed me inside. I tried not to wince, even though her touch was incredibly gentle, and let Zean begin. I was starting to get that overtired feeling where living zombie becomes a reality.

The inside opened straight into a living room of wide oak floorboards, and panelling on one side of the wall. The other side was a mass of dark oak-framed French glass, turned into a mirror by the night, but the outline of overgrown vines on the other side was just barely visible, pushing against the panels. The far wall was just a mass of shelves, covered with yet more books, photo frames, deco statues, and other bits and bobs. That was where Jackson seemed to end. The furniture was low, overstuffed and covered in multi-coloured striped blankets. Half-burnt candles of every colour imaginable were scattered everywhere in hand-painted glass holders; fluffy red and white shag carpets were spread between the sofas with stray books left on them; and beautiful abstract, antique oil paintings of nude women hung on the wall. The mix of Loraline and Jackson bizarrely worked in an eclectic, almost sophisticated way.

Loraline led me over to the couch, sitting me down, holding on to every word Zean said, her eyes getting wider and darker with each word.

"I knew it. That guy just oozes trouble. His aura is about as dark as it gets, plus he gives me the goosebumps," she said, Zean nodding vigorously to agree with her every word. I was starting to guess why he did so much work for Jackson, especially as he really didn't need the money.

"I tried to get her to go to the hospital, but—"

"I have a thing about places where they like to insert tubes into openings they make themselves," I muttered.

Jackson, clad in green and white plaid pyjamas, rubbed his eyes and got up. "Alright, alright, let me have a look." He came and sat next to me, aiming a light over so he could look at it. Every touch he gave my clenched fist felt like a saw.

He looked over to Loraline. "Get me some bandages, and, ah, have we got any lolly sticks?"

Loraline was already up. "I'll improvise if we haven't, and I'll make some tea, and maybe some tonic for the pain. I think I have some kava and turmeric mix left over that'll send her off as well."

Zean sprang up. "I'll help you," he said, a little too eagerly.

Loraline shrugged and hopped off, still in her underwear. I wished I could prance around that confidently half-naked.

"Do you know why he tried to hurt *you*? Was it sexu—?" asked Jackson.

"No!" I broke in. He was looking at me down his nose with such warmth and tenderness, I felt like I might cry just for that. "I think he thinks he knows me," I said carefully.

"Do you?"

"I hope not." My voice was very small.

He nodded slowly, his eyes still on me. "Your hand should be fine. I'm no physician, but you're not the only stubborn girl I know who's broken something and doesn't like doctors."

We both smiled at each other as Loraline and Zean re-entered with arms full of white bandages, brown bottles with handmade labels, and what looked like a pack of cocktail sticks.

"Qualified butchers playing with vile artificial concoctions," Loraline declared, perching on the arm of the settee. "There's nothing that can be done to the human body that can't be healed with Mother Nature." I didn't have the heart or the strength to say I disagreed entirely but had a history with people in white coats.

"The guy should be behind bars, though. I think we should call the police; if he's got it in for Khyle, then he's going to be dangerous to others, right?" Zean said, handing over bandages and sticks – and I tried not to cry or scream.

"Very true," said Jackson, "but there's little the police can do at this point. They'll file the report. But, Khyle, how precisely did this happen?" He gestured to my hand.

"I hit him," I choked.

He nodded. "You see, we have nothing on him, and if Khyle is truly against the idea, then it's stirring a hornet's nest for the sake of it. I do think we should keep a careful eye on both him and Khyle, though."

I wanted to hug him. I didn't want to involve the police more out of fear *for* the police. Marcus was dangerous in a way that I knew they couldn't handle. I just felt the truth behind the impossible. He was the guy, he was a predator, he was lethal and just like in my dreams, and I was drawn to him. I had wanted to go with him, to be with him. My mind was going to be the end of me, clearly.

"Do you know whether he's ever done anything like this before?" Zean asked as I screwed my eyes closed.

Loraline brushed back some of my hair. "Hold in there," she said softly to me, and then to Zean, "No. I mean, he's all dark and dangerous and straight women say he's handsome or whatever, but he keeps to himself, he's never outright attacked someone."

I heard the hesitation in her voice. "Outright?" I asked.

"Well, he hangs around at the bars a lot, and at the local whorehouse, but it's normal for whores to go missing so the police do nothing."

"That was why I asked whether it was sexual," Jackson interjected.

"There's nothing wrong with a healthy sexual appetite," I burst out. Jeez, was I defending him; had I lost all reasoning in my pea-sized brain? "Where's Jaz?" I blurted out to change the subject, now more preoccupied by the idea that she might overhear and never sleep again.

"Asleep. She can't hear us," Loraline crooned.

"Do you think he has something to do with that girl Delia who went missing in September?" Zean said.

My eyes snapped open, shooting Zean a warning look through the pain. If he brought up encounters of the third kind I'd break the other hand on him.

"Why?" Loraline exclaimed sharply.

"No reason, just wondering," Zean replied coolly.

She sighed, sounding a little defeated. "I don't know. He goes to Casper's, and everyone thinks that place had something to do with her going. He… I don't know, I really just don't."

I don't know what possessed me but I took Loraline's hand. Still not a lesbian.

"He just doesn't fit. There was something about Delia's disappearance that meant more than one person was involved. That sort of brutality – what happened to Catharine – is difficult for one person to cause in such a short period of time, in the open. This Marcus may be an unhealthy character but part of a conspiracy. Besides, the police already checked him out. Apparently he had an alibi."

Trust Jackson to give such a more useful answer.

The kettle started to whistle from the other room. "Khyle, I'm going to make some herbal tea and put this" – Loraline held up a thumb-sized brown bottle – "in it. It'll stop the pain, I promise, and it'll send you straight to sleep within an hour. I promise it will help. Would you like a shower? You're, eh—"

I finished for her. "A total train wreck. Actually, a shower sounds lovely. Thank you, both of you. This, beyond anything, I don't know how I can ever say thank you enough for."

Loraline laughed, walking into the other room. Jackson finished wrapping my throbbing mummy hand.

"Finish indexing. You wouldn't babysit Jazmine for me a little next week too? She's taken an uncharacteristic liking to you, and I have to do a few seminars," he said, practically smiling ear to ear.

I laughed, feeling, bizarrely, a little flattered that Jazmine liked me. I knew those creepy pictures of the resident ghost must mean something other than that she was trying to annoy the hell out of me. "Of course, I'd love to. Erm, doesn't she go to school, though?"

Loraline shoved a cup of some overly sweet smelling liquid into my good hand that I half expected to be green and bubbling. "Quickly, down it, and then I'll show you to the bathroom upstairs. You can have a shower, and then you can have my bed for the night. You look like you're about to fall asleep any second."

I obediently did as I was told, forcing the scorching hot syrupy mixture down in as few gulps as possible. In comparison to my hand,

I barely noticed the rebellious throbs of my tongue and throat as it seared going down.

I was too tired to press about Jazmine, or ask what Zean would do, or say thanks, or even take in my surroundings, as Loraline took me gently by the arm and steered me to a (surprise!) thick black oak staircase to the left. My legs were intolerably heavy to move, and each step felt like an anvil was attached to my feet. "I've got an en suite you can use. You don't want to use the guest bathroom. The last time Jackson cleaned it he still had red hair," she laughed.

"Jackson had red hair?" I had just enough energy to find that a little funny.

"Oh yeah. He was the picture of Ron Weasley-ness!" she said, opening a door from the hallway, and then another inside that, and pulling a cord to give a flickering purple light into the bathroom. Anyone else, you would have thought that a bit eccentric. Loraline? You'd expect it.

She hovered a moment. "Everything's in there. Eh… " She disappeared a second, and came back holding a green wool jumper and black underwear. "You can sleep in these. They might swamp you a little; I'm a bit taller than you. And I'll put your clothes through the washer." She smiled, her expression growing sympathetic. "Do you need any help or anything in particular?"

I didn't know what I needed so instead I just wrapped my arms around her, breathing in lavender and primrose. "Thank you so much. And no, I'm fine." She left me to it, probably the kindest thing anyone had done so far.

I let the door swing closed on its own, and looked around. Loraline's bathroom was small and colourful. A tangerine threadbare rug filled most of it over the grey-green tiled floor. Every inch was cluttered with bottles of different shampoos, conditioners, organic bubble baths, homemade soups, shower gels, strange vials of leafy creams. She'd even gone as far as to paint any wood red or green, and border the mirror with a pattern of blue and lime diamonds. It made my already sore eyes water. I stripped off my muddy clothes, taking a quick glance in the mirror. My eyes were wide and bloodshot, and there were bruises, already turning bright hues of grey and purple, around my neck and down my chest and ribs. There was a cut above my eyebrow encrusted with dried blood, and leaves and dirt streaks in my hair. I looked totally grotesque. I grabbed the nearest bottle of shower gel and another of shampoo, pulled back Loraline's glittery shower curtain, and let myself sink to my knees under the soft trickle of heat, watching as mud and blood fled down the drain.

I refused to cry. It wouldn't have been out of fear or shock anyway; it would have been through exhaustion. The thing that was the most draining was that part of me was horribly aware that something in me hadn't wanted to run from Marcus, hadn't thought of what he was planning to do to me. Part of me just wanted to stay with my human magnet. I wanted those answers. I started scrubbing, digging the nails of my good hand into my already raw and battered skin. How could I have been so stupid? How could I still be so stupid as to be so upset that I'd run? He could have killed me. Was I suicidal now, or had I just lost all sense? Angry thoughts, one after the other, until I was scrubbing and scratching so hard I was drawing new blood, fresh scratches. Immediately, I stopped the water, breathing hard and scowling down the drain. I didn't take enough time to push the shower curtain away; I stumbled out of the bathroom, feeling around for the jumper and knickers Loraline had supplied, and clumsily pulled them on. I didn't make it to the bed. My body gave in, a protective device, to safeguard me from what had happened, and probably, from myself. Or it could even just have been what Loraline had given me. Either way, I curled up on the soft carpet and let the world drift away.

Smells tart. Like lemon. Lemon and sugar and cream. They were the only beautiful things that this place produced, the only thing that was truly harmless, and they were shaped like roses. Each one the size of a child's fingertip, and the colour of his eyes when he was angry: deep, deep black with silver specks like the sky. I crouched in a patch of them, trying to concentrate only on them, but failing badly. I had my back to them, but I could still hear them, almost twenty feet away and still too loud. Twenty feet was as far as I could make myself go. I'd tried hundreds of time to go further, but it was no use; my feet just stomped on the spot while I silently cried. So instead I had to sit curled up in the grass and flowers, my hands over my ears, rocking back and forth to try and ignore their moaning. It seemed like forever since he'd taken the girl to his favourite spot. The place he took all the girls. I knew I shouldn't know what was happening. Once upon a time there was someone who would have protected me, let me stay a kid. But you had to grow up fast here, in spirit.

There were cries from behind me, echoing around the clearing, and then it all stopped; nothing but a rustling of movement, and the sound of petals being squished as I rocked. I felt, rather than saw, the girl rush past me, felt the hem of her robe brush me and the sound of her feet in the grass. Then there were just heavy footsteps, and a thud as he sat down beside me. Oh no. I hated it when he actually recognized that I was there, I hated it when he actually paid attention to me. Incredibly, so softly it could have been a breeze, he pushed my hair behind my ear with one hand, the other pressing down on my shoulder to steady me. I stopped immediately, frozen, too scared to look up.

"You've been abandoned, little one, you know that? No one will ever come for you, as much as both of us wish they would." I didn't say anything; I didn't know what to say.

"How old are you?" he breathed. His tone had changed from icy to... warm? That wasn't possible. When I didn't answer, two fingers gripped my chin, forcing me to look at him. I hated his eyes.

"I don't remember. I can't tell any more, there's no birthdays here." I could hear my voice trembling but I couldn't stop it. Weakness was worse than blasphemy here. I saw it then: actual sympathy. Pain for me flashed behind his eyes, his fingers brushing my cheek.

"You're so small, just a little girl. You shouldn't have to—" He broke off as he realized what he was doing. He was showing me pity, caring. His touch immediately dug into my cheek and I cried out, wriggling away, sending petals flying up into the air.

"I've never done anything to you. You said it yourself: I'm just a kid," I said desperately.

He shook his head. "You exist. That's your only fault, and for both our sakes I am so sorry."

I rolled over onto my back. Lemons. And honeycomb, sage, camomile, green tea, mint, incense, oil, scented candles. I'd either woken up in an Eastern brothel or Zean was cooking again. I opened my eye, the world tilting left and right and making my stomach churn. The brothel. Suddenly everything from last night, or rather this morning, started to creep back into my being; the mass of silks, velvets, fluffy pillows, Asian replicas, candles. Make sense, it was just Loraline's kaleidoscope bedroom. But still, lemons. In the mass of smells, lemons were the only scent that stuck out.

I crawled up off the floor trying to shake the grogginess away. It didn't work. Whatever Loraline has shoved down me was still running around my system, playing havoc. The world was spinning and I almost felt numb from the tips of my hair downward. I ran a hand through my hair and then realized which hand I was using. "Shit," I muttered immediately, removing it as it began to throb lazily. If it hurt this much under God-knows-what, I hated to think what it would be like when I wasn't witchy and spaced out. My stomach lurched.

I was starving; all the adrenaline last night had sapped the energy from every cell in my body. Gingerly I felt around towards the door, accidentally knocking over stray bottles of nail polish and other clutter that had the audacity to get in my way,, and that I couldn't properly focus on, my knee finally colliding with a chair as I literally hit the door. What the hell had she done to me? I felt like someone was putting me through a cheese grinder while on a rollercoaster ride… Ah, even my similes were off.

It was brighter out in the hallway, and immediately that bitter lemony smell was replaced with one of grinding coffee and slightly burnt toast. My mouth watered. I crept down, slowly but steadily dragging my hands against the thick flowery wallpaper, leaning most of my weight there as a counterbalance against the need to fall to the side dizzily. One step after the other, I looked down at my feet, creamy white against the rusty dark oak. Bad idea. I lost my concentration and my balance, fell to the right expecting the wall to steady me; but rather than wallpaper, my hand touched wood (no pun intended) and a door swung open, letting me fall face-first to the floor. "Shit," I muttered again. Clearly witch *healer* was not Loraline's job description.

Groaning, I got again to my feet using an antique desk to pull my rebellious body back up. As I hoisted myself level with the desk surface, my eyes came face to face with an almost identical pair in black and white. I blanched, jumping almost a foot in the air. I'd literally fallen into a small study. The books Jackson had been unable to fit into his shop and living room had found their way into here. The walls were white, but covered with equations and notes written straight onto them, along with a mosaic pattern of yellow sticky labels. This oversized antique desk took up most of it, covered in papers and notes and mathematical calculators, and an A4-sized silver deco photo-frame. It was one of those ones that they had back in the seventies and eighties where it was a mixture of dulled colours and black and white. A mass of people were posed in front of a huge building, perched on the stairs to a double door entrance. It looked like it could be the outside of a college or something. I didn't recognise anybody, except one. They ranged from twenty to fifty, but there was a twenty-something woman perched right at the front, her long mousy-brown hair braided and swinging down to her elbows where she sat, laughing.

I'd never seen my mother laugh, but her plump cheeks spread to encompass a massive full-toothed open smile, little creases appearing around her eyes, which looked back at me full of warmth and hope. She was wearing flares and a crisp white shirt tucked into them, and she was holding a couple of books loosely in her hand. A man was kneeling down beside her, one elbow resting cockily on his knee as he whispered in her ear. He was looking away from the photo, but even in profile I could tell he was handsome, in a cocky playboy-loves-himself kind of way. I gripped the corner of the table, managing to force one shaking hand to pick it up and bring it closer, rubbing my thumb over her face. She looked just like a normal girl. When was this? Where was this? Who were these people? What was Jackson doing with a photo of my Mum?

"Khyle?" There were footsteps behind me and then a gentle hand on my shoulder. "What are you doing in here?" Jackson sounded like he was trying to hide a healthy dose of bewilderment. My immediate response was to apologize for snooping but I couldn't manage it; after all, it wasn't my fault I'd been drugged by his lodger.

"What is this?" I managed.

Jackson looked at the photo, frowning. "That was taken in the eighties outside the MPLS division of Oxford University, back when I was still an ignorant graduate student rather than an ignorant old man." He smiled.

I felt like I was choking. "MPLS?"

"Mathematical and Physical Life Sciences Division. Have you ever visited Oxford University? It's split into a dozen or so sub-colleges. They're beautiful places. Are you alright?"

Mathematical and Physical Life Sciences? My mother? Not possible, surely. Jackson tilted the photo to look at it, pushing his glasses up slightly.

"Were you all students there?" I croaked.

"Most. Some were professors who like to spend their hours with their students for some bizarre reason." He laughed. "And some" – he pointed at the man kneeling by my mother – "weren't students at all. He was actually a son of a dean at the university, but rebelled with every last ounce of his being. We were all friends. Whether educated or not, all connected with a need to understand, in our own clumsy ways, how the world ticked on." He chuckled to himself again, his eyes lost back in another place and time.

"And her?" I pointed directly at the smiling figure I'd seen so many horrible times before, but never like that.

"Oh, Jane Exeter. Your mother, I believe. She was brilliant. Brilliant *and* beautiful. Traits I believe or I think she may have passed down to you, though I dare say you may be abusing them a little." His words were kind, but the moment he looked at my face he seemed to get a grip on what was going through my head. "Ah" was all he came out with.

"You knew my mother and you never said anything?" It would have been a screech but my voice no longer reached that octave.

"You never asked," he said matter-of-factly.

Not good enough. I turned to go, furious, but had to grip something to stop from falling on my face. He took my shoulder.

"You're still disorientated. Let me—"

I shook him off. "No, get off me. Jeez, I thought you were helping, like I could trust someone or, at the very least, that someone was normal, or as normal as a witch and the mad professor get." At the back of my mind I knew this wasn't as much Jackson's deceiving me as his touching on a very tender spot of my life.

"Khyle, breathe. You'll make yourself faint. I wasn't sure how much you knew of your mother, and it was not my place to tell you. For all I knew, you hadn't seen her since you were a small child. You may not even have known of her at all," he said steadily, peering at me down his long, crooked nose in that calm warm way he had about him.

I breathed as he said, feeling oxygen start to pump back to my brain. "She was brilliant?" I breathed again, unsure of what else to say. Part of me didn't want to know, part of me didn't want to have to mourn any more than I already did. To feel the loss of an actual person was ten times more difficult than to mourn a vegetable.

"She was, in her own way. But then, aren't we all? Brilliance, after all, is something totally subjective to person and circumstance. She was a student; she struggled; she found her heart wanted other things than knowledge. She was young and free, as most of us were in the eighties. This, perhaps, is a conversation for another time. When you feel more together, have less to deal with... know whether and what you truly want to know."

I admired how a physics professor could be so attentive to the inner working of the human mind. Weren't those kinds of people meant to be entirely objective to balance out such high intellects? I suppose, of course, he was primarily a person and then a genius;

that's what one tends to forget about smart-arses. Considering I'd grown up you'd think it would have sunk in by now.

As he led me out of the study, shutting the door firmly behind him, I was compelled to ask, "Do you know—?"

He cut in. "Of her condition? Of course. That's why I wanted to offer you the job so badly; you deserve what help anyone could give you to start out in life. Your mother loved you, Khyle. I'm sure she still does."

That last sentence was it. I didn't want to know any more if I didn't have to; I could already sense the feeling of being choked with buried emotions. And all I could think to say was "Small world, huh?", my voice devoid of any emotion.

Jackson nodded, and smiled half-heartedly, but didn't say anything. I wondered whether he could guess the thousands of questions I should, but never would, ask.

Chapter Seven

The hand is composed of twenty-seven bones including those in the wrist, some as small as a few centimetres long. Looking down at mine, it felt like I'd broken each in turn. Over a week had gone by since the incident with Marcus and it seemed, in my opinion, to be getting worse. It kept swelling, so Jackson had to remove and re-apply the bandages, but he only tried once to persuade me to go to hospital which was met with a "you-know-exactly-why-I'd-rather-have-my-hand-placed-in-a-blender-than-go-to-a-sterile-butcher's" look, and had given in immediately.

I hadn't asked any more about Mum and he didn't push me to find things out. At the moment he was right: I had too much on my mind anyway, without that pain to deal with. As for Delia, Zean had told Loraline everything, though I'd made them both swear not to say a word to Jackson. The fact that he knew my mother, and what condition she was in, now made the idea of him thinking I was going down the same route about as painful as my hand. Loraline, though, had marvelled. She'd believed me without question, and said I must have a strong psychic connection with Delia that no one else in the coven did, and therefore I should focus more on trying to find her, and less on what had happened to her. She was oblivious to my desperate need for a story out of this whole mess. As it was, her and

Zean had been off together, continuously trying to find things about spirits and about Delia herself, but neither of them wanted to (and refused in all manner of ways to let me) go near Casper's.

All in all I was slowly being smothered to death to the point where I was wishing I was doing this alone still, at my own pace; though of course Delia's pace was probably a lot more vital, and for Delia the faster the better. The only good thing that had passed was that now, for the first time in my life, I was having new dreams, of Delia alive happy, alive broken, somewhere between alive and dead, and seriously pissed off. No more Marcus. At least, not in my dreams anyway. Whether it was Zean, Jackson, Loraline or, to my horror, very recently the painstaking Adam, I was being chauffeured everywhere. Of course Adam didn't know why. He was just happy to be acting like a five foot ten inches high golden retriever. It made no real difference, though; I could feel Marcus. For the first time in my life I could safely say this wasn't paranoia; he really was there. Sometimes I caught his eye out of the corner of my own, but by the time I'd turned fully to see him he'd disappeared into the shadows. Okay, when you put it like that it did sound like paranoia. His Jaguar, which in all fairness was pretty distinctive, had been parked a little way away from GUTs a few times, which Adam had commented on, admiring the car while I wondered whether I was going to have a knife pulled on me.

Now I was walking home – for the first time in what felt like a lifetime – alone. I'd managed to ditch Adam by telling him I wanted to pop by the chemist's and buy tampons. Men. The temperature was dropping by the day, frost and black ice covering windows, and the pavement and crisping leaves turning to spade-shaped icicles. It was all over the news still, except storms had turned to gales of ice and sleet. It wasn't particularly the weather that had the world baffled; it was just that it was the world with both hemispheres the same temperature, and with the same weather conditions: an apparently possible impossibility.

I rummaged in my bag for my keys. I felt completely calm; cold but calm. I wasn't as scared of Marcus as it would probably have been sensible to be. I wasn't saying he didn't scare the shit out of me because he did, but not in the life or death way that should have had me hiding under the sheets all day and night. The thing was, I'd faced him each night of my life. I couldn't properly remember the dreams, but I remembered his face, the feel of him, how he made me feel; and those feelings weren't life or death, just scary and painful. Something inside me, something naive and misled and suicidal, was desperately, achingly, curious.

I shoved the door open, a wash of heat hitting me like a welcoming dog, and I felt every muscle in my body (other than my hand, which preferred things numbingly cold) release and uncoil. I quickly closed the door behind me to keep the cold out, flung my jacket and bag in the living room, and started to make my way upstairs. Zean and Loraline should be home pretty soon after visiting the art college Delia (sometimes) went to, and we were all going to have a brainstorming session to see if we could put some of this puzzle together; and I just wanted to take some of the painkillers Jackson had given me before I spent an hour going over stuff we already knew, getting more frustrated by the second, and watching Zean make moo eyes at Loraline. I really should tell her that all this time she'd been spending with Zean, who was totally oblivious to the fact Loraline was more gay than Ellen DeGeneres, was giving him the wrong impression.

I stopped just outside my room. The door was ajar and the smell… I used cinnamon air freshener because the smell of lemons, I found, gave me a horrible sickening feeling of terror and pain. Lemon. Sugar. Cream. I wanted to run down the stairs screaming, or throw a match into the place without so much as a step through the threshold., Instead, bracing myself, I kicked the door open, ready to run if need be. My heart kicked into overdrive. Eyes wide, I stepped into my literally gloomy room. On the bright side, it was empty of people: on the downside, I didn't know how the hell I was going to hide this from Zean before he hired a personal bodyguard. Millions of unopened rosebuds, dyed the colour and matt finish of black pearls, littered my room. They were piled over my bed, stacked together in heaps almost a foot high on the floorboards, over my desk, and sprinkled over the window-sill where the wide glass panels were ajar, letting the cold wind freeze my room and blow them about, a few dancing past my ankles and out into the hall.

I tiptoed into my room, almost scared to squash or step on them, they were so beautiful; beautiful and petrifying. I ran my fingertips over one, its satin-like petals breaking off under my touch, they were so delicate. Just its touch conjured up images, spinning wildly behind my eyelids, of people screaming, a child, just a little girl, huddled in their midst, too scared to look up There were women, beautiful and dark, their arms outstretched. My eyes snapped open. I gasped; memories from my dreams, monstrosities I never remembered now painted in my mind's eye. I dropped to my bed, gasping for oxygen but only getting lungfuls of that tart sweetness making me cringe and gag. I moved to get up and start hiding them before Zean got back, but my hand crushed against something that crumpled. I looked down, and there on my bed was a drawing: a sketch, serenely lifelike and unsettling. There I was, my eyes closed, my hair brushing my cheeks, and my brow furrowed, almost pained. Beneath it, scrawled in italic old-style letters was "You are rather enchanting when you sleep. It's the only time yet you haven't answered back while I've been with you. Mark."

I felt dizzy, nauseous from the smell, sick with something between horror, alarm, and even worse, excitement. I jumped up, my mind and body kicking into overdrive, running a shaking hand through my tangled hair and gathering it at the base of my neck, a reflexive habit of mine for as long as I could remember. I stood in the middle of my room, looking desperately around. Should I tell Zean? Should I show him? No. He couldn't handle any more before he got too worried for me and called the police. He was the sensible one, clearly. I would deal with this; it was, after all, between me and Marcus. Mark? He'd called himself Mark for short. Jeez, woman, of all the things to notice at a time like this. I started grabbing armfuls of rosebuds, kicking my suitcase over with my foot, and stuffing them in madly. When the suitcase was full, I ran down to the kitchen and grabbed a black bag, returning for the rest and shovelling them in. The dregs were pushed into the closet just as I heard the front door unlocking, Zean's and Loraline's voices drifting up from downstairs, Zean calling, "Yo, zombie, it's us, you home?"

"Yeah, I'm up here; I'll be down in a sec."

I looked wildly around, grabbing the drawing and shoving it under a pillow as Loraline appeared in the hallway.

"Mm, what's that smell? It's gorgeous."

"Eh, new air freshener," I blurted frantically, out of breath.

Loraline smiled, nodding slowly, her eyes examining mine, reflecting on how mad the look on my face must be.

"Hey, wow, you alright?" Zean appeared in the doorway, his cheeks pink from the cold.

Some distant part of my brain registered that Loraline was clad in a thin camisole and denim hot pants. She was totally insane.

"Yeah, I'm good. How'd it go?" I asked, trying to wipe my face bare of freaked-out-ness.

"Not much we didn't know. Either of you want a beer and nachos?" Typical Zean, stomach first, everything else second. I shrugged.

"So this is your room," Loraline said, ignoring Zean.

"Yeah, needs decorating. I think you could help with that, Miss Technicolor decorator," I joked, pushing past her to go downstairs and away from that freaking smell.

She laughed, coming down behind me and dropping onto the living room floor cross-legged, as if this was her second home and not a house she had never stepped into before now. "Oh, absolutely, I'll have you kitted out in seconds. How do you feel about pink? Or plaid? I could definitely see pink and purple plaid."

"Do you want to vacate now or later, K?" Zean laughed, coming in with a six-pack and a bowl of spicy nachos.

"Later. That way, after she's created me a brothel of a room she can pay for the hotel I'll be staying in." I laughed, grabbing a handful of nachos to avoid any more conversation until I could get my pulse running steady again. "So what did you find?" I muttered, covering my mouth to avoid crumb spray.

Loraline sighed and shrugged, placing her delicate chin in her hands. "Same old thing: how nice and sweet Delia was… em… is… most bubbly girl they've known, great art student, really promising, always talked about opening her own gallery or designing eco-friendly designer clothes." Loraline laughed. "Yup, no dangerous ex; in fact, no guys at all, ever, as far as anyone knows. Didn't go out clubbing, no hardcore drugs. In fact, the only reason she was meant to be hanging out with Catharine was for an Aids fundraiser."

"Which could be saying something about Catharine, but nothing unexpected," Zean added, on sitting right behind Loraline as if more than a two-foot radius was unthinkable.

I nodded, getting up to look at the 'Finding Delia' zone we'd created in the corner where all the newspapers and books and our own notes and ideas had been spread across two tables, and some pieces, like Delia's missing poster, had been stuck to the wall. I ran my fingers over the newspaper photocopies, picking one up to read. It was the newspaper article the library women had been going on about. Why on earth had she photocopied this out? Mind you, she'd also included a copy of a Baxter's soup ad so I guessed she wanted to make the total photocopying fee up to a nice round figure. It was dated October third and headlined 'Schizo in Oxford bistro'. Tabloids.

"I was thinking, maybe, if you both were up for it, maybe we could do a little spell." Loraline's voice was very small, but not a bit unsure.

"A spell," I stated, sarcasm oozing from every syllable as I turned back to them.

"Ay, hear her out, will you," Zean snapped defensively. Blimey, next he'd be writing poetry.

"Yes, a spell. Nothing big. I mean, we at the coven have tried scrying a dozen times and we never got anywhere—"

"Scrying?" I interjected.

"Yes, scrying. You know, to see the future with crystals and a map or fire. You know, alchemists did it all the time, back in the sixteenth century, with water," she said, so matter-of-factly she could have been stating the Earth was round.

I nodded. "Bet the church loved that," I muttered, sitting back down.

"Well no, actually, but I'll give you a private history lesson later if you're eager." Mee-ow!! "I thought a spell to enhance your, our, psychic link and ability, channel it towards Delia. If she's trying to contact you anyway then it should be a breeze, and best of all, it would be for all of us to see so we might all notice different things. What do you think?"

I thought, if you were born to any other century we'd be informing the vicar to have you burnt alive at the stake.

"Why not? Got nothing else to do tonight," Zean said, stuffing more nachos into his gob.

"Khyle?" Loraline asked tentatively.

I hesitated. Truth was, I didn't really want to *enhance* any connection me and Delia were having, even if it did help. They hadn't seen it, felt it, and it wasn't exactly a trip to the flicks; more a trip to hell.

It could help Delia, Delia the arty hippy, who everyone loved and who wanted to save the world and wouldn't hurt a fly but probably nurse it back to health to buzz around someone's head another day.

I groaned, flopping back on the couch. "What do we have to do?" I was defeated.

Loraline jumped up immediately, beaming as if she were going to hug me. "I knew you'd want to try it" – because I looked and sounded that eager? And Zean was just nonchalant? – "I've got everything in my bag. It shouldn't take long to set up. We're going to have to make some space, though."

Twenty minutes later we'd moved the furniture, the evil TV and the coffee table against the wall, and a chalk and salt circle had been drawn in the middle. I felt like I'd stepped onto a Buffy set, with Loraline as Willow the lesbian witch minus the red hair. We sat cross-legged in the middle, forming a lopsided triangle with a Jack Daniels glass of water, a yellow candle, mugwort incense, and a seven-faced stub of a clear quartz crystal carefully set up between us. Loraline explained carefully what we had to do, Zean concentrating hard on her every word, his tongue pointing out of the side of his mouth like it did when he was dealing with one of those equations he sometimes worked on that involved two walls of his bedroom and a serious lick of paint afterward.

"Okay, join hands," Loraline sighed, straightening her back and shaking her mane of silky black hair over her shoulders. "Close your eyes, breathe, calm yourself, release any tension, starting from your toes, your calf, your waist" – and Zean was going to be getting an erection if she kept up like this – "focus on the world around you, the energies, our energies."

I was focusing pretty hard not to giggle, but other than that I was failing in the relax department. Nothing about any of this was encouraging me to relax, not the idea of seeing Delia, not the echo of Mark hovering constantly at the back of my mind, not the incense, nothing. And I noticed the smell of lemons was creeping downstairs now. I concentrated on my surroundings.

Loraline began to chant, her voice winding like an invisible ribbon around us, connecting us. "Fire burning true and bright, let my second sight ignite, water clairvoyant and clear, let mental barriers now disappear."

Zean broke in. "Earth join, steady us three. One, future, past, present we see." His voice was serene and soft, not very Zean-like.

I was very aware that it was my line, but I didn't want to open my mouth. What if it worked? Then what? I didn't want to go through it all again… Delia, it's for Delia, it's for Delia.

"Air, pure and forever wise… " I paused. I could feel the air crackling around me. "Sort now" – I lost my breath as a vibrating tingle ran through my fingers to Zean, and then back through Loraline, and then back again, a current growing with each breath – "fact from lies," I breathed, barely loud enough to hear.

It built, pushing up under my skin, flying around us like a tornado, encompassing us, joining us. I could feel myself spinning inside my own head. Then, as if someone had broken down an invisible wall, foreign emotions started to sweep into me, lust, excitement, withdrawal, alarm, pure undiluted kindness. They blended; I couldn't tell which ones came from who; and then it burst, the tornado dying in under a heartbeat. A flood of images sprang into my mind, like a snapshot of scenes from movies I'd never seen; a little girl, her hair curling around her shoulders as she played in a field; Loraline, looking radiant and scantily dressed, sat with a group of other women, with her laughing as the kids played and the sun shone; a gangly teenager, her hair longer and tied back with a scrunchy, as she laughed and spooned soup out into plastic cups as the biting cold tried to freeze everyone. Older still, the girl from the photo, now crying, holding another girl, her hair short and dyed electric blue, as she rocked her back and forth, desperation oozing from them both; and a figure lying on a grey flagstone floor, naked, bleeding sores so red they looked like burns.

I was just aware enough of my body to feel myself double over as that figure's pain knocked into me. She was so alone and lost. Nowhere could or would anyone ever find her where they would send her; she'd never eat Bakewell tarts again, or kiss a guy, or hold her mum, or play basketball with her dad. The figure vanished into darkness before a flame the size of my thumb, blue and gold, started to dance in the dark, growing steadily taller, running up two things: bare legs spread at a strange angle, up a torso, illuminating a square white dress so stiff it could have been paper. Finally, the figure burst into flames, her face distorted and spread tightly over swollen black eyes; her once-straight strong nose was crooked, arched and pink around the sides; her hair had been shaved leaving a short crewcut around her scalp. Delia stared at me, her eyes lost in shadow. As she started to fade I could feel her soft cries. She'd given up crying out to me, to anyone. This was her life now, a world of pain and of disbelief and confusion. I watched the fire flicker, watched her fade, her dress flapping in an invisible wind, a last flicker of light shooting over her, throwing a label on that dress into light. I pulled back, disconnecting my hands from the other two and knocking the water over onto the carpet.

I jumped over to our investigation corner, wiping out the story I'd been looking at… what, ten minutes ago? An hour ago? There had been a label on the dress, or rather her paper surgical gown. It had read 'Patient Jane Doe, St Matthews'.

I heard Zean groan, and then a shuffling sound as he ran out of the room; I could hear him throwing up violently in the kitchen. My own stomach was churning, but after the past three weeks it had learnt to be strong. Loraline was swearing under her breath, her voice trembling.

I found it, whipping it out from the mess: 'Schizo in Oxford Bistro. Oxford. Sunday. Police arrested a young female after she burst into The Tearooms bistro in Oxford High Street, naked and screaming of the "end of days". The girl was reported to be battered and disfigured beyond any immediate recognition by the Missing Persons Department. The young woman has been identified as being seventeen years old, and Caucasian. She had sustained three broken ribs, deep punctures to the left temple and frontal lobe, with a face that patrons described as "a thing from nightmares".

'The girl knocked over several tables, and attempted to assault a waitress who had been working at the bistro. After police removed the girl from the site, she was taken to hospital where doctors believe that she had been a victim of brutal and terrorising torture and that she had been lucky to have survived at all. Jane Doe has been moved to St Matthew's Psychiatric Clinic, Cheltenham, where she has been admitted to a new specialist section of the clinic designed for cases such as her own… '

I didn't have to read any more. "I know where Delia is," I muttered, walking over to the couch, perching on the arm, and passing the photocopy to Loraline, who scrambled to get up, snatching it out of my hand and scanning it.

Zean came in, pressing a wet cloth to the back of his neck. "That was intense," he said. "Is it always like that? I mean, wow, talk about abusing the known and observed laws of sweet science." He laughed, oblivious to the look on my face

"No. It isn't usually like that. Khyle? She's like a sinkhole for Delia's energy or, well, *any* energy, I think. You think this is her? It fits. God, that vision. She's just a little girl."

She sounded close to tears. I moved to get up and hold her, but Zean got there first, wrapping his arms around her. The boy was trying, that was for sure, though Loraline didn't exactly fall into his arms, remaining stiff as if he wasn't there. He didn't seem to notice at all.

I pushed the hair impatiently off my face, pacing to the window. Specialist ward, people of her condition; she was with Mum. Could that have something do with why it had been me? I didn't know how far I believed in all of this, but coincidence was starting to sound a bit far-fetched. The horrible thing, though, was that I wasn't sure I could do it, not for Delia or a story. I would rather have gone to hell and back to help her than go to that place, with its plush carpets and chandeliers for one side of the world, and its cold white rooms and cages for the other. Was I that bad a person? I would leave an innocent girl, a kid who was calling out to me after being brutally treated beyond all belief, and was so close to giving up all hope because I was a coward, and a selfish one at that.

I leant my head against the cool glass. The street outside was dark and empty, televisions pulsating behind the curtained windows of people leading normal lives, watching soaps or the football or sitting down for dinner, not having freaky séances with the non-dead. The street lamps cast warm orange halos across the parked cars in the street. My lips tightened as I felt an anger explode through me, beating any common sense to a fine pulp. One of the cars outside was a sleek, glossy black Jaguar. And worst of all? Lemons! I could still smell the bloody lemons. I'd never be able to have sherbet again.

I ran for the door, Loraline and Zean shouting out behind me as I stalked out into the cold, goosebumps erupting along my bare forearms. Zean grabbed my arm. "No! Go back into the house. I'll deal with this, you hear me," he said sternly, attempting to steer me back as an orange glow shone behind the Jaguar's windscreen, showing two drawn, dark brows as he lit a cigarette and cranked a window, clearly getting himself comfortable for the display. I raged; how dare he? Could he not tell I had a little too much on my mind at the moment to deal with him? Could he come back in a month or so and then try and kill me for God knows (and I'm not willing to question) whatever reason?

I shoved Zean's hand away with so much force, he was actually thrown back off balance for a second. "You go the hell inside, Zean. I'll be the one dealing with the complete psycho-bastard!"

"Khyle, like hell you will. He'll tear you apart."

"Oh yeah? Well, he hasn't yet, has he? And trust me, and don't read anything into this, Zean, but he's had enough bloody opportunities before now. Now, back off before *I* hurt you!"

Loraline called him back, saying something along the lines of 'there-there' as if I needed them. I wouldn't; I wasn't going to give Mark the gratification of thinking I was weak like that. I grabbed the smooth black handle, yanking it open with all my strength. "Get out!" I seethed through gritted teeth. He looked up at me, his expression not changing from light amusement, calculating every move I made. I shook my head. I'd never felt like this. You could say I'd never given anything enough actual passion or care to feel any emotion this strong. I didn't know what I'd do when, if, he ever got out, but I knew one thing for certain: that I was going to make damned sure he knew.

"I'm not scared of you, you know that? I don't know who you really are, and at this precise moment I don't really care either. I. Do. Not. Have. Any. Bloody. Patience left for this!" I shouted, jumping back from the car and throwing the door back closed. I never heard it slam shut. A choking iron-like grip yanked me by the back of the neck, throwing me back against the car, his hand tightening around my throat, cutting off anything resembling an airway.

Zean immediately lunged forward, grabbing Mark's arm and raising his for a punch. Mark barely moved. One quick and clean movement, and Zean hurtled through the air, hitting the front wall of the house. Maybe confrontation had not been the best policy. I told the idiot to stay away!

"You don't have the patience for it?" He leant in, his voice barely above a whisper, tilting my chin up to meet his eyes. "I have waited a long time, Khyle. Trust me when I say, when it comes to you, I'm going to enjoy taking my time."

"How long *you've* waited? You really think you're intimidating me? You have no idea who you're dealing with, mate." I had to stop to try and suck in some air to continue. "You can threaten to kill me, threaten to kill me slowly. How do you know you wouldn't be doing me a favour? I mean, why on earth do you think that I have an endless ambition to live in the first place" – okay, things going blurry here; breath would be good about now – "because my life is just roses?" Something like confusion or, eh, well, fuck, worry showed so blatantly through him as I said the words, he actually released his grip just enough to let me draw in some air. "Look, you can bleed me, break me, bruise me. I don't really think I care any more; I'm being mentally beaten up every second. But you ever do anything to remind me of my nightmares again, I'll be the one killing you." I tried to push past him and make my grand exit, but he was like marble, stunned marble.

His brow furrowed. "Nightmares? Khyle, what exactly do you think is going on?" he asked evenly; no threat, just pure reason, almost comfort in his voice.

I shrugged. "Actually, I'm trying my best – and failing, may I add – not to think about it," I muttered, rubbing my throat. I would be bruised in the morning.

He reached over to me, taking my throat in his grip again, but tenderly this time, rubbing his thumb gently over where his fingers had been effortlessly squeezing the life from me a few moments before. "You are not scared or intimidated. In the least." He was studying my throat now like he might have his car, intently, almost gently.

"No? I'm scared shitless, just not particularly of you. You could hurt me, Mark. I know you're capable of it, and something in me tells me you might actually be sick enough to enjoy it. But, I don't know, something tells me you won't," I ended lamely.

He laughed. "Wishful thinking." His eyes finally focused, embedded themselves, in mine. I felt myself begin to tremble, the adrenaline of the night finally becoming too much running through me.

"Who are you?" I asked.

He shook his head slightly. "Wrong question, kid. About now it's time to ask who you are."

I stared up at him. I could feel questions replacing the anger. "Marcus, get out of here before I call the police."

"Khyle, please, Zean's hurt." I'd forgotten Loraline was there. I stood where I was, staring up at Mark. "Khyle," Loraline pleaded. Mark rolled his eyes, turned on his heel, and stalked over to where Zean lay. Loraline backed off a bit as he crouched beside him. I ran over to where Zean was lying crumpled and unconscious on the floor. Mark took his arm, pulled his head up by his hair, and then let it fall limply to the floor.

"Give him some ice, he'll live. He's probably had worse hangovers," he growled, getting to his feet and walking back to his car as if he hadn't just assaulted someone.

"Wait," I shouted, but he'd already started the ignition, pulling the car out and speeding off with a deafening screech.

I watched the car turn the corner. Gone in an instant. Loraline came back to crouch by me glaring. "That was stupid. Brave. But stupid," she hissed.

I pursed my lips. "Let's just get him inside," I sighed, starting to feel guilty. Poor Zean. The overgrown panther was right; he'd live, but with one hell of a headache.

Chapter Eight

'A ghost, that loved a lady fair,
Ever in the starry air.
Of midnight at her pillow stood;
And, with a sweetness skies above,
The luring words of human love,
Her soul the phantom wooed.
Sweet and sweet is their poisoned note,
The little snakes of silver throat,
In mossy skulls that nest and lie,
Ever singing, "die, oh! die."

'Young soul, put off your flesh,
and come With me into the quiet tomb,
Our bed is lovely, dark, and sweet;
The earth will swing us, as she goes,
Beneath our coverlid of snows,
And the warm leaden sheet.
Dear and dear is their poisoned note,
The little snakes of silver throat,
In mossy skulls that nest and lie,
Ever singing, "die, oh! die"'

"Thomas Lovell Beddoes, 1803 to 1849. Do you know what gets me the most? It's not that you're making me read you this stuff, coz I've already accepted you're a creepy little pixie, but it's that you understand it. I just can't decipher what it's on about." I lowered the poetry book to look at Jaz, who was tucking deep into a jumbo pack of chocolate buttons. She smiled her little cherub smile.

"Grandpa says it's not about content, but inter-pre-ta-tion" – she stumbled over the word – "like that one. It's not just a girl being haunted by a ghost, it's about a ghost wanting what he shouldn't because her world is light and his is dark, and eventually she decides she loves him too and lives with him in the dark."

I looked down at her. Jackson had obviously passed most of his smarts to her. I sighed. I was on babysitting duty. Zean was fine, but pissed off to the thousandth degree and giving me the silent treatment I totally deserved. I hadn't seen Loraline since yesterday, or was it this morning? After we'd sorted Zean out she'd said she'd best get home, and gone off also looking really pissed off. I didn't get why she was angry, though. Zean, fine. I'd been reckless and got him hurt, but at the end of the day, in my opinion, I would rather have taken the risk than spend each time I opened the door to my room wondering what was going to be staring at me next. That would cause a slow mental breakdown. As it was, I couldn't sleep last night because of bloody lemons. The first chance I got when I was alone in the house, I was going to be putting Zean's fireplace to good use with those flowers. I'd inspected them closer last night; they were just dyed rosebuds, but he'd soaked them in lemon essence or something because the stench had now penetrated my clothes.

I hadn't decided what to do about Delia. I'd even gone as far as to ask Jackson to go for me, but I knew in the end it would probably be me. If Loraline was right, and I doubted the witch would be wrong, then it was me Delia had connected with, Christ knows why, so it was me who was going to have to face a real-life nightmare.

"Khyle?"

"Yup?"

"What do you wanna be when you're properly older?" Oh fabulous, another one who didn't consider nineteen an actual milestone for maturity, and this one was under ten.

"Properly old? Hopefully, snuggled up tight in an old people's home, surrounded by fat, ugly grandchildren, all products of IVF." I laughed, hoping this didn't get back to Jackson. Well, he'd been stupid enough to leave the impressionable angel-genius with me for the day, having offered to do a seminar in Reading.

"What's IVF?" she asked, looking up at me with big eyes, chocolate smeared around her mouth and on the tips of her gloves. Hmm, finally, something she didn't know yet. No need for the sex talk any time soon then.

"What do you want to be when you grow up?" I changed the subject, flicking the book closed as she'd finally, thank God, lost interest.

She smiled. "In love, and pretty, and… em… and a story-teller."

I laughed and stopped walking, crouching down beside her. I'd decided to take her out of the house as me and Zean had pretty much nothing for a kid to do. Zean didn't even own an X-box or anything. Unfortunately, the only place I could think to take her was the park where Mark had taken me. It was one of those bitter white days where it was so cold the rain just stayed up in the clouds, frozen too solid to fall to earth, and the park was empty and a little solemn. I'd hepped her out on so much sugar, though, I really had no choice but to take her somewhere unless I wanted to have her hanging from the lampshades.

I zipped her coat up to the chin and rubbed away the chocolate, unable to stop myself smiling. "Well, you're already pretty so that's one. Love, well, you probably know more about love than me, but I'm sure Prince Charming is out there somewhere. Trust me, though, you'll be kissing a lot of toads first."

She stuck her tongue out and made a face. "Gross. And the story-teller? I'm good at telling stories, you know? I capture the audience." She made a dramatic Shakespearean gesture with her fist.

I sighed. "You know, I wanted to be a story-teller too when I grew up. Still do. I want to be a journalist and inspire people to think differently, break the mould."

"Why aren't you?"

I sighed again. From the mouths of babes, huh? I stood up, tapping her on the back and gesturing over my shoulder. "Go and work off some of that sugar before I have to face your dad, okay?"

"No. Answer my question first." She crossed her little pink raincoat-covered arms over her chest.

I scowled, groaning, "It wasn't as easy as I'd like it to be. We're not the only ones who'd like to be story-tellers, unfortunately. Now go. I need an adult moment."

She gave me one of her infamous quizzical looks, but to my relief actually went to go and play. I kept my eyes exactly where they were: on the black Jaguar that just pulled up across the road. I'd felt his eyes on me for ages; literally been aware of him hearing me, but of course, that was impossible, just like everything else my life had become. I fumbled in my coat for my battered packet of fags, shaking one out and putting a light to it, not once taking my eyes from that spot, daring him to... Jeez, he was going to and all! The door swung open, and one powerful dark denim-clad leg swung out, but when I saw his face, his eyes, they went straight past me into the park. A look of distorted worry echoed within them. I frowned, glancing over my shoulder. Jazmine was looking into the trees, standing on tiptoes, her hands fumbling around in the bramble bushes to steady her.

I frowned deeper, torn between going to her and stopping him from coming here. I didn't really want him near Jaz, and I was a little weird with guilt over last night. I didn't want to make the feeling worse by talking to him, and thus putting myself in danger and betraying Zean again, now. I took a step toward the direction Mark was crossing the road from, only intent on telling him to back off, but at that moment a glossy rich blue Ford Mondeo started to slow, coming in from the direction Mark had, almost stopping completely in the middle of the road. I watched as Mark stopped dead too, giving it a... Seriously, how can anyone pull off a bluntly *sarcastic* look? As if it was a pathetic little fly that was slowly getting on his nerves and ruining his meal. He gave the spot he was staring at behind me an angry glare, his eyes flickering just momentarily to my own, something changing there (hope?) before he turned quickly, jumping back in his car and speeding off, swiftly getting into fourth gear. The Mondeo, which had just opened a door for someone to get out, jolted, the door flinging shut before it had fully opened, someone leaning on the horn as it accelerated in the direction Mark had driven off in, its engine growling rebelliously in the quiet winter morning gloom.

I stood staring, my fag dropping forgotten between my fingers. "What on earth was that?" I muttered to no one in particular.

"Khyle?" Jaz was calling from behind me, sounding a mixture of alarmed and unsure. I ran over to where she stood looking through the brambles into a thicket of patchy dark forest. Butterflies erupted in my stomach; flashes of Mark's fingers around my throat. I swallowed.

"What is it? What do you see?" I placed a hand on Jazmine's back; she was shaking, pointing one little finger into the dark. I tucked my hair behind my ears, not knowing what to expect taking recent past experiences into account. "Stay here, you hear me? If I call you, fine, but otherwise don't move from this spot, Jaz," I ordered, raising a leg clumsily to get over the thickets. I scrambled through, tripping on a tree root and having to steady myself. There was a whining sound the closer I got to where she'd been pointing, but looking straight ahead there was nothing but mossy oaks and shadows. A growl crept out from a dip in the ground. I started leaning forward to look straight down.

There, nestled in the dip amongst rotten leaves and sticks was a sand and white-coloured wolf, different from the one that night. Her head was smaller, her limbs longer and spreadeagled on the ground. God, she was in pain, raising and tilting her head, letting out tiny moans of desperation. It suddenly hit me what Mark had been after. Did that mean he had listened to me and wasn't stalking me any more? Well, Zean would be thrilled; his swollen head wasn't entirely for nothing. I jumped down into the dip, skidding and raking up earth as I went. The moment I came close to her, she let out a throaty growl of warning, her eyes following mine with a predator's integrity. I put my hands up, half bent over, half encircling her.

"It's okay, girl, I wouldn't hurt you. I just want to see what's the matter. It's okay," I breathed, trying to keep as much eye contact as possible.

I had no experience as a veterinarian and no idea about the anatomy of a wolf, but I knew what was wrong because it was peeking out at me: slime- and blood-covered, she was trying to have a pup and she was straining. "Oh blimey. See, this is where males get you," I said to her, more to soothe myself than her. I ran my hand through my hair, an involuntary reflex for when I was thinking. "Jaz!! Come here, I need your help," I cried up at her, beginning to pull off my coat, jumper, scarf and gloves, leaving me exposed to the elements with only a T-shirt and my oldest pair of worn jeans. I felt my lips go blue instantly. I threw them about a foot away, crouching low to the ground as I went up to her. She growled intensely, but her pain was almost contagious, her moaning greater than her growls. I placed one hand on her neck, feeling the fur thick and bristly beneath my fingers. She smelt of the woods, of being wild and untamed, and for an instant I wanted to be her, free. I understood the affinity Mark felt for them; he was just about as wild and untamed.

Something deep inside me suddenly broke. It would cause him pain if she died. For any other person that may have given them an inclination to let her die. For my twisted self the idea of him in any form of pain made me feel sick. "You're going to live," I muttered adamantly, as there a was tumbling of earth and mud as Jazmine jumped down, her eyes welling up with tears. How had she been able to see her in the first place? How had Mark known she was here? I rubbed my temple. Enough questions; time to focus.

"Jaz, you see over there?" I pointed at the bundle of clothes. "I need you to take my coat and jumper and make a bed right by my side, okay. Quickly, and then come over here and put your hand on her neck."

Jaz nodded, quickly bundling my coat and jumper by her rear and coming to crouch beside me. I took her little hands, placing them gently on the wolf's neck. Her fingers automatically started stroking the strands of fur there. "If she snaps for you, jump back, no hesitation, you hear?" I'd never sounded so stern. She nodded, eyes wide. "Just try and soothe her." I touched her cheeks briefly, and then got to my feet, whipping my scarf from the ground and going in behind the wolf where her legs were spread. The moment I touched her thigh she lifted her head to snap. I went to shout to Jazmine to move away, but she held the wolf's gaze, gently rubbing her, soothing her. The animal looked almost transfixed; hypnotised, even.

I grabbed the bundle of clotted mess and amniotic fluid, which the pup was somewhere encased in, with the scarf, giving a good tug. The wolf cried out instantly, but didn't bite. Its eyes stuck like glue to Jaz's. I braced myself, this time propping one foot up so I could put a bit more muscle strength into it, grabbing hold again, careful not to pull it out of position, and keep it coming out at the same angle to prevent breaking the little thing's neck. I tugged again. My foot dug into the dirt. The wolf wailed, Jazmine cried, and the little pup started to slide out, the mother's muscles contracting as it came, helping to release the trapped creature. It slid out onto the earth along with a handful of blood. I cringed, reaching over to my jacket pocket to pull out my lucky penknife. This would be the first time I'd ever had to use it. What a way to break it in.

I cut through the amniotic sac, ripping it away with my hands and brushing it off the slick wet form of the almost human baby-sized pup. Cutting away at the umbilical cord with one hand, I started to untie my shoelace with the other, cutting it into two pieces and using one to tie off the cord. I leant back. Well, improvisation was better than nothing. Just as I dropped the pup into the makeshift warmth of my coat and jumped, mother wolf let out another whimper, this one echoing back around the trees, eerily. I hesitated just long enough to consider how utterly gross this was going to be, and then slid my hand into her, cringing at the response whine. I felt around in the warm moist interior, feeling as muscles pressed and released around my fingers. I pushed deeper, cringing, unable to feel anything I was brave enough to acknowledge.

Gotcha! There, nestled in the heat, was another gooey form. I wrapped my fingers around it the same way I had before, guiding it out, and into the harsh cold, ripping it out of the amniotic sac and tying the umbilical cord. After two more reach, rip and wipe sessions, I was sure I would never get rid of the gloop from beneath my fingernails, but on the brighter side, four wriggling little pups were searching for tits (and one of which had already desperately locked on, its jaw working desperately), beginning their first steps in the struggle for survival.

Jazmine released the mother's gaze to look down at the pup, the mother immediately snapping back to life, out of her trance, and starting to lick and pull the pups towards her, guiding them to where tufts of fur had fallen out so they could find nourishment. They were big buggers too. The smallest, which had been the last, looked just under three pounds.

"They're so cute," Jazmine said, stroking one behind its ear as if it were a new-born puppy and not a wild animal. I sat back on my heels looking at them, my hands held out in front of me. I felt the smile tugging at my lips, the corniest swell of emotion flooding through me. The miracle of birth; turned out it *was* a little bit of a natural miracle.

"Yeah, they are actually," I laughed. "And what about you, huh? Little Miss Midwife; what was that about? You were amazing." I felt almost obnoxiously perky; totally uncharacteristic. Jaz shrugged, giggling and crossing her legs beneath her so she could comfortably alternate between stroking mother and pups.

I wandered a few feet away to find the stream that had been splashing about in the background, and wash the gloop off my white and blue fingers. Up to now, the adrenaline had kept me warm; now I felt like I'd walked into the scene in *Titanic* where everyone's paddling around in the Atlantic. I swore as the icy water hit my fingers, but at least I could move the fingers of my good hand without them sticking together. There you go, Khyle. Not only did you just help deliver wolf pups, you did it one-handed! I laughed to myself, getting up to get back to Jazmine, when I could have sworn I caught a pair of silvery eyes looking back at me from behind a tree ten feet away, but when I looked back quickly there was nothing. Mark had driven off, right? Had he doubled back? Another wolf? My imagination? God knows. Because I sure didn't.

★ ★ ★

Five o'clock. There was a precise sequence of three taps on the front door. I rolled my eyes, uncurling myself from the couch. Jackson had picked Jazmine up an hour ago, to be delighted by the thrills of our wonderful afternoon. Jackson, to my surprise, had believed every word she said, turning round and looking at me with such admiration I'd wanted to crawl under the mat and die. He'd asked whether I could take her again tomorrow and later on in the week, and then left, thanking me with a nice crisp cheque for my pay. I might be a glorified babysitter, but the cash was good and Jackson was great. He wasn't going to press me for anything, or press anything on me even when he could. I was starting to think of him as the makeshift, scatty uncle I'd never had.

Zean was due back about now. Probably forgot his keys. I swung the door open to be met by Zean walking up the road, right at the end of the road. "Huh?" I muttered, looking up and down the street quickly for who'd rung the bell. I crossed my arms, sighing, "Someone rings the bell, no one's there, and this is so damned cliché." I left the door open, storming down the hallway to where the back door led off to the courtyard. I had unlocked the rusty bolt, really putting my elbow into it. Zean obviously hadn't been out since the summer. The door was only plywood nailed clumsily together, and smacked the wall so hard when it finally came open I was afraid it might shatter, and I'd be losing my first load of pay to Zean. The courtyard outside was just black and grey paving with weeds growing in between, an unused washing line and three sides of seven-foot-high fence. If someone was going to get in here they'd have to be a good climber, but there it was lying on the floor right at the doorstep: a three-by-one massive red box. "That is unbelievably tacky," I cried out into the grey, empty courtyard. Funny thing was, it may have been empty, but I would have bet I'd heard a snigger echo around it.

I knelt down and picked it up, slamming the door closed and running upstairs to my bedroom before Zean could get home and freak yet again. He really was taking his role as over-protective big brother seriously. I dropped it down on the bed, flicking off the heavy cardboard lid to reveal an explosive mass of red dead-nettles, their spiky leaves starting off green at the base, and growing into a glowing red colour like little fires burning at their tips; some the size of my little fingertip, others as large as my palm. Dotted in between were the soft teardrop icy lilac flowers that glittered in all the woods around this area like fairies dancing above the shrubbery. They were beautiful, wild and untamed; they didn't sting, hence the name 'dead-nettle', and best of all, they weren't roses, and they smelt nothing like lemons. Lying on top of the array was a thick white envelope with that spindly black handwriting scrawled on the front *Thank you. For helping her.* I flipped it over and ripped into it, not sure whether to be worried and alarmed or... An A4-sized letter, neatly folded, flopped out into my palm:

Dear Miss K. Exeter,

My name is Steve Blain, and I am the senior editor of Oxfordshire Onslaught. We recently received an assortment of your previous work, and believe you may have the wit and individuality we here at OO look for in our writers.

We are about to introduce a new section in our publication that deals with news, culture, subjects of debate and several individual columns revolving around the younger adult and student population of Oxfordshire. We were hoping you would be interested in coming in for an interview, to write long-term as a new recruit to our programme, and discuss which areas would be most appropriate, and of course pay and other formal conditions.

You came most highly recommended, Miss Exeter, and I am notifying you that this is not an opportunity regularly offered to previously unknown writers. I personally have been assured of your professionalism, individuality of character, and your writing speaks for itself.

Please do call to arrange that appointment. This opening may be considerably time-limited.

Sincerely

Steve Blain, Senior Editor

I gaped at the letter. I'd aced my English and was brilliant at reading between the lines, and Mr Blain either had a rod stuck up his arse or was being pushed into something that had not originally been his idea. Come highly recommended? There wasn't anyone to recommend me; no one knew me in the writing industry, and I'd never heard of this paper, let alone sent my work to them. I wasn't exactly an expert on Oxfordshire papers (or was this a magazine?), having not yet completed a full month here (and might still not).

"What the f— is the door doing open, Khyle?" I heard Zean shout from downstairs. "You're letting all the warmth out."

I quickly replaced the lid on the flowers and shoved the box under the bed, removing the letter from its envelope, and padded down to find Zean at lightning speed. "Have you ever heard of something called *Oxfordshire Onslaught*?" I called out, finally finding Zean in the kitchen searching the empty fridge for nourishment. "And don't look at me; it was your turn to shop. Have you?" I urged.

Zean grabbed a beer and flopped down at the table, snorting. "Ah, Oxford's equivalent of *Private Eye*, with even less fact in it. Yep, can't get enough of the thing. Their reports on what the Dean at O. Uni gets up to are both hilarious, and perfect works of fiction," he laughed.

I was so giddily excited I didn't think about the repercussions, or the questions it would raise. I slapped the letter down on the table. "Guess who just got offered a job there?" I gloated, the embodiment of both smugness and happiness for what felt like the first time in forever.

Zean grabbed the letter. "What! How? I didn't even send your work to them. No offence, K, but they're an exclusive lot; they never take in new writers." He read it through, his eyebrows rising with each line. "Well, he sounds like a great boss. Who on earth pulled this for you? It says someone recommended you… "

"Oh, who cares, Zean? This is what I've always wanted! Finally I'll actually be able to use my laptop again. It's been so long since I've written something I was starting to worry I'd forgotten how to type," I blurted, snatching the letter back before those cogs in his head could really set off.

He looked at me patiently, obviously not going to let it drop that easily. "So that's it. You're going to forget all about Delia now you've got what you want, right?"

I stepped back, shocked. "No, of course not, I wouldn't do that. I mean, I guess I *don't* need the story any more, but, eh… " I trailed off. Was I that evil that I would leave Delia to dwell in her misery now that I really had no use for her? Yes. But I wouldn't, of course, and Zean seemed to see that very clearly in my face.

"Good. I bumped into Jackson, in the sense that I ran by his house to see him. I'm taking Jazmine tomorrow; you can have the car. That girl needs you. I can't stop thinking about her face."

Only now did I notice how pale he was.

Chapter Nine

It was almost an hour's journey from Blackleigh to Cheltenham, long enough for me to get myself so worked up that, by the time I cut the engine of Zean's submarine-like car, my hand was shaking so badly I had to steady it with the other to get my fingers to operate properly. I'd never been to visit my mother of my own accord or on my own, my whole life, though now I thought about it, it wasn't really of my own accord even now. Zean had been shaky and distant since the séance, spending more and more time down the pub. I was having trouble believing that it was just Delia that had shaken him so badly; something else must have been going on inside him to make him like this. I'd felt so bad for him last night, hearing him stroll aimlessly around the house while I pretended to be asleep. I'd given in. Screw me; hell, screw Delia. Zean was my family and I would do anything to stop his distress. Besides, I was in such a good mood after the editor's letter for *O.O.* that it seemed like the best time to do it: kick myself while I'm up and I'll end up roughly where I started, right?

I pulled up outside, hunching myself in against the weather. The stately manor house that contained one of the UK's best specialist psychiatric clinics; and out of the non-stop hail and sleet that had been chucking down since I'd woken up at five that morning. The place was massive. Originally built by some duke or something, it was now under the British Psychology Society, and any of the new wards they'd added on, I'd read, had cost millions to perfectly replicate the sandy-white, elegant Edwardian exterior and interior. I wondered what the BPS had thought about their experimental 'white rooms' in preservation terms, but then I suppose the people of centuries past drilled holes in people's heads when they thought they were a tad looney so the white rooms were in keeping with history.

The foyer was equally as cold as it was grand, the silence so stark you could almost hear the patients' drool hitting the tiled floor. My stomach clenched, empty but hurling. Breakfast had been too big a risk for this. Chandeliers, cream walls, wedding cake ceiling, white and black marble floors, big windows, seats turned to look out of those windows, with people as white as sheets staring out at the world, not seeing a thing; or at least, I hoped they didn't. Nobody should have to suffer a place like this and know they were here. I walked over to the secretary's desk where a large woman, her hair pulled so tightly back in a bun she looked like she was trying to give herself a cheap yet painful face-lift, sat flicking through papers.

"Hi, good morning, my name's Khy—, em, Kahlillyne Exeter. I'm here to visit my mother, Jane Exeter," I somewhere between stuttered and croaked.

The woman made a show of navigating her massive bulk to the computer screen. She reminded me of a toad in brown lipstick and a wig. "I'll need ID. Just let me check her session schedule. You'll have to wait a while if she's with a doctor."

I nodded as politely as I could while fishing out my driving licence and flicking it her way. A sudden loud cascade of crunching gravel interrupted the silence, making both me and Mrs Toad jump a little. She frowned, scrambling out from behind the desk to see who had arrived, shouting over her shoulder, "Room 215, third floor, to the left, she may be sleeping" just before I went to find the lift. I caught a glimpse out of the windows at the front car park where a shining new four-by-four had just pulled up, flanked by two imposing black vans, seemingly out of place given how official-looking they were. As the lift doors touched, I caught the secretary pushing a button on the desk and saying something in a hushed urgent tone. I frowned. Would government health inspectors arrive in a tax-guzzling four-by-four and black vans? Talk about political hypocrites.

This part of the clinic, the 'living' quarters and part of the old house, was still plush carpet and cream walls and bad lift music. I walked on automatic, passing door after door. I hadn't really needed the secretary to tell me which room. I'd never responded to the letter I'd got from them a couple of weeks ago, which meant, though her treatment sector may have changed, until they received a pre-payment on the raised rent, Mum would have lived in the same room since I could remember. Two, one, five. The door was open; I walked into the dim grey and cream interior. There was a desk (unused) and dresser (unused) and a bed (used, constantly), Mum's long willowy figure lying flat on her back under the thin sheet, her head turned to the windows where a crack of light shone apologetically through the curtain onto her face.

I could have hoped it was the rain's gloomy light that made her skin that placid green-white; I could have hoped the deep etched lines and sallow cheeks were a reaction to a change in medication, or the product of lack of sleep. But none of it was; it was just my Mum as she'd always been: a hollow shell, eliminated from within by a darkness sucking the life from her, slowly but efficiently. I gently sat down on the bed beside her. I just felt so numb; any tears had dried up years ago. Her long wispy dark hair, still a glossy brown but now streaked with silver, was spread out on the crisp white pillow around her head. My Mum had once been beautifully full of life – I knew that from Jackson's face – but that woman didn't exist any more, because the thing that was here was unsightly.

"Mum," I whispered, pushing her hair back from her face. "Mum, can you talk to me? It's Kahlillyne. How are you?"

Her eyes darted from one side of the ceiling to the other, frantically.

"Lilly?" she gasped in her raspy murmur.

"Yeah, Mum. It's Lilly," I whispered, despairing already. She couldn't really tell I was here. She knew my voice and my memory, but she was gone in her own world. How could I think she'd know about Delia if she couldn't take in her immediate environment?

"The… they… they're whispering, louder now, excited, excited," she stuttered.

"That's nice, Mum. I'm glad you're all happy to see me. I haven't been to visit in a while; sorry for that. I've been busy, getting set up, own life. I might have a potential job as a writer; remember I told you I wanted to be a journalist?"

She'd returned to the ceiling view, her eyes darting ever faster.

I was already exhausted. At least I could tell Zean I came and tried.

"Anyway, this new life's been interrupted by a girl called Delia who—"

"Bronzebard!" she cried. "She's young. I told her; I told her you'd find her; you're an angel. Lilly my angel."

I stared, my mouth dry. Holy Mother of God. "You know Delia? Is she here? Is Delia in this hospital now?" I asked carefully, bending closer over her and gripping her papery hand, something I hadn't done for years.

"With me now, yes, right here."

My stomach sank, and then her hand clasped mine with a grip

I wouldn't have thought she could muster, her whole body lurching up. I immediately jabbed the emergency call button on the wall while getting up off the side of the bed.

"She cries. Oh, Lilly, she cries, she screams. Help her, help her." She was lurching up off the bed. I tried to push her back down, but she was frantic, crying out "Help her!" again and again, her sallow face contorting.

"Yeah, Mum, I'm trying, but I don't know where she is, do you hear me? She's not here. I need you to tell me if you know where she is," I cried, emphasizing every word as clearly as possible, still trying to push her down to the bed. Damn! I'd worked her up like this.

"She screams," she cried out again, tears rolling off her cheeks and into her flying hair.

And then I actually heard it: a high, blood-curdling scream, penetrating the stagnant feeling that hung everywhere in this place. I stopped trying to hold Mum down, for a moment thinking I'd gone mad, but then it was followed by a loud thud and a crash like glass from outside. I jumped up, leaving Mum where she was, and burst out into the hall. I didn't have to go far. As I swung the door open, I ran into a green and black camouflage jacket, almost tumbling over backwards. The guy spun round, and before I knew it a long Tech gun was being pointed directly at my chest, a narrow pair of eyes glaring back at me.

"Stay where you are, ma'am." The voice was harsh, and I immediately, almost beyond reflex, raised my hands in the air, wavering backwards. The door opposite stood ajar. There were three, including the gun pointer, of what looked like army. In the hallway, one had his gun pointed into the room; the other was pointing at a group of very startled-looking employees. I recognised two as doctors here because of their coats, and another was the secretary from downstairs.

"What's going on?" I cried, but at that moment a thin white foot came into view through the doorway, kicking and flailing in mid-air, followed by a white surgical gown and two arms and then a familiar, battered-but-healing face, her hair about an inch long and sticking out around her head in an auburn halo. She screamed again as a massive black-clad figure tried to restrain her, holding her thin form five feet in the air.

"Grab her arms, will you! And get a doctor in here to sedate her or something," a gruff, accented voice exploded.

I didn't even hesitate, the lie coming so easily and naturally it may have been that someone had written it and placed it in my head without me knowing. "I'm Jane Doe's doctor. I'm off leave today. I can sedate her. Let me through. She gets easily distressed, you know!" Even my voice commanded a bundle load of authority.

The guy pointing the gun at me immediately lowered it, grabbing my arm in an uncomfortable (but certainly not Mark-worthy) grip, and let me into the room. The tip of his gun worked into the base of my back. I slowly circled the mess, not sure where to look first though my eyes were instinctively drawn to the other gun pointed from the opposite side of the room directly at my chest.

"Young for a qualified therapist," came that heavy accent I now recognised as Russian. A middle-aged man; aged, but extremely well, his hair a whitened grey as was his bristly beard, but he held himself straight and his arms were ribbed with muscle beneath the immaculate white silk shirt. He had an antique revolver shoved into his belt and a narrowed expression, aimed directly at me, on his blocky square face.

I shrugged. "Degrees these days, huh? Practically take them in preschool," I said breathlessly and more than a little hysterical.

"Who gives a crap? Restrain this thing, will you," came a, by contrast, barely understandable accent I simply couldn't place, it was so harsh. I didn't look around at the speaker; instead I jumped straight to the crash table at the corner, grabbing the first syringe and unrecognisably labelled bottle I could find, and pretending to look like I knew exactly what I was doing. In reality, for all I knew, I could be directly injecting adrenaline into an already frantic girl.

I swirled around, tapping the syringe and squirting a little out, pretending to check the quantity. I looked up at the now partially restrained Delia, but all I could do was gape. The black-clad figure in front of her was an enormous white bull of a man, rivalling Mark in height, and beating him in width with shoulders the thickness of my calves (and they weren't thin). He was albino-white: white-pink skin, stark blond hair shaved at the sides, mohawked on top and left long in a ponytail hanging halfway down his bulky, hunched back, but his eyes, framed by blond lashes and a black-and-green African tattoo where his eyebrows once were – they were just a clear white, no iris.

I actually stepped back involuntarily. "Whoa," I muttered under my breath.

"Get a move on, doctor," the Russian barked, the sarcasm drowning the word 'doctor'.

I took a deep breath and then grabbed Delia's thin arm, scared to hold it too tight in case it snapped. I found the vein and, eyes closed, I stuck the needle in and injected her with God knows what. My hand still pressed to her forehead. She instantly calmed down, her unseeing hazel eyes scanning the surroundings and not taking in a thing. I took a step back, shocked, but the moment my touch left her she started looking around desperately, beginning to be frail again. This time I stepped forward, encompassing her in my arms.

"Delia, it's okay, I'm here. Just relax, remember the sessions." If she could hear me still, I hope she got the hidden message there. As if she could feel without seeing me there, she sagged into me, almost falling to the floor so that I had to grab her beneath the shoulders, the breath being knocked out of me.

The white dinosaur backed off, raising an eyebrow and turning to the Russian. "She's coming too," he said, so bluntly I almost laughed.

"Of course, Cryon, if you're unable to handle a girl one sixth your size," said the Russian, pocketing a few of the syringes, grabbing Delia's chart out of the slot at the end of the bed, and gesturing for Combat Guy at the corner to follow. Guns pointed into the arch of my back, Delia partially slumped on my shoulder, and flanked by a Russian and the Creature of the White Lagoon, we started to leave. Just as we were turning the corner of the hallway the Russian stopped dead, turning to the army man beside him.

"Kill them all." His voice was an icy knife on its own.

I jolted. "What?" I cried, but before I could react there was the blistering sound of gunfire, and screams burst from down the hallway, echoing around the empty walls. This place had never had so much noise. Delia blanched. Whether she sensed something or was just startled by the screams, she started convulsing.

"She's going to throw up. I need a bathroom," I demanded, pushing past the Russian and into room 201, knocking into the bathroom just as Delia began to hurl. I managed to aim her over the bath just in time. Trying to hold back my own nausea, I pulled her hair back at the nape of her sweaty neck. "I need a saline drip, now," I demanded of the Russian, who stood nonchalantly at the door watching Delia as if she were sleeping, not throwing her ring up.

"We don't have time," he said blandly.

I got to my feet, walking up close to him. "If you do not get me that drip this very second, this girl will dehydrate and she'll be dead before you can get her anywhere. May I stress, a drip is portable."

The smallest of tilts appeared at the corner of his mouth, and he turned on his heel, shouting, "Cryon, stay by this door. I'll be back; let's make this quick."

Cryon was adamantly watching the blood spill. I slammed the door behind him, unable to watch. Quickly, I fumbled in my back pocket, pulling out my mobile; I hesitated, and then hit a speed dial I'd very recently added, begging that it would hurry up. Delia was muttering between hurls, her entire body turning inside out.

"Hello," came Jackson's crisp R.P. accent.

"Jackson, it's Khyle. I don't have too much time. I'm at St Matthew's Clinic. I've found Delia. She's in freaking awful shape. And we are being abducted by an albino giant, a Russian with a bad attitude and the military. Help! Oh, and they're killing everyone." I hesitated, the last part my voice shaking with hysteria, and trying to keep hold of Delia at the same time.

Jackson's sharp command was surprisingly unshaken and efficient. "Do you know where they're taking you? What state is the child in?"

I groaned, Delia's moaning growing louder; and I could hear heavy footsteps outside, drawing close.

"…bluebirds over white, he's coming, it's so high… "

"What's that?" Jackson asked on the other end.

"It's Delia. She keeps repeating 'bluebirds over white, high'. Someone's coming, Jackson. She's out of it. I—"

The door to the bathroom opened. I flicked the phone, ready for it, jabbing it down my bra (closest place), and jumping up to take the drip from the Russian before he'd fully come through the door. Thankfully, I'd had so much food poisoning by Zean's diabolical cooking, a drip I actually knew what to do with. Once the drip was in and Delia was empty, we were escorted out through the clinic. I tried not to notice how the blood spread thickly across the smooth white floors.

Chapter Ten

I'd never been abroad, not to France or even Scotland, but the colossal white cliffs of Dover felt rather than looked familiar. We'd been driving for almost four hours and as five o'clock drew nearer, it was getting darker outside and edgier in here. The Russian, Zambruski, kept glancing at the clock and barking at the driver to speed up. Good luck with that; this was the UK. Severe over-population affected traffic. Go figure.

We were driving up them now, the view over Dover a mass of twinkling lights, and the boats from the docks riding the icy, foamy sea, the wind growing more and more wild until the van shook a little from side to side, matching Delia rocking back and forth. She'd grown quiet about an hour ago, resorting to a petrified look and muttering under her breath. I wrapped my arms around her, whispering meaningless words of reassurance in her ear.

The van pulled to a rocking halt, Zambruski jumping out and grabbing Delia before it had even stopped. I jumped out too, very tired of having a gun pointed in my face. We hadn't got all the way to the top, but we were still fairly high, massive rocks the size of small cars dotted here and there amongst the grass. The vans, and now the four-by-four which Cryon pulled to a skidding halt, had stopped in front of a decrepit stone outbuilding, glowing orange from its crumbling stone windows. A gun nudge in the back forced me and her forward into a surprising amount of heat, and shelter from the gale. Turned out a small fire had been started on the mud ground with yet another camo-covered commando huddled by it and… eh, Dolly Parton.

Dolly stood up the moment we entered, her fluffy stilettoes tapping against the floor impatiently. Okay, now she'd stood up she was more transvestite Dolly. She came equipped with false beauty mark, peroxide blonde candyfloss perm swaying to her waist, my share and every other flat-chested girl's share of breast, and size eights on a size twelve arse. She could have been Angelina Jolie, beautiful with her heavy features, large yet graceful frame and thick neck. Instead, well, ouch.

"You're late. We have less than thirty minutes until sunset. Who's that?" Ohmigod, it was Malibu in Dover. I sniggered. She raised her eyebrows.

"She's the Vessel's doctor; put up with her for now. You can have her later. Get it ready," Zambruski grumbled, pushing in to get near the fire.

I reflexively put an arm across Delia.

"Sentel, Ilati, miss me?" Cryon walked in, sweeping her literally a foot off the floor, their faces plastering together.

"O-o-o-okay, too much tongue for the casual viewer? Ilati?"

"Sumerian for goddess. Trust me, doctor, you're not the only one who has trouble finding the resemblance," Zambruski said, crouched in front of the fire rubbing his fingers together.

Cryon gave him a look that even made Zambruski blanch, then turned, pulling Delia out of my grasp and throwing her to Sentel.

"Hey! Watch it, she's fragile, and I've put a lot of work into her," I burst out.

"A lot of work into her?" Sentel murmured. Her gaze narrowed on me. I'd so been hoping she'd be a dumb blonde. Like Cryon, who I'd expected to be all brawn no brain but, it turned out, had had brains. I didn't need Miss Peroxide to as well.

"You have no idea how much work *we've* put into her," she murmured softly, snake-like, running shock-pink fingernails across Delia's cheek, who just trembled, unseeing.

Sentel led the way outside, across the clearing and to the rockside. For a horrible moment I thought they were going to push her over, but it turned out there was a shallow dip and pathway running through the white, chalky rock and leading into a cave. It curved in on itself, a smell of musk and damp heavy inside. In its depth dark enough that you couldn't see your hand against your face.

"Back in Napoleon's time, the people of Britannia built these caves through the peaks to hide and fight. The cliffs themselves were a symbol of power, unity, Britain's front against foreign lands, facing the world at large across the shortest part of the Channel. You see, doctor, anything, even something as tiny as a few lines joined together, can be a symbol of great power. All that it requires is great belief."

"What exactly do you mean by power?" I asked sceptically, trying not to bump into anyone, or Zambruski, or fall over the grooves in the man-made ground.

"A woman of science. I think perhaps it will be worth keeping you alive as long as possible. So you can have a momentary, personal appreciation for exactly what I mean by power," he replied, with additional sniggers from behind and in front of me.

Light shone up ahead as the cave opened out into a flickering dome large enough to park a lorry. Crystal needles broke the light cast by a scattering of orange lanterns into a cascade of colours, making it look as though the white stone ground glistened with diamonds. I didn't gasp – I could stop myself that much – but just for a brief moment, like when I'd helped mother wolf with her pups (Christ, was that yesterday?), I marvelled how beautiful our world was, all on its own.

Now I gasped. A slab of white stone was placed right in the middle, and hovering a foot above it was a teenage boy, his skin the colour of ebony and his eyes a shade of topaz that reflected the crystalline roof back at me. He reminded me of a cub panther, sleek, patient, ribbed with lean sinew, and highly dangerous. His feet hit the ground the moment we came in, little puffs of chalk wafting upwards as if trying to get away from the feel of his feet

"Cryon, the moment dawns. Were you planning on leaving Ti Ilu pondering your incompetence on the other side?" he almost hissed, striding towards Delia and swiftly reaching up to grip her chin, and pulling her down, burying his nose in the nape of her neck. "Dress her," his voice screeched, throwing her back down to the floor. I jumped towards her, but the click of the safety of a gun being released stopped me, mid-stride. "It was not on my day plan. Sepsu, Sentel…" Dolly nodded, dragging Delia by the hair. I swallowed. Delia didn't seem to notice.

Sepsu turned to me. "And that is?" he hissed, fixing me in his gaze.

I rolled my eyes. I didn't like being treated like a zoo exhibit. "Hi, my name's K… Doctor Khyle Exeter. It's lovely to meet you. And you are…?" I butted in, in a mock-polite voice.

Sepsu's eyes flashed wide for a second. "And what is it exactly?" he said, his voice breaking out through his clenched teeth as if the very sight of me was causing him physical pain.

"An obnoxious, insignificant, and only slightly cute female human."

I spun around at the sound of that familiar slow sarcasm. He stalked out from the opening, those eyes flashing into quicksilver. "M—" I began, but Cryon spoke over me.

"Maraknight?" Cryon's voice was flooded with awe as he dropped to one knee, his head bowed low to the floor, and Sepsu actually inclining his head, polite, though suspicious. I gaped, taking a step back from Mark and closer to Sepsu, clearly totally freaked.

Mark's cool calculating expression ran over Cryon until he seemed perfectly satisfied that the guy was offering up total devotion. "Get up, man, we are not at court here. You and I are equals." He was trying and failing to keep any smugness from his voice.

"Never." Cryon spoke to the floor.

"Well, very true," Mark responded reflexively, that devilish smile slowly sneaking over his face.

Cryon laughed, rising hesitantly to his feet. "How are you here?" he asked.

"Yes, I would like to understand that," Sepsu broke in.

Mark shrugged. "I was in the neighbourhood. I could practically feel the energy crackling in the air over my fish and chips. Why such a small party? Who are you bringing through who could be so unpopular?" he said stalking further into the cave and taking in the surroundings.

"Your father," Sepsu replied.

"Ah," Mark muttered dryly.

Sentel dumped Delia's small form onto the white stone. Her surgical gown was removed, and replaced with a practically see-through cotton robe. She was convulsing from the cold. Sentel was looking at Mark appreciatively. I snapped, running up to where Delia lay and taking her hand. A bullet ricocheted about an inch from my arm and I hunched slightly, cringing. "Consider that a warning, doctor,"

Zambruski snarled.

Mark coughed. "Eh, doctor?" he all but laughed, his gaze probing me with so much incredulous amusement I felt that familiar infuriation ignite.

"Yeah, doctor, it could happen," I snapped.

"Step away from the Chosen, Unclean One, or death will not be what you have to worry about," Sepsu hissed, his hand hovering in mid-air. I heard the air crackle between his fingers.

I pursed my lips, glancing at my watch: five to five, five to sunset?

"Speak for yourself, yob," I snapped, gripping Delia's hand tighter even as I felt the beginnings of something stark and electric rush through the air.

"It has been too long, sire. A long time needing your presence." Cryon seemed transfixed by Mark.

"Well, that is the idea of exile, my brother; you don't hang around," Mark muttered to no one in particular, his eyes running over Delia's limp form as though he were only mildly interested.

"Brother, the time is coming. You know your birth; you know are the strongest to lead ou—"

Mark cut him off. "I did not leave a full pint for a pep talk, Cryon, but thank you, your words are noted." He bit out the last words, turning them into a rough threat that Cryon, though a good two inches wider, actually winced at.

Sepsu had moved in front of the altar, his hand hovering over Delia. His eyes very quickly met mine. "You chose to stay where you are," he said, so softly I strained to catch the words. Mark, on the other hand, was much louder.

"Khyle. Move the hell away. Now!" he between roared and ordered.

Mark was tense, his body ready to lurch toward me, his face a mask of anger and worry. I pulled my hand back, letting it hover in the air like a retreat, and then the first of Delia's screams filled the cavern. I reared, feeling it before I saw it. A light like live fire danced between Delia's chest and Sepsu's hovering hand, his other outstretched above him, eyes closed tight. I stumbled backwards a little, feeling myself collide with someone. Sentel pushed me away like a rodent, and to my horror she was strong enough to actually propel me a few feet forward to the base of the white stone, which I now realized was acting as a certain kind of altar; a sacrificial one. Yes, I was dim on the uptake.

This close I could feel the air itself wavering, spikes of invisible electrical force trembling in the air like hot currents swirling around the base of the altar. This was familiar, I could see the memories; I could feel a breeze with so much heat just a few seconds exposed to it would scorch you, but I couldn't, didn't want to, remember… Another of Delia's screams. I stumbled to my feet, no longer bothering to understand, a whirlwind of the blue, sparkling ribbons tinting black and enraged in the air, twisting and fusing together into a statically charged tornado from Sepsus' other outstretched hand. Feet above us they began to gather in a swirly disc dominating the scene beneath it.

I jumped back, even as I heard something like thunder echoing down the cave tunnel. I couldn't look around. I stood staring up at the disc in horror. Something was distorting the world around it: hair, colour, light twisting into the image of a head, a hand, human-sized and reaching straight for Delia. I heard Zambruski cry "Yes!" repeated by several of the troops, and thuds as a few people sank to their knees. Only one person muttered, "I wonder, if I go now, will that pint still be there?" Mark sounded seriously put out.

The thunder grew louder, bursting into the cave, except it wasn't thunder, it was… wheels. I tore myself away as a motorcycle, a leather-bound figure loosely gripping the handle bars, back-flipped mid-air and skidded to a stop at the end of the cavern. The lanky figure jumped off, removing a black and gold helmet to reveal tiny blue goggles, a balding head, and a greying goatee twisted into two braids at the end.

"Sorry to break the moo' bu' I luv n' entrance," he said in a cigarette-damaged Bristol accent, as his motorcycle-gloved hands twisted his goggles up to beam at the charade like he'd just crashed a Sunday picnic.

There was loud running behind him as a group of people burst into the cave, slightly out of breath. Two I didn't recognise, three I did: Jackson, Zean and Loraline, all looking dishevelled, scared and shocked, almost tumbled over each other as they burst in.

"Yo, Khyle, you alright?" Zean didn't sound angry any more.

"Oh yeah, I'm great, time of my life. We should do this on a daily basis; I'll cut that pesky life span down by ten years."

I'd reached full-blown hysteria. Yippee!

"Yeah, right, get your point. Bad question," he said in a rush, looking frantically around.

"Oh God, is that Delia?" Loraline breathed.

"Yeah, she's looking healthy," I cried, watching as her whole torso arched backward, rising off the altar and into the air, straight for disc world minus the elephants.

"Hysterical girl. Step away from the altar. Let us, the professionals, take care of this," said a Malibu Ken lookalike, with dark sunglasses and a torn sleeved shirt, holding his hand out in my direction. Professionals. Blimey.

"Nice to see you again, Ross," Sentel said, positioning herself between me and him, flirting so hard I thought Cryon might explode in frustration.

The last person was older, late forties, and strangely familiar like I'd seen his face somewhere, or someone like him. He had that look like he'd been very handsome once upon a time, but time had taken its toll, creasing his face so it looked like a permanent scowl, and thinning his blonde hair which was pulled back in a short pony tail at the nape of his neck. His eyes ran over everything, calculating it, making an instant decision and focusing on Zambruski.

There was a sniff from the corner as Mark leant against the wall, rolling a blunt. "I have a feeling things just became potentially entertaining." He smiled, lighting his fag. He caught my eyes, and offered the tin to me across the room. Absolutely; I hadn't had one all day.

Get a grip, girl. You don't have a chance.

The room exploded into havoc. Cryon lurched at the motorcycle guy who rolled his sleeves up, grinning widely to show yellowed, and then altogether missing, teeth. Ross and Sentel began something so elegant it could almost have been a rehearsed dance. Ross moved inhumanly, predicting Sentel's every move, dodging her, moving past her effortlessly. Jackson took Loraline by the shoulder, navigating her and Zean to the side of the room, Zean gesturing at me frantically to get over there.

I wanted to go. The sense part of brain screamed with each synapse: *Move your feet or you will die*. But something else, something much stronger kept me rooted where I stood. I looked around. The cavalry were engaged and Delia's screaming had died down. I whipped around, turning my back on Zean and the rest. If I'd had the nerve to scream I would have been bellowing my lungs out. Delia hovered in mid-air, inches away from the rip. In reality, the thing jumping from it wasn't an inch from touching her. Sepsu had his eyes closed so tight I doubted he'd even noticed the parade of violence and bad puns which had just begun. Something caught my eyes: a speck of pink and green and lilac shone in the midst of the swirling mass of energy, a radiating warmth of goodness, of kindness, of Delia.

I ran my fingers through my hair, thinking fast. I could feel eyes pressing in on me, hearing the mental cogs turning. Delia was going to die. She wasn't dead already; she was somewhere else, somewhere she could haunt me. No one except me could get to her in time.

"What's the worst if I let her die?" I said out loud, immediately feeling bad as if I was causing my own damage to her battered and broken self. The energy was building stronger with each microsecond. "I need some motivation! Worst that could happen, worst that could happen. Think, Khyle," I screeched to myself, trying, knotting my hands in my hair. I stopped. "She could freaking haunt me in the shower, the toilet. I'd never have any more privacy again… Sod that, she isn't going anywhere."

I'd found my motivation.

I jumped up onto the altar. The air here was so thick I felt I couldn't breathe it, my heartbeat erratically jumping. I cringed, gasping, shower, shower, shower. This'd better work or there'd be two dead bodies on this slab. I jumped, reaching out, pulling; my eyes stung, feeling like they might explode in my skull, or boil out. I could literally see the spark turning from Delia to me. How kind; it preferred me. I ignored it, ignored wanting to breathe, the pain, my own tangled agonizing screams or the screams of my friends, desperate as they watched me practically send myself to my own grave. One blood-boiling groan of anger stood out in the midst of it all, though. "You little idiot, what the hell are you doing?" Mark sounded furious. And admiring.

Blindly, I clamped one hand onto Delia's neck, the other reaching for that part of her lost in the mass. If all this energy wanted to channel through me, it could through her too, straight to her body.

137

I felt the spark latch onto me. I was right; this wasn't just pure energy. Thought, spirit, soul; this was Delia, and Delia wanted out. And if I could survive I wouldn't have to worry about any shower issues. It grew until a second bright ghostly white hand erupted, gripping my own, sending ripples of something through my skin and into the lifeless shell I gripped with my other hand. Two problems though: one, my lungs were straining for oxygen, my head fogging from irregular blood supply, my brain starving; and two, my legs being pulled from the altar.

I was already screaming so hard from the pain I couldn't scream any louder from fear; but abruptly, two steel-like hands, so strong I felt a rib instantly crunch under their pressure, wrapped around me.

"Remind me again. Your incentive for getting yourself killed is…?" Mark hissed into my ear, his teeth gritted, as he wrapped one arm around my waist and reached with the other for Delia's ghost-like hand. He was going to help me channel her. Oh, thank God.

"You try being haunted by a seventeen-year-old who's seen one too many horror movies in her living years, Mark. There was a reason you paled in comparison," I gasped, as one final pull broke the connection. Mark and I flew back in the air, his arm still wrapped around my waist, pulling me to him.

The energy died instantly, followed by an incensed cry of rage nothing human could make.

"You traitor."

I rolled over onto Mark, suddenly very aware that I was pressed tightly to his chest, very able to feel every muscle underneath his thin cotton shirt. He rolled his eyes, seeming not have noticed me, his head flopping back on the floor. "Ex-i-led!" he called back, bored. I didn't get this, and I wasn't even beginning to with the freaky magic-monster thing going on, but him! One minute he was threatening to kill me, then next he was saving my life, albeit begrudgingly. I mean, no one was forcing him to do either here!

He's really big, I thought, my fingers absently brushing down the abs, pushing up under the material. "Comfortable, are we?" he smirked, one sharp dark eyebrow raised.

"What? No," I lied, badly.

He laughed, throwing his head back, showing off a thick bristly neck. "That's fine, kid. I like it on top anyway." He laughed, his eyes smouldering, two hands pressed on my hips. I winced; everything ached.

"You hurt." The humour fled from his eyes, but was then replaced by a quick surge of something much darker. With an effortless lift he twisted me right over, plunging me on my back. I braced myself, waiting for hands around my neck in one of his usual mood swings, but instead he kicked his leg right up, throwing Sepsu back across the cavern, hitting the wall with an explosion of chalk particles, the knife Sepsu had been holding dancing across the floor. He'd saved me again. I groaned, letting my head drop back. I was going to faint. I could feel the heady darkness coming over me as my body gave up on me.

I heard Sepsu scream, but was already falling.

"We have to go now. Grab Delia." Zean?? Someone scooped me up in a tight and warming embrace. My body responded instantly, registering safety.

Just before I went off, I got a glimpse of those silvery eyes looking down at me despairingly.

Chapter Eleven

When I pulled back to consciousness, my ribs ached so hard that just breathing was a punch in the intracostal muscles, as I found out when I was foolish enough to try. Before I could stop them, I felt tears welling up under my eyelids and leaving down my cheeks.

"Khyle? Khyle, it's Loraline. Please, sweetie, open your eyes." She sounded sick with worry. Hesitantly, I blinkingly opened my eyes, immediately met by a curtain of black hair obstructing my view as Loraline bent, an inch away from me. "She's awake!" she cried, literally crying, pulling herself up to scream at the group of people scattered around.

We were gathered in what looked like a hospital ward, filled with beeping machines and uncomfortable flat-pack white beds, and that disturbing clinical smell which clung to everything. My stomach lurched; this was not what I would have liked to wake up to. I tried to move to hoist myself up and out, but my ribs shot pain right through me; and worse than that, my arms actually shook at the effort. I felt terrible, just terrible, like someone had stuck a vacuum against my body's energy stores and pressed 'suck'. Loraline pushed me back against the horribly hard mattress. "No, stay down. You're really weak at the moment, Khyle."

"Where are we?" My voice was shaking too.

"Romney Marsh's Off-Centre Project Base," came a stern, ruined voice. I looked up. The man who'd gone straight for Zambruski was standing over me, checking my vitals.

"Military?" I breathed.

"Not exactly. Government, yes. Gun power, definitely. Military command, no," he said, sharp amber-brown eyes surveying me speculatively. I frowned subconsciously; I hated feeling weakness of any kind.

A heavy steel door across the room swung open, hitting the wall, as Motorcycle Man, Ross, and... Mark came in, looking windswept and dishevelled.

"That thing Cryon is an animal. The fucker followed us all the way up to Hythe before we lost him!" declared Motorcycle Man to the room, looking more exhilarated than pissed off.

I hoisted myself up just enough to see who else was here. Loraline and Zean sat by my bed and across from me. "Thank God," I muttered, slumping back down as if I no longer had any need in life. Delia was lying in a bed opposite me, with Jackson and a woman wearing a white coat standing nearby. She was safe; I was surprisingly alive; this day should be made a national holiday.

"Yeah, but thankfully we've found ourselves an animal of our own. This guy almost ripped his arm off when he got close to the jeep outside Dover. It was brilliant," Ross boomed, jumping onto the bed next to mine and slapping Mark on the back. Mark looked somewhere between amused and belittled.

"What the ruddy hell is going on?" I cried, surprising myself as much as anyone else that such a shout could come from someone so dilapidated. "Sorry," I muttered. "Maybe left over from any hysteria I felt earlier," I mumbled to the ceiling.

"No, she's right. What the f-u-c-k is going on?" Zean demanded from across the room, face shadowed by something close to rage.

"That shit was terrorising, and totally beyond the laws of nature I've been taught. You lot obviously know, and me and her have been dragged through the hedge backwards. We have a damned right to know," he continued, his voice almost falling to a low growl; and then he jumped off the bed as if just for good measure. "And that" – he pointed in disgust at Mark – "is no *hero*, he's a low shit who threatens innocent girls."

"Sit down, Zean. I promise you will get your answers. You just have to be patient. Now Khyle is awake, we can begin," Jackson said sternly, rubbing the crease between his eyes beneath his glasses as he walked away from Delia.

"With all due respect, professor, you'll tell us now," Zean hissed, but he lowered his lean form back down, his gaze not leaving Mark, who met it, blank and dark.

"How is she?" Loraline asked, shifting on the bed.

"Go to her," I said. "I'm good. Not planning on dying any time soon, at least not *here,*" stressing the last bit with disgust.

"K, look at you. Where did you want me to take you? If it's any help, this is a medical ward, not a hospital," Zean said, as Loraline gave me a small smile and walked over to Delia, saying something to Jackson; and he nodded, looking more like death than I felt.

"Close enough! I'd rather be in a morgue than a hospital."

"I remember that from last time, you little prat. What came over you? Since when did you become heroic, anyway? You didn't even want to go to that place to see if she was there, let alone throw yourself headfirst into an abduction!"

I hoisted myself up quickly, the pain sickening but worth it being able to shout at Zean face on. "It's nice to know you think so highly of me. What was I supposed to do? Leave her to die? Well fine, but then she'd actually be a ghost and I truly wouldn't be able to save myself from that whole haunting-in-the-shower scene. Only one person sees me naked, Zean. I don't even have a gynaecologist!"

Zean looked at me for a second, and then he, Motorcycle Man, Mark, and Ross burst into hysterics. Even Jackson smirked a little.

I felt myself blush slightly, pressing one hand to my ribs. "Change of subject: who are you people? And who are *you*?" I asked the last bit directly to Mark who responded immediately.

"Maraknight, Marcus, or Mark for short. You haven't got temporary memory loss, have you?"

I glared at him, but Motorcycle Man jumped up, grabbing Mark's fist and shaking it in a huge sweeping movement. Mark looked down, bewildered, at his hand being jerked up and down.

"You are Maraknight?" said Motorcycle Man. "You were the man who saved those off Columbus in 1930. It's a true pleasure, man," he growled.

Me, Zean and Loraline exchanged looks of real disgust, but none matched the actual look of disgust on Mark's face, as if he'd happily kill the beaming leather-clad man in front of him just for mentioning it.

Jackson ignored them. "We, or more accurately, they" – he gestured to the men, and around him, at the ward – "are a governmental project called Nomas 12. It's now an international project with branches all over the world, and it's been in place for long over a hundred years—"

"Way more active recently," Ross drawled, cutting in, examining a graze over his knuckles, bored, like he'd heard it all before. "And it deals with the end of the world."

I blinked. Zean burst out laughing, doubling over, but stopped when every other face remained still. I was watching Loraline across the room. Her ivory face seemed to have grown grey, and she was staring at the floor. I felt my stomach crunch.

"Professor, you are not serious." Zean tried to joke, but the humour was fading fast, dampened by the grave air everyone else in the room was exuding.

"Zean! He pretty obviously is; they all are. End of the world? How?" Even to me I sounded disbelieving, and in my opinion, rightly so.

Jackson pulled himself up from the bed, heaving a sigh. "I don't know where to begin."

"How about that energy-sucking flying saucer," I offered, trying not to become hysterical again.

Jackson shook his head. "Right." He got up off the bed, beginning a steady circular stride to end facing the front of my bed, fingertips clenched like when he was doing one of his backroom discussions. "Our world, our universe, is made up of energies. Matter, energy, are interchangeable. This is one of the most basic physical laws defined by $E=Mc^2$." I heard Zean groan and flop back flat on the bed. Jackson ignored him.

"Those energies originated from a peak point of refinement, of concentration which we call, inaccurately, Lexis, which exploded, so to speak, to give us our universe—"

"Big Bang," I added, just to show I was following. He nodded, smiling at me a little.

"In laymen's terms, to every action there is a reaction, to every particle an anti-particle, to the Lexis an anti-Lexis, which at the point before the Big Bang, we believe, was concentrated at that same point, and had expanded therefrom. Now the only reason matter is what it is, and that which we call antimatter is not matter, is due to one kind being produced in slightly excessive quantities, meaning that, after all annihilation had occurred, one was left dominant. This happened; our Lexis won; anti-Lexis – energy unable to be destroyed, only transformed – fell into a reality parallel to our own, and continued a process of evolution, as did we."

I was stumbling behind somewhere back at $E=Mc^2$. This wasn't written anywhere in any physics book I'd read and, more importantly, he was speaking as if this was fact, not theory. And nothing in science was fact. You could call it the penultimate, educated pessimism: theories can only be disproved, never proved.

"The question becomes: what happened in the process of evolution of anti-Lexis? Well, humans are vessels of energy, energy which originated from the beginning of time, and which is one with everything created by Lexis. What we call, what ancestors called, monsters of myth of legend and folklore are the vessels – animals, humans – of anti-Lexis."

Zean fell off the bed, staring at the professor as if he'd gone mad.

"The bugger is that they're homesick," Ross laughed.

Jackson glared at him. "Thank you, Ross. It is not quite that simple." He removed his glasses again. "Humans are unbelieving creatures. We have never wanted to believe in any other life or action that we are not every day familiar with, so why over the centuries would we have changed from story-tellers to factual bores? Well, we didn't. We look at ancient civilisations as being simple, lower grade early man. Well, in a lot of ways they were perhaps more intelligent than us, for they found much more with far less to work with, and they were no story-tellers; the demons of stories are the demons of reality which gradually have been lost from *this* reality."

I was starting to agree with Zean: the professor needed a vacation or rented accommodation at what was left of St Matthew's.

"Lester, can I—?" The gruff man put his hand up.

"And you are?" Zean broke in rudely.

"Christopher Leeds. Christ. Shorter, easier to remember, less pansy-like, and you can't deny the irony in it. Any other questions, son? Save them. Our universe is like a dam, or two rivers with a log separating them. The log is slowly being pulled away in a cycle that works every twenty six thousand years—"

Oh bloody hell, I knew where they were going with this, and so did Zean because I saw his jaw slacken and his eyes roll.

"—and as the log moves, water spills until the log is gone for an instant; that instant when a planet, any planet, any solar system, any place in our universe, is in exact alignment with the dark rift where we think the Big Bang happened. And unfortunately, kids, this year's when that alignment occurs for us, and the anti-Lexis right beside ours has an opportunity to flood back in and try again to get back what it lost."

Christ finished. Hm, he was right about that irony thing.

"It's happened before, right," added Ross, "and each time, humans, or energy beings that dominated Earth at the time, won out. I mean, serious consequences: Ice Ages, Neanderthals; it's all happened but they never got through. Until now. They've developed like humans. They're more dangerous; they look like us, but they're more powerful in some ways, blunt as thick posts in others; but they feed on us, on our energies. It does something to them… " He trailed off, his eyes on Loraline, and then darting quickly; and darting away just as fast, I may add, to Mark.

There was a long moment of silence, mostly filled by Zean opening and shutting his mouth, obviously searching for something either useful or just totally derogatory, and finding himself stunned silent. I thought I'd cut in.

"Okay. Let's just stop for a second. Process, rewind, try and close your mouth, Zean, and for all our sakes keep it shut for a minute." I ignored his glare. "What you're saying, that has any relevance to why I'm limp and lifeless on a bed, is that they tried to take Delia's energy. Why? And what was the discy thing, accumulation of energy in the atmosphere? And for that matter, assuming I believe you which I don't, I think you all need serious help because you're making me feel good about my sanity, which is saying something. If, eh, lethal expats…" – Mark snorted – "are trying to get in, how come we aren't seeing them?"

"They weren't trying to take Delia's energy; they were trying to transfer it. The disc you saw was a channel between the two Lexis. Delia is a witch, which is one way of describing a human who has an extreme connection with Lexis. She can channel her own energies, and those around her, which makes her a perfect way of getting through what they want to get through. She wasn't powerful enough, though, otherwise the transfer would have been relatively instant and you wouldn't have been able to save her the way you did." It was like Jackson had just slapped me with objective honesty.

"And they were trying to transfer?" Zean added incredulously.

I bit my lip. "Mark's father, right?" I blurted.

"Not quite. The buggers are trying to get through what the good people of centuries past called Ti Ilu, which is Sumerian for 'life god' or 'oh fuck'. I'm sorry, little Wonder Woman, I ain't introduced nothing 'bout meself. I'm Skinner. Nice to meet you, angel cakes." Moto Man grinned gappily at me, and held out one still-gloved hand. I took it out of politeness.

"Ti Ilu is the embodiment of Lexis in human form," Christ added. "You see, Lexis is like God in the sense that it's not aimless; it has intention and protection. Anti-Lexis has been harnessed by its inhabitants; that's what makes them stronger. It's also what makes us snacks."

There was dead silence. "So, Git Features over there. He's not human." I gasped at Zean, tempted to laugh or roll my eyes, but there was still silence. I frowned, looking back and forth, and then met Mark's eyes. He was staring right at me, something working behind his eyes: a yearning. I felt awful.

"Neither am I."

Everyone whipped around. Loraline was still staring at the floor. "I've been in this world thirty-five years. It's my home. I feel like I've been adopted by it, by the energies. My home, our home" – she glanced up at Mark – "feels like hell."

There were tears in her voice, but the look on Mark's face said he didn't exactly agree with that. Zean looked as if he'd been betrayed. He dropped his head into his hands, and then jumped up from the bed.

"You are all loonies. I don't want anything to do with this shit." He reached in his pocket for a fag. "K, you coming?" he shot at me, as if I could just jump up and follow him. I looked at him helplessly, but no one was stopping him and it didn't look like anyone would stop me.

My head was spinning, and personally I thought I, unlike Zean, was taking this very well.

"Zean, you are a completely, *blindly*, hapless idiot even though you're a genius." I didn't know where it came from but I knew I meant it. "Okay, I'm lying on a frigging hospital bed out of my own choice and you know that. Something weird was happening. I felt something like, I don't know, I guess it could have been an energy. Christ, man, did you see Delia? They're right: humans are idiots; we are all idiots; we don't want to believe anything except what we think falls into a set scale of what can and what can't be." I was clearly hysterical again because I could swear that had just sounded like I was

148

defending these mad men. These mad men who had saved my life.

"That's a no, then," Zean said evenly, and walked out, slamming the door hard behind him. Loraline jumped up and ran after him. I wanted to tell her it was more than her life was worth, but I was so freaked I could barely speak more than two words.

"Why me?" I freaked.

Christ and Jackson exchanged looks, worried looks. My eyes narrowed.

"What aren't you telling me? Why did Delia come to me? How could I help her?"

My voice was shaking again. Jackson came over to the side of my bed, putting a hand on my shoulder. "It could have been anyone; anyone can manipulate these energies because we're all—"

"Don't you dare give me that crap!" I cried, struggling to sit up properly. "How did my mother know Delia? And how the hell did I know what I was doing, because I did. I didn't scream or run. It all felt very bloody familiar!" I was literally howling at the top of my lungs. Jackson looked awkward, looking away now.

I felt the tears again, welling up out of nowhere. All my life something had been haunting me and I knew, I just knew, the answer to what it was and how to get rid of it, or at least understand it was in this room, and I wasn't sure they were going to give it to me. I flung myself off the bed, feeling my knees buckle and my legs threaten to give way. Jackson jumped up. The doctor started walking over briskly, but I ignored both of them. Gripping my ribs, I walked wearily over to Delia.

She was a horrendous sight to look at still, but her skin had become a soft shade of pink, the circles gone from her eyes, and the black and blue patches of bruising were already fading. Energy, energy we see every day, energy which makes and surrounds us, and is just life for our world, was healing, helping, nurturing her now that it could.

"I'm not a hero, I'm not particularly honourable, or at all actually. I'm certainly not Wonder Woman. I hate my mother for what she is; I have dreams every night so horrific my brain has literally found a way to block them so I don't lose my mind. I would have left Delia to die to escape this conversation. I know him." I pointed to Mark but kept my eyes rooted to Delia. "He's threatened to kill me, and I'm not the least bit scared because there's nothing new about it. It's familiar. I'm no hero, I'm the extra in the movie that gets beaten and bruised to prove a point and no one give a shit about. Please tell me that this is all coincidence, that non-hero me had nothing to do with any of this, and I was just in the wrong place at the wrong time, and that I'm losing my mind."

Jackson and Christ exchanged one last loaded look, and then Jackson shifted and replaced his glasses. I'd seen him make this move twice when responding to an awkward question by a student at his backroom conferences.

"You need to understand, Khyle; Delia was here in our dimension, our Lexis, but her astro-psyche, her spirit if you'd prefer, was there. The energies that make up her personality, make her who she is when in the anti-Lexis plane—"

"Which is why to you, to us, she was like a ghost."

I glanced up. I hadn't even heard Loraline and Zean come back in, both looking only semi-here. Jackson went to continue but I cut in. "You knew about this, all of this, and you played dumb?" I accused her, eyes narrowed.

She stared at the floor. "I didn't know Delia was… was made part of it," she muttered.

Jackson jumped in to save his roomy. "It's not exactly uncommon, and a lot of psychiatric patients and psychics, and even children who cry about the monster in the wardrobe exhibit the same thing." I knew where he was going with this and I immediately shrank to the side of Delia's bed. "Your mother. You saw her in the photo. There was a time when she was a beautiful, logical woman. When we were all at Oxford together, our work became high profile, and Nomas 12 became involved. She became fanatical about helping them." He paused, drawing the mental line under how far to go in detail. "In 2001, for reasons I'm sure you can guess, the barriers temporarily shifted and something came through, or came very close. By this point your mother had developed a strong connection with, and understanding of, Lexis and as a result she became a highly developed psychic of sorts. She was involved when this being tried to come through, and in unison with other society members she offered to—" He broke off, his eyes lost, searching for something frantically.

"Plug the hole," Christ growled, staring at Delia's ECG like it was the most fascinating device in the world.

"She exists in anti-Lexis, and it is possible she connected with Delia, and you were… an easy method to get through to the other side as you were the only one who she has a blood connection with, and can feel the presence of. You were the only one she knew was alive, and had faith would help her." He finished, explanation over, done, no more information required. But there was. That didn't even begin to touch on the questions I had, or the loose ends that needed tying up, and he expected me to swallow it, shut up and stop causing a hassle in the grand scheme of things.

"Well, blimey, K, your mum's like an unknown hero," Zean said, lighting another blunt.

I shook my head. "You're telling me my mother, this miraculously courageous woman, gave up everything, she gave up her daughter to save this world? This world filled with terrorists and gunmen and serial killers and Barbie?" I muttered, unable to look at anyone.

Silence. I got up. "My mother is a vegetable, but more than that, she is dead to me. I don't care if she's the freaking female Winston Churchill of the twentieth century to planet Earth, she chose this world over me, so she's dead to me. It's not that much of a loss. I never had her anyway." Christ looked furious. I ignored him. Nothing he was feeling could match my own fury. "Are we going?" I shot at Zean, who was so shocked his blunt was hovering an inch in mid-air as he stared at me.

"No ride. Why the hell do you think I'm still in a room full of freaks?"

I appreciated that his despising tone matched my own. I shook my head. "Sod that, I'll walk," I declared, getting up from the bed and immediately feeling like I'd done four rounds with Muhammed Ali.

Mark shook his head, stabbing his own fag out on his palm. I cringed. "I'll drive you. You! Not lanky over there, he'd offend my car." Out of total desperation I followed him.

The halls outside were as sparse as possible, a cascade of iron-clad door after door so that I felt as though I'd fallen into a futuristic spin on *Pan's Labyrinth*: no windows, each door barred and closed tightly, each footstep echoing like a dropped anvil. It was a relief when we burst outside into the salty air, where a small car park was almost empty, Marcus's Jaguar standing out like a black diamond amongst the few grey-pebble vans parked in it. Mark was dead quiet as we slid out of the cold into the equally as sharply frosty interior. I wrapped my arms around myself, wondering what had happened to my coat in the last… how long? The sky outside was bluey-grey, just before morning broke. Mark's dash read 4:45 a.m. It felt a lot longer than that; it felt like a lifetime.

Mark flicked the heater to full even though he had his sleeves rolled up to his fist-sized upper arms, and I could feel the heat waves rippling away from his bare skin. I started to feel a whole new fear. Here was this whole new world, this whole new reality, and there were people in this world who wanted me, any human, dead. These things weren't human and one of them was driving me home. Hopefully. I leant my spinning head back.

"So you're not human. How 'bout that?" I asked hesitantly, looking at him out of the corner of my eye.

He shook his head a little, smiling. "With respect, in my opinion you handled all that... with dignity."

I felt my eyebrows shoot up and tried not to laugh outright. "So what are you?" I scoffed.

He shrugged. "Apparently, a lethal expat. O.O. is going to be thrilled with you."

Yeah, I get it, mate. You want to change the subject. "You really aren't telling me anything I didn't know. I always knew you were lethal, Mark. It's just the expat part that's new."

He laughed; that deep throaty one I was hating myself for adoring. "Namlugallu, that's what we call ourselves back... " He hesitated.

"Back home?" I offered.

"Sakhush. Yes, my home. I'm told Namlugallu actually means 'civilized man' in your Sumerian. My people probably stole it from a past field trip. We're not very inventive."

"They don't say men with great cars know how to appreciate beauty; they say they have no imagination, just to set that straight."

He shook his head again. "I do, though."

"You just admitted yourself you have no imagination," I laughed

"No. I know how to appreciate truly beautiful things."

There was something about the way he said it, the way his eyes shifted to search for mine that made me whip my glance out of my window to hide behind a shield of tangled hair. How could he do this to me now? When I say freaked to the millionth degree, exhausted emotionally and physically, how could he suddenly make me feel alive?

"What's wrong with you?" I snapped. "One moment you want me dead so bad you leave bruises on my neck and attempt to freak the life out of me, and the next thing you're saving my life and acting all sweet and getting me the job of my dreams. Make a decision because I'm getting emotionally egg-beaten!"

"It was me. I couldn't bear the idea that night that you wouldn't care if you were alive or dead."

"Why? You hate me, remember."

His lips drew together into a cold hard line. "Oh, more than you can even begin to understand. For reasons you will also never understand. Surely you've had enough for one day or are you just a sadist? Christ, woman! Look at you; you could fall asleep in that seat, you're so wiped out. It's done. I've done what I've done. You have nothing to fear from me any more!" he said through clenched teeth.

I suppressed the urge to hit him. "But why? You didn't know me to hate me, did you?"

No answer came, but the car sped up with a subtle purr. I shook my head, feeling close to tears. "Mark! Are… you… the… guy… from… my… dream? Please, I promise I won't break. I just need to know that much."

"What dreams?"

I sighed, not sure how far I could go with this. It was impossible beyond the point of physics behaving badly. "Nightmares. Or just dreams, horrible dreams that I can't remember but know are horrible because I wake up sick, or terrified… or heartbroken," I whispered.

I stared disconnectedly out of the window feeling like I was confessing a lifelong sin.

"If you don't remember them, how would you know if I was in them or not?" He sounded generally interested and confused.

I frowned. "I remember a face, eyes, how strongly he—"

"Felt?" Mark cut in, almost defensively.

"—hated me. Just like you, apparently. Well? You?" No answer. "I wish I knew everything. They're keeping pieces of the jigsaw back."

"I know." Startled, I turned in my seat to try and make him out in the darkness. I wouldn't have believed he could infuse that level of softness into just one word. "No, I have no idea. I'm not lying to you, Khyle. I don't know what this has to do with you; not your mother, but you."

In spite of myself I believed him, I was even silly enough to almost have believed he cared. I watched his profile in the dusk light, how hard his cheekbones were, and how his chin concaved up ever so slightly underneath. Was this normal? That a person could have this sort of physical effect even when it was against all your better judgment?

"But for the sake of your sanity and your complexion, I swear I'm going to do everything in my power to find out for you."

Chapter Twelve

Columbus, an immense beast of metal and shiny, polished wood, was wedged and protruding from the grey-black soil like a lop-sided mountain, spilling ants out of its cracks and crevices. Except these ants were crying or trembling, these ants were humans, terrified humans, so small in comparison to the crashed ship throwing us into shadow because of how it blocked out the suns.

I was trembling too. I didn't have to feel their fear directly because I lived it every day. It was the fear of facing death or worse. Soldiers were rounding the passengers up, not caring if they knocked them over or even if they broke them in two; they were cattle to be herded and enjoyed one at a time. HE was watching me as I trembled beside him, looking pathetic as per usual. I wasn't like their women. I shook, I cried, I screamed, and felt no shame in it because that's what my mother had taught me made us human: the ability to think and feel, an ability that would stand the sea of rounded humans in good stead.

A bald man, smaller in comparison to the other, and with a sharp chin and goatee, stood with several other troop men counting and noting down as they threw blood-encrusted chains around their necks, his emerald robes blowing in the fiery wind. HE was here; just here to monitor one of the biggest imports they'd ever seen, but HE seemed about as interested in it as anything that didn't involve women, fighting, feasting or learning. Anything practical HE said it was better to hire people for. "What this time? We have to eat. Practically you should just be sighing in relief that no one can eat you. Not that it would be much of a meal." He turned around in his seat at the vantage point a little above where the mass was gathered.

There were so many. We were close enough that I could see how the wind had already begun streaking blood red sores onto cheeks, and how they huddled together. There were two older people, old to a point that you never saw here. They looked elegant, dressed in long black coats, and the woman had a brooch that sparkled like the moons in dual colours of silver and topaz. He held his arm up to protect his eyes, and huddled the rest of his body around the small frail frame of his wife, desperate to protect her from it, to stop her from coming to pain even as they were ushered forward brutally by the barbaric, authoritarian guards.

There was a sudden breakout right at the front where they were counting and assessing age and usefulness (how long they could keep drawing energy from them before they gave up). One of the guards had ripped a young blonde woman's baby from her arms. She'd fallen to the floor, screaming desperately, her arms flailing, not even feeling as the bare exposure pulled skin from bone. I burst into tears at the same time as the people around her. Some of them could even be strangers, confused, scared, and hurting themselves as they pushed through the crowds. Two women cradled the mother while three men ran forward to where the little withering bundle had already been towed off somewhere else. Probably to the farming facilities, I thought, that's where all the young ones were kept until they were old enough to be taken and eaten, or grained.

One of the guards, his expression unalarmed by the outbreak, twisted one of the fighting men's heads right off and then turned to the others. The display didn't go unnoticed, but after a moment's hesitation the two men and others further back in the crowd hurled themselves forward, ready to fight a battle they just couldn't win. They just could not win. *That was the human race for you; no matter how much they disgraced themselves, when it truly mattered – not all of the time, but some of the time – they amazed you.*

Brave and stupid, but full of love and care and everything everyone here had had sucked out of them.

"They're really here. Look at them, they're scared. They've done nothing, they'll do nothing," I moaned, beyond tears of despair and on to hollowed-out numbness.

HIS eyes shifted from them to me, his expression taking in each twitch of a muscle in my face. I heard another scream, followed by a little girl's cry of "Mummy" lost in the bustle of shouts. At the sound of that word I felt the numbness fill me with a new mixture of pain and anger as my own mother's face flashed into my mind's eye. Below, it broke out into a full rally. I turned to HIM.

"Help them! I know you can, you're really strong so help them!" I ordered, stamping a foot for good measure. He stared at me blankly for a moment and then doubled up laughing; he was the guy who gave orders, not me, after all. I stood still, waiting for him to get it out of his system before he straightened up again, swallowing the rest down as he realized that I was serious, but still looking as if this was the best joke he'd ever heard; and said, "Absolutely. Stop haunting me, midget, and I'll save the pigs from the slaughterhouse."

"I would if I could, but I can't so I won't." The moment I'd said the words I deeply wanted to take them back. They brought back the most vivid memory I had of Mummy, laughing when I'd first come out with it. The anger flared further. Those children down there would lose their mummies or daddies and they'd be alone and lost like me. How could I stand here and not beg or fight for them?

"Well, no deal, then," he laughed, and picked up the accounts sheet, looking on the verge of falling asleep any second. I struck out. It would make no difference – he could touch me, but not the other way around – but I was hoping the very effort would make me feel better. My clenched fists flew right through him one after the other, furiously. They barely disturbed the air as they sank through him.

"That's very distracting," he muttered, not bothering to look up.

"Distracting? They're not just numbers on those papers, you know. They're dying; help them. I want you to help them. I don't want to be alone or hurt. Please, for me." I fell to my knees, feeling pathetic again.

The rickety chair he'd been perched on wobbled as he got up, crouching down beside me.

"The only thing they're good for now is a high. Listen to me." He pulled my chin to look at him. I directed my gaze stubbornly at a rock by my toe; I hated meeting those glittery eyes. "Stop hurting yourself over this. It's how it works. It is the system, midget. Honestly, just be thankful you have the advantage of not being part of it." I realized that, for the first time, I could remember he'd taken pity on me, tried to ease my pain instead of make it.

"I hate you," I muttered through my tears, for the first time truly feeling the boiling inferno, hotter than the wind here or the sun beating down on us. I hated him and I would embrace it just to have to concentrate on something other than hopelessness.

The moment the three words left my lips, he recoiled as if I'd struck him with the strength of three of the soldiers down on the plain below. His whole face crumpled and his chest rose and fell, erratically and deeply. I immediately felt guilty; had I hurt his feelings? Well, he always said it to me so why should he care if he'd finally managed to make me loathe him the same way?

He recoiled, focusing on me calmly now. His mouth was open just wide enough that I could see how his teeth were gritted. An awful seething, an enraged growl burst through them, and he whipped around in a gush of scorching wind. I watched his imposing figure stalk fast down onto the lower plain, but he held perfectly upright fists clenched into balls by his sides. There were twenty soldiers down there to deal with a mass of at least three hundred humans. Five were ripped into shreds within a minute. Moving like a jungle cat, he cut through the crowd, as people literally leapt out of his way to leave feet of empty space between his predatory form and themselves. Five other *soldiers caught on quickly. Bewildered, they sank to their knees, surrendering instantly, and saluting in obedience to royal authority, though it was a lot more likely they were prioritising their lives over their regimental status. The other five didn't have a chance to surrender, his teeth ripping deep into sinew and bone, not lingering long enough to draw blood, but just enough to let them bleed to death; or to pull apart limb from torso in a horrid shower of acid-green sparks, crimson raindrops, and a crunching of bone.*

I heard people screaming. I could see them huddling together in groups, now transfixed with fear, their eyes watching this new, much worse, danger.

"Mark, what are you doing? Maraknight!" the man in the emerald robes screamed from the hill, shouting something to the men at his side, who ran away before he'd finished. He looked utterly shocked and utterly furious at the same time, but Maraknight didn't seem to notice him. Maraknight stood staring upwards at the ship, right at the top of its bulk where, at the angle it was balanced, railing met horizon, and a thin rainbow of sparks and swirls distorted the sky. I'd seen the same spread of light every time they had brought humans through, sparks of energy like little floating bombs. He held out one immense hand up toward the sky, shouting words in their language that I didn't understand.

The world rippled around where he stood like a painting that had a breeze brushed across it. He had to spread his feet to secure his stance as if he might actually be ripped apart by the energy rippling through the ground and sky; and then nothing. The ship, the people gone, with just a dot of beautiful sparkling white light hovering high in the air like a bird made of diamonds. He gave no obvious sign of effort as his hand dropped back to his side and the dot up ahead blinked right out, but there was a sense of heavy weariness emanating from him now. "Wow," I muttered, watching dumbfounded as he fell to the soil, raising a spray of dust and a dull thud. He rested his elbows on his knees with something like a stifled groan. I hesitated, jumping a couple of steps forward, thinking better of it and jumping right back again, then giving up: self-preservation. I landed beside him, but for me there was no disturbance of either air or soil, my obviously not being solid and all. He thumped down onto his back, glaring up at the sky, his face drawn. "Thank you. Thank you so much," I cried, voice wobbly. He didn't say anything but I could see the bones in his jaw grinding away at an internal battle.

A shadow fell across us. Neither of us looked up; we both knew who, no, what it was.

"Son, pray tell, what happened to our food supply?" A voice, clipped, cold, soft, and come to deliver punishment for something completely unheard of.

Betrayal.

My eyes flew open. I didn't know what I'd been dreaming about, but frankly I didn't give a shit because my stomach, if not my mind, was telling me it had been bad. I tried to fling the sheets off quickly, but they stuck to the thin sheen of cold sweat that covered me. I gave in, half jumping, half crawling to the bathroom as quickly as I could, my hands like claws on the floorboards. I flung my head over the toilet and let everything inside me pour out in a twisting sting of pain and wrenching, and something that looked suspiciously like Chinese takeaway.

I rolled over onto the cool tiled floor, breathing hard, sweat beading on my forehead and running down my cheeks like tears; or *were* they tears? I reached down to untangle the bed sheets which I had dragged with me to the bathroom. My fingers were shaking so hard I couldn't hold them still long enough to get a grip. I gave in, putting my head in my hands and trying to stop the cold shivers. I could still hear a child screaming for her Mummy in my head, my whole body contorting with fear. "Snap out of it, let it pass," I breathed, chanting it over and over in my head when I could no longer manage to say it out loud. The feeling wasn't going as fast as it usually did, as if something inside me wanted to rear it up. Like I could handle that much more at the moment.

I hadn't left the house in two days, too scared to go to work in case of facing Jackson and the thousands of hidden questions I had a right to know the answers to. Zean had been great on letting me stay in bed all day and pretending not to hear me cry at night. I didn't know whether I was crying for Mum, the sake of the world, or sheer frustration, but for the first time in my life I had no problem bringing tears to the surface.

There was a loud rhythmic knocking from the front door. I jumped a little. "Zean," I shouted, hearing it echo off the bathroom's shiny surfaces.

Another knock, except this time a little louder. I groaned, crawling over to the bathroom door, kicking at the sheets to come off.

I glanced at the clock as I swept out of my still unpacked room: 3:12p.m. Zean would be at work. Wow, there went another day. I opened the front door a crack, but my attempt at being able to judge whether I wanted whoever was on the other side to come in or not was thwarted when a bone-thin body threw itself through the door and straight at me, wrapping its arms around my shoulders and forcing me a few steps back. My first instinct was attack before I caught sight of Loraline at the threshold, staring at me and the hugging demon, rolling her eyes.

"So you're alive. Well, nice to know we've established that much even if you do look like hell warmed up," she chimed, looking almost pissed off.

"What the—? Get off me!" I said, muffled, but then the figure pulled back, and a rosy-cheeked though still gaunt Delia, head wrapped in a tie-dyed scarf, beamed back at me. "Oh my God," I gushed, feeling my mouth slack open. "Delia, you look… "

"Horrible! I'm bald. I miss my hair; it took me ages to grow that. So is there where you live?" she beamed, pushing past me. "Where's your room? Is it upstairs? Where is it? Tell me, tell me." She skipped upstairs, not waiting for an answer.

I turned back to Loraline. "She's—?"

"Yep."

"Was she always so…?"

"Apparently."

"Wow."

"Oh yeah, you haven't had to live with it since the moment she woke up. About an hour after you ran off with Mr Dark-and-brooding."

I sighed, and stood back to let her elegant form in, a floor-length dark denim skirt trailing behind her.

"Yeah, sorry about that. I was… freaked, I guess. You want a drink or breakfast or something?" I asked as we went into the kitchen, the sounds of Delia thudding around as she rushed around upstairs echoing through the ceiling. It sounded to my very fragile ears like thunder.

"You're not the only one who was freaked, you know. I'm friends with Delia's mother. Think how I feel." She stared at the can of Coke I passed her.

"Yeah, so what did you know?" I tried not to look at her; this wasn't really a conversation I wanted to have yet. I would have loved some time to just process.

"Nothing. I don't know anything about Namlugallu any more; I've been human for decades. You know, I wasn't even Namlugallu when I was in Sakhush… erm, that's where—"

"I know," I cut in, absently.

"How do you know?"

"Mark."

Loraline pressed her lips into a thin, tight line. "Marcus? You do remember he tried to kill you?"

"You do remember he saved me? And besides, he's not the one who's kept secrets. *He's* never hidden anything."

Loraline's lips trembled, and I immediately felt guilt, pulling out a chair next to her. "I'm sorry. I don't know what I'm talking about. So, you, eh, didn't fit in, and decided to go on a dimensional road trip?" she laughed, tears stuck in her throat as little pixie Delia, hazel eyes glowing, flew through the beaded curtains.

"We so need to decorate your room. We'll go out and find paints this afternoon, yeah? Oh, what's the matter, Lorry?" She hopped onto the table, brushing long strands of ebony hair behind Loraline's ears.

"Women like I was in Sakhush, who weren't warriors, were bred *for* warriors, kept sheltered away, veiled in public. We were educated in worthless crap and most of it was just how to fulfil our duties on how to please men."

"Yuk," both me and Delia muttered almost in unison. All three of us smirked.

"Yeah, well, we knew nothing of what our, erm, government planned. Everyone knows about the dimensional shift between the two Lexis, unlike here, but as to the specifics of what they do, they're clueless. But anyway, I couldn't exactly feel much for my duty… "

"Why not?" Delia asked blankly, inch-long tufts of woody-brown hair escaping from under the scarf.

I touched Loraline's hand. "Because she's a lesbian," I muttered softly, suddenly feeling an overwhelming feeling of sympathy. Loraline nodded.

"There's no such thing where I come from. Women have two purposes: fight or breed. And they're so civilized. So I ran; the day of my wedding I ran; and I sensed something so pure and accepting, a world of creativity and freedom and uniqueness – and then I was here. Jackson and some of the others were at the site where I came through, and he's helped me ever since. He taught me everything here, taught me how to be me. So, yeah, I, the me I've learnt about and discovered and become, I became this place, this place where I'm not suppressed."

So she wasn't Namlugallu in spirit even if that wasn't the case by birth. I liked Loraline and that was good enough for me. I flung my arms around her, Delia giggling and throwing her arms around both of us. We stayed like that for about a minute before I heard my stomach growl loud enough for the other two to hear. Loraline pulled back, her eyes running a once-over on me. "When was the last time you ate?" She didn't wait for a response, getting up to rummage around in the fridge.

Delia clapped her hands. "Snacks!" she chirped, flopping down in the free chair.

"You sure she was always this perky?" I asked, slightly worried her brain could still be a little scrambled.

"Oh, me and Lorry didn't really know each other. She lives all the way over here in Blackleigh, after all. Oh, by the way, you're invited to dinner. Mum doesn't know any specifics but she can sense you were the one who saved me."

I tried not to grimace. "Do you remember, I mean, do you want to talk…?" Please say no.

She shrugged. "I don't really remember much at all. It's like Lexis is in my mind and is trying to block it out to save me from the pain. I remember you a lot, and being afraid, and I don't like to sleep, but nothing much specific."

I stared at her. Nightmares? Nightmares her mind tried to suppress?

"What makes you think some all-powerful Lexis is what is trying to help you?" I scoffed, acting lighter than my heart felt at that moment.

Delia shook her head at me like she was my mother and I was her ignorant toddler or something. "Lexis protects its own. It is like our abstract energy mother of everything! Honestly, Lorry, what *have* you told her?"

Loraline was chopping ham at the counter and just rolled her eyes. "Delia, I'm begging you here, stop calling me Lorry," she moaned.

"Loraline is way too long," Delia moaned back, swigging from Lorry's... I mean, Loraline's Coke.

I rubbed my already bursting head. "And before?" I urged. I wanted this cleared, just out of principle.

This time Delia looked a bit more bothered. "Well, Catharine came to me asking for help. She said she'd been on smack and was too scared to go to the doctor. I was hoping I could give her some alternative. We got friendly a little and went down to Casper's a couple of times. I guess, thinking back, they probably offered her money or drugs or something to get me for them, and in the end they just killed her for the sake of it. Sentel? The blonde one... She's horrible."

I wanted to say something. I shouldn't have asked; all the perky glow had drained from Delia's cheeks.

"Well of course she is, honey. Have you seen her? She looks like Pamela Anderson meets Barbie meets... " Loraline stopped, her lips pursed at one side as she stirred the omelette.

"Triple H?" I offered. Delia burst out in a small laugh.

"I was thinking more Jabba the Hutt, you know, green complexion," Loraline said very seriously. We all doubled up, cackling like three real witches as Loraline put three plates of cheesy meaty omelette down on the table, Delia immediately picking at hers with her fingers, her knees drawn up on the chair, totally ignoring the fork.

"So, Casper's is what? Capturing people to try and bring Nam… eh, lethal expats through?" I asked through a mouthful of cheese and egg goodness.

Loraline sighed. "Nomas are looking into it. Jackson said they've known about Casper's and a couple of other places like it around the country, but the level of powerful activity is so dangerous they just can't get close to do anything. They always knew they took, like, homeless people and stuff like that to eat or drain, but this is new. He said we shouldn't get involved, leave it to Nomas, it's what they're there for." She made a face, but I got the impression she wasn't entirely disagreeing.

"What do you mean, eat or drain?" I asked hesitantly, watching Delia, but she seemed totally discombobulated in a cheery, energetic kind of way. Loraline, on the other hand, visibly cringed.

"Eat is self-explanatory. Drain: well, just take their energy for themselves. It's exhilarating and empowering, and because of the way they're bred, they, we, evolved so that we need it to survive," she said quietly, playing with her food again.

"How'd ya drain someone?" Delia suddenly asked, leaning in, totally unaffected. Jeez, if her ghost had been that freaking scary, and she was like this in person, mine'd be a Voldemort–Hannibal hybrid. Loraline seemed to be thinking the same thing because she was gaping at Delia in disbelief.

"What? Curious!" Delia said defensively, holding up her egg-drenched hands.

Loraline shook her head. "Directly tap into an energy sink, like electrical impulses over the heart. Brain: tap into blood—"

"Whoa! Like vampires?" I gasped.

Loraline didn't seem pleased with the comparison. "Well, that way is more intermittent because it keeps the other person alive, and it's more used as a strong stimulant, you know, like between love—"

"You know, we don't need to know this!" I cried, feeling totally grossed-out, looking at what was left of my oozing cheesy omelette with total distaste.

"Uh-huh. I agree. Real life Bram Stoker; not good," Delia said, making Loraline giggle a little.

"Wait. Rewind and click; slow motion. That must mean you do it! You look like a vampire. All you need is red lipstick and a trashy outfit. If you're a vampire, can I be a pixie?" Delia cried, bouncing up in the chair, overjoyed at the prospect.

"Wait. *Trashier* outfit," I added derisively, only to receive a nudge in the ribs and a stuck-out tongue from Loraline. "Oh you just love that. You get such a good view."

"Yeeeaaah!"

"No, Delia, I am not a vampire. I'm good with the sun, I like garlic, and I have a lovely pair of gold crucifix earrings, thank you very much. Blood transfer is just a means of chemical energy transfer. There's a lot of nice things carried around in it. And when I need to have it, I have pigs."

Delia gasped. "That's murder! Poor piglets!"

"Wait. You're alright with sucking humans to death, but put a pig into the equation and it all gets too much for you. You eat pork, right?" I laughed.

"I do not. I'm a vegetarian!" Delia exclaimed, outraged, leaning back in the chair.

"Oh, brother," both me and Loraline managed at once, both rolling our eyes.

One moment our shabby little kitchen had been filled with

laughter and giggling and, frankly, the best moments I'd had since arriving at Blackleigh; and the next, both Delia and Loraline were sitting straight up in their chairs looking as though someone had set off a fire alarm my ears were at the wrong pitch to hear. Delia hopped around like a baby kangaroo on the chair to look into the hallway. "We got company," she mumbled distantly.

"How do you know?" I demanded, bewildered.

Delia snapped back, looking straight at Loraline, one hand held out to me. "We totally have to teach her something. She knows nothing; it's like being around an infant!" she cried, giggling a little through her words.

"Teach me w——?" I was cut off by a loud rapping on the front door. Both me and Loraline got up at the same instant. Loraline's eyes narrowed.

Loraline got there before me, every muscle in her shoulders bunched tensely. I placed a hand on hers.

"I'll do it. I do live here, after all. Just in case it's not demons from hell, sorry, home sweet home, coming to attack." I flung the door open to reveal an imposing looking black woman and a middle-aged policeman standing patiently on the doorstep, and looking almost too normal after what all of us had been braced for. Then reality struck. Police, not good. I hadn't driven enough to get a ticket. Was this about Delia? The woman stopped that thought in its tracks straight away.

"Kahlillyne Exeter?" she asked in a voice of steel. Oh, shit.

She was just slightly shorter than Loraline, muscular shoulders underneath her very brown suede coat that mixed in beautifully with the deep cocoa colour of her luminous skin. With the protruding cheekbones and with those distinctive Jamaican lips and eyes she could have been very attractive, but the way her hair had been pulled tightly, slicked back into a bun, and how she'd buffed up so much that her neck and arms, if not for the occasional delicate curve here and there, could have belonged to a man, made her look hard, like iron. The man behind her, with his greying eyebrows and chubby rose-coloured cheeks, almost looked like a cherub next to her androgynous majesty.

"Ye… yes," I stammered as an inspector's badge was whipped out in front of me.

"Inspector Dashay Green. This is Sergeant Chance."

Chance nodded his blue and white hat at us. "May we speak with you, please?"

Loraline reached out in front of me, almost snatching the inspector's badge from her and scanning it with narrowed eyes. The inspector raised one perfectly groomed eyebrow, her gaze fixed on Loraline.

Delia was hopping behind us, trying to see what was going on. Loraline passed the badge back.

"Of course." I pulled Loraline back a little so she'd let them pass. Clearly, of all our customs, she was a little rusty on how to deal with law enforcement officials, especially when you lived in this area of Blackleigh. I glanced beyond the inspector. There was a group of skinhead chavs on the corner smoking God knows what. Great impression. As I closed the door, my eyes hooked momentarily on a deep blue Ford Mondeo parked right outside. I started to feel that omelette churn rebelliously.

I led through into the living room, the inspector and Chance refusing to sit as Delia flopped down onto the couch, looking a little pale and distracted. I wondered whether to offer tea.

"May I ask what this is about?" Loraline said, a bit icily.

"Of course. I'd like to enquire whether you know this man?" Green held up a Polaroid of a man in motion, his thick brown-gold hair blowing in a breeze and his eyes glaring at some invisible annoyance. Mark.

I took a deep breath. "I do. Mark, erm, Marcus. He lives here in Blackleigh, I think." I sounded very guilty already.

"What's this about?" Loraline demanded, glaring at the snapshot like it was a rodent.

Green placed the photograph in a pocket of her coat. "Would you mind coming down to the station for a general enquiry?" she asked crisply.

"What!" Loraline exclaimed. I wished she'd cool off.

"No, I wouldn't. But I've only been here a little over a month. I haven't even known him that long... " I trailed off, already looking around for where I'd chucked my coat last night. When Mark had driven me home.

"Of course, Miss Exeter. This is just a general enquiry for your own safety," Green said coolly, looking at Loraline out of the corner of her eye.

"What's this got do with Khyle?" Loraline asked, her own eyes locked on Green's.

"I'm afraid I'm not willing to share that information with you, I'm sorry. And you are...?"

"Loraline."

"Loraline...?" Green pressed.

"I'm afraid I'm not willing to share that information, inspector," Loraline half smirked, half snapped back.

The inspector pressed her lips to stop an amused smile. "Are you Miss Exeter's partner?" she asked graciously, while Chance grew more and more uncomfortable in the corner, shifting his weight from foot to foot.

"No, I am not. Would it be a problem if I was?" Loraline started with raised eyebrows.

"Not at all." Green stressed every word as if she were thoroughly enjoying this.

I grabbed my coat from behind the couch, but I suddenly caught sight of Delia. "Eh, Loraline?" I cried, worry seeping into every syllable.

Sweat had beaded on Delia's lightening green-white brow, and her eyes were closed.

"Honey, what's the matter?" Loraline was there in an instant, crouched beside us.

"I feel a little… " She trailed off, gulping hard.

"Bathroom's right down there," I quickly said to Loraline, not sparing a moment, grabbing Delia by the arm and almost lifting her to the bathroom, from where the sounds of Delia giving a mixture of crying and heaving immediately erupted.

"Miss Exeter, I am sorry, but if you wouldn't mind leaving your friend to the, I'm sure, more than capable hands of Ms Loraline… " She gestured to the door. I nodded, absently pulling my coat on and grabbing my keys as they led me out into the brittle wind and into the car. God, I hoped Delia was alright.

Chapter Thirteen

Blackleigh, though small, had a fairly large police station, probably due to all the crime activity in downtown, but it was about twenty years old, all white-greywashed walls and that patchy blue and green faded carpet you see in doctors' waiting rooms all the time. The outside car park was full to the square inch with police cars and motorcycles and off-duty vehicles, and the inside was even more bustling. I followed Green. Chance had gone on her orders to collect something from her office. I'd only been in a police station once and that had been to collect one of the younger fosters who had been caught shoplifting. It was very different being on the other side; people who were waiting, looking ashen-faced or nursing fresh wounds, shot me questioning glances and I could feel my cheeks burning.

Green led me into a square box of a room which came equipped with the notorious two-way mirror reflecting back my own pale, stricken face. "Please sit." Green gestured with one surprisingly small hand at the white plastic and metal table and chair that dominated the emptiness. I pulled out the chair, feeling a massive relief as my legs no longer had to support my exhausted upper half. I was really starting to wonder how much I would be able to take before my brain hit a previously unknown self-destruct button to save it from any additional atrocities this place was going to throw at me.

"Chance should be back in a moment. Your friend Loraline, she was very… abrasive." The inspector's eyes were a clear sea-green like bottle glass, and they were about as empty of any emotion.

"Yes. Sorry about that. She's defensive, I guess."

"As long as I shouldn't be looking at it as over-defensive in Marcus's case."

"No. No, not Loraline. She hates Mark's guts, really."

The inspector gave one curt nod. "Well, just for that reason I'll forgive all the viciousness. Can you give me a reason why she would be so defensive, though? Does she have feelings for you?"

I scoffed despite my self-control. "Not that I can see how it's relevant to your investigation, inspector, but I doubt it. I am not lesbian. We've just been through a lot recently, is all."

"Like what?" she asked sharply, so quickly I hadn't finished the sentence properly.

I was relieved when the foggy glass panelled door swung open and Chance handed Green a stack of thick brown folders. Green never took her gaze from me as she slipped one from the bottom. An A4-sized photograph slid out onto the table towards me. "Recognise this woman?"

It took me a moment to break Green's stare. I think I'd forgotten how scary people can be. I'd much rather be wrestling a deadly tourist. The photo was a school photograph of a girl, thick tousled brown hair falling in a shiny mane a few inches below her blazer collar. The bridge of her nose was lightly freckled, light brown eyes rimmed with very dark thick lashes. She had one of those naturally doll-pretty faces. I should know; I was forced to glare at one whenever I looked in a mirror. She looked about sixteen. I shook my head. I'd never seen her before in my life.

Green raised her eyebrows. "How about now?" She slid another photo across the smooth surface. I felt my breath catch in my throat. It was the same girl, except this was a crime scene photo of her sprawled, tied to a chair, flopping forward, that hair falling over her drooping head. She was in just her underwear, her arms and legs cast into an awful black and white of bruises by the harsh light used by the CSI forensics. Her throat had been torn out, literally a gash about the size of a small fist, and deep enough; I could see how her windpipe had been ripped and exposed.

Bile rose in my throat and I pushed the photo away. "God!" I breathed, disgusted.

"I'll take that as a no." Green flicked open another folder, sliding another photo across the table. This was a family photo. She jabbed it with one dark finger, pointing to a girl standing by her father, a sturdy-looking man. It had been taken in what looked like a very high-class family's backyard. Long, thick tousled brown hair, brown eyes, doll features. I shook my head, feeling my eyes widening.

Green slid another photo across the table, wordlessly. This time, the girl was hanging from a chandelier in a very grand entrance hall, her nightgown hanging in tatters at her bare feet. I swallowed, pressing my hand against my mouth. I felt a cool pressure on my hand. I glanced up. Green was leaning across the table, her expression almost soft. "Breathe," she said calmly and commandingly.

She slid open the other folders, filling the tables with befores and afters of pretty brunettes, ranging from fifteen to twenty-five, all petite, brown-eyed. They all looked like me. There were five in total, and the only inconsistency among all of them was the earliest: it looked like it had happened back in the Sixties. The girl was so mod she would have put Twiggy to shame. The newest was dated about five years ago, in 2007.

"Two of these women reported being stalked, death threats,

strange flowers, family members brutally killed. She" – Green pointed to the mod woman – "had her father dismembered in front of her and her kitten nailed to a wall. They were all tortured eventually; slow-acting poisons, drugged, hot, cold, sharp, and blunt. Brutality is the way to describe these murders, and cause of death is the same in each. Can you tell me, Miss Exeter, what you think that may be?"

I swallowed. "Throat wound?"

"In three, yes, and the resulting blood loss; blood that has, without explanation, evaporated. And these two" – she pointed to two I couldn't describe with words – "were apparently eaten."

I looked up at Green. "How didn't this get to the Press?"

Of all the questions to ask. What on earth was wrong with me? Thankfully, Green looked more bewildered than disgusted.

"You'd be surprised how much the Press *doesn't* actually get hold of. We believe that there is one murderer between all of these women."

"And you think it's Mark, erm, Marcus? That's ridiculous. This one must be about sixty years old. Have you seem him lately? I doubt he could be wearing that well." My voice betrayed me by quivering. Green saw the challenge.

"A lot of serial killers take inspiration, and mimic; those who don't have any imagination anyway. How many times have you been in touch with Marcus?"

I was about to say "Didn't you just say you believed they'd all be done by the same person?", but I thought better of it, and began to count mentally. "I've seen him on five or so separate occasions, I guess."

"Alone?"

I'd never been interrogated before; turned out I wasn't good under pressure. "No, I mean yes, yes, yes, alone," I stammered, debating how bad it would look if I bolted.

"Has he ever made a move on you, sexual or otherwise, any threats, suspicious behaviour?"

A few death threats, plenty of suspicious behaviour; in fact, he's never actually acted normal if he knows what that is, I thought.

"No. No, he's never done any of that stuff."

The blind and deaf could tell I was lying. And so could Green.

"Those are some nasty-looking bruises you have there." She gestured to my neck; my hand went there reflexively. I couldn't think what to say that wouldn't have them put me in witness protection. Why shouldn't they, after all? They were trying to help. Any sane person would beg for a bodyguard. Me? I defended him. Did I think Mark had done this? I couldn't admit that to myself; there was no proof it was him.

"Why do you think Marcus is behind this?" I asked faintly.

"He had contact with two of these victims and we think he lived close to two of them, plus other evidence I'm not—"

"—willing to exchange," I muttered absently. Yeah, there was a lot of unwillingness to exchange information with me lately. Green sat back.

"If he is threatening you or hurting you in any way, I can assure you that I will offer you full protection if you testify to his advances. This man is very dangerous, Miss Exeter—"

"Khyle, please. Anything to do with Exeter reminds me of my mother," I interjected, tired of wincing every time she addressed me.

Green said, "Khyle, you must see I am not accusing you of anything. Look at these women; look in that mirror. Can you tell me you believe so fully in this man that you would deny all this at risk to your own life?"

"Yes." The word escaped so fast, so instinctively, I was left wondering if it had been me who had actually said it, but when I realized it had been, equally I realized it was true. I was suicidal, clearly.

"May I enquire why you think he would, other than the obvious resemblance; and, I mean, assuming he was guilty, why me?" Green surveyed me over clasped hands. "I mean, Blackleigh isn't massive, but it's large enough to have at least five brown-haired, brown-eyed girls between fifteen and twenty five. Why me?" I pressed.

A flash crossed Green's face as she made her mind up about something. "We monitor Marcus very closely, Khyle. *I* do. I have been on this particular case a great deal of my career. He's recently become very interested in you, your background, running checks into your history, gaining your phone number from records. I have been told that he has even been to your foster homes. Are you interested now?"

I felt what was left of the colour in my face drain away. "Are you having me arrested, Inspector Green?" I sounded just as sick as I felt.

"No," came a sharp, tight response.

I got up, wrapping my coat closer around me. "Then I'm leaving. Thank you for your concern, inspector." I forced each word to come out sounding robotic.

"I'll be keeping an eye on you, Miss Exeter, and I may ask you to bring in a few of your friends for questioning. If you are withholding something for his protection and you do not wish to be charged, now would be the time." Green stood up, her perfectly toned and ribbed figure making me feel very unfit and unkempt in comparison.

"Good afternoon," I muttered, walking out.

Outside, I managed to swipe a fag off a guy in a Man. United T-shirt who appeared to be trying to chain-smoke any potential charges away. I took a massive drag, my brain screaming *thank you* as nicotine penetrated each individual synapse in turn. The only good thing that had come from the last few days was that my smoking had been seriously compromised; if I considered that good, that was.

I fished out my mini-Nokia. Loraline answered immediately as if she'd been expecting the call. I was starting to think I wasn't giving this whole witchy thing enough credit.

"What was that all about then? Are you okay? Where are you?"

"How'd you know it was me? I've never called you before. It sure as hell weren't caller ID," I grumbled.

"Do you really wanna know?" Loraline laughed.

"Probably not. How's Delia?" I sighed.

It was Loraline's turn to groan a little. "Okay, I think. She hasn't eaten much since she got back. I took her to Jackson and he just says it might take a while for her system to come back online, you know? Regardless, she's back to her insufferably happy self. You're avoiding the question, Khyle. What did they want with you?"

God, I didn't want to talk about it. "Does Mark strike you as serial killer material?"

"Do birds fly?" Loraline replied dryly.

"Not all of them."

"Then I guess you have the answer," Loraline snorted, sounding unimpressed. I groaned, stubbing out my fag. "Come to dinner tomorrow night at Eliza's. Jaz 'n' Jackson are gonna be there and, of course, so am I."

I laughed. "I don't know."

"You clearly didn't hear me. I said *I'm* going to be there."

"Tut. Well, then, how could I resist?" I said. "Other than that, I don't know where on earth she lives, and I have no way of getting there unless you invite Zean, and no offence, but I don't think he's going to be up for a nice sit-down wi—"

"With us freaks," she finished bluntly.

I sighed, trying to think of something comforting, but Zean had made his blunt-ended feelings pretty clear. There was a beeping as the other line came in. "Lorry, I have to go," I said. "It's the other line. I'll see if I can make it okay."

"Oh, you'll make it or you'll have the hysterical Delia to deal with. Oh, and call me Lorry again and I'll bite you." I laughed, praying to dear God she was kidding. "Khyle?"

"Yup?"

"I'm begging you. Be careful; with Marcus, with everything." I yoohooed her and then flicked the 'call waiting' button.

"Miss K Exeter, I hope for your sake as a writer you're in intensive care," came a deep, arrogant voice on the other end.

"Excuse me!" I cried, making a group of officers sipping coffee from plastic cups nearby look round.

"My name's Steve Blain, of *O. O.* We had an appointment at three you missed because you were hit by a bus, and rendered unable to move your unknown, unaccredited and, I may stress, unpublished arse, down here."

Oh, this guy sounded like a bundle of joy. "Well, excuse me, Mr Blain, but it helps if you inform someone precisely of the time and date of an appointment if you want them to make it. Am I wrong when I say that letter you sent me said nothing precise other than to get in contact with you?"

"No, you are very right; that letter said nothing. The three messages on your landline, on the other hand… "

I gasped. "How did you get either of these numbers anyway?" I screamed into the receiver.

"Be thankful I did. You want this job, Miss Exeter?"

The cockiness was practically oozing from my mobile, past my fingers, infecting as it went. I swallowed. "Yes," I managed to spit through clenched teeth.

"Then get down here by six. I'm working overtime tonight, and

I'm cutting you a very unique piece of final slack. One minute after six and you can sign yourself up for a McDonald's uniform." The line went dead, leaving me gasping and seething so hard I could have ignited myself into a ball of flames. It was clear: I'd gone through nineteen years where the most interesting thing that had entered my life was the X Factor, and now I was making up for it by being thrown into such a rush of turmoil I wouldn't even have time to process it.

I made an instant decision: if the world was here in eighteen months or not, whether Mark had me on a list of brutal ways to knock someone off or not, whether demon equivalents would be walking on Earth or not, I wanted that job.

★ ★ ★

The *Oxfordshire Onslaught* editorial office I found after asking around at the police station; and a twenty-minute debate with a cab driver later, I was in downtown's high street at the top of a Thirties-style rundown block of apartments. At 5:45pm this was not the best place to be. The shops had eerie fluorescent flashing signs hanging blinking in the late afternoon light, the pavement was littered with cigarette butts, crumpled beer cans and candy wrappers, and as I climbed out of the cab and handed over the fare there was a group of kids break-dancing outside a tattoo parlour at the end of the street. Welcome to the real Blackleigh, I thought half-heartedly, running up to the buzzer and pressing it a couple of times.

There were three corporations in this block. Sally's Nail Salon and Antique Furniture Polishers and Co. were on the bottom floor. It looked like *O.O.* occupied the other three floors. It took a while for an unfortunately familiar male voice to answer.

"Exeter?"

"Yeah. Is that Blai—?"

The man didn't wait to hear my question as a buzzing ran through the heavy glass double doors, which looked as though, before the metal bars had been placed over the scratched windows and the green and silver paint had chipped, they may once have been grand. I pushed inside into a surprising amount of stuffy warmth. There was creamy beige carpet running through the entrance hall and up the deep mahogany staircase. A cork board opposite the door had faded flyers of special offers and town shows and fairs. I noticed one of Loraline's for the past fair where I'd met Eliza and had slipped off onto the floor. Omen!

It was a steep climb up and I wasn't sure how far I was going. On the first floor I glanced through the smoked glass window in the door to see a massive area of printers and photocopiers and filing cabinets and a couple of over-cluttered desks. It was empty. The second was much larger, about the size of a tennis court, and flooded with table after table with neat computers and printers, and a whole rainforest of paper spilling over tables and pinned to walls. Every last person in the room seemed to be attached to cups of steaming hot coffee. There was a woman at one of the desks, her fingers typing away so fast they were a blur of tan over the black keyboard. I pushed the door open a little, peeking in.

"Excuse me… do you know where I might find Steve Blai—?"

"Upstairs, honey. Good luck."

She didn't look up from the computer screen, but something about the way she spoke gave me the distinct impression that I'd already been stamped 'new girl'.

Another flight of stairs up, and I came to an old-fashioned wavy-glassed door with the words 'Steve Blain, *Oxfordshire Onslaught* Senior Editor'. I knocked, forebodingly. "In!" Mr Blain, I assumed.

Inside was mostly dominated by a huge pine table with a state-of-the-art Apple Mac perched on one end, copier fax, picture frames facing away from my view. Old covers and past and future stories were overflowing from their folders, old-fashioned posters and blown-up photographs of Oxfordshire countryside and farms had been stuck to the brown and white walls, and the room stank of sugar, fresh print, body odour, and stale coffee. I was home.

Behind the desk stood a red-haired man, somewhere between forty and forty-five, his eyes scanning something in his hand with an exaggerated look of shock and disgust. Blain had very thin lips and freckled skin but a frame that said he spent every other waking moment at the gym. It also said he was unmarried and considered himself Oxfordshire's most fortunate bachelor. He was chewing a cigar beneath his ginger and brown speckled moustache. I had a sneaking suspicion that the cigarette ban had been the equivalent of the UK's anarchy in his opinion. In fact, his whole appearance, down to the deep lines around his nostrils and eyes etched in from excessive snarling, was so cliché, if he stood up to reveal suspender belts and knee-high black cotton socks under loafers I would be in danger of falling into side-splitting giggles.

He looked up at me quickly, gesturing with the paper he was holding to the seat opposite him. He put the paper down to chew on his moustache while staring at me.

"And this is actually good considering you look as if you just walked out of a chess club, Exeter."

He threw me the paper he'd been reading. I picked it up hesitantly. It was a piece I had written on England's increasing dependence on brainwashing language in order to wring the necks of its public in a consumer society. How the ruddy heck had he got this? And what did he mean, chess club? I was wearing light skinny jeans and my black jacket. How did that result in chess club, if at all, and not what I would choose to go to an interview in.

"How old are you?" he barked, removing his cigar a moment to dash out the ash.

"Nineteen." I had to stop myself adding 'sir' as if I was at the principal's office again.

"Big opinions from somewhere so young. Good. That's what I want. That's why I want you. What I don't want is moaning, excuses, sloppy work and unimpressive writing. You give me that, I'll either cut your wage or cut you. Got that?" He didn't give me time to respond. "Good. We here at *O.O.* value originality and we expect that from each of our full-timers. There's a lot of people who have begged to be where you're sitting and you decide to sit there almost three hours late. Anything to say for that?" No time to even draw a breath. "Shame. You want this, you fight for this. Fight for it hard enough and I'll reward you. I take care of my own. Now do you want to know what you're signing up for?" Were these even questions, because he seemed, for a man who valued opinions, to be neglecting any need for one? "We've always been aimed at an older generation which I've never liked. I'm just taking over, you see, Exeter, from my predecessor, and I've thought, for a place like Oxfordshire where, yes, there is a farming community, a political community, and a general community. what is the *main* community? The *student* community, and it's time to open our pages to *them*; not just the pompous Einsteins down at the unis but *all* of your generation. I will take this to a new level. Are you with me?" He sounded like he was proposing the salvation of mankind... If only he knew. I nodded.

"A little bit more than that would be good," he barked.

"Yes, right, opening your doors to the next generation." I nodded, a little spinelessly. I wanted to point out that the student population could be considered part of the general community and, for that matter, came in all shapes and sizes of age. I didn't, but only because I wouldn't have got a sentence that long into the answering intervals he was allowing me.

He sniffed. "We'll cover lifestyle, scandal, politics. You name it, we'll bring it, and what I want is to bring it in a way no other of those magazines talking about where to spend their government allowance for the night does. We have to get the dirt, Exeter, you understand; go deep, be brutal, you understand? That's what this newspaper is about, pushing limits, and that's what we're going to do." He held out one hand, gruffly. "You with me?"

Yes sir, no sir, three bags full sir. "Absolutely."

"Brilliant. Now, so far I have three others working in this new department. You're going to be doing the legwork for me. Its nine to five officially; unofficially, you work until the story's on my table by deadline as standard. You'll have a press card that allows you access to library resources, etcetera; it also allows entrance into a few distinct theatres, restaurants, the photographers down King's Street too. I pay a pretty price for that so use it well. Questions?" When he paused for more than ten seconds I dived.

"Pay?" I asked, a little sheepish.

"Seventeen grand a year. Bonuses if you get me something damned good; otherwise it's flat, no dental."

"That's fine. I've already accepted cigarettes will have me in dentures before thirty anyway."

To my surprise, he actually barked a laugh that reminded me of a ginger terrier hound. "I like you already. Right, this is what I want and I want it by Friday. There's a new party scene going around: Goth meets dominatrix meets just plain freaky. Get me a review, and your opinion. If it's cruel enough, you get your first bonus. In cash.

There's a list over there of the best-known clubs in Oxfordshire which are drawing them in. Ten thousand words, cynical, sarcastic; bitter, even. Questions?"

There was only one I could think of. "What's the day today?" I muttered quietly.

"Wednesday. Good start. Now get out. My personal trainer wants me by seven."

Told you: exercise freak, even with those lungs.

As I left Blain's office I glanced at my watch. It was six. I'd barely been in there five minutes. It had been like the Spanish Inquisition. I hadn't really had to say anything at all. He might as well have had that conversation with a wall and he would have got more feedback. Wednesday. I had two days. Ten thousand words; brutally honest review? Piece of very sweet cake. I glanced at the list, and as my eyes trailed downwards I felt myself deflate as the cake suddenly became equally as sour. Right at the end of the list, one word: Casper's. Well, it was an excuse to check it out for my own curiosity, I guessed, but then the sensible, less self-destructive thing to do would be to pick one of the other clubs, and stay as far as possible from a firing range that seemed perfectly adept at finding me without me literally walking towards it. But then, I'd always admitted to being self-destructive, hadn't I?

Chapter Fourteen

As I handed over the crumpled twenty-pound note to the stud-eyebrowed taxi driver, I'd swear he spent that second too long looking at my bare thighs. I pursed my lips and jumped out of the car into the dark, almost deserted downtown street wishing my coat was thermally padded. I'd never been to a club before, but obviously, not being totally socially retarded, I'd seen clubs in movies and I knew the sort of stuff you should wear. Well, after an hour and a half, and the entire contents of my wardrobe spread over the floor, I'd decided that maybe... I was entirely socially retarded. Eventually I'd snuck down the hall into Zean's and found the 'Jessica drawer', or in theory the Jessica drawer. It could just be strays from many past ladies who'd liked to walk out in Zean's clothes rather than their own. I'd ended up wearing a pair of micro-mini fake black leather hot pants, a neon UV lime skin-tight vest top, thigh-high black high-heeled lace-up boots, and my own painfully flimsy black wrap jacket. I'd even gone so far as to apply actual make-up so now, in my attempt at sexy, I'd managed beaten-up panda. In fact, the only thing that had gone right was that I'd managed to tame my hair to a nice smooth mass that was behaving itself in the frigid cold rather than frizzing.

I had my Nokia in my pocket, cash down my bra, and an empty stomach full of butterflies. I was screwed: not only would everyone be able to tell I'd never been to a club, let alone a notoriously push-the-boat-out danger zone one. As I stood alone staring at the deserted cobblestone street where the taxi driver had left me, I was painfully aware just how far from home I really was, especially as I'd been too much of a puss to tell anyone for fear of the disapproving argument it would ignite. Suicidal. A couple laughing, arm in arm, suddenly appeared out of nowhere down from the darker end, the girl's heels flicking viciously as she almost doubled over laughing. I stuffed my hands down in my pockets, and walked in the direction they were coming from. As I went past them the guy, a punk-looking twenty-something, caught my gaze. It could have just been funky contacts, but I could have sworn his eyes glowed with an eager luminescent jade to match the colour of the top I was wearing.

I swallowed, shaking the hair off my neck. Maybe not the best idea, considering what I might be walking into. As I walked further into the darkness, I could hear the steady beat of heavy R 'n' B drifting out the wind. It turned out they'd come up out nowhere, rather than just out *of* nowhere. There was an iron cast staircase descending sharply, a lustrous amber light bursting from its depths. I walked down, desperate not to trip or catch a heel. The bouncer at the bottom was huge on the human scale, his skin midnight black but tattooed tribally in gold and red. He was strangely beautiful. I expected him to ask for ID, but instead he asked in a deep rich ghetto accent, "Number?"

Seven. "Eh, seven?" I stuttered.

The guy smirked a little and picked one of two stamps in front of him, jabbing it in a glittery blue ink and stamping my hand with it, before releasing the robe and letting me through into a swirling mass of sound, bustle, heat, and alternating shades of scarlet, amethyst and sapphire.

As I pushed in, I tried to look at the word stamped on my hand, but the light wasn't really strong enough to pick up on the rich dark letters on the stark white of my skin. A gorgeous woman, dressed in mock leather suspenders and a bad, bad interpretation of a maid's outfit, took my coat without asking, allowing me just enough time to whip my phone from the pocket and clasp it in my fist. I was consumed in a flood of bodies bustling around, leaning into each other, groups talking and laughing, gathering drinks from the bar, heading towards the dance floor… It didn't look that bad. The place was like a huge basement/ cavern/ snug, the walls covered with a silver and green wallpaper like something you'd find in a bad Indian restaurant, but the floor, when I looked down, was a metallic silver glass, and underneath it a mass of trapped water, with tiny multi-coloured lights flashing in the constantly rippling waves beneath the hundred or so feet stamping around on it. I instantly felt unstable just standing, imagining myself going straight through in a blur of shattered glass and electrocution. I waded through the crowds of people, flicking my phone to camera and clicking away at the chaotic mass of energy.

There were over-stuffed couches and chairs packed into corners with Eighties-style hanging chairs dotted here and there, and high tables and chairs spray-painted a multitude of colours and textures. The ceiling was a good twenty feet up with a whole second storey walled off with an iron-railed balcony, bodies hanging over it looking down on us. Most eye-catching of all, though, hanging in mid-air, exactly parallel to the second storey, were cages of what could be kindly described as male and female exotic dancers twisting in and out of the bent and twisted bars, their legs going in directions I thought only circus performers could pull off. I felt my mouth fall open as I backed up, my camera held a foot in front of me.

"You aren't supposed to take photos in here, sweetie."

I spun round, accidentally hitting a bar stool and almost toppling it over. A long-haired, gothed-out barman, who looked way too sweet for his outfit, was smiling kindly behind the bar.

"Oh, sorry," I cried over the music, showing him as I tucked the phone into an invisible back pocket in the hot pants which was actually the gap between the leather and my knickers.

I pulled up the stool I'd almost knocked over to perch on and look around at the packed crowds. If I felt naked, that was nothing compared to some of these girls who were practically in their underwear, with accessories. I watched one girl, her hair ringletted to Alice Cooper-esque levels, as she pranced by in fluffy leg warmers, a ballerina skirt, and a piece of pink-coloured ribbon. The place was so crowded I couldn't really actually see much of anything, everything blending into blurs of grinding bodies and UV-lighted clothing.

"What'll it be?"

I glanced around to the gothic barman. "Erm, I don't know. What do you suggest?" fiddling awkwardly with the tips of my hair.

He laughed, beaming. "Yeah, you don't come here often, huh?" Thankfully. I doubted he could tell how red my cheeks were. "Well, let's start at the beginning: drink, or be drank/drink??" He laughed again at my expression. "Look, give me your arm. I'll give you a shot on the house and send you up. It'll be a ride."

He reached out for my arm which was leaning on the counter. The light by the bar was a bit stronger, a kind of bright citron, just strong enough for me to make out the word on my arm: 'human'.

What the—?

The barman had turned my arm over, and was fiddling for something under the bar, suddenly appearing with a thin, viciously sharp, syringe. I reflexively pulled my arm back but his grip was like a vice, and in a heartbeat I felt the sting of metal as he penetrated my skin, a teardrop of blood exploding upwards.

"Khyle! What the fu—? Aye aye!!!"

A red-leather-clad hand flung out, tearing the barman's grip off me and gently, efficiently, removing the syringe in one quick gesture. I looked up from my arm which I'd been gaping at in complete horror, helplessly. Flash Gordon sunglasses and a mass of now spiked-up, bleach blond hair looked back at me.

"Ross, what are you doing here? I thought Nomas couldn't get in here," I stuttered dizzily.

Ross's boyish features looked somewhere between shocked and outraged as he flung the barman's hand away. "Back off, Ace, yeah? She's with me unless you want 'assle." He turned to me. "What am I doing 'ere? What the f— are *you* doing here? Does anyone know about this?" He pulled my arm, steering me away from the bar and through the crowd to a secluded corner table cluttered with stout, empty glasses, all with the remnants of what my skilled nose could detect as whisky.

"Does anyone know you're here?" I countered.

Ross perched me on one of the chairs like a china doll, and then pulled up the other. "Of course. I'm on duty tonight."

"Duty?"

"Yeah. We can't infiltrate this place. One: too high profile; two: too much work for little product. But we still keep surveillance; make sure nothing too big goes down. And your excuse; you know what Casper's is 'bout, right?" His brow was furrowed in candid concern above his glasses, and I felt an immediate surge of warmth towards him. He seemed really… genuine.

"Yeah. I mean, I know it's infested with lethal expats and all. But I'm doing a story on this whole new club scene and Casper's was one of the places to check out. Plus, I don't know, I was curious. I know it was stupid and crazy… " I trailed off.

"Nah, girl, you got balls. Curiosity's still a killer, though bloody hell, if Christ knew… " He shook his head. "Why should Christ care?" Ross looked as if he'd happily swallow his own tongue. "What kind of story do you want?" He changed the subject, signalling to a waitress in a bat outfit and ordering a whisky and an unopened bottle of water for me… Okay, maybe too unfeigned.

"I don't know. What was that about 'back at the bar'? Drugs? Erm, do they know about the surveillance?"

"Yeah, they know, but they can't do jack. I order drinks, I don't cause trouble. What do they care? They do all the big stuff in the back rooms" – he gestured to a set of curtained doors at the far back of the room dwarfed by two bulky looking men – "and no, that wasn't drugs. You don't get what they do here. They feed off the humans who come here, drug most of them up, and then send them upstairs. The humans get left with a massive high, completely out of it and unable to remember a thing; the ones who get left down here get a general good time and cause no fuss. Those back rooms are a mixture of in-house brothels, ceremonial chambers, and conference rooms, but none of us have ever been able to get back there to find out what's actually going on." He thanked the waitress, strategically checking the bottle of water hadn't had its seal broken.

"What do you mean, feed?" I asked.

Ross looked up, or at least his chin tilted up. "Straight energy drain, blood exchange. It's more a high for the, eh, lethal expats. That's good, by the way. I can see why you want to be a writer." We both exchanged a smile.

"That's terrible. And you can't do anything about it?"

Ross groaned. "I've tried to get our operation to. But we've tried before. Loads of times, but the truth is the big boys like to hang out back and up there. We always end up getting more humans worthlessly slaughtered with very little good actually coming out of it."

"Big boys? Like Sentel and Cryon?" I took a sip from my water, absently wondering whether you could smoke in there.

"Yeah, they hang here, but no bigger than that, and before you ask, no, you don't need to know. I think I'll call someone to pick you up before you become li'l girl chowder."

"No," I snapped, "you can't. I need my story and I don't want anyone knowing. I'm tired of being the reckless one with no care for her own neck." I groaned. "Can I ask? Isn't a bit dark in here for sunglasses?"

He laughed, removing them and shaking the hair off his eyes. I gasped, alarmed. His eyelids were disfigured, shrivelled-over, closed in, a mass of red and white scar tissue.

"Gross, huh? I'm officially blind and deaf."

"What?" I actually shouted, amazed. "But you… I mean, you can hear me and you move like… "

"I'm one of the most powerful psychics Nomas has ever seen. They picked me up in a military orphanage in Ireland when I was six. Trained me up from there. My parents were killed in a massacre by LEs."

"LEs?"

"Lethal Expats. I was contracting it for you?"

I giggled at how easy he was to be around. "I'm sorry. That's terrible."

"No, it's not. I've seen a lot worse than that, and I couldn't really fit any other lifestyle than this even if they hadn't done this to me. This has made me what I am." He took a swig of whisky, absently checking women as they passed. How could he actually check someone out?

"You've heard of auras, right? Well, every person leaves something like that – an energy print – and we all attract those that match our own. That's what I can sense."

Whoa, psychic. "Like a soul mate?" I muttered, finally catching a 'no smoking' sign hanging in the corner. Fab drugs good, nicotine bad. What was wrong with this country?

"Yeah, something like that, I guess. I suppose an actual soul mate is when the connection is perfect, a perfect fit, two magnets, no control. Cool, huh? Brings a tad more magic to our jaded world, and a tad more hell, I guess. So what you done with no care for your own neck?" He downed the rest of his whisky. He looked so young, it didn't seem right he could already be this grown up.

"Mark," I sighed.

"Yeah, what about him? He seemed effing fab from where I was at the time. Christ has been on his back ever since, asking him to help out, but he won't have nothing to do with it. Mangled history or something."

I snorted. "Yeah, serial killer history, it would seem, for girls who look, well... And he threatened to kill me a couple of times when we first met, and Zean and Loraline think I'm stupid for not calling the police or locking myself away or something. I don't know."

"Hm." Ross was nodding, his non-existent gaze pointed directly at me. It was weird, like he was seeing more than what a normal person would. "What?"

I groaned. "Nothing."

"Don't you dare lie. I've so had enough of that lately." Ross sat back in his chair. "Well, from what I saw, I've never seen anyone treated as something so precious, not like he was planning on ripping you in half."

I bit my lip. "Yeah, well, apparently he changed his mind. He hates me but I couldn't understand or... Oh, it's all very confusing," I sighed.

Ross shook his head. "The best thing about being the way I am? It simplifies things. And it couldn't be more simple, you and him. Perfect fit."

I burst out laughing at how serious he was. "Me and Mark? I don't think so, somehow. Your psychic radar's playing up, boy."

He laughed too, his whole body moving as he did. Legitimate was the best word for him, something I'd been in desperate need of. "Come on, Khyle, you can make something up. You've seen the place. Write a good bit of fiction and let me call you a cab. My boss'll rip my balls off and wear them as earrings if he knows you're here. And come on, I need what assets I've got, right?"

I smirked, nodding in agreement. The idea of having yet more needles in me was enough to completely put me off. "Mmm, something tells me it would take a lot less effort to pull off a piece of fiction than to write this place up as fact."

Ross led me to the front door, stuck on my heel like a golden retriever. "The taxi should be waiting," I heard him shout as he grabbed my coat from the, well, maid with 'added bonuses' at the door.

"How? You haven't even called it yet."

"I called it the moment I spotted you from across the bar," he smirked. "That was like forty minutes ago!"

"Then I guess you're pitching in with the fare, huh?"

It felt too quiet outside, after the explosive rhythmic displays inside, to just be the sound of the breeze whistling through the alleys and the plugged-out ghost of the music.

"Are you coming too?" I turned to Ross, looking at the way the moonlight cast silver flashes over his sunglasses. A dose of livid outrage smacked me straight in the stomach that these… demons could do that to him.

Ross's eyebrows jerked upwards. "Don't. I told you, not being able to see the world; it's messed up, but I consider the way I *can* see the world a lot easier, a lot kinder, and a bloody sight more appealing to put my neck on the line for."

"Is this like a revenge kick for you? I mean, do you know who it was who did it, exactly?"

Ross nodded, but his body had grown still, his head turned, nose raised as if sniffing for something. I followed his dog impression. A glossy black limousine had just pulled up at the end of the alley next to the washed-out cab, which I guessed was mine as the thin trail of cigarette smoke wafting out of the window indicated that it may have been waiting a bit.

A door opened and slammed, and a familiar hulking albino, dressed in a ripped black shirt stretched taut over his ape-like chest, and a clear indicator that he couldn't possibly be human to wear something like that in this weather, walked around the car. Ross edged closer to me, his nose still twitching. "What? Do you have psychic nostrils?" I joked, but I was rewarded with a gloved hand clamped hard against my mouth. "Mph, wuz wng?" I said, muffled. Ross pulled us both into the shadows, not removing his hand. Cryon opened the other door, one glossy tan hand extended out, followed by Sepsu's boyish form, and then a snake of a woman uncoiled herself from the limo.

She didn't strike fear into every sense of my being just by the look at her; it was more the way Ross stiffened his hand, clasping down harder on my mouth. Like he wasn't already making it difficult enough to breathe. All three of them were walking towards the cab. The woman looked like she'd stepped out of *The Matrix*, her emaciated thin body clad in a polo-necked black snakeskin dress contrasting with the brilliant coffee and cream of her skin. Her Afro-styled hair was bundled into a turban of braids high up on her head, but rather than being a rich black it was the kind of beautiful white that was only achieved by age rather than peroxide. Her long face, straight nose, and black eyelined cat eyes made her probably the most hideously elegant sight I'd ever seen in or out of the cinema; but when those eyes landed on us, both huddled in the shadows, I felt the hideous part was a lot more dominant in her character. She held out one long bare arm to gain the other two's attention, who immediately glanced up, Sepsu actually speeding up.

"Shit," I heard Ross mutter.

"I fuf yu seth ay wuldnt do anything u us?" I managed, getting a mouthful of leather.

"She's a Higher. And I said they wouldn't need to. I didn't say they wouldn't for sport."

He released me, wandering out of the shadows. "Oh, that's relieving!" I called, running up after him.

"Rosswell. A pleasure as always," the woman said, her eyes madly wide and filled with an exaggerated, practised take on affection. I took a step back, praying to become invisible. "And this is Kahlillyne. I've heard so much of your potential, child. Are you coming inside? I'd love to appraise you myself."

"You and me both," Sepsu hissed in his cat-like tongue.

"No, just leaving actually, Anna. Well, she is, anyway." Ross attempted to walk past them but a quick exchange of looks between Anna and Cryon put a white-bodied brick wall in front of us.

"No. I believe Sepsu has unfinished business with the girl. I believe we all do. How is Delia for that matter? Strong stomach lately?"

"What did you just say?" I burst out, stepping forward.

Ross placed a hand on my shoulder, flashing his coat behind him to reveal a very lethal-looking automatic. "You won't be getting close enough to sort any finished business, Sepsu. You lost, mate. Deep breath; accept it. I can always suggest counselling if it's eating away at your shrivelled little heart," Ross mocked, beginning to pull me behind him, but just before even he was able to sense it, a splitting crackle of white-hot electricity hurtled him back three feet and flat on his back, his glasses skidding off down the alley. I staggered, my shoulder stinging like someone had poured acid on it. Really it was only where what had hit Ross flat on had skimmed me.

Anna cocked her head at Ross. "Anyone thirsty for shaken, not stirred?" she laughed, extending one hand towards me. "Sepsu, I believe that's yo—"

She was cut off by the sudden, extraordinarily loud, pop/rock of my ringtone exploding into life in the quiet alley. I must have jumped about a foot in the air, fishing it out automatically, caller ID registered as unknown. One long-nailed hand extended into my line of vision. "May I?" Anna had the practised mad look in her eyes again. I wordlessly dropped the phone into her grasp, everyone falling into silence as she answered, her eyes going from eager to confused to a lot more eager. For a minute she just stood, the other two's eyes following her every movement and then, startling her apprehensive audience, she burst into a cackling laugh, allowing my phone to slide from her open hand and clatter on the cobblestone floor. She gestured for Cryon and Sepsu to follow her. Sepsu hesitated. Anna glanced over her shoulder at the entrance of the club.

"Not now. I promise, son, when the time comes, you'll have your fun," she near-whispered on the breeze.

Sepsu's small narrow face widened into a disgusting rat-like smirk, and he turned on his heel and disappeared. The bouncer replaced the rope as if nothing had happened, looking straight ahead absently.

I stood there a moment in the quiet, adrenaline pulsing, mind strangely numb. I crouched down and picked up my still-registering in-call phone. "Hello," I squeaked.

"Hello," drawled a painfully familiar voice.

The moment lost all its suspense in a heartbeat. "Mark! What the hell are you? What was that? How did you…?"

"Which would you like me to answer first?" He laughed.

"What did you just do?" I asked, wondering why I sounded ungrateful as I stared at the spot where they'd disappeared into the club. Perhaps it was just the fact that *he* had saved me. Again. It was annoying!

"Do you really want to know?" He sounded a little exasperated at my question.

"Eh, no, no, you're right, I probably don't. Where are you, how did you know…? Oh, you know what, just forget it. You're right: I don't want to know squat!" I exploded, spinning around to check on Ross who was groaning on the floor.

"In that case I could say you were finally learning what's good for you, but then, look at where you are. Rather puts a dampener on any beginning of sanity within that cute little head of yours," he sighed.

I could practically see him in my mind, trying not to roll his eyes. "I object to cute and little," I grumbled, bending down to check Ross's pulse.

"You would," he jibed, enjoying himself. "By the way, we need to talk. Are you free tomorrow for dinner?"

"If you insist on existing, Mark, yes I agree, we do need to talk, and no, I'm not free tomorrow or any other time for dinner with you."

"Why's that?"

Because you're a serial killer. "Because I'm having dinner at a friend's."

"Hm, I must be slacking in my stalking abilities," he mocked, absently, "or I just can't go near that damned police station without having Green call half the CID."

"Well, on the bright side, I know where I'll be able to take a shower with complete peace of mind," I mumbled.

"You clearly have a deadly fear of being watched in the shower," he said dryly, making fun of me. I smirked, wanting to slap myself as I did. "You're smiling." His voice had grown soft and I felt a butterfly wing tickle the inside of my stomach

"Are you watching me?" I tried to make the accusation fierce but it came out flimsy. Maybe this was a weird case of Stockholm syndrome.

"Of course I am. But I can hear it over the phone; you bite your lip when I make you smile, you see, because you know I shouldn't."

I shook my head, lips pressed. "Marcus, stop it! You're freaking me out. I've got an inspector telling me you're gruesomely murdering young girls, and you just scared away the freaking she-Satan from over the phone. I don't need this right now!"

"I'm sorry, but I didn't scare Anna away; I only promised her something far better than the sight of having you ripped to shreds in front of her eyes for stopping my beloved daddykins from coming through. Now, are you going to say thank you?"

"Wel—"

"Nope, didn't think so. We do need to talk. Not about Green, though. Oh, and take care of Ross; he's quite fun to watch, really."

The line went dead and I felt like throwing the phone against the wall. Not because he infuriated the hell out of me, but for just being the most confusing part of the whole mess that had become life, and also because… because I was totally schizo. I didn't want to stop listening to his voice.

Ross shook his head, grunting. "Wha' 'appened?" he grumbled, still out of it. I helped him pull himself to his feet.

"Scared them away," I muttered, still glaring at my phone.

"No you didn't. What actually happened?" he said again, a little more with it.

I stamped my foot, frustrated. Why couldn't I have scared them away? It could happen! "They got bored."

"Ye-e-es, more likely; but no, I doubt it. Try again," he said, massaging his chest with one hand and the back of his head with the other, spiking up the golden strands even more. I groaned, kicking a pebble and grabbing his arm to steer him to the taxi.

"Oh, shut up and get in. I don't want to talk about it," I grumbled, opening the car door and flinging him in. He scrambled to get back out.

"Wai— No! I told you, I'm on duty."

"Look at yourself, man! You are being relieved of duty for tonight due to being totally f—ed up, okay? Good." I slammed the door shut and went around to the other side, massaging my temple. Well, in a way I had been asking for this just by coming to Casper's. Maybe I *was* a schizo with Stockholm syndrome who was becoming addicted to emotional frustration and pain.

Chapter Fifteen

"Wow, what happened to your shoulder?" Loraline reached over from the driver's seat to touch the place where the energy thingy last night had scraped me and taken with it the first three layers of skin. I quickly pulled my jumper up where it had slipped down off my shoulder before she could touch it.

"Ran into a wall," I muttered, tucking some hair behind my ear.

Loraline withdrew, looking a little hurt and a lot more suspicious. "What were you running away from?"

I groaned. "Zean. Naked," I snapped, a little too loud.

Loraline snorted, pulling the car over outside the tiny little cottage off the main road with, by the steam it was letting out of the squat redbrick chimney at its peak, the promise of heat.

"In that case I'm just surprised you didn't knock yourself into a coma," she mocked, eyes narrowed, as we walked up to the front door which had a hand-painted sign on the front reading 'Merry meet, merry greet'.

We were at Delia's. Delia had asked Loraline if we could come a couple of hours earlier because she had something special lined up for us. We were both painfully well prepared to have our hair braided and toenails painted multi-colours before the end of the night. The best part of the idea was that Jackson had to stay and wait for Jaz's babysitter to arrive so I wasn't forced to endure a forty-minute-long car ride with him and an awkward silence, or the constant fear that Ross had betrayed me and let him know where I was last night, even though I'd made him swear on his freaking sunglasses that if he said a word I'd find a way to make him pay beyond his imagination. He, being psychic, should have been able to tell I really wasn't kidding. The only catch was that he'd made me tell him about the Mark phone call which, almost to my annoyance, had only succeeded in making him think Mark the Ripper was even more cool than before, brushing off my persistent reminders of what Green had shown me by saying that it's not our past that makes us, it's our present, and what we do with it to create our future. Bull.

The front door swung open, releasing the smells of roasted pork and rosemary and potatoes out into the arctic pre-winter air. My mouth began to water; I could hardly remember the last time I'd had something to eat that could actually be considered a real meal. Eliza was a different person from the woman I'd met a couple of weeks ago: her skin was plump and flushed red from the heat of cooking, and her eyes were glowing with what could only be described as pure content. I was immediately pulled into a chest-aching hug, her apron sticky and smelling of gravy and syrup.

"Oh, Khyle, it's a charm to see you, my dear."

"Hey, Mrs Bronzebard," I said into her shoulder as Delia came bundling around the corner.

"Thank you," Eliza whispered into my ear before releasing me to literally almost pull Loraline off her feet to hug her too, pushing the door shut with her foot. "And Loraline, sweetheart, how are you? How's the parsnips?"

She gestured for us to follow. Delia had already skipped off into the kitchen ahead of us. Their house was a typical English cottage material, small, beamed, crooked, spread over a dozen levels with a dozen hit-your-head-or-fall-to-your-death lumps and bumps in the low ceiling and carpeted floors. Every inch was filled to the brim with pure clutter: handmade pottery bowls, flower arrangements, half-finished knitting, an entire family tree of photos spread on counter tops and hung on any available space of wall. It was cute, the home I'd always imagined I would have had. A complete mess of love and cringe-worthy photos.

"They're doing very well. All that manure James got for me has worked a charm. Mind you, my manicure has suffered horribly. I'll never get that smell off my fingers!"

Eliza led us into a cramped brown and red kitchen filled with the aromas of drying herbs hung like bats from the beams, and half-chopped food spread on the bare wood counter tops.

"My husband works at the local farmer's shop and gets great deals on the sort of stuff you see, Khyle. I hope you girls are hungry; I've got pork, roast potatoes, baked apples stuffed with bacon, roast parsnips just to rub Loraline's pretty little nose in it, peas, honeyed carrots, and sticky toffee pudding for dessert, or apple pie, or both. You look like you need it," she laughed, flicking a dishcloth at my stomach and tutting. I started to feel every muscle in my body uncoil from last night, general normality oozing into every pore.

"Would you like some tea or Coke or—?" she asked.

"No, it's alright. I got it, Mum. We're gonna be upstairs, K. I loooove you," Delia burst out, grabbing a carton of orange juice, a packet of Jaffa cakes, a packet of custard creams, jammy dodgers and some Viennese swirls. Her arms bulging, she kissed Eliza hard on the cheek, making exaggerated smacking sounds, and kicked Loraline with the back of her heel to follow us.

"Oi, where are you going with that lot, Delia?" It was useless, of course. Delia had already skipped upstairs and was calling for us, sounding impatient.

"Sorry, Eliza. Wouldn't want to upset the elvish demon," Loraline laughed, grabbing my arms and steering me up a handmade wonky oak staircase.

"Have you been here before?" I whispered.

Loraline shrugged. "Once. But once Eliza takes a liking to you, you might as well be her own flesh and blood. There's no escaping it; you'll leave her five pounds heavier. Trust me on that," she whispered, smirking wonkily.

Delia's room looked like it hadn't been redecorated, but just added to, since she was seven, as a mass of purple, gold and frill. The room followed suit well with the rest of the house: cluttered, with just a hint of chintz. From the patchwork quilt slung over her bed to the army of assorted stuffed animals that were perched on every available inch of surface that wasn't in turn covered with family photos framed in equally chipper frames. There was a wall of Disney videos and chick flicks, out-dated girl band posters stuck to the walls, and the whole room smelt suspiciously of Oreos and rosemary, a match only Delia could come up with. All I could think was, the hell was she going near my room with a paintbrush.

Delia had perched on her bed and was flicking on a little TV perched in the corner.

"Welcome to my haven, ladies!" she chimed, picking the chocolate off a Jaffa cake.

"Hungry, are we?" Loraline sounded a little disapproving as she pulled out Delia's desk chair, removing a pile of clothes first. I slumped down beside Delia on her bed, nicking a Jaffa cake and winking at her. I was starting to look at Delia as my little, and Loraline as my big, sister. I'd be the peacekeeper.

"Yeah, I'm always hungry like mad, and I still can't keep much down, you know. No one knows what's going on. I mean, the police made me go and see a doctor—"

"Wait. The police have been to see you?" I gasped through a mouthful of chocolate and orange. Loraline closed her eyes as if I were severely testing her patience.

"Yep. They didn't ask much. I think Nomas have stopped them asking too many questions, and they've got so much on their plate anyway, one missing teenager just, like, slips through their fingers. Oh, that's it. Quick, look at this."

She stopped flicking the TV, leaving it at Channel Four news where a bitterly cold-looking man was standing in front of a manor house or… I swallowed my Jaffa cake whole, only hoping I'd be lucky enough to choke on it. St Matthews!

"What is it?" I groaned, forebodingly.

Delia shrugged. "It's just about the break-in; you know, with Zambruski. Except they don't know it was Zambruski. They think the missing Jane Doe went mad and killed a load of people. Not everyone was hurt, you know."

"Oh my God, Delia, that's serious. What if they trace it back to you?" I blurted, alarmed.

Loraline shook her head.

"No, Jackson told me Nomas planted false leads for them. They're not going to find anything conclusive. In fact, I think the only loose end is that you were there. I mean, you're registered as the very last visitor there, I think. Hey, have you been to see your mum yet? Jackson went this morning. She's been moved to a different sector until the damage has been cleared, right?" Loraline clearly thought she was being polite to ask, but the look on my face was very easy to read and she quickly changed the subject. "So, what did you want to show us, Delia?"

The truth was I hadn't even thought about going to see Mum. Actually, since finding out she'd once been sane and well and given that up for the greater good, I didn't want to think about her at all, let alone be in a room with her only. The thing was, it had been so much easier to mourn a characterless charity case than the saviour of mankind. I wasn't sure the loss of a mother worth having was something I could actually take, plus I could sense how easy it would be to love her, truly love her, as my mother, and not just out of instinctive blood bond.

Delia beamed, swigging orange juice, and hopping over to her bookcase. Me and Loraline exchanged a different kind of look. The more I looked at Delia, the thinner she looked, if that was possible. She still had colour in her cheeks and was bursting full of life, but she really did look like she was fading, draining physically to nothing. Anna's comment from last night kept repeating in my head. I wanted to tell Loraline in case it meant something, but that would mean telling her I'd gone to Casper's, and though seeing her as my big sister might be lovely, it also meant I feared her wrath like one would fear being pushed off a one thousand and fifty foot high skyscraper.

"Got it! Right, I think I've got everything here I assembled beforehand 'cause I wasn't sure how much time we'd have before dinner." Delia danced over to the middle of the room, passing a thin silver and gold book to Loraline, who smiled faintly as she read it, her face thoughtful. She glanced up at me.

"She's not going to like this, Delia," she said, but got to watch as Delia arranged three eight-inch white candles in a triangle in the middle of the room, her tongue poking out of the side of her mouth.

"What?" I thought. I already had a fair idea.

"Well" – Delia sung the word, stringing it out – "I thought, as you've seen all this gruesome stuff of this new world that's been chucked at you, or, erm, you've been chucked into, or, eh, either way, badness, I thought I'd show you something a little nicer. Come on, you'll like it. Can you get the light, Loraline?"

Delia skipped over, grabbing my arm and dragging me into the middle of the room to sit cross-legged with her just as the room went pitch-black. A rustling and sighing beside me told me that Loraline had joined us.

"Shouldn't you light the candles before you turn the light off?" I scoffed.

"Sure." Delia sounded way too excited. I heard someone take a deep breath and then let it out in a low, steady gush, just as a spark ignited, mid-air, like a fairy and danced over to one of the candles, illuminating Delia's beaming face, her lips puckered as she watched the candle ignite.

"Whoa!" I leant back, but Loraline grabbed my elbow.

"Relax. She's just showing off."

"How d'you do that?" I burst out, having to admit to myself I was just a tiny bit tipping the scale for fascinated rather than freaked.

Delia shrugged. "Make particles move fast enough by supplying them with enough energy. They heat up. Heat 'em up enough and they'll be able to light the wick. The little fairy thing they do is just a consequence of heating them up. All things emit photons when they're at a higher energy state than usual."

I nodded, no clue as to what she'd just said except that it sounded a lot more like physics than witchcraft. "But you're not making something move, there's nothing there to heat up," I challenged.

Delia gave me a smug look. "We're not in a vacuum; there's particles of air everywhere, and even in a vacuum there's neutrinos and virtu—"

"We get it. You've been around Jackson too much," Loraline broke in, shaking her head. "That man takes all the magic out of the world. Thankfully, I bring it all back," she giggled, extending her palm out.

A tiny, penny-sized luminescent blue spark exploded in the air, and hovered over the third candle, igniting it. "It's easy; it's just a manipulation of the energies around us or, in other words, playing with the magic that's all around us and in us!" She smiled warmly at me, nodding at the other candle.

"Wait. Why did I blow and you didn't?" I stalled. There was no way I could light a candle with my mind, but I was smiling all the same.

"From birth we're taught to trust what people smarter than ourselves tell us, which is usually along the lines of 'The world's grey, no magic. Everything you dream of, or play with, as kids? Forget it, and start paying taxes'."

I felt like the little girl I could never really remember ever being.

Delia giggled. "Blowing? That was just for witchy effect. Lorry's right, I'm a show-off."

"Now you try," Loraline almost demanded.

I shook my head. "I can't, come on. I'm not even sure I believe in all this, and I've seen it first-hand. In fact, like Delia said, I've been flung in headfirst."

"Well, contrary to popular belief, not all little miracles require pure faith. Lexis isn't that picky. If it was, all the atheists out there would never have anything they really hoped and wished for. In fact, most of the twenty-first century human population would have pretty shitty lives. Now close your eyes."

"No, I ca—"

"Don't argue with us, Missy. Do as Lorry says and close those peekers."

I groaned, but it was two against one, and Loraline and Delia were both terrifying in a way Anna could never manage.

"Now just breathe. Stop thinking how ridiculous this is. Open your palm."

I held my palm out, lips pressed, feeling Loraline's eyes drilling into me.

"You're a bully, you know that?" I muttered.

She laughed like bells chiming. "How long have you known her and you're only just getting that?" I didn't have to see to know that Delia was giving an exasperated look. "Listen to your heart beat, feel the energy running over it with each contraction, feel it running through your veins, and also a new energy; not the one running through you, exactly, but close, built into everything around you, pressing in on you." She was going to tell me to open my third eye in a flipping second. "Now think of something that gets your pulse racing like, erm, cookies or, erm, clothes."

Delia broke in. "What?"

"Just do it," Loraline sighed.

"I don't get excited about much," I whined, regretting it the moment I heard them burst into sniggers.

"Oh come on, there's got to be something? Sex?" I heard Loraline throw something fabric-like at Delia. I tried to rack my mind for something but there was nothing. I was a fairly placid person. I mean, sure, I like biscuits and I guess clothes. I had a thing for loud music and cheesecake, but they weren't exactly adrenaline-builders. Loraline sighed. "Marcus?" She didn't sound happy to have to say the word. I scoffed, but in my state of calm and connectedness I felt my heart jump a little. I bit my lip, letting the idea slip a little into my very badly wired brain; the way he laughed, how he could make me laugh when I really did not want to give him the satisfaction, the way his one eyebrow was always that little bit higher than the other when he looked at me, like he was highly amused at something I didn't know I was doing.

There was a sudden shout and movement around me. My eyes flew open, heat so intense pressing against my face that sweat started to bead at my hairline and run down my neck. A scarlet and gold ball of light the size of my fist was spinning in mid-air. Loraline rolled her eyes, looking very upset that what she had tried had worked. Well, that was nothing compared to the shame I felt. Delia flapped around, grabbing the carton of orange juice and dumping it in mid-air, dosing the little ball of energy, and dosing me in sticky orangey goodness at the same time.

I jumped up but it was too late; the whole of the front of my jumper and a good three inches of the ends of my hair were already glued up in Tropicana. Loraline got up and turned on the light, standing across from me, arms folded.

"I'm very angry that worked, you know. I mean, honestly, Khyle, that man is intolerable. I don't know what you see… " she trailed off, flapping her arms.

"What man?" Delia chimed in, looking excited.

"Eh, excuse me. Has no one noticed me auditioning to be in the next *You've Been Tangoed*?" I shouted, stamping my foot, my arms outstretched in front of me. There was a moment of silence while the other two looked me up and down, Delia walking over and picking up one long sticky strand of my hair. She sniffed it then looked at Loraline. They both doubled up, Loraline actually having to sit down and clutch her sides.

"Well, on the bright side, Khyle, you know you can do it, right?" Delia gasped between giggles.

"Yeah, and best of all maybe this whole experience might put her off the Prince of Darkness," Loraline cackled.

I shook my head, exasperated and still dripping. "Yeah, or orange juice, and I'm going for the latter. Have you got a bathroom?" I cried.

Delia showed me to a tiny but clean bathroom outside, just as the front door went and I heard the stumbling apologies of Jackson for his lateness. As I detangled and rinsed orange juice from my hands and hair, and changed into the ivory sweater Delia had lent me – the only thing we could find in her wardrobe without either pink or something weird and colourful on the front – I caught a glimpse of myself. Regardless of the weirdness, end of the world factor, and the general complete gut-wrenching fear, I was actually happy. I felt like I'd found a comfortable little niche where I had friends for the first time, and people around me who, yeah, were witches or mad professors, stalking murderers, ex-ghosts… I'm going to stop now before I depress myself. But my cheeks were pink (not the least from lusty energy balls) and my eyes were glowing.

"Girls, get your butts down here for food," I heard Delia's mum call out, and the sounds of footsteps and someone banging on the bathroom door as Delia and Loraline walked by. I cupped a handful of water, spraying it over my heated cheeks, and quickly cracked the double-glazed window for a swift breath of fresh air. The sun had gone down, and the whole of the front of the house had been cast into varying shades of black and greys and oranges from the house's lights. A new car, that looked like it had been on the road since the late seventies so it had to be Jackson's, was pulled up next to Loraline's. I took in a lungful of chilly air, wondering at the back of my mind how long it would be before I could sneak off for a quick nicotine kick, when headlights flooded the front yard and a sleek, smooth and presumptuous, well-known Jaguar rolled jaggedly off the main road. I winced. "No, Mark, bad, bad Mark, go away, Mark, it's more than your life's worth, Mark," I chanted under my breath just as

I heard the front door slam open, and watched Loraline's feline figure stalk towards the car, fists clenched. He really was asking for it.

I flung the bathroom door open, taking the steps two at a time, and almost falling out of the front door just as Delia made her way out; and Jackson, who I tried not to make eye contact with, hovering back to watch, confused. In all fairness to Loraline, she would probably take this as more stalking from Mark, not to mention a complete invasion of James and Eliza's home. But still I was starting to think that the controlling-of-temper aspect of being human was lost a little on Loraline.

"I mean it, Marcus. Get yourself and your piece of male gratification out of here. She doesn't need any more of this at the moment."

She was screaming at him through the window, looking very banshee-like, her hair flying. Mark was leaning slightly back in the driver's seat, looking somewhere between bewildered and arrogant. If there was such a place? I put my hands on Loraline's shoulders as gently as possible in case she flipped and had my head off. "It's okay, calm down. I'll get rid of him. Just remember to breathe. You know, if you have to and all," I added awkwardly, suddenly unsure whether I'd actually ever distinctively seen Loraline take a breath. She certainly shouted like she didn't need to.

Loraline shook me off. "No, you don't need to have anything to do with him, Khyle. I swear I've got half a mind to call that loathsome Green."

"Oh come on, Loraline, you and I both know you found her far from loathsome," came Mark's egotistical voice as he unfolded himself from the car, holding a massive tattered brown envelope to his chest. Loraline's eyes bulged, but she looked as if she'd become so overwhelmed with dislike she wasn't capable of saying anything mean enough.

Delia appeared, a massive grin on her slim face. "Okay, who is the hottie? Wow," she said, exaggeratedly fanning herself. I felt myself cringe and blush simultaneously. Mark grinned, his eyes half-lidded, and smugly extended a hand to Delia, turning it upright and kissing her palm.

"Marcus," he said. "We were never formally introduced. You are looking far better than the last time we met, Delia."

Delia looked as though she might turn to butter on the spot.

"Okay, okay, smoothie," I hissed, knocking their hands apart, a little too obvious in my jealousy for my own pride to fully accept it. "Delia, take Loraline in before she detonates and say sorry to your mother for me. I'll be in in just a second, I swear." When she didn't move but looked a little dreamily up at Mark, I added for good measure, "Go! Now!" in an octave very close to a shout. Delia pouted a little, but steered the red-faced Loraline with two hands towards the door, Loraline's feet dragging a little. I planted one hand on Mark's chest, grabbing a handful of shirt and dragging him a few feet further away from the house to not risk being overheard. "Do you speak English, Mark, because for the love of God I swear I keep telling you to back off or bugger off, whichever you prefer."

"Mmm, and I keep telling you to stop lying to yourself, that that's what you really want, so I guess we both have issues with English. Would you prefer Sumerian or Arabic?" He just didn't stop with this whole high and mighty mock-the-patience-out-of-you thing, huh?

I took a step back, grabbing handfuls of hair. "Mark, please, I'm begging you. Just go. I don't want to have to deal with your insane arse at the moment."

Mark's eyebrows rose. "Insane," he stated, all amusement lost.

"Yes, insane! What Green showed me. What makes you think I want you within ten feet of me? Do you think I'm blind or just dumb? Get out of here!"

"A little bit of both at the moment, actually, but *Green* is not the reason I'm here."

The way his eyes had iced over to a dangerous degree made my heart skip. "Oh yeah? And why are you here, then?"

"To show you who you can and can't trust."

I shook my head. "Oh, that is just rich. Is this the part where you tell me that there's no one else out there except you I can trust?" I hissed, jabbing a finger at him. He took a quick step forward, grabbing my finger in a painful grip and pulling it to his chest. He looked to be at the point where Loraline had been, where you were so angry you could no longer find words. "Ouch, stop it! And you think I can trust you? Go on then, let's just get it out and finished. Was it you who did those disgusting things to those girls?" I could feel tears in my voice, but tears of what I didn't know. He didn't have to say anything; the way his chin lowered, his face tilting away from me, showed a level of shame too easy to read. I tried to yank my hand away, but he was holding it too tightly, right over his heart. "Let go!" I swallowed, my voice wobbling.

"Marcus, I've got my answer now," I continued. "Leave me alone before I do the smart thing for once and take Loraline's advice, call Green, and put you in hell where you clearly belong, you monster!" I shouted right at him in a way I'd never cared enough to shout at anyone in my entire life. His eyes shot down at mine, and for just a heartbeat I thought I saw a quiver of glassy tears over the molten silver. He dropped my hand, and I felt my heart ache horribly at the loss of his touch. I hated myself. He flung the heavy brown package at my chest, almost pushing me backwards.

"Lie in your bed, then, you *ignorant* little girl," he snarled, almost pushing me off my feet with just a movement as he jumped back in his car, screeching sounds echoing through the quiet, quaint street as he disappeared off.

I stood there, staring towards the end of the street where he'd left, sobbing so hard he may as well have tied me up and tortured me right then and there. I looked down at the envelope in my hands, feeling its weight. Something in me was more hurt by what he'd just said than I could put into words. My brain told me I'd for once done the right thing, my heart was bleeding in unthinkable agony.

After a while I became aware that warm hands were stroking my hair away from my shoulders as I sobbed. I glanced around, Eliza's soothing, knowing eyes looking at me with a motherly care I'd only seen in movies. I fell onto her shoulder, sobbing and feeling like a complete pathetic idiot as I did. I let her lead me into the comfort of inside, and sit me down in one of the cat-hair covered couches, Loraline immediately settling down beside me and cradling me to her chest.

"Well done. You were right to do what you did. That dirt bag…" she muttered.

"Cute dirt bag, though," Delia sighed, perching on the couch arm.

"Honey, would you put on some tea, and stick the pork and roast potatoes in the oven so they don't get cold," Eliza said to a plump balding ginger man with thick-rimmed glasses, who nodded very sympathetically and walked off, taking Jackson with him to my great relief. I'd once felt safe around Jackson; now, I didn't know how to feel any more.

I sat up straighter, rubbing my eyes. "No, don't, please. I'm sorry I don't mean to make a fuss. Let's just eat. I'm fine." I tried, my voice still wobbly with emotion.

Eliza shook her head. "No, you are not. I've seen that look on a lot of people's faces in my time and you are not okay."

"What look?" Delia asked blankly. No one answered her.

"I don't know why he affects me like this," I muttered stupidly.

Loraline shrugged. "Because you've got a sadistic mind. Infatuation is a cruel thing," she said matter-of-factly.

"Infatuation? Are you sure that's all it is?" Eliza said, peering at Loraline with knowing eyes.

Delia suddenly looked up. "Oh was *that* Mark? Oh, Khyle, I see what you mean," she laughed. I shook my head absently, feeling the weathered brown paper under my fingers like a bomb or a dear gift. Question was, did I have the nerve to find out which it was?

"No, Delia, not well done," Loraline scolded. I cringed, placing my hand on my chest. My heart felt like someone had put it in a bear trap and was letting it come down very slowly, my whole chest constricting in on itself. This was ludicrous; there was no rational reason for me to feel like this.

"Khyle, are you okay? Do you want me to get you some pudding? That always makes me feel better." Delia crouched down in front of me, her big dough eyes looking panicky up at mine. I shook my head again, my throat too dry to talk. Loraline was right: I'd done the right thing, but the look in his eyes... All he'd done really was very clumsily tried to help. Less comforting than they should have been at that moment, flashes of the photos Green had shown me popped into mind; those girls, their bodies broken barbarically, their lives slowly dismantled in an unjustifiably cruel way. He'd done that.

"What is in that thing anyway?" Loraline whispered into the silent room.

I sniffed, turning the heavy package over in my hands and then, with one deep heavy breath, I reached inside. My hands enclosed a stack of papers which, when I slid them out, materialized into a grey folder, bursting at the seams. Something slid out of it onto the carpet with a muffled clatter: a CD. Delia got there before I did.

"Oh, cool!" she exclaimed, immediately turning on her heel to fiddle around with the DVD player.

I ran my fingertips over the front. There were stamped, faded black letters on the front that read 'St Matthew's Psychiatric Clinic'. Right at the top was a dog-eared yellowing sticky label with typed letters which read 'Exeter, Taylor Kahlillyne'. Loraline read aloud over my shoulder. The bare shock and disbelief flooding me echoed in each syllable. I don't know what came over me, but I was suddenly desperate to not see what was on that CD. "Delia, get away from that," I gasped, jumping up to press the eject on the DVD. Too late. The screen flickered; a black and white camera, a recording, the time rolling by in black digital letters in the top right hand corner, appeared on the screen. I felt myself fall to my knees, not even a foot away from the screen. The film was from a camera hung from the ceiling of one of those horrid white rooms at St Matthews which they had to keep the most out-of-control patients in. My mother was usually admitted to them twice a year on a good year, and I was always notified with a crisp, nausea-invoking letter. Now the padded white cell held a small figure captive: a little girl, unruly hair lying in silky waves on her small shoulder. She wasn't strapped down at the moment though the restraint chair was there in the middle of the room, the leather bonds loose and hanging. The girl couldn't have been more than six; seven, maybe. Her blue and white square-printed gown was too large for her, and hung way off one shoulder as she stood, little doll-like face staring straight, blankly, up at the camera, seeing and yet not seeing.

I reached blindly for the remote, unable to take in any oxygen. I felt someone place it in my fingers. I held down the fast forward button, watching the little digital numbers increase rapidly; and with it a horrific movie unfolded. One moment the little girl stood staring up at me for six hours unblinking, and then suddenly her head went shaking left and right violently. The next moment she was running from wall to wall, her whole body hitting each wall like a rag doll, and then mindlessly getting back up and starting all over again. The screen went black, and then a moment later burst back into life. This time the girl was restrained, her whole body flailing up and down madly, three doctors having to hold the little thing back just to get a needle into her arm. I took it off fast forward for a moment, and a burst of erratic high-pitched screams erupted from the TV along with a chorus of doctors yelling orders for more medication, more restraints, and a cascade of educated, countless curses. I recoiled, hearing someone whisper something under their breath that sounded a lot like "Dear God". I pressed the fast forward button down harder, the sound of the plastic remote actually crunching in my grip. The clock was moving rapidly on and the little girl grew still. The screen went blank several times, the clock resetting it at different recording times, different sessions. Same idea each time, except the little girl was very slowly getting older, her limbs a little bit less pudgy, a little bit lankier.

"Wait. Go back." Loraline was suddenly by my side, pulling the remote forcefully from my fingers and reversing it to a night-vision part, the screen a mass of luminescent green, black, and a ghostly white. "What was that?" she whispered as Delia crouched down beside us both, Eliza with one hand clasped on her daughter's shoulder in horror. God knows what horrific images were going through Eliza's mind with respect to what her daughter had gone through.

Loraline let it play. I watched as the little girl sat quietly restrained in the chair, whispering to herself; and then the whispering cut out. I blinked, and one moment there she was, the next she was gone, the restraints lying limp on the wooden chair.

"Where'd she go?" Delia whispered in suspense.

Two eyes suddenly appeared, barely inches from the camera, a high-pitched screaming, like cat's claws on a blackboard, bursting through the TV and giving me a horrible flash back to that night when I'd first arrived in Blackleigh, and Delia had first found a way to get to me. We all fell back, Loraline, Delia, and Eliza crying out in fear, Delia actually scrambling across the room, grabbing a cushion to hug, eyes wide, as she shuddered. I jabbed the eject button, watching the screen go to blank blue.

There was dead silence. I could feel everyone's eyes on me. I crawled over to the folder, mindlessly flipping through the pages. They were hospital records; *my* hospital records. I'd been diagnosed with extreme monothematic delusional disorder including something called reduplicative paramnesia and Cotard delusion. I flicked further through, trying to ignore the pictures of the pale, dead-eyed, wild-haired little girl strapped to beds and staring, mad-eyed, at the ceiling.

'Admitted, December 30th 1999'. I was six years old, and that was the same day my mother had been admitted. I'd been released on June 21st 2001, and put immediately into foster care after a complete but unexplained recovery. Doctors described it as a complete medical miracle. I crossed my legs, scanning the dozen or so doctors' notes, no longer caring how the room was still deadly silent or that this evening was now officially beyond salvability. I'd been subconsciously convinced I existed in a brutal, vicious, and inhumane parallel dimension with an 'imaginary captor' who was never given a specific name. I'd been susceptible to mild and extremely violent outbreaks twice, breaking several of my own bones; four self-inflicted mild concussions; and had once suffered inexplicable near-death loss of blood. I'd spent the whole of 2000 in alternating white rooms.

I leant back on my heels, letting Loraline very gently prise the folder from my fingers to look through it silently, Eliza leaning over her shoulder to look as well, her brow furrowed and her mouth taut with worry and deep thought. If I'd had the strength I might have been able to register that I didn't want them to see it, that I was ashamed of something I had no memory of, that it was none of their business anyway. But I didn't. Instead I stared up at Jackson, who was standing in the doorway to the kitchen, his hands on either side of the doorframe as if he needed the support to hold himself up. His weathered face was ashen, his eyes wide and horrified as he stared at the TV screen.

"You were there, Khyle, you were there. Just like I was. Like your mother… "

I got to my feet surprisingly steadily, glancing at Delia who was rocking back and forth on the couch, hugging the pillow as if the whole thing was more traumatic, raking up too many memories for her rather than me. Well, in fact it was not raking up any memories for me at all; it was blank. I stumbled over to where Delia sat, enfolding her in my arms, afraid if I didn't she might fall to pieces on us again.

"You knew." My voice was cold as I glared at Jackson from across the mute living room.

Jackson regained his composure, drawing himself up to his full height and pushing his glasses fully onto his nose.

"Yes, Khyle, I knew." His voice shook. "It's what you didn't want to tell me before; after we found Delia." These weren't questions, they were numb, hollow statements of burningly painful fact.

"Yes," he said again, not meeting my eyes.

"Explain," I hissed. I wasn't sure, to be honest, whether the shaking was me or whether it was Delia.

Jackson nodded. "You're your mother's daughter, you share her blood. Half her energy pattern, half her soul. When she sacrificed herself she sacrificed you too. We didn't know it would turn out that way. We would never have let her, and *they* would never have let her. My God, you were just a child." He swallowed, his eyes fluttering shut for an instant, clouded with memories. "You were in the same state as her, worse in a lot of ways. We didn't know where you were, there, but you weren't with your mother because she would cry out for you in her delirium, screaming for her lost girl. You were insane, vicious in a way we'd never seen in a cross-over, and then one day you woke up and you cried; not screamed or raged, you just cried. You saw what was around you, you saw people. Where you were you'd made a full recovery. I and three others of your mother's appointed guardians went down to St Matthew's to see it was true: you had made a full recovery, with the exception that you cried like someone had ripped your heart in two."

He sat down.

"It was as if you were being emotionally tortured, and it was far worse. Worse than when you were in that psychotic state, because you could see us and you were in real agony, and there was nothing we could do to help you." He broke off, squinting as if he himself wanted to cry. "You kept repeating 'Where is *he*? I need *him*'. Then four days later, out of sheer exhaustion, you just fell asleep. When you woke up it was like the last two years had never happened. You were just a normal, confused little girl who had a craving for ice cream and peanut butter and banana sandwiches." He laughed to himself and I did actually see a tear make its way down the wrinkle in the corner of his eye.

"As far as we can speculate, Lexis saved you when you slept, in the same way it has done to Delia. It smothered the memories in the dreams so you could regain some semblance of sanity. I'm sorry I didn't tell you, Khyle, but we immediately put you up for foster care.

Technically you have guardians in Nomas, friends of your mother, but we didn't want you to have anything to do with this world. We, I, didn't want to watch you suffer like that ever again. And then you turned up in Blackleigh and… " He trailed off.

"And I brought that world on myself all over again," I muttered, watching Jackson cringe and massage the bridge of his nose, avoiding my gaze.

"I still don't want you to have anything to do with that world," he said.

I ignored the essence of care, concern, even love that was infused into his voice. I looked away. "Neither do I. I know my world. If I had any way to protect myself from the memories of it, I would, but I can't."

"You can, which means you can have *absolutely* nothing to do with it. Khyle, maybe, maybe you should leave… Eliza, James, you could take Delia and Khyle and go so—"

"Excuse me?" I shouted, jumping to my feet and scaring poor Delia out of her skin. "Run away? You want me to run away while the world falls to pieces? Just pretend it's not happening?" I cried, wondering how poorly they must really think of me.

"Nomas, hopefully, won't let it get that bad," said Loraline. "As long as they stop it at the right times, the right milestones in the other side's plans, then it'll never happen. They're a big operation, Khyle. It would be easy to just go on, get a normal life. Haven't you been through enough? Look at your mum! I don't want to see you like that, I don't want to watch my world break another person." Loraline finished on a sob, and Eliza had to enfold her in her arms.

I wondered absently how much of this Eliza actually understood. "And what if I can't? What if it follows me and I can't escape it?

What if they can't stop it and the world does tumble down around us, and I knew that there might have been some way I could have done something… " I wasn't talking to anyone in particular; I was more trying to figure it all out in my own head. What if the world did come to that peak and I knew that locked away in my head might be some knowledge, some past memory, that could have helped due to two years in hell? What if I remembered? What if my nightmares became my memories and I went mad like in the video? I suddenly understood my mother. Sometimes, when put into retrospect, we as humans have an inbuilt love that wasn't aimed at anything in particular, it was just there. It was the love of our world and everything in it, and that why she'd done what she'd done. That's why I'd gone to Casper's: I wanted to help because I was human and I loved, and I didn't want the world, my world, our world, to suffer. And now they were telling me to run away and let it bleed.

Above everything else, above the secrets, and the fact that Jackson and God knows who else from Nomas had known about a past that ripped my childhood as well as my mother from me, this, this idea that they thought so little of me that they would have me run away because they didn't think I couldn't handle it; that was the ultimate betrayal. "I'm part of this now. I know that. Not a very big part, but big enough that I can't and, God damn it, I won't, run. Do you hear me?" I was silently crying, but I shook it off quickly, gathering the folder and CD. Flinging my coat on, I quickly pulled Eliza into a brief hug. "I'm sorry for ruining the night, Mrs Bronzebard. I'm sure it would have been lovely," I mumbled as fast as I could get the words out, and walked toward the door. I heard Eliza, Delia and Jackson call my name, trying to object, but it was Loraline who ran after me into the frigid night air.

"Khyle! Please listen to me! My world will break you. Now you know your past, this is the crucial instant where you can make the decision to have a life to live, or to go down in flames!" she begged desperately.

I spun around, spreading my arms out wide. "Then, out of respect for the mother I'll never know, Loraline, this is the kind of person I apparently am. I wish I was a coward, but apparently I'm not, because frankly" – I gasped through my tears – "burn, baby, burn!"

Chapter Sixteen

I'd screamed at Loraline not to follow me, but by the time I'd reached the end of the road away from Delia's house I was agonizingly aware of just how far from Blackleigh I really was: too far too walk. Especially on an empty stomach, and shaking from tears, shock and left-over adrenaline. I could have called Zean or a taxi, but shamefully there was only one person I stupidly needed to see. I jabbed numbly for my phone, retrieving it and flicking into recent calls. Thankfully few people actually called me and last night's alley incident phone call was my last incoming call. I punched the call key, holding it up to my ear, wondering what on earth I was going to say if he even answered at all.

"What could you possibly want?" came a hostile voice on the other end.

"Mark, please… " I couldn't bring myself to say the words 'help me' in a teary voice to a potential serial killer. Even in its tattered battered form my ego simply wouldn't allow that. Mark's response was instant, his voice going from aggressive to urgent but with that almost unsettling gentleness. "Where are you?"

"Down the road from Delia's," I sniffed, now too tired to cry any more. There was a massive screeching sound of tyres burning tarmac on the other end of the phone as Mark calmly whispered "Fifteen minutes."

I found a stout brick wall, damp from the general dampness that was a constant in England, and sat trying to keep my mind as blank as possible. I was shocked and terrified at what those papers had said, what that DVD had shown, but mostly I just felt crushingly guilty. My mother, the mother I had considered to have abandoned me, who I'd always thought had never fought hard enough. And I was no better than her. I had been in the same state as she had, if not worse… And yet, somehow, I had got out, hadn't I? I had no memories of it to lean back on; I had no way of really being able to understand everything that was happening *now*, at this very moment, because it was buried deep inside me and I had no way of getting to it. It was only just occurring to me that in all the time I'd wasted discriminating against and blaming Mum, I'd never once tried to sympathise, or now, empathise with her, even.

But if I had somehow found a way to get back, didn't that mean there could be a way to get her back? I swung my leg back hard against the wall, a torrent of anger and self-loathing swamping me. If I'd stopped for a second in my self-pity I could have had a mother, couldn't I? If Nomas, if Jackson, if the people who called themselves my mother's friends hadn't hidden me because of the *possibility* that knowing could have broken me, then I might have found a way to understand and bring my Mum, my only known family, back to me.

I didn't know where Mark had been, but it could barely have been ten minutes before a sliding, screeching sound indicated an intolerably rapidly moving vehicle was on the approach. And then there he was. As I pulled myself up from the wall, desperate to get into the heat of the car, I hesitated, a thought striking me like a boxer smacking me down. Had Mark really shown me what he'd shown me to help me, or was it part of what he'd done to the other girls, to hinder me?

I didn't care. I was tired of running or pushing things to the back of my mind. Everything from now I was going to face head-on, and I most certainly would not be running anywhere. Mark got out of the car as I came up silently, opening the passenger door as if on reflex action. I couldn't help but be a bit shocked; Mark didn't strike a girl as a guy who'd been taught a specific way to treat women. The inside of the car had clearly been preheated for me on his ride over because Mark had his sleeves rolled up, and I swear I could just make out a faint line of sweat on his brow.

"This is too hot for you. Let me t—" I started reaching over to the heating. His hand gently touched my own to stop me.

"Leave it. You're white enough to be the walking dead," he smiled.

"I don't think that's the cold. Where did you get that stuff?" I asked absently, the brown envelope a weight on my mind, let alone in my arms.

"I borrowed it from St Matthew's Clinic. The woman was very helpful considering all the trouble they've been in since Zambruski."

"Borrowed?" I cringed.

"I have every intention of not giving it back, but considering she showed me where the folders were and helped me find your case specifically, I just can't see that as stealing."

"The police would." I stared blankly.

"The police want me for mass murder, Khyle. I think they'd have to get their perspectives right if they took me in for this."

He had a point. "So what drama did I miss?" he sighed, cracking a window a bare centimetre and lighting a roll-up.

"I can't believe they hid this from me! It's my past, regardless of whether they thought I'd end up a genuine raving loony! I mean, they didn't think that maybe being able to know, to remember, might help... people." I stumbled over the last word a little, Mark's eyes slanting sideways and calculating the hidden meaning in that stumble. God, he didn't miss a thing in reading me. "And the worst thing of all, Loraline—"

"Breathed and inevitably made it worse. Her only talent as far as I've discerned," Mark muttered very seriously, a deep edge of sarcasm buried in his words.

I ignored it. "She wanted me to run away, to take it as an excuse to bury my head in the sand and hope that it all goes away, like I could even do that if I wanted to. This shit just finds me!" The interior of the car was pretty roomy, but I wasn't sure it would be able to hold my shouting or my anger, even if it was so huge.

Mark nodded, looking deep in thought, and then swiped out a packet of fags, offering me one. "Cheers," I sighed, taking the pack and cracking the window.

"So… What, Khyle? What do you want to do with what you know?" He was stating the obvious question and I wasn't sure I'd formed an answer yet. I leant back, savouring the nicotine rush.

"I don't want them to be just nightmares. Forget the possible outcomes. They hold something, in my being able to both understand my past and make sense of this whole freak show and maybe help mu… people… And… " I choked on the last part.

"*And?*" he urged in a deep, husked-up voice.

"And maybe make sense of you," I finished in a very small voice. There was dead silence. "You're him, aren't you?" I said. "You were there, wherever *there* was, with me."

"Sakhush. Yes, Khyle. You haunted me the way Delia haunted you."

"How come I can remember bits of you and nothing else?"

Mark shook his head, deep and brooding and lost to any semblance of positive feedback I might be requiring. I sighed, impatient.

"Well, is there a way?" I snapped, wanting him back where he was useful.

"A way to what?"

"To remember!" I cried, throwing the rest of the fag out of the window for something to vent my anger on.

"If it's what you need. I know something. But it would require you to trust me, which you've made clear—"

"I trust you, Mark. It's just that it happens to be against any better judgment I might have," I cut in, watching him flex his fingers on the steering wheel. I got the impression not many people would just have been allowed to interrupt him and keep a limb.

"Fine," he hissed through gritted teeth, stepping down hard on the accelerator.

"Slow down; my heart's already on an adrenaline overload," I groaned, pushing back into the seat.

"I'm sure that's just the effect my presence has on your little self." The ego was back.

"Ha! Only if I was worried for my life," I retorted.

"Aren't you?" he tested smoothly.

"I don't really know any more," I sighed, defeated.

"Khyle, give yourself a break. Maybe you just know how to prioritise. That doesn't make you stupid, that makes you brave." All sarcasm, all ego, was gone. Just admiration. I stared at him, stunned. Shamefully, I was flattered and a little bit comforted.

"So is this where you kill me?" I only half-joked as Mark pulled the car over and popped his seatbelt out.

"Only if you ask nicely," he grinned, and even in the dark I could tell it was the creepy wolfish one that made the butterflies in my stomach keel over from overdrive. "No, kid. This is where we get your answers. Welcome to my place," he laughed, walking around to get the door, but I jumped out quickly, not giving him the chance to open the door for me. We weren't in the eighteenth century, after all.

Mark had pulled into a thicket of unidentified trees in this darkness, and I had to let him guide me through. "Should I be suspicious that you can see so well in this light?" I mumbled, concentrating on not tripping.

"If you still have the energy," he whispered darkly into my ear.

I wasn't sure whether he could see me or not, but I gave him a good glare just for good measure. A quick mental calculation told me we shouldn't really be far from Blackleigh; fifteen minutes, maybe? And in the thicket of all this forest I'd say we were at the north end where most of the built-up city-ness of it gave way to the Oxfordshire wild green. After a sharp turn where Mark had to place both hands on my shoulders to attempt to steer me right, we came into a small clearing cast in glittery white moonlight, where an immense Georgian shadow of a house was perched, flanked by overgrown trees and forest on every side. A cast-iron fence, finger-like spikes adorning its top bar, surrounded it and a small courtyard where weeds pushed the chalky-grey flagstones aside to grow. It was beautiful in an eerie, ghostlike, extraordinarily-badly-kept kind of way. Mark pulled out a ring of keys holding everything from compact modern silver ones to three-inch-long rust encrusted beasts, flicking between the modern ones to undo two heavy padlocks and chains wrapped twice around the gate's deco-patterned bars.

Though the moon was shining at its brightest, and spread fully over the house because of a slight gap between the trees, it was still dark enough that I could only just make out where to put my feet, tripping once on an escaped flagstone and having to grab hold of Mark's sleeve, who sniggered without even attempting to hide it. It was too dark to make out much detail of the house's exterior, but once we got inside I was somewhere caught in a mixture of devastation and awe. The house wasn't mansion-sized; more tall than wide, with three storeys, but the inside had been entirely knocked through to create one massive room boarded on all four sides by the original long, elegantly panelled Georgian windows. The floor was all white tiles with black diamonds evenly placed in between, but a good four inches of thick dust marred it; and worst of all, the huge space was almost completely bare except for smack bang in the middle, where a brown leather deco-style couch, low-slung cluttered coffee table, and five enormous wooden trunks rested, looking lost in so much space.

"Not big on decorating," I muttered as I followed him across the room.

"You remember, Khyle, I've been in your room," he said bluntly and pointedly. He stopped by one of the trunks, staring at it for a moment and then carrying on across the room to a pair of double French doors, the wood a rich but worn pine.

"What was that about?" I asked.

He held it open for me. I could have complained about the cold but in all honesty I think it might have been warmer outside than inside that place.

"I was deciding whether I needed anything."

"Needed anything for what?" I spun around, but I must have taken the step with too much stride, letting out a yelp of terror, Mark grabbing me one-handed around the waist and pulling me back a foot. There was a ten-foot drop of uneven grey- and moss-covered stone wall to a pool of mirror-still water, which I'd almost fallen into headfirst; the distance between the French door and the drop was barely three foot wide.

"It's best to use the stairs." He rolled his eyes, his hand sliding from my waist to lace his fingers through my own and tug me forward.

If it hadn't been for how cold it was I would have sworn his skin would have scorched my own. Touching his hand was like touching hot metal with a thin velvet coating over the top, hard and burning.

"We're going down there?" I hissed, quietly, weirdly feeling a need to whisper "yes."

That was it, just a yes. Oh boy, he was going to drown me alive. He turned quickly on his heel, holding me with both hands. He slowly descended a set of dilapidated stone stairs built into a wall, walking backwards ready to catch me. Okay, he was a considerate killer, I'd give him that much. At the base it was mostly just a foot of mud, upturned grass, weeds, and mossy wet stones at the water's edge, the water so still I could see a perfect brilliant orb as the moon was reflected in it, its misty rays of light hitting the oaks, willows, and billowing tall pines at the water's edge, and painting perfect echoes on the water surface.

"Okay. What now?" I turned to look at Mark who was pulling his shirt over his head, pure ribbed muscle flexing over bone as he did. His skin was a creamy white in the moonlight. I turned away so fast I lost my balance, and went hurtling face forward into the water, it hitting me like being flung into an iron maiden and tightened to the maximum. I gasped, going straight under, the banks of mud and stones breaking away under my flailing feet as I kicked to get up to oxygen, but the cold seemed to want to freeze every muscle. I vaguely heard a loud groan from above me, and then something that felt like an explosion in the water overhead. Two uncomfortably hot arms wrapped around me, dragging me to the surface, air filling my gasping lungs and heat seeping into the iced-over crevices of my body. In spite of myself I nestled closer to Mark, desperate for the heat. Mark went a bit stiff but recovered, pushing the long damp strands of hair off my face in a gesture that, if I hadn't been smart enough, I would have described as nurturing. Obviously, from Mark I doubted that would be possible, and he probably just wanted eye contact so as to be able to mock me to the best of his ability.

"Are you ready for this?" He didn't sound sarcastic, just... shaken?

"Ready for what?" Despite Mark's immense body heat, my teeth still chattered wildly. His eyes searched mine for a moment, looking like perfect miniatures of the new moon up above. He looked worried but serene, not like the mock-the-world careless Mark I'd come to know and loathe.

"Close your eyes, kid, and just keep them that way."

I did as he asked. "How is floating with you, fully clothed in a freezing lake in the middle of the night, going to help me remember squat?" I managed to say through chattering teeth. I felt him move in the water to go behind me, his hands placed very lightly on my hips to stop me floating off.

"Water is an intermediary, a barrier between everything, and universal to everything. We need to reopen that blocked-up mind of yours to both worlds. Like I said, Khyle, trust me on this. I'm here."

For the first time since opening the package Mark had given me what felt like a lifetime ago, I was scared for the immediate moment. I didn't know what was going to happen, what that world was like, whether I would somehow be hurled back there, trapped and mad here. I swallowed.

"I do, I trust you."

My breath caught in my throat as I felt his lips brush my ear, his breath warm against my cheek. "I know, Khyle. But I wish you didn't."

Mark's hand left me, spreading out in the water. I could hear him almost singing something so quietly under his breath I could hardly make it out. Whatever it was it was not English. The cold immediately started to seep away, entirely inflamed warmth seeping through the water. I gasped. I could feel the water bubbling as it reached boiling point, gathering and bursting against my arms. I squirmed to get away from the first needle pricks of pain building and blistering my bare skin, but when I pushed through the rippling water to get away, I came back to a solid wall of unmoving muscle otherwise known as Mark.

"Mark?" I questioned, unable to keep the whimper from my voice.

"Concentrate, Khyle," he demanded sternly.

I swallowed, screwing my eyes up, but what I was supposed to concentrate on I didn't know, and the water was really starting to hurt my eyes. They were watering from the steam rising and coiling around us.

"Deep breath." I heard him whisper it, but I didn't believe he was actually seriously going to… He did. With one quick push I was straight down in the water, my face like someone had just stuck it in an oven at two hundred and fifty degrees. I gasped, which was a terrible idea because scalding hot water swamped my mouth and throat, my scream gurgling up. I felt Mark's grip falter a moment but he recovered, pushing my thrashing, wriggling self deeper. I opened my eyes. The water was parting, from bubbles bobbing up the surface like an underwater explosion from one massive orb of heat; a break in the water energy crackling around the opening, heating the water and causing the boiling. If I'd had any oxygen left I would have screamed again as the parted void grew and my vision went blank.

Mummy's arms wrapped the opening of her heavy cream wool coat around me as the sea-salty breeze burst at us over the ship's railing. I snuggled closer, watching the pale cliffs that towered over Dover port grow smaller and smaller.

"Are we going home?" I asked in a high-pitched child's voice, straining my neck back to look at her face. Her long hair was blowing around in the gale, her beautiful soft face serene as she watched England grow smaller.

"We're going to a new home, Lilly."

I frowned, confused. "But I like the home we have already with Snowzy." Snowzy the ancient sneezing white cat of ours that I hadn't seen in the last three days since Mummy had started folding everything away into boxes and putting them in the car.

"So do I, Sweet Pea. But we're going to make a new home now with a new Snowzy." She absently stroked my hair.

"Snowzy Two," I muttered, watching as her beautiful smile broke out on her face, wide and radiant even as tears rolled silently down her cheeks.

"Yes, angel, Snowzy Two."

The ocean and the wet railing of the ship melted away, replaced by a filtering sunshine and the smells and warm breeze of spring bursting through small kitchen windows covered with delicate white lace curtains. I ran through the old stone villa's kitchen and out into the little garden outside, which had been cast in red and amber light by the sunset.

"Khyle, sweetie, hurry up with the rosemary," Mummy called from back in the house. Rosemary, rosemary. Was that the sweet-smelling one with the small leaves or the prickly one? I stared down at our herb patch as our neighbour glanced over the fence, watering her roses.

"Bonsoir, Khyle, il y a quelque chose qui ne va pas?" she called, leaning over, her worn flowery hat slipping lopsided.

I frowned. "Lequel est du romarin?" I asked in my clumsy French. She laughed and pointed to the small-leaved sweet one. I quickly grabbed a handful, turning on my heel to rush inside calling "Merci" over my shoulder as I went. But I wasn't looking where I was going, and I bumped into someone standing in the middle of our garden, so hard I fell backwards, the rosemary crumbling beneath me where I fell. I looked up at the snake-like woman, her coffee skin glowing in the scarlet evening light and her white hair left loose to swing to her hips.

"Fais attention, ma petite, no te fais pas du mal," she hissed as I quickly gathered the crumbled rosemary and ran inside, looking over my shoulder as she turned very slowly, her cat-like eyes green, wide, and insane. Be careful, little one, don't get hurt now.

"Mummy, there's a woman in the garden," I cried, entering the living room where Mummy sat cross-legged in front of an iron pot filled with herbs and salt, her eyes flickering open. She took the rosemary from me.

"I know, Khyle; that's why we need this. It's a protection spell. She won't bother us any more" she whispered, her face drawn and troubled in a way I hadn't seen it for months, not since we first came here.

I ran back to the kitchen to close the doors out to the garden. As I pulled with all the strength in my arms and the doors slammed shut, the dimming light showed my reflection in the glass, which cracked slowly, like a snake moving across my terrorized little face. I jumped back, the woman in the garden throwing her head back and laughing like a banshee. I spun around as the mirror over the little wooden table in the kitchen corner, where Mummy made me eggs on toast, glowed an emerald green and then shattered into thousands of pieces, exploding like knives over the table and onto the floor. I screamed, holding my hands over my head and running to the living room calling out for Mummy. There was no response. The small satellite TV in the living room was flickering static, actual sparks flying from the plugs and dancing in mid-air like the fairies the villagers said watched the gardens. I stopped as though hitting an invisible barrier; Mummy was lying in the middle of the chalk circle, her body convulsing back and forth. An invisible tug of war was going on between her legs and her head. Her eyes were screwed up in pain, her mouth opened wide, choking and gasping for air. "Mummy," I cried, falling to my knees beside her, reaching into the circle to grab her spread tensed hand, her head jerking from side to side. Something caught my eye:

from the living room window two glowing, cat-shaped eyes watched me; the woman was still laughing, her face eager, excited.

Mummy finally choked something out. "Lilly, remember... nursery rhyme," she choked. I nodded desperately.

"Y..., ye... yes, erm, Mother spirit holds me still, with her strength in my will, I am hers and she is mine, with these words we entwine, I ward you off now, foreigner, You may not have this Exeter," I chanted over and over again, my voice growing louder and louder, cracks running up the windows like cobwebs being spun against the glass. Mummy had taught me the rhyme every night since we'd been here; she'd said it would keep us from the dark. Mummy stopped convulsing, lying still on the floorboards, the contents of the iron pot spilt over, leaving a mess of herbs across the floor. The woman behind the window stopped smiling, her face twisting into a snarl, her eyes drowning an iridescent green, like cats. Mummy reached over and took my hand, breathing hard and shivering horribly, but otherwise still as the air before a storm. Was whatever it had been leaving her? The woman on the other side of the window screamed, a ringing so high-pitched and horrible that the windows, the TV screen, and any other crystal in the room shattered, shards of glass slashing gashes in my cheeks as they flew past. I stopped chanting to scream and block my face, but the moment I did the world blackened. The last thing I heard was Mummy's cry of "No!"

I blinked against a scalding wind, desperately looking around. "Mummy, Mummy, where are you?" I cried, desperately looking back and forth. I was standing in a cavern of running waters, and clear, mirror-like glacial ice making up the ceiling and walls.

"Who are you?"

I spun around. There was a desk piled high with thick dusty books bound with something like dyed snakeskin, though not quite the same texture. Shelves had been carved into the glacial walls, holding bottles and vials and weird objects like dried claws; and – I swallowed – an eye was bobbing up and down in a jar filled with a green pickling liquid. It was looking right at me from where it floated.

"Eww," I muttered, momentarily distracted.

"Who. Are. You?"

I started. Sitting behind the desk cluttered with books and bent over it, a sharpened owl feather quill in one hand, was a young boy; older than me, perhaps, in his teens, and glaring at me lividly.

I shuddered; his silvery eyes were equally as cold and cruel as the woman behind the glass. "K-K-Khyle. Who are you?" My voice sounded weird like it was being smothered. It didn't echo around the room like the boy's, but was muffled dully, like it was behind a pillow, the words having no effect on the world around me. "What are you doing here?" He ignored my question entirely.

"Who are you talking to, boy?" A brown and gold-robed man, so old and withered he reminded me of a wizard, strolled over, glaring down at the boy. The boy raised an eyebrow, obviously unconcerned about the sternness in the old man's face.

"Her," he said bluntly, with an air of answering the most retarded question in the world.

The man glanced in my direction, but didn't focus on where I stood. Blankly, he turned back to the boy.

"Who?"

The boy rolled his eyes. "Her! Oh, forget it!" he snapped, raising his hand in a snap. A mass of blue and silver sparking flames built on his palm. He launched it in my direction. I screamed, a rather pathetic muffled sound, throwing my hands in front of my face and bracing myself, but the ball went straight through me, hitting a glacial wall right behind me and digging a hole a foot and half deep, scorch marks spreading in a perfect magnified hand mark up the wall.

The man nodded speculatively. "Very nice work. Continue your studies. Oh, and next time refrain from needlessly damaging your workroom for...

the need to show off." He strolled off, returning to a seat in the corner next to the floating eyes, and snuggling down in his robes like a deflated balloon as if to doze off.

The boy's eyes were huge, his upper lip pulled back in a hideous snarl. "What… Are… You?" he hissed.

I took a step back from the monster. "I, I'm me. Where am I? Where is my Mummy?"

The boy didn't answer me, obviously choosing to ignore that I was there now that he'd sussed he wasn't going to get any remotely interesting information from me.

A painful rush of images hit me, coming faster and faster, as though a floodgate had been opened too fast, to the point where it was difficult to keep making sense of them. The boy was growing older. I was watching him study, being able to do things with his mind, like move things or burn the skin off a monster's bones slowly, savouring watching it cry in howls of agony; watching him learn how to kill; watching what he was taught to do to humans who'd been brought through from my world. He was trained to be lethal, the worst. They took pride in him because from what I learnt, he was the best by right of birth, the one that was destined to bring his people to their feet in an upcoming 'awakening' that the people around him spoke of constantly. And he never failed them, never failed to impress. He killed mercilessly, taking pleasure in it, and I was forced to sit by, unseen, watching those quicksilver eyes warm only when he either got a chance to watch something or someone suffer, or when he found a new way to scare or hurt me. He may not have been able to actually touch me, but he soon learnt that his hurting other people, draining their energy, or finding new ways to torture a living thing until it begged for him to just end it, hurt me; it made me cry from sympathy or fear or disgust, and my pain was the pain that drove him the most wild of all, that gave him the most exhilaration. At first it hadn't been so bad; he'd finally acknowledged that I existed once he realized that even if I'd wanted to, I wasn't going *anywhere, and he'd devoted hours of time consulting his teachers, millions of books, elders, oracles, to figure out, one, what I was; and two, how to get rid of the annoying little moaner who kept preaching at him what was right and what was wrong to do.*

But then it happened: after what felt like a lifetime there he'd been sent to somewhere to train. Out, away from the towering glistening cities that made up this world, and into the barren, dry and starved deserts… where there was a school, if that was what you could call it, where they taught you how to lose what I thought of as what humanity was: emotion, love. Instead you were taught how to 'prioritize' emotions. They taught them how to fight with weapons I didn't have names for, how to channel energy to stimulate every nerve ending in something to make it feel like acid was pulsating through its blood vessels. But they also taught them how to control pain, how to ignore it. After seven sunrises of him being trapped, screaming and crying, in that chair, I couldn't take any more. I'd seen him inflict pain, but seeing him in pain had killed me a thousand times over. He was, after all, everything I had. I'd run up to him, whispering anything I could to make him laugh, or support him, and after a while it had worked; he'd found a way to ignore what they put him through, but it hadn't been along the lines it was supposed to work. He'd never left the final lesson. Whatever thread of humanity had still existed there I'd kept alive, they hadn't been able to turn it to ashes. And he'd learnt to hate me for it. So I would suffer. Dearly.

I jabbed Mark in the ribs with any strength I had left, and to my distressed, frenzied relief he actually did respond. I broke the surface of the water which had already begun to cool, gasping for air and pushing armfuls of water out of my way, to swim and get away from Mark. I grabbed hold of the bank, my fingers digging inches into mud and sliding through slick, lichen-infested stone, dragging myself up, heavy with water, and so sore that just the feel of the stone and earth's rough surface was like sandpaper against an opened wound. I rolled onto my back, then crawled on my shaking knees and backed away, keeping my gaze focused on Mark. He floated motionless in the water, unmoving, his head bowed slightly, casting his face in shadow. It didn't matter whether I could see him or not; I knew that prickly feeling that sent the hairs on the back of my neck up. I remembered it perfectly after being subjected to it for so long, his eyes boring into me. I shook my head which was pounding like a full orchestra in my ears.

"You monster, you demon, you bastard!"

Chapter Seventeen

I half ran, half loped across Mark's empty living room, pulling off my shoe to dislodge the mud from my toes.

"Khyle, please; this is my house."

I jumped a foot back, losing my balance and falling flat on my arse, spreadeagled. I struggled up, ignoring his extended hand. "Oh, excuse me for dumping filth on your, erm, streaked filth," I grumbled.

Mark withdrew his hand, his eyes narrowing. "Alright, would you prefer an argument to a talk?"

"Argument? Not possible. There'd have to be something up for debate, and the fact you're a brutalistic, murdering demonic arsehole isn't it."

"How about the fact that you're a hot-headed ignorant little shit with more pride than I have ever seen in a single person in my entire life. Besides, have you ever heard me deny that I'm a monster?" I winced at how loudly his voice echoed off the panelled walls and high ceiling. "You can storm off like the headstrong, reckless child you are, but how better off will you be? You'll have been betrayed and lied to by everyone around you. You'll be all alone. Now I might be a brutal murdering bastard, but when have I lied to you?"

I stared at him. He was right, of course, as much as storming off sounded like an appealing idea. If he could clear some of the mess that was swelling up under my skull at that moment, then grinning and bearing it, without the grinning part, was what I would do. I slumped down wet on one of the couches, smirking a little as Mark winced. They were 30s vintage and I knew it.

"What do you remember?" He straightened up, standing in front of me and looking down. Dominating as well as demonic; it figured.

"What don't I remember?" I muttered.

"Khyle," he warned.

"Okay, okay. I'm not sure; it's jumbled a little. I remember you, a lot of you. I remember you being taught all those things and hurting all those... And hating me... You know, the more I think about it the less staying appeals," I finished, frenzied, and quickly looking for the door. Mark saw what I was doing and stood between me and the door, arms folded. "Who are you?" I whispered exasperatedly.

Mark sighed, grinding his teeth. "Technically? I'm formerly the lieutenant-colonel of our Sakhush's royal army, son of Ventram Ti Ilu, and the Alal in my own right—"

"The what?"

"Alal. Eh, exact translation would be 'destroyer'."

"How nice. Suits you well."

"Thank you. The Ti Ilu, life god, was a sort of human who took the Lexis, sorry, anti-Lexis, into itself, and I am his only son."

"That's why you were trained the way they trained you."

"I was trained to live up to my name, Khyle. I am a vicious killer."

I shook my head. "Mark, the things you did, which are still foggy but I'm very sure were very, very bad... you say it with pride almost," I whined despairingly.

"Yes. Sakhush is my home. I have no loyalty to this place. Everything that is in my father exists in me. I have no remorse for what I've done; it's what I was born for." His face was completely

244

blank as if he were just stating that he had brown hair!

"But, Mark, that's a *bad* thing," I cried.

"No. It's a point of view. If you were one of my people and I was built to protect you, to ensure your continued existence, would it be bad?"

I shook my head violently, my wet hair flying around my shoulders, spraying water everywhere. "No, because you take too much pleasure in it and your way of survival is to kill us, kill people. Christ, you sort of, like, eat us."

Mark laughed. "I've seen you dig quite happily into a plate of steak and chips." I gaped at him, then just gave up, and dropped my head into my hands. He was actually defending this, wasn't he?

"Before I was interrupted," he went on, "you showed up, to haunt me—"

"Yeah? Excuse me, you were the scary one—"

"If you don't stop interrupting me I swear I will lob you one. Don't put it past me, Khyle—"

"Oh please, how mundane! Are you sure you wouldn't prefer to rip my tongue out?"

He laughed, inclining his head. "Touché."

I smiled a little. It was just so natural to talk, to be with him it was very – almost – unnatural. I suppose with that much constant time together it would get a bit like that.

"Mark, did you just hate me because you were bred to hate my kind, because you really…"

A muscle twitched in his jaw, a sign I was learning meant he was trying to decide on something in his own mind. "I never hated you, Khyle. It wasn't long before I realized I… " He stopped, eyes narrowed, looking off darkly somewhere.

"Hey, not the time to brood," I snapped.

He looked down at me. "In my religion and, I'm sure, in some way in this world too, there is what we call Isten Duranki, one bond, a perfect match for a soul... "

The conversation I'd had with Ross suddenly flashed in my mind.

"Soul mate!" I forced the word sourly through gritted teeth, not liking in the least where he could be going with this. He took a deep breath and I decided to let him run with no more interruption. I think I could remember him actually pulling a tongue from somebody's jaw.

"I didn't hate you, Khyle, and that was the problem. I have been born and bred with one purpose and that is to loathe and destroy each one of your kind."

(Okay, reckon forty seconds to get to the door if I really leap for it.)

"My birth was placed into legend, preordained," he carried on, bitterly, "and I was good at it. I enjoyed it."

(Thirty seconds, if I throw myself at it.)

"And then, you. Your precious Lexis knew exactly how to protect itself. It made you, the exact equal and opposite to... You're a liability, Khyle, that's what *you* were made to be: a passive saviour. I was taught not to feel emotions like guilt, remorse, need, and you inspired all those things in me. You made me incapable of fulfilling my destiny. There was one moment." He swallowed, lost in memory. "We'd captured a massive quantity of people off a ship, and you were there during the accounting. The pain in your eyes—" His teeth were on edge as if just the thought ate at him inside. "Needless to say, *Columbus* of the 1930s was sent right back to where it came from, and I betrayed everything I was, everything I am, for a pathetic little girl who, for my life, wouldn't leave me bloody alone."

I blew my cheeks out, eyes wide, heart racing absurdly. When he put it like that I thought I'd hate my guts as well. "And all those girls that Green showed… " I trailed off, swallowing back a sob.

"They tortured me, ripped me open and introduced me personally to my entrails, and then exiled me; and you just left." He jumped to his feet, his voice a full shout, and full of a kind of agony I'd only imagined from wounded animals. "You just disappeared. When I was going to fight for you, you abandoned me. So I came to find you, to make you pay and—"

I jumped up too so there was barely an inch between us.

"But you *didn't* find me, Mark! You found a bunch of innocent young girls and you destroyed them!" I screamed back, furious. "You can't think for a second that any of this delusional shit you're filling yourself with justifies any of what you did," I seethed, but as *delusional* popped out I saw the raw enigmatic fury race into him.

"Delusional! Do you think if I'd had a choice it wouldn't be *you*?" I backed up a step as if someone had knocked the air out of me. "Why do you think your spirit was tied to me? A soul is drawn to its other half when it has nothing to stabilize it on a solid plane. You couldn't be more than seven foot from me without feeling agonized. I know, because you inflicted the same thing on me eventually! If I could find a way to be rid of you I would do it. You make me weak and yes, yes, I hate you."

"Then what the hell is stopping you, Mark? I'm right here." I threw my arms wide. "Go ahead; you know I'm no match for you in the slightest. Do it! Do to me what you did to those other girls!" I was so full of emotion I was shaking on the spot.

Mark shook his head, teeth clenched, but rather than pulling out a cleaver or wrapping his fingers around my throat, he finally fell to the couch, head in his hands. "I've tried. Those other girls… " He laughed bitterly. "The only reason I could hurt them was because they weren't you." He licked his lips in a thoughtful kind of way. "I waited a good hundred years to have you dead, thinking, planning what I would do to you, and then I finally have you. You don't scream, Khyle; you charge out of your house with your friends screaming in fear behind you, and shout at me, a hot-headed, insane, wild *child*, and I can't lay a finger on you because you're *her*." I stood, arms still spread, gaping at him as he eased himself back onto the couch, staring at me, making my already burning skin feel that much more alive. "I never truly had you, and when I first met you a month ago I knew exactly what I was going to do and how I was going to do it. And then you impressed me at every turn. And then, suddenly, as you were jumping to your death, so that a *ghost didn't watch you while you showered*, I realized the idea of losing you was a very new type of affliction."

"It wasn't just so a ghost didn't watch me while I showered. And Delia wasn't a ghost," I muttered childishly. Mark raised one eyebrow. "Okay, so mostly it was the shower thing," I muttered again, slumping down, my turn to put my head in my hands. "Mark, I don't, I can't begin, at the moment, to get my head round this, I just… " I just couldn't think about this; I'd barely known him a month and he was saying what? We were preordained soul mates? I was made for him by our all-powerful energy source so that he could lead their people to crushing us? No. No way. It was ridiculous, laughable; and yet wasn't most of my life so far becoming ridiculous, laughable? And the way I felt around him… He was a murderer. It came down to that, regardless. I didn't know how I felt about Mark. I didn't know if I knew what love was or was not, truly and in the end. Could anyone love someone like him anyway? Who would want to? Wouldn't that be like suicide, emotional or otherwise?

"What else?"

I glanced up, still lost in despairing thoughts. "Sorry?" I breathed.

"What else, Khyle? What else do you remember, other than me?"

I shook my head, letting a long breath out. It suddenly hit me mentally, square on, and my head shot up. "Oh my God, my Mum." My breathing picking up instantly as actual memories came back to me, actual memories of my Mummy, my caring, strong, hot-tempered, erratic mother who liked to make upside-down cakes, and decorated my room with paint balloons we threw at the walls. I was hyperventilating, tears welling up inside me as I fought for oxygen. Mark was by my side in an instant, one hand pressed to the back of my neck, the other taking my arm in a sobering grip.

"Breathe, just breathe. What is it?" he soothed, and it really did; my breathing started to calm, my body just reacting to his reflexively, reacting just to his touch.

"I remember her," I said in a very small voice. "She wasn't, she wasn't a vegetable, Mark. She was... lovely, she was like me."

Mark sniffed. "She was like you and you're describing her as lovely."

I giggled a little though the tears caught in my throat. I turned to him. "No, she really was. She was messy and all arty, and she let me eat really badly, like Oreos and peanut butter right out of the jar," I gushed excitedly at a very awkward-looking Mark. Something told me sarcasm, irony, pain, and hatred he was good with, but when it came to giddy happiness he might be having a few problems quite comprehending. I was smiling through the sobs; all these things I'd lost and I now had back. "And she loved cats, she was a creepy cat woman and she loved Fra—" I stopped, choking on the word.

"What?" Mark was able to efficiently read and understand *that* particular emotion in my voice.

I swallowed back the tears. "Oh my God. They lied to me. She ran; she didn't sacrifice herself at all," I gasped. "She ran away to

France because she was scared, she wanted to protect us, she wanted a normal life. Why would they lie? And that snake bitch Anna, she was there, she was the one who, who… " I was suddenly furious. "I'll kill her," I muttered.

"Anna?" Mark sounded more than a little doubtful at that idea.

"What?" I snapped defensively, finding a new target for my anger.

"Well, she's an elder… I mean… " he trailed off, and took a deep breath. "I'm sure you'd be able to take her," he sighed, obviously not wanting to get into *that* particular fight with me. I narrowed my eyes nodding in a yeah-I-know-how-sarcastic-that-was kind of way.

He shrugged. "Wait, a house in France?" he said, eyes narrowing. "That's where I came through."

"I know. I remember watching, I think, but I mean, the house was derelict and you said a hundred years. Well, I haven't been around for a hundred years. Wait! How old are you?" It suddenly hit me that there was a serious problem with those calculations.

"Hmm. It must be a memory from Lexis," he said.

"A what?"

"Sometime the Lexis to which we belong gives us past memories like… psychic visions. I believe quite a few fortune-tellers of this world make their living by them."

"Are you avoiding the age question?" I asked suspiciously.

Mark rolled his eyes. "Your years or mine?"

"Yours."

"Four hundred or so. I lost count."

I nodded, eyes wide. "Yeah, I guess that would happen after the first three." He smiled a sinful grin. "Wait. How long was I with you in…?"

His brow furrowed. "Two hundred."

I felt very ill. Two years here, two hundred there. My God, Mum had to have endured that for so long. "You have no idea how I came back, then?" I asked, searching his eyes desperately. "Well, how did you come through?" I burst out.

"I opened a gateway. I was taught to: that's how I sent *Columbus* back, but I had no control as to when; that's why I was a hundred years or so out. You have no idea how you came back?"

I shook my head. The problem was, if I had no idea, I also had no idea how to get Mum back, and half the reason of going through all this was lost. I felt like crying all over again. I'd never wanted to know about my mother from fear of feeling this kind of loss, and I had taken the risk of feeling this way in the chance that I would know a way to get her back. But I didn't and I was going to have to suffer the torment anyway.

I was suddenly very tired. And hungry. I wondered whether Mark would have anything that wasn't raw and bloody. My awful ringtone suddenly exploded into the silence. I closed my eyes, wondering who on earth it was that I probably really didn't want to talk to. Mark reached over and pulled it out of his re-applied jacket pocket. I frowned, taking it from him.

"It fell out as you fell in," he said.

I glanced at the caller ID: Loraline. To answer or not to answer? The responsible thing would be to answer, of course. I let it ring until it finally cut out. "Not in a talking mood?" The sarcasm was back in his voice. The phone started ringing again, this time an unknown caller. I groaned and flicked it open.

"Hello?"

"Khyle?"

"Yes. Jackson?" I thought I might just die at the sound of his voice.

"Khyle, we need you. It's Delia."

"What?" I was suddenly alert, jumping forward in the seat.

"She's back in the Nomas medical ward." His voice sounded as if it had already started to mourn her, it was so clouded with remorse.

"What? Why? How? She was fine just a few hours ago?" I cried, hitting overdrive for what felt like the millionth time this night.

"After you left, we went to try to eat and she started throwing up again, except this time she was throwing up blood. It also looks like her kidneys have shut down. She is asking for you. I know and I understand that you don't wish to be around any of us and I respect that decision but, if you would, do it for Delia. Now would be the moment, just a moment, to forget everything else and come for her."

I swallowed. "Where are you exactly?" I asked urgently.

Jackson gave me directions for yet another Nomas military base just outside Farringdon, about twenty minutes drive away, and then we hung up. He seemed to get, by my tone, I wasn't interested in speaking to him more than bare necessity required. I sighed. Now that I'd stopped shouting I was able to realize how badly everything was throbbing. I glanced down at my hands where burns the size of thumbprints spotted my fingers and palms, blisters and boils running up my wrists. I thought I might start crying all over again just at the sight of them. "Can you give me a ride?" I asked Mark, still looking down at my hands.

"Where to?"

"Farringdon. Something's gone wrong with Delia and they've taken her to a Nomas base close by with a hospital ward. I guess they can't take her to a normal hospital in case it's... I don't know, supernatural or something... "

"What's wrong with her?"

Jeez, what was this, the Spanish Inquisition.

"I don't know," I said. "Jackson didn't say, but I mean, she hasn't exactly been right since she came back, she hasn't been able to keep anything down. Look, can you give me a ride or not?" I snapped.

Mark looked for a second as if I may almost have come close to hurting his feelings. Like I cared if I hurt a murderer's feelings… Problem was, I actually did.

"Yes. You're soaked, exhausted, quite hungry, I imagine, and covered in rather painful-looking blisters is what I was getting at," he hissed.

"Well, so what? Afraid I'll mess up your car seats?" I hissed back, starting to feel the beginnings of some hatred of my own. He didn't get to play the considerate caring one, not after everything he'd done, everything he was.

"Yes, Khyle, I'm worried about my car seats, not your comfort or the fact you may faint on my floor. Car seats." His eyes had that insane wide look filled with an obscene level of scorn. I looked at the floor, unable to keep eye contact. I heard him sigh. "I have some clothes. You can change into those and we can pick up some food on the way there. Bound to be some grossly processed fast food joint open this time of night." He got up and went towards a beautifully carved mahogany staircase that I guessed would once have been quite a focal point for this dilapidated building. For a man who loved his car…

"Thank you," I croaked in a small voice, making him pause, one hand on the banister. "After this, that's it, we're over. No more contact, Mark. I don't want anything to do with this." I didn't look up as I said it but I felt, rather than saw, that terrible, scary mad glare boring through me, and then it was gone in a heartbeat. I never got a response, and I had a feeling I could have got down on my knees and begged; it wouldn't have made any difference, because he was right: we both knew, in the end, it wasn't what I really wanted. Whether I would ever admit it to myself or not.

Mark's change of clothes turned out to be a very soft silk black shirt of his and a pair of actual women's jeans. I didn't want to know where they came from. In fact I purposefully blocked myself from thinking about it. The trip was dead silent, with just the sound of me working my way through the heaps of gooey delicious Thai food Mark had grabbed on our way up there. He was impassive, and I was scared of him, for Delia, but mostly I was preoccupied with revelling in actual memories. I tried to put the ones of Sakhush aside and concentrate on the little girl's perspective of my Mum. It was true torment, but it was also blissful. No matter how terrible a past it was, there had been beautiful pieces, and for a girl who had spent so long with nothing, no strings, it was indescribable. It was past midnight before Mark pulled up outside a massive warehouse-looking building about a mile out of town from Farringdon. A tall boy dressed in combos came up to the car.

"Miss Exeter?" he asked through the window in a clipped voice.

"Yes," I sighed.

"Just you, please," he said, stepping back from the car.

"That's fine," I muttered, placing the empty plastic carton remnants of dinner back in the brown paper bag and climbing out. Mark reversed the car the moment I was out, and was gone so quickly I barely had time to breathe. Well, what would I have said anyway: Thanks for the truth; I hope you end up behind bars for the sake of all humanity?

"This way, Ma'am," said the boy, and you could only describe him as that because he didn't look all that much older than me. He punched a security code into a pad beside a barbed wire fence that went around the warehouse, and led me through. This base was a lot like the one on the downs: narrow grey corridors, blocked-off rooms. Some I noticed required security card as well as code just to enter. Finally, he opened the door to a massive, shining white hospital wing. My stomach clenched automatically at the sound of beeping machines. I now wondered vaguely whether that was a subconscious result of my *own* hospital experiences that I'd just never been aware of. Only one bed was filled; Loraline, James, and Eliza were crowded around it. Eliza was crying so hard she looked as though she might break in James's arms. How much could she take? This was her daughter, after all, her sweet, overly-perky, slightly crazy daughter who didn't deserve any of this.

I walked over, Loraline's head immediately turning to look at me. A wave of emotions crossed her eyes; all ended in disgust.

"Really, Khyle?" she hissed, jumping up from the seat as I approached.

"What?" I asked, clueless.

"You went to *him*. I can smell him all over you."

"You can *smell* him?" I was more than a little grossed-out at that. And then, bizarrely, I just wanted to ask what he smelled like. That was before I caught sight of poor Delia. Her face was ashen, and the whole of her tiny frame was covered in a thin sheen of sweat as she moaned in her sleep. "Jesus," I cussed under my breath.

"Yeah, she's been out for about half an hour," Loraline said from behind me.

"Do we know what's wrong with her?" I asked, touching her forehead. I really didn't want to lose my theoretically adopted little sister. Especially not at the risk of being haunted all over again. Loraline glanced up at Eliza; I got the message. We walked to the end of the room where there was a water cooler.

"Well, apart from the fact that her digestion has just all-out stopped so that she's been running on empty the last three days, she boiling from the inside out; her body temperature is rising through the roof and killing off her internal organs." Loraline rested her head against the wall.

I put a hand on her shoulder, tenderly. "What is it?" I asked gently.

She sighed, eyes full of tears. "My world; it just destroys everything."

I wrapped my arms around her even though she was a good foot taller than me. "We'll sort this. I'll sort this. Do we know what's causing it? I mean, it's not natural or of-this-world, is it?"

"Jackson's talking to the re— Wait. He's here."

Jackson came through the doors, closely followed by Ross in shocking pink sunglasses. I know it was totally inappropriate timing but I couldn't help but snigger a little. I wonder whether Ross was…? It wasn't totally out of the realm of possibility in comparison to everything else going on, I mean.

"What do we know?" Loraline asked them as they walked over to us, shooting glances at Delia and her distraught parents.

Jackson looked awful, his usually well-kept self dishevelled, with bags under his eyes the size of potato sacks. "Not much. They've got their researchers on it, but… "

"Researchers? Like paranormal experts?" I asked, curious.

"Yeah, kind of. We've got a whole research facility for this type of thing, full of mythology records and databases of past experiences and what we know about the beings in anti-Lexis—"

"Sakhush," I broke in, reflexively. I received four blank stares. "Sorry," I muttered.

Ross shook his head. "Nah, I'm glad to see you've done your research, eh? Yeah, so the problem is, Delia has no idea what's happening to her. She's not hearing voices or feelings or seeing images so we have nothing to go by in a sea of possibilities," he finished, shrugging.

"Well, can we help? More heads?" Loraline sounded desperate to make up for something she wasn't in the least guilty for other than by association.

Ross and Jackson shook their head in unison, Ross saying, "Classified information; authorized personnel only. You wouldn't guess the amount of times I say that a day."

"Oh, I would," I muttered, pacing on the spot.

I blew the air out of my lips. What did I know that could help, if anything? My mind was more filled with gruesome scenes involving Mark's callousness. "Do they have a broad idea?" I asked, a little desperate.

"Well, the most likely is that it's a parasite. Sometimes lower beings, sometimes even higher beings – but she'd be dead already if it was one of those – latch on for a joyride, see if they can cross over. But without knowing which kind it is we have no idea how to extract it or fight it." Ross's tone was hopeless. If he'd been speaking to Delia's parents like this, then it was no wonder they were already mourning their daughter as if she'd died.

"That's no help then, is it? What about magic; could we try and exorcise it?" Loraline burst out. I thought exorcisms were Christian.

"That's if it's a demon, and the amount of energy she's lost she hasn't got more than an hour, maybe a bit over." Ross's voice was growing smaller and smaller.

"Well, that's not long enough. We need more time. We can—" Loraline broke off, sobbing too hard. Jackson pulled off his glasses, wrapping her in a fatherly hug, whispering something comforting and probably totally useless in her ear. I exchanged a look with Ross. We needed more time; that, we had. Delia needed more time, but she didn't have the strength, she didn't have the… energy. I paused; I knew what these memories could help me do. I mean, I'd seen Mark do it. All I had to do was the opposite, right? I could stand here and debate it… and I'd watch Delia die if I did.

"Well, sod that," I muttered, walking over to where Delia was. "Eliza, James, would you move back for me for a moment?" They both exchanged a look. I put a hand on Eliza's shoulder. "Please, trust me."

They stepped back a few feet hesitantly. "Khyle, what are you doing?"

"Khyle?" I heard Loraline and Jackson shout behind me.

I glanced around. "Ross, eh… ." I waved him over, sick with nerves. Amused, he appeared by my side in a moment. "You got a knife?" I whispered at him.

He raised his eyebrows but didn't move. "Explain." He drew the word out.

"I don't have time."

"Make time, Miss," he snapped.

I stamped my foot. "Fine. We need time, which we can only get if Delia has enough energy to last more time. You think she's possessed by a demon, which would mean the reasons she's fading away in front of our eyes is because that demon is what's eating away at her. And it's" – could I make myself say it? – "not getting the right kind of sustenance, so if helping it means buying more time, then… Oh, just give me your damned knife." I shouted the last bit, totally exasperated, as a lopsided grin grew on his face.

"You're insane. You've watched too many horror movies. You're a stupid imbecile for risking your own life. Here's my knife, you're a genius, well done."

He didn't change tone once as he held out his knife. I swear it seemed like he mentally winked at me. I smiled, taking the butterfly knife he held out to me.

"What the hell is she doing, Ross?" Loraline cried from behind me.

"Relax, Lorry, I've seen this done a thousand times," I muttered.

"What?" she shouted behind me.

Ross moved over to grab her in case she lunged. I took a deep breath. For Delia I could do this. I held out my left arm, the scorch marks still bright rosy patterns. I pressed the knife against the main vein in the crook of my arm, pressing deep and swishing down the length of my arm in one rapid gesture. An animalistic hiss burst out behind me. I whirled. Ross and Jackson had both grabbed hold of Loraline, whose eyes were massive and bulging, her body prancing low to the ground, trying to pounce, hands and fingers spread wide in front of her like claws raking the air. I heard Eliza scream behind me; how much of this did she actually know? I turned back to Delia, bending over her, placing my arm right beneath her nose and mouth. She twitched, her nose jumping, lips pulling up into a snarl. I bent down, whispering very lightly in her ear.

"Come on, you know you want it, you need it. What happens if she dies? Are you sure you can exist without her?" I didn't need to say any more because Delia jerked, her eyelids flipped backwards showing white canvases where her muddy brown irises had once been. She latched onto my arm, her fingers digging like claws where the cut was, squeezing the blood to make it slosh up and out abundantly, and straight into her gaping mouth.

I gasped from pain, but mostly I was too transfixed in a mixture of horror and complete disgust as she gulped deeply from my arm, tongue lashing out to sop up what she could. I cringed, looking away, feeling myself go pale. "Oww!" I moaned. Okay, Khyle, don't be a wuss; that's not the end of it. I felt my other hand, pressing my eyes shut. It was just like the fire, except very different. I listened to my own heart thudding softly against my ribs, imagining the sparks of electricity – chemical and electrical – igniting there, pulsating through me, through my veins, my bones, the muscles, my very skin, down my arm and into my hand.

I quickly spread my hand over Delia's chest while I still had my concentration, feeling the energy crackling there. I directed it straight through the air to her, willing it to go into her, please go into her, I don't need it…

Eliza screamed again. "Hell!" I yelped, out of surprise.

A line of deep purple sparks like mini coloured bolts of lightning shot from my fingers, hitting her like a defibrillator, Delia's entire chest rising up towards it even as she, it, clung onto my arms, still drawing as much as it could. I don't know how long I managed to keep it going, but eventually I was exhausted, and a pain like being shocked by five hundred volts in a continuous stream broke through my concentration and I slumped away, Ross ready and catching me coolly. The problem was, the Delia demon didn't want to let go. The moment the energy stream was broken, it was broken, but she dug deeper into my bleeding arm, her fingers so tightly knotted they dug and disappeared inches into my arm, spilling new blood onto the crisp white bedsheets.

Ross was quick, hooking Delia with two fingers in the nostril. She screamed, reluctantly unlatching herself from the now very open wound, and Ross pulling away instantly, his face screwed up as he looked for somewhere to wipe his fingers.

"Man, that's nasty," I murmured, nursing my arm to my chest. Loraline tossed me a roll of gauze bandage, seeming to have totally recovered now that the temptation was gone. She was a bit pink in the cheeks, though no doubt humiliated for showing the demon half she spent her life trying to hide.

"We have to talk," Jackson suddenly demanded, sounding shaken, his brow knotted. I nodded, wrapping my arm in gauze. God, I felt dizzy, like I'd just run ten miles at full sprint on an empty stomach.

Ross led me to a hospital bed across the room. "Sit. I'll get you some water, eh?" He shot a glance at Jackson and Loraline. "Good luck."

"Cheers," I mouthed.

"Khyle, may I ask how you knew how to perform that task so efficiently?" Jackson asked, removing his glasses yet again to rub them on his shirt, his grey hair falling over his face.

"Have you been bloodletting to Mark?" Loraline snapped furiously before I had a chance to answer Jackson.

"Blood whating?" I blurted, shocked.

"Giving him blood for his pleasure," she burst out, exasperated at my ignorance.

"What the fu—? No! Ew! Ew, ew, ew... May I stress this? EW!" I think I'd reached lightheaded hysteria all over again.

"Does it matter how she knew? That was a brilliant idea." Christ had come in at some point, his thick sandy hair-covered arms folded, with a look of something that, if I didn't know better, could be described as pride.

"Maybe not to you, Christopher, but it does to me. I like to understand things fully," Jackson snapped, his accent growing even crisper and clearer when he was mad.

"Then for your own amusement, professor," Christ muttered.

Every eye turned to me. "I've seen it done a lot of times" – that wasn't going to placate them. "Mark! Me and Mark did a spell so I could remember. Everything. Every last thing before I was in Sakhush and... during." I said each word clearly and precisely, watching Loraline's eyes grow drier, and Jackson visibly age in front of my eyes.

"Khyle," he whispered, his eyes closed. Even Christ's eyes had widened.

"But you're, I mean you're not... " Loraline trailed off, awkwardly.

"Walking on the walls? Oh, give me time. If I don't get a fag and sniggers after that little incident, there may be some wall walkage." I tried to lighten the mood, but the only one who was kind enough to laugh was Ross who, after a look from Christ, silenced instantly.

"I can't believe he would let you do that, let alone help you," Loraline seethed.

"What?" I snapped. "It was what I wanted and if I wasn't going to get answers from you lot then, well, he was a good choice really. Doesn't give much for my feelings, you see." I swallowed back the tears as I said that. I shook them away; I'd cried too much for one night as it was. I'd cried enough for one year actually. "I mean, you wanted me to run away! That's what you thought of me. Well, that's not me. I can't, and even if I could, I wouldn't sit back and watch; I have to do something to help. I want to be part of this. Besides, this is the most interesting my life has ever been."

That received a little smirk from Christ but Jackson shook his head.

"Khyle, this is not an interesting lifestyle. It's not a lifestyle I would choose for anyone, especially not you. You've been through so much already. If you were my daughter—"

"Well, she isn't," Christ barked fiercely, making me jump a little unexpectedly.

Thankfully, before an argument could fully blow up there was a moan from across the room. Eliza was immediately by her side.

"This isn't over. We need to talk about this *decision* and we need to talk through what you remember," Jackson said very seriously, holding his hand up to keep everyone's attention before we went running to Delia's side. Well, seeing as I already had everyone's attention…

"You're right, we do need to talk. I was just thinking it should more be about the lies you all spoon-fed me about my mother."

I jumped off the bed before I forced myself to meet their gazes. I felt betrayed enough. Delia's eyes were hazy but she was there; I could barely believe it had actually worked.

"Khyle?" she whispered, her voice raw and raspy. Eliza looked up at me desperately, her eyes wet. I took Delia's hand.

"Shhh, conserve your energy, hun," I whispered to her, stroking my thumb over the back of her hand.

She swallowed, shaking her head a little.

"Please, Khyle, you did it before; do it again," she breathed rawly, sounding so broken. "I'm asking this time. I'll even say please."

"No, Delia. Just, just sleep, okay," I breathed, feeling something I was too tired to identify rearing up inside me.

"No. Please, Khyle, I'm not ready to go, I don't want to go yet. Please save me."

Eliza burst into tears beside me as Delia's eyelids fluttered shut. I looked up at the group gathered around me.

"Delia, can you tell us anything about what's... erm, hurting you?" Loraline crouched down beside her. Delia nodded.

"It doesn't like me very much," she whispered so sincerely, as if above everything else the idea that something could exist that didn't find her totally adorable was the biggest hurt of all.

I got back from the bed, unable to take any more. I started pacing, grabbing a handful of hair and pulling it tense reflexively. "We're not getting anywhere," I sighed as Ross came over to me.

"What do you suggest?" he asked quietly.

I shook my head. "I have no idea." It was a lie; I knew exactly what I was going to do. I just didn't want anyone in this room to know. Because they'd stop me.

"You got a fag? Can I go outside? I just need to breathe, process, you know."

Ross nodded sincerely, opening the door for me as he led me down the claustrophobically narrow hallways and outside into the wide open air. I took a massive lungful, feeling sobered already. Maybe they were all right, maybe there was something in this world that took care of us, comforted us; we just were so used to it we didn't notice any more. The night certainly felt like an ice-cold embrace. Ross passed me a fag and a Zippo with 'Gucci' written on it in diamante. Okay, now I really was suspicious.

"You need a minute, sweetheart?"

"Yeah, please." I waited until I was sure he'd disappeared from view before fishing out my phone and hitting speed dial.

"Yo, stranger." Zean's sleep-clogged voice came on the other end.

"You know all the massive favours you owe me?" I said.

"No. Must be a figment of your imagination, especially as you owe me rent."

"Shut up. I need a favour and I need it quick, Zean. Really. Quick."

Chapter Eighteen

"Do I want to know what happened to you?"

"No."

"Do I want to know where we're going?"

"No."

"Khyle?"

I sighed, lighting up yet another cigarette. I felt completely drained, slumped down in the patched, threadbare front seat of Zean's car. "Okay. Going to Casper's to make a deal with a demon to save Delia."

Zean sniffed. "Try saying that ten times faster" was all he muttered in the dark car. I'd convinced the same boy who'd let me in to let me out, and had got away before anyone could realize that I was gone, agreeing to meet Zean at the end of the road away from the warehouse. Zean, unfortunately not to my disbelief, had turned up with his leather jacket thrown over his blue and green pinstripes which meant I was in this alone. "It's three in the morning," he said pointedly.

"Good, the party should just be starting." I wasn't really being fair to Zean but I didn't want to have to explain, I didn't want have to talk, I didn't really want to get up off this seat for the next decade, but there you go.

"And Delia is? Taking another ride to bizarroland?" Zean turned the car with a rebellious jerk, the engine spurting. I wondered whether we'd actually even get to Casper's.

"No, actually, she's seriously ill because something's eating her up from the inside out," I snapped. Zean had no idea what he was on about.

"Jeez, K, what's the matter with you? I came, didn't I? I've got a right to ask why I'm here."

I ground my teeth together, pointing to the alley which led down to Casper's. As Zean pulled the car over, I sighed.

"I'm sorry, mate. I… I'll explain, but at the moment I just can't. More than anything I just don't know how, I don't know how to make sense of what I do know."

Zean turned in the seat to face me, his expression full of a confusion and worry that I'd never seen Zean wear in his life. "You should never have got so involved with them, Khyle, you should—"

"Have run away?" I snapped.

Zean's eyes narrowed. "No, should have given yourself time to process, to figure things out at a normal pace."

"Yeah, well, Delia doesn't have time," I said as I started to climb out of the car.

"Casper's is here. Bit secluded."

I laughed. "Zean, I don't think they go for passing trade."

He laughed. Best thing about old friends? You can treat them like shit one second and then the next you'd be on even better terms than before.

I got stamped but could barely get through the door, the place was so packed. I'd been right: Casper's was at its peak. The dance floor was packed solidly with bodies twisting and grinding together, radiating waves of heat and sexual energy. As I waded through the sea of mostly naked bodies, the music pounding out a gothic rock that was enough to make your eyes water, I figured another reason why the Namlugallu were attracted to this whole scene: the place was like an explosion of raw energy, a juicy, intoxicating, candy factory to chocoholics. I was relieved it was so busy; it allowed me to go unnoticed for as long as possible. I didn't want to draw more attention than I needed; it would take up too much time that I didn't have. I didn't honestly know how much time the energy transfer had given Delia, but if she'd been on an hour before it, even if it had doubled her levels, then I was eating into a ticking bomb clock. Would one of the others try giving her more?

I bounced on tiptoes to try and see over the crowd of shining multi-coloured heads bobbing up and down. There was a staircase, sealed off with a thick black rope, with a bouncer standing by it, his arms clasped obediently in front of him. He looked human, but the blank look in his eyes was more than simple obedience, it was complete emptiness. I had to get to the second floor; I had to get past him. From what Ross had told me, the only people who knew anything that could help me were on the second floor looking down at the ice-cream counter, dancing their lives away below them. I ducked into a corner as a dominatrix-esque waitress, her eyes imitating a beaten-up Cleopatra, came over to me. I ordered a vodka on the rocks; a little liquid courage was needed without saying. Waiting felt like a lifetime. There was no way I was getting up there without proof I'd been drugged and given the stamped seal of approval which I'd seen partyers flash at the bouncer to go up. Vodka I was willing to flood through my veins: whatever was in that syringe, I so was not.

The girl brought my drink, flashing me a nonchalant smile, just as a group of longhaired, rabbit ear-wearing, playboy wannabes, swaying a little on their feet, walked up to the bouncer. I jumped up, grabbing my drink and pushing myself in with the five of them. The girls were so out of it, their glittery eyes wide, shining and focused on elsewhere. They didn't even notice me push against them, and the bouncer was already re-hanging the rope behind me in a heartbeat. I closed my eyes for a second, letting the five girls go up a little ahead of me. I took a sip of vodka, savouring the feeling of it burn as it ran down my throat and into my stomach. It helped.

Gripping the iron railing, I ascended to hell. Upstairs was a bit of an anti-climax at first glance. It was set out like a paradoxically Indian boudoir with beautifully coloured and patterned pillows spread around low multi-coloured plastic tables, and floating candles bobbing up and down, shining eerie orange hollows against the concrete walls, which had been decorated by spray-painted, iridescent weird symbols, and words I could pronounce. At second glance you started to get the weirdness. The whole floor ran round as a balcony overlooking below and directly level with the caged dancers who, up close, were too pale, too thin, their eyes closed dreamily and their heads lolling backward at horrible angles on their necks. Their wrists and ankles were clad in heavy metal chains which left horrible friction marks rubbing raw into the skin there. Silk curtains hung in various places from ceiling railings, blocking off whole seating areas, which would have been fine if the one directly opposite where I was standing hadn't had a limp, white arm flopping out from beneath the heavy fabric folds. Involuntarily I took a step back, wondering if I could get back downstairs, back to Zean and the hell out of here quick enough to get back to Delia and think of a new idea. I didn't have enough time, of course, and besides I could already feel the beginning of eyes making fine hairs on my arms and on the back of my neck stand on end.

I threw my drink back, the ice rattling in the low tumbler. I realized, vaguely, I was shaking from adrenaline again. A quick scan had almost a dozen sets of iridescent, unnaturally glowing eyes looking up and staring at me. I spotted the sleek, sylph-like Anna, clad in an all-in-one yellow leather jump suit that glowed like the sun against the warm chocolate of her skin, literally sprawled on the floor in a darkened corner. The curtain was slightly drawn and those incandescent eyes were wide and looking at me, the cream for the cat.

"Kahlillyne." How the f— did she know my full name? "You finally decided to leave Ross and enjoy yourself," she laughed. I guessed she wasn't sincere.

"I don't think so, Belum. She is sober… aren't you?"

Someone pushed me hard on the shoulder. I glanced around as I stumbled forward; Sentel's peroxide cloud of hair was pulled back and flicked down right to her scalp, making her look like a chav trying to pull off goth very, very badly.

"Hey, demonic Barbie," I jeered through gritted teeth.

"Don't forget you are the lamb in the slaughterhouse, enfant." Anna's French was perfect. I wondered whether…

"Je n'oublierai pas, probablement, ce que j'ai vecu avec ma vie entiere." *I'm not likely to forget what I've lived with my entire life.*

One eyebrow rose. "Ah, memories. No, cherie. Tell me, how did you manage to regain them? It's not of any importance, of course. Just curiosity." She took a sip from a martini, actually caressing it with her fingertips. I prayed, but didn't hold out much hope, that it was a Manhattan considering its colouring. I shook my head, ignoring the onlookers' building interest.

"I need a favour, Anna." Just get it out in the open.

She laughed, her whole body lurching forward. She tilted the curtain back, the thick velvety fabric rolling off a young girl, younger than me, slumped dreamily. Bite marks, actual animalistic deep gouges, marred her soft exposed skin. Anna ran her long bony fingers over the girl's cheek. "I'm afraid you do forget. Why would I do anything to help you and not…?" She gestured to Sentel who smiled, baring gleaming white teeth.

"Well, I'm sure I would taste terrible and, well, I'll give you whatever you want; anything you ask, I'll give it to you."

"And I would want what from you?"

"Let your imagination flow free. I don't have time for this. Do you know why I'm here?"

Inside I was trembling, but I'd be damned if I'd show even an ounce of weakness in front of this evil cow. "The girl," she stated too eagerly. "What precisely do you want me to do?"

I paused. This was a test. She'd given me only what I asked for this very moment. I had to word this carefully.

"I need to know what's hurting her and how to stop it." I chose each word carefully.

Anna sat back, fiddling absently with the strawberry blonde strands of the junkie on the floor. "And you will give me *anything* in return?"

The silence up here was deadly; it felt like every living being in the room that wasn't totally spaced-out had its eyes on us.

"I will give you one thing in return for the information I ask for. You can ask whatever you want, but only one act for one piece of information." I felt like a lawyer trying to keep a contract as clear as possible. Anna leapt to her feet, freaking the life out of me and making me stumble back a bit. So much for keeping my intimidating cool.

"You ask for two pieces of information," she hissed, stepping closer, her head moving back and forth like a hypnotized snake to take in every ounce of me. I swallowed.

"It's more of a block of related information, really," I breathed, wondering whether my life would be passing by my eyes any time soon.

She smirked, pulling back. "I want a spell," she suddenly snapped.

What kind of spell? Did I know how to do a spell? "Erm, what kind o—?"

"An unbinding. I need you to break a spell, rather." She seemed to be getting bored at a rapidly increasing pace.

"And you need me to do it bec—?"

"Because I am not Kashshaptu," she snapped.

"Not wha—?"

"A witch. Does the girl have time for you to ask these questions?" she hissed.

I winced. "Done," I sighed, a little bewildered. I'd more been expecting to sign my soul away or end bleeding to death on the floor, not to have to say a rhyme.

"Goody," she chirped, turning without her feet seeming to touch the ground, two fingers indicating for me to follow her. Had she just said 'goody'? I smirked.

Anna led me through a curtained opening set into the concrete wall right behind where she'd been sprawled. The moment we passed the threshold it was like someone had clamped a two-feet-wide concrete block over the door, not a few centimetres of worn wool, the way the music just died. The back was just a mass of interlocked rooms, all of whose doors slammed shut as I went by, like automatic lights, making me jump a little each time. Was it magic? More bouncers? Anna? Either way, it was like a trip to Disney's haunted house.

Anna continued down a set of concrete steps, finally sending a chipped, baby-blue painted iron door right back with just a flick of her wrist. It probably had been her, then. The inside was what looked like what had once been a storage area, maybe. The floor was bare concrete, and the walls bare, thin iron scaffolding that did nothing to keep the cold away. A lone, dusty light bulb flickered progressively as she approached it.

"What are—?"

She held up one finger, silencing me instantly. She spun on her spiked heels, locking gazes with me for scarcely a heartbeat. My stomach fell. Her face was alight with something along the line of triumph; luminescent, radiant triumph. She swung one elongated toned arm out to her side. A plastic bucket, which had been on the other side of the room, flew into the air following her actions perfectly, as if an invisible string were attached from it to her. The bucket sprayed water everywhere, gathering unnaturally in a puddle where her feet were planted on the concrete. The next instant her hand and head shot straight up and backwards toward the light bulb hanging above, which snapped off from where it had been attached, spinning to the floor and smashing right into the shallow puddle of spilt water. I yelped, jumping back as fire and sparks flew feet into the air while water and electricity mixed. Anna seemed unfazed by the flames rippling against her skin. She spread her hands over the gathering of free electricity swirling beneath her in the spilt pool of water. It wasn't going to ground, or dissipating, or even running into Anna, but it seemed to be building at Anna's command until I could hear the static discharge crackling in the air and inside my ears, like that sugar pop candy all kids eat and then regret after the subsequent five trips to the dentist.

"Hmmm, where is the little one?" Anna hissed, concentrating intently on the radiating swamp of charged embers at her feet. She smiled cruelly, one hand rising slowly above the other, fingers drawn together, pulling a string puppet of blue sparks up from the ground. I gaped as a giant angel of blue and silver crackling lines spun around in the energy, growing, building until it was the size of a small van, dominating the entire room until I had to shrink back against a wall to stop my eyebrows getting singed. It turned left and right, dancing wildly in the air, wings spread, a human face like that of a Grecian sculpture, eyes closed and tranquil. It was only when it flipped full frontal from my vantage point that I realized with a sharp intake of break that what I'd thought was the figure of an angel wasn't anything like that. A gruesome mixture of birds wings and talons ascending to the bare upper half of a woman, flexing back and forth in mid-air as if dancing to some music only it could hear.

"What holds the girl Delia is a harpy," Anna snarled, flicking her hand back, the image and the electricity flooding to earth instantly, the room, which had lost all source of light, folding away into a dim grey gloom cast by the cracks in the flimsy walls and roof where moonlight filtered in.

"The only way to banish a harpy is for one of the rank of at least high priest to separate their energies, and pray the girl's soul has not been engulfed beyond the point of saving," she drawled, stepping through the water and striding over to me, her hand held out towards me. She stopped about a foot away, a thick piece of folded white parchment held out to me. "Do it now," she hissed.

My eyebrows shot up as I tentatively took the paper from her. "You had it already?"

She smirked the strangest of challenges in the way she tilted her chin as she looked at me, daring me to put two and two together.. "It's in the blood, you see. Your mother never learnt either. You're just the pawns. We" – she spread her arms wide – "are the board."

I scowled at her, repulsed. "Never. Never talk of my mother, Anna. I swear to you, one day, you'll understand your part isn't quite as significant as you think it is. *You* are a player, Anna. And any piece can be captured by a pawn."

She looked at me for the first time with something I had the great pleasure of interpreting as hatred. Good. I could assure her the feeling was mutual.

I unfolded the expensive white parchment. "All I have to do is read this?" I hissed through gritted teeth. The tiniest inclination of her head was all I was going to get. "Blood to blood this command rises, life spirit my will devises, release now your hold, your protection, forever severing your connection." As the last syllable left my lips, Anna spun round, hurtling something square and flat into the fading flames in the middle of the room. My chest constricted. I had no idea what I'd just done, but the swell of emotion that constricted inside me felt like I'd just suffered a loss I had no way of putting a face to.

"What was that?" I asked, a little shakier than I would have liked.

Anna turned her back on me, holding herself stiffly as she started, heading for the door.

"I don't think you'll have to worry about that," she called over her shoulder. "You see, you won't be alive long enough. Well, you *may* be. For your sake I hope he kills you quickly." She paused, her eyes darting to something at the other side of the room. "Have fun, son," she whispered.

"Wait! We had a deal," I screamed after her as she went through the door.

"And it was fulfilled. You said nothing about getting out of this building alive afterward." She slammed the door closed, the sound of metal sliding rapidly against metal indicating the sound of the deadbolt.

I blinked hard, begging my eyes to adjust better to the darkness. Two small beady yellow orbs watched me from the corner. Sepsu. I swallowed, backing up into the darkness, but my legs failed me, my kneecaps locking involuntarily. I shrieked in surprise as I toppled straight back, my head ringing as it hit the hard concrete floor.

"Your people are not very forgiving, are they?" The hiss resonated through the room. I tried to kick my legs, but they were lead blocks attached to my hips, heavy and totally immobile. "You see, I've been doing my research. Have you been taught what they did to witches in your world. I found it most... inspiring." There was a flash of blazing light from where Anna had performed her magic, casting Sepsu as a hovering shadowy figure just behind it.

"I'm not a witch, Sepsu, I'm an atheist; or at least I'm trying to be. It's difficult these days to believe in nothing," I called out over the sputtering, infuriated flames, hungry and growing to the ceiling, eager for their feed.

"Do stop fighting, Khyle. You'll only speed the process up." The sound of his words mixed so well with the hissing of the now crackling flames it was unnerving.

"Process?" I whispered to myself, horrified. He was right: my hips had gone dead on me. Even my ribs felt like some invisible force was pressing in on them, squeezing the muscles into ridged lumps around my bones.

"Where was I? Ah, yes, hanging, drowning, spiked headlocks, induced insomnia. All are promising, no? I thought we'd start with burning." I gasped as my neck muscles strained, closing my throat, my whole body forced, yielding, to a stiff board flat on the floor. "You see, Khyle, I am an enormously obedient servant of our master, and you obstructed my ability to fulfil his preliminary requirements. So..." There was the softest brush of feet nearby, before a dreadful, suffocating, constricting feeling filled my throat. "I thought you may like to pay penance in a manner... traditional to your own and your people." He tilted his head, bending over me, his perfectly straight, almost stone-like boyish features bare of all emotion as he stared, barely an inch from me, into my eyes. "Would you like that?" he breathed. His breath smelt rancid.

I wanted to tell him to go and screw himself, but obviously I was a tad disadvantaged. He was smaller than me, his bones thin, delicate, and childlike, but like lifting a feather he flung me so high in the air I felt my back hit the iron-beamed ceiling, and then hit the floor face-on, tasting the coppery heat of blood running across my lips. Worse than that, I'd landed less than a foot away from the raging fire, the heat reminding me uncomfortably of the scene with Mark in the lake, which felt like a lifetime and a half ago. Sepsu twisted his wrist and my body was flung back up, hovering in mid-air.

"Do you want to know what the breeze in my world feels like, Khyle?" he whispered softly, almost lovingly, into my ear.

I felt furious tears mixing with the blood as very slowly, just with the tiniest of twists of his wrist, he moved face-on into the flames, smoke already brushing up against my watery eyes, ash filling my nostrils and mouth, my body and brain desperately demanding of me to convulse, but I couldn't.

I hoped they'd find a way to save Delia.

There was thunder from outside. Had it started raining? I wished it would rain in here. Wait! That wasn't thunder; it wouldn't last that long, and besides, I knew that sound. That was, that was... Zean's sputtering engine. It didn't matter. I screamed out as the first tendril of heat tickled my stomach, the smell of burning cotton mixing in the air. Next it would be burning flesh.

There was an eruption from the other side of the room, pieces of wood and plastic and shards of iron flying over the flames, some brushing my already agonized skin. I heard something like a mangled cry, and then I was falling straight into the flames, not slowly any more but… Arms wrapped around my waist, catching my falling body in mid-air.

I hit the ground flat on my back, my head ringing once again. I raised my palm to massage it, and then realized I'd just raised my arm.

"Khyle! Bloody hell, girl, talk to me, open your eyelashes!"

My eyes snapped open: Zean's long smooth face, his hair messed and hanging in unkempt greasy tendrils down his flushed cheeks.

"Oh my God, Zean!" I cried, clamping my arms around his pyjama-clad self. "I thought I was dead." I sobbed into his shoulder.

Zean pulled me up in his arms, almost carrying me. "Nah, couldn't let that happen. I told you, you owe me rent, girl," he mocked, his eye looking wide across the room. I followed his gaze, my heart immediately kicking off on its marathon race. Mark had Sepsu around the neck, his fingers ripping slowly through flesh and sinew, literally tearing him apart. I gasped, burying my face in Zean's shoulder. As Zean kept walking, into the refreshingly cold morning air, I heard a mangled, gurgling scream.

"How is she?" Mark was there, instantly prising Zean's protective fingers away, his hands brushing my cheeks and pushing hair off my sweat- and ash-mangled forehead. I looked up at him. The whole of his face was filled with nothing but sincere worry. Zean pulled me back a little, glaring at him. Mark didn't like the fact that Zean was pulling me away from him, I guessed, because he responded, not with a glare, but a full-out animal throaty growl, his teeth bared. Zean looked as if he'd just been hit, but held his ground.

"Please, not here. We need to get to Delia," I choked, my voice raspy from pain and clogged ash. Zean nodded, but Mark looked like he'd quite happily waste a moment to rip Zean to a few zillion -pieces just for the closure. "Mark," I whispered, unable to bring my voice any higher. His eyes met mine, and he pulled back, though reluctantly, from Zean, taking me around the waist and lifting me almost off the ground, entirely effortlessly. Zean didn't relinquish his hold. I felt like a chew toy between two puppies. If I hadn't really needed someone's help I would have shaken them both off and told them to grow up.

Zean's battered car was standing looking abused with the hood collapsed inwards and little tendrils of smoke rising from the engine. The screen was cracked, and glass had splintered and spilled inside onto the dash. Zean took one look and forgot all about me, groaning and swearing under his breath like someone had taken his whole purpose in life and driven it through a warehouse wall. Oh, wait, they had; that was his car.

"You effing arsehole, look what you've done, you kidnapped me then towed my baby!" he shouted at Mark as Mark carried on, now Zean had relinquished his hold, fully carrying me and striding fast to the end of the alley outside.

"Would you prefer to have charred Khyle?" he said, bored.

"No, but—" Zean began.

"And your car was pretty fucked anyway. I wasn't going to drive *mine* through *there*." He flashed no one in particular a grin at a personal joke at that thought.

"Zean, hurry up, they'll be coming," I cried as Mark loaded me into his car, jumping into the front seat and starting the engine, about to speed off just as Zean yanked the back door open, lunging himself in as the car climbed to thirty. "What are you doing here?" I asked, not sure where to start inspecting the damage first. I had a nose bleed; I didn't think it was hurting enough to be broken. Mark shrugged.

"Midnight snack," he said bluntly.

I saw Zean repulsively cringe in the backseat. "Did you get what you needed for Delia?" he asked me, leaning over the back seat, and tearing off the rim of his pyjama shirt. "Put that on the back of your head; you're bleeding. As much as I'd love you to cause a nice dry cleaning bill for this prat, I don't think you can lose much more blood."

I murmured "Thanks," trying to ignore the glares they kept throwing each other. I was scared for Zean if he kept that up. I knew Mark would only find it amusing for so long.

"Yeah, it's called a harpy," I said, choked.

"Harpy? That's Greek mythology, right? Wronged women or something; turn into hideous monsters? Reckon could be an ex of mine?"

I laughed, which was a bad idea because it turned into a violent, rib-shaking cough. Mark shot me a look something like a panicked glare. Jeez, he really didn't know how to do anything but glare, huh?

"Yes, that's just one of the many ancient civilizations who tried to warn your sorry selves of the remnants left over after the last Lexis–anti-Lexis alignment. They're common in Sakhush when a woman can't fulfil her duties." He waved a hand, like saying when a kid was rebellious they got expelled from school.

"Her duties?" I croaked hoarsely.

Mark took a deep breath as if he could see the conversation that was coming and would rather avoid it.

"Yes; was strong enough for the warrior trials; couldn't please her man properly; fulfil the female's soul duties. They went for punishment, one of which is to be transformed from a beauty to a hideous monster. Women are rather second to males where I come from. They either do their job or they're disposed of." Both me and Zean stared at him, gaping; horrified. He glanced at us, drawing a breath through his teeth, a pained look on his face. "I didn't say it was right… exactly." He'd tried but failed to clear the air.

"Exactly?" Zean cried. I hit him in the ribs, unwilling to go into this at this particular moment.

"Well, come on, Zean, it makes sense. Since women are so superior in this world, then maybe in the, like, *opposite* world… " I joked a little.

Zean snorted. "Yeah. You keep telling yourself that. Women think they're superior," he shot back, nodding sarcastically.

"Men just like an easy life," Mark sighed under his breath.

"Yeah." Zean nodded, exaggeratedly.

"Oh, well, it's nice to know you guys have found common ground," I drawled. "Can we get back on track please? She said, like, something about separating energies, high priest status? Do you reckon anyone at Nomas has that or can do that?"

Zean shrugged, looking helpless. Mark glanced at me, lips pursed.

"What?" I asked, forebodingly.

Mark shrugged. "I can." His voice was totally devoid of all emotion.

Zean narrowed his eyes, opening his mouth, no doubt to say something derogatory. I put two fingers on his lips before he could. "Would you, eh, help? If no one else can," I blurted out awkwardly.

Mark was silent for a moment and then said in a strained voice, "For you?" Zean's eyebrows shot up.

"Yes. Okay, for me," I sighed.

I saw that familiar twitching muscle in his jaw. "Of course, it's without question," he breathed, sounding a little hurt.

"Well, don't put yourself out, like, mate," Zean spat cynically, slumping back in the rear seat.

"Harpies are hierarchical creatures, not your average dimensional hitchhiker. It's not a simple spiritual separation," Mark snarled.

I frowned. "But Ross said it would have to be a lower-class creature-thingy for Delia to have held on as long as she had."

"Well, you see, harpies are assigned as guards to the spirituals such as Ti Ilu. It's never been heard of, as far as I know, for one to leave a guarding post," he thought out loud.

I followed him. "Could she, eh, it, be a bodyguard for, say, Ventram if he's the Ti Ilu?"

"The Ti what?" Zean chimed in.

"All-powerful human god for their world. That's what they wanted Delia for before, to bring him through," I clarified.

Mark kept his eyes intent on the road. "Possibly," he finally muttered, strained, "and if they don't leave their wards, then…?"

There was silence and then Zean finally groaned from the back seat.

"Daddy's a-knocking."

Chapter Nineteen

"Only Miss Exeter has clearance, I'm afraid."

The young boy was still on guard at the gate and as stubborn as I feared he might be. Zean climbed from the back seat, putting an arm around the guy's shoulder.

"Look, a friend of ours is in there, and she's possessed and dying and we all need to get in to knock the *hell* outta her. Now, I'm sure there's something you can do." Zean folded a twenty, patting it down in the boy's combo jacket. I cringed, groaning and leaning back in the seat. Mark snorted, clearly enjoying the display.

"Sir, you're aware bribery is a crime," the boy chirped, pulling the twenty from his jacket pocket. We really didn't have time for this, starting to feel desperate. Mark unclipped his seat belt, jumping from the car.

"Yes, well, I, well, that, not, eh," Zean stammered.

Mark's arm shot out in a perfect clean swipe, colliding with the boy's chin, the boy slumping to the floor instantly. Zean jumped back. "Bribery might be a crime, but assault's a bigger one," he sneered at Mark.

Mark shrugged, opening the door for me and pulling me out in a gentle but firm grip. "I am truly terrified at the prospect," he droned, bored.

The gate was hanging loose, thank God, so we could make our way inside fairly easily for a place that was meant to be government secure. Loraline's bowed head shot up like a bullet just as we entered the door, her red-rimmed eyes blazing to life as she caught sight of Mark.

"What in the world is he—?"

"Shut it, Loraline, he's here to help. We know what's got hold of Delia. It's called a harpy."

"A harpy? Not possible." Ross swung after us through the double entrance door followed by Christ and three armed military personnel. I gulped.

"I'm here to escort you gentlemen out," the largest of the men (though a good foot shorter than Mark; even Zean rivalled him in height) said in a clipped, stern voice.

"How is she?" I asked, rushing over to Delia's side.

Actions spoke louder than words. Eliza was sitting stock still, her face bare as if she'd finally retreated to a level of numbness to save herself from any more pain. James's hand was on her shoulder, silent tears rolling down his plump cheeks. Delia was flat on her back, staring up at the ceiling, her eyes blank, her body twitching spastically.

"Her heart rate's at sixty. She has minutes," Loraline whispered brokenly in my ear.

"Well, she won't do if you believe me and let him" – I shot a finger over at Mark – "help! Look, I know it can't be a harpy, it shouldn't be a harpy, but, well, I just almost got flambéed to discover that the impossibility was actually, who knew, possible! Now you can arrest him for assault, murder, breaking and entering, petty bribery, I don't care, but first give him ten bloody minutes," I cried, finding just enough strength to add a stamped foot. A few shot glares, and there was some arm waving before I slumped down onto a hospital bed of my own, feeling faint.

Mark didn't wait for anyone to respond, shrugging off his coat and covering the distance from the door to Delia in three long strides. I couldn't help it, but every move, every time a muscle on his shoulders flexed under his cotton shirt, or his eyes narrowed or sought mine, I caught it. Like I was a satellite built just to monitor his every move, I lied to myself, putting it down to fear and cautiousness, but really I could feel that just having him here in the same room meant we could save Delia. He rolled each of her sleeves up, absently, his eyes, searching Delia's face, narrowed by concentration. He ran his fingers over her forehead, hovering over her wrist, tiny in comparison to his own, fingers finally pulling back her eyelids to look into the stark white globes of her eyes. He smirked.

"Hm, fun," he breathed bitterly. He straightened up, hands spread a foot above Delia's body. A minute passed; then another. I started to feel my thoughts go dry, forced to watch as Delia continued to slip away, and Mark stood as still and imposing as a dark-marbled Greek statue, carved and placed smack bang in the middle of the ward. Then he started singing, his voice deep and rich, the words a lattice of unintelligible syllables wavering in the air, crackling with a raw, dark power that seemed to match Mark's very essence.

Delia started flailing, her body distorting, arching up off the bed and then ricocheting backwards again, a rag doll on strings. Her sharp-angled jaw sprang open, her mouth gaping wide and growing even wider still until large enough to fit a fist in. Her body gasped, sputtering and choking. Eliza whimpered in despair, but Loraline wasn't that far gone. She jumped to Mark's side.

"Stop it!" she shouted, her arms pulling at Mark's spread hands and having about as much effect as though he was really just a solid statue. But then, to my amazement, he didn't actually stop chanting, his eyelids flashing open, a crackling of liquid silver pools swirling

284

where his eyes had once been.

"Get me a generator," he growled, his voice strained.

I felt my breathing sapped up, sweat building on my forehead even as I heard scrambling, as Ross ordered the military men to go and do it. This was hurting him; I'd asked too much. Sweat beaded and ran down the side of his face into the crook of his neck, disappearing under the rim of his shirt, the tendons in his neck and forearms sticking up under his skin. I jumped up from the bed, pushing a surprised and a little hurt Loraline away to stand in her spot. "Tell me I can do something," I moaned, feeling like the weight of the world was crushing me to the floor.

Mark reclosed his eyes, his lips twitching ever so slightly at the corners.

"You are," he said, swallowing, as the doors were once again flung backwards, a black and grey monster of a generator being rolled in by two of the men.

Mark worked instantly, one hand shooting upwards, the choking Delia giving one last forward convulsion, droplets of blood spurting up and out over the sheets and speckling the ceiling. Mark slumped instantaneously, just as the generator started rumbling, bouncing up and down on its wheels as if it was coming to life; coming to life in a foul mood. I went to grab Mark in case he fell over, but it was he who had me under the arms, folding me to his chest like I was a child.

"I'm fine," I muttered to him.

"Consider for a moment that I'm not holding you for you." His voice was tight and dark, like the strain of what he'd just done was nothing compared to the strain it caused him to admit that he had something even resembling weakness. My eyelids fluttered, along with a feathery light brush of wings in my chest. Just the heat seeping through him to me was healing, every tension-riddled taut muscle uncoiling against my will, the burns easing their intense throbbing for just an instant.

And then I was hurled back to reality with the sounds of heated metal expanding and bursting, flying like low velocity bullets off the wall and ceiling. Mark shoved me down to the floor a little too harshly, making me wince. The rest of the room shrank to their knees too, arms over their heads. Jackson was on the other side of the bed, pressing his glasses deep into the crooked bump of his nose. "Energy to matter," I heard him whisper to himself, his eyes wide and transfixed on the rocking generator. Ross was bustling across the room, Christ shouting orders, but what they'd been I had no idea because, before the men could respond, or even Eliza could scream out, there was a flash of light like a miniature lightning bolt dancing on the spot where the generator had been. And the light particles began to gather together in clumps, building until they were more than just clumps of light, more solid, flexible... They'd become flesh.

As the light faded there was a bare instant of utter silence as each pair of eyes processed the thing crouched in the middle of the room. Wings, clawed hands attached, spread out in front of it as predatory eyes watched us back. A pearly ivory colour and a texture somewhere between solid and a thick viscous liquid, a half-woman with long white silky straight hair gathering at her scaly, taloned hawk's feet, her face a masculine sculpture of hard angles, devoid of all femininity and certainly of anything resembling humanity. The arms were embedded within feathered wings that moved in ripples, more liquid than solid, and moved down into the rock-hard torso of a woman, the occasional feather sprouting through skin and slicked back. Its eyes were bulging golf balls, too large and too out of place for its otherwise human-like face.

Like I said, the silence lasted only a second. Bullets whined through the air, hitting the harpy with ringing, clinking sounds, and bouncing off like feathers floating above the ground, the thing literally sucking the momentum away. Delia had suddenly sprung bolt upright, grinning from ear to ear. Eliza had started off screaming and ended in hugging the already overly perky Delia like mad.

"Now that is so cool. Has anyone got a camera?" Delia cried, bouncing in the hospital bed; as the first round of bullets ran out and the men started immediately reloading.

"And they say my people are brutal," Mark muttered, scowling as he pushed my head back down, the chink and slide of metal signalling the upcoming fire.

"What do you expect? Them to pelt it with pillows? This is the military, after all," I muttered, kicking over the hospital bed, on its side this time so that I didn't have to use him as a shield. Just the feel of him close to me made my stomach twist in a mixture of disgust, hate and… well, let's leave it at those two, for my pride. "Oh, I forgot, your armies only know how to justify themselves when they're holding a firearm," I said to him. I could remember seeing him do a lot worse to people than shoot them. "And excuse us if we don't have a mouth full of daggers, brute force, and magical shit to fall back on. I'd call shooting men down a lot more humane than tearing their throats out and grinning down at them as they slowly bleed to death," I shouted, barely noticing as bullets began flying through the air again.

"We don't kill unless necessary. We're taught to calculate, keep one's honour, understand the decision you're making by killing. What are they taught? How to aim?" he roared back at me, the tendons in his neck sticking out. I leapt back, falling over behind the upturned bed. A bullet rocketed past my shoulder so fast I felt the air displacing, rippling. Mark scowled, grabbing my ankle and yanking me back. I scrambled to all fours.

"Don't give me that bull," I said. "If that's what you were taught, then you must have failed every class!" My yells were almost louder than the dying gunshots. Mark's mouth opened suddenly, for the first time showing an impressive array of sharply pointed teeth that curved inward and were half an inch long; but before he could either retaliate or bite some extremity of mine off, there was a high-pitched cry from above us. Delia? Oh my God! She hadn't seriously been sitting up there still, the dozy little...? I jumped up, quickly dodging Mark's shocked attempt to pull me back down, but Loraline had already leapt over, throwing the army men one of her prized glares as they held fire by one raised hand of a very angry-looking and put out Christ.

"Knock it off, you metal heads. Look at that thing!" Zean leapt across the room, circling the still-crouching, utterly unfazed harpy to get to Delia who was sobbing from a scratched shoulder. It seemed like a hell of an anti-climax to get upset about *that* after everything she'd been through recently. Christ barked something, and three of the personnel ran from the room, two others still perched ready to fire useless bullets.

"Who are you, harpy? And what is your purpose here?" Christ's voice was practised, stiff, as though this was not the first time he'd said these lines, and that they were being said more to stall or out of protocol than any actual interest. The harpy ignored him like he wasn't there. Instead, its (her?) eyes had grown ever so slightly wider, staring directly behind me. I swerved. Mark had just stood up and was retrieving his coat, rubbing dust off it, made by the bullets slamming into the walls, with an extremely vexed look on his face. The harpy hesitated, and then lowered its eight-foot self onto one knee, head bowed.

"Maraknight, my Alal." Its voice was surprisingly feminine, but had an echo like the sound waves didn't quite know how to manifest in our dimension. Loraline's head shot up from Delia, eyes massive.

"Alal?" she half-screeched, half trembled. Hm, nice to know his reputation wasn't just a figment of my imagination.

Mark cringed. "Aralia. What a pleasure." The way he said it didn't sound like he was pleased; more disgusted or horrified, or just really, really bitter.

Aralia inclined her head. "I beg you, sire; it is mine. It has been many years. But of course your power is as recognisable as ever," she said to the floor.

"Ah, yes. I thought you came a bit easily. Curious, were we?" Mark said cynically, hanging his now grey-from-dust-particles coat over his arm and strolling over to her, placing one finger under her chin to tilt it back to eye contact like dealing with a child.

Aralia met his eyes, her own now wide with shock.

"You may meet my gaze. We are equals here," Mark muttered stiffly.

"What the fuck is this?" Christ shouted, bemused, from the door.

Both of them ignored him. Not the best idea: the man looked like he might explode from the indignity of someone with the nerve to ignore him. Aralia shook her stone-like head rapidly, long hair swishing out around her, landing in a perfect veil over one side of her face. "Never, Alal. I am forever your servant," she gushed, her gaze returning to the floor.

Mark groaned, exasperated. "Yes, I never get tired of hearing that. Exiled. You all seem to have forgotten. And no, Aralia, I believe you were promoted. To the Ti Ilu. Or was I misinformed of that honour?"

If sarcasm could kill, that one statement would have been a nuclear bomb, putting the sea of bullets lying dormant and bent on the floor to shame. Aralia looked as though she'd have done a lot not to answer, but something told me by the way her lips parted stiffly, almost painfully, that she was obliged to answer whether she wanted to or not.

"Correct, sire."

Mark cocked his head impatiently. "And you decided to take a holiday?" – that wicked grin moving in on his lips.

"I am needed," Aralia literally choked out, her eyes wide.

"What the hell?" Christ bellowed, striding over to Mark's side to peer down at Aralia, obviously unable to control himself a moment longer.

"Oh, excuse me. Christopher, Aralia; Aralia, Christopher. Christopher is a commander in an obscurely small section within a governmental organization called Nomas twelve. Aralia is bodyguard to the stars… or otherwise, me, most of my life, and apparently now my father," Mark put in dryly, eyes half closed.

Christ's face had swollen at the word *obscurely*. Once Mark had finished, he deflated. It was like watching a burst ruby-coloured balloon "Ti Ilu? She's needed here?" he seethed, cocking his weapon reflexively to load a fresh round.

"Well, no, not directly here." The dry note had evaporated further, to something worthy of the Sahara desert. Aralia's eyes were darting round efficiently to every crack in the room for an escape point, wings flexing involuntarily, ready to attack. She was either very desperate to get away from fear (which somehow, given her size or the sheer power behind her eyes, seemed unlikely to me), or she had somewhere far more pressing to be. Christ watched her like a hawk, his eyes narrowed and darting between her and the door where the men had vanished.

"Ti Ilu? That's the big bad guy from before, yeah?" Zean pitched in.

"Shut up, Zean," Loraline and Delia snapped together.

"What? I was just clarify—"

The doors to the ward burst open, Ross jumping in, throwing something out of his gloved hand and shouting, "They've tracked it. We have to go, Christ."

"Tracked what?" Zean mimicked my thoughts perfectly. Before Christ even went to answer there was a sizzling sound like bacon frying. The harpy froze, perfectly statuesque in mid-stance.

Ross smiled at me from across the room, gesturing for the three commandos to follow him, the full five men positioning themselves around the statue-like harpy, each grabbing a different angle and straining upwards, chests heaving back and forth as they tried to manoeuvre the enormous bulk out of the room.

"Sector fifty-three, sir?" the eldest, forty-or-so, crewcut man huffed at Christ, who gave a curt nod, not particularly interested. Ross came over to my side, picking up what he'd thrown out and handing it to me. I ran my thumb over the smooth-faced flat quartz crystal, watching in amazement as tiny flaws broke and reformed in its depths, ever changing.

"Energy traps. Literally sucked the consciousness right outta Bird Girl. Cool, huh? Got it from our psychic department. We're always creating neat little natural gadgets like this. I should take you down there sometime; you'd have a blast. Emotional incense, my own personal—"

"Ross, we don't have time." Christ shook his head, annoyed, striding to the door.

"Emotional incense?" Zean laughed, appearing beside me to take the crystal.

"Yeah, mate, brill aphrodisiac. I'll lend you some," Ross shouted over his shoulder.

"Wait! Where are you going?" I called after him, but he'd already gone.

I slumped onto Delia's bed. "Does it look like I need an aphrodisiac?" Zean sounded the most worried he had all night since I first brought his pyjama-clad arse down here. I rolled my eyes.

"Countless sleepless nights assure me… you need no help," I groaned, wrapping Delia in a hug.

"Well, what can I say…?" Zean shrugged smugly.

"You could admit it was porn," Mark sneered, ignoring the finger Zean shot him.

I shook my head. They were never going to stop. "How are you?" I muttered into Delia's pixie-spiked hair. She shrugged, bouncing a little as Loraline tried to put a bandage on her shoulder.

"Actually, I feel great, like I've been plugged in, on charge or something or, like, I'm on a high. I can't explain it!" she giggled, rosy-cheeked.

I cringed a little. "I can," I muttered to myself, ignoring Loraline's pointed look.

"What do you mean?"

"Nothing," I groaned putting my head between my knees. Everything was throbbing like I'd been beaten up repeatedly, starved for a week, and then beaten again for good measure. I knew exactly why Delia felt great; she was walking away with her energy plus mine, and I felt like mashed potato.

"What is that on your arm, K?" Zean pulled at my arm where the sleeve had slipped down. The cut I'd thrashed into myself so long ago was shining red and black, and looked Frankenstein-ish.

"Noth—" I began, but a painful grip was suddenly crushing my elbow. Mark pulled me to my feet to see it properly, his whole expression smouldering. Moving to my face, he grabbed my chin, tilting it backward as if trying to see up through my nostrils into my brain. I tugged away, but his grip was too strong.

"You idiot," he breathed. "How the hell are you still standing?"

"What this time?" I sighed, too drained to bother any more.

"You're human! You can't bloodlet to someo—. You didn't stop her!" he threw at Loraline, on fire with anger. Loraline pushed the seat back as she jumped up to look at Mark eye to eye.

"Have you met her? Was I supposed to strap her down? Because that's the only way I could have stopped her! It's your fault she knew anything about that anyway! What right did you have to show her those memories, my dear Alal?" she snarled, the last part bitterly, but there was a slight break which Mark read oh-so-efficiently as the fear that he knew ran through her veins like ice water.

I rested my head against poor bewildered Eliza's shoulder as she absently patted my hair, wondering whether I had enough strength to shut them both up, when Zean's voice, very serious and very loud, broke in.

"Shut up, both of you!" He had his phone pressed to his ear, his eyes narrowed, focused and staring right at me. He removed it, looked down at the keypad and handed it to me.

"Wh—?"

"I just dialled into the answer machine at home. There for you." There was such a stern concentration oozing off him that the room had grown still in anticipation. Hesitantly, confused, I held up the phone to my ear, thumbing the call button into our house phone. A clipped female voice told me we had eleven missed messages since only three hours ago. The first was Steve, barking at me because of the absence of my story on his desk; the second was a panicked female's voice.

"Miss Exeter? Hello, my name is Jane Symore. I'm a new secretary at St Matthew's. I'm afraid something terrible has happened. Your mother is missing. According to our records she hasn't been seen for the last two or so hours. We've contacted the police and I expect they will be in touch. Please, we'd like to call you in to discuss how dangerous she may be to herself and oth—"

I missed the rest of the call, feeling my breath become shallow, the air thickening around me, too heavy, too tight against my chest.

"Khyle!" Eliza exclaimed, cool hands pressing in on me even as I watched the world blink blissfully out. The last thing I felt was the acidic burn of bile as it rose in my throat. But, thankfully, my body clearly didn't have the energy left to vomit. I faded.

★ ★ ★

The speckled green-and-white tiled ceiling blurred in front of my eyes as I came to, shaky, hot, and dizzy. My whole body felt awful beyond anything I'd ever imagined.

"Khyle," I heard Loraline gasp beside me. I groaned, trying to prop myself up on the hard hospital bed. I'd been on one too many hospital beds lately.

"What happened?" I moaned, trying to raise a hand to my forehead. Loraline stilled my efforts, shaking her head at me to not bother.

"You fainted out of utter exhaustion," she seethed, more pissed off than worried.

"How long?"

"A couple of hours," she sighed. "We're pumping you up with saline and glucose. Demon boy here wanted to go all vampiric on us and let you drink his blood, but… "

Zean was sitting by my other side looking grossed-out and censorious. Mark was pacing about, glaring at everyone at the end of the bed.

"This is not going to work. She needs raw energy. Look at her," he growled through gritted teeth.

Alarm bells burst into life in my head, my gaze shooting down to my arms where two tubes had been injected and taped into my skin. Animal instinct, reflexive and over-powerful, exploded. I clawed at the tubes, Zean acting too slowly as I ripped them out, screaming in pain as blood burst from the messy tears, and I scrambled up, almost knocking Loraline on the floor away from the bed. My teeth gritted as I pressed my hand over the gaping hole, a doctor rushing across the room, white coat flapping behind him.

"Are you mad?" Loraline gasped.

The doctor, who looked more military than medical, with bulky muscle and a choppy ginger crewcut, grabbed my arm.

"Miss Exeter, what on earth are you—?"

"Are you all mad! You will never have any of those fucking things attached to me again. I was helpless, and you just start shooting drugs through me," I cried, utterly hysterical, backing a few feet away from the doctor. Mark stepped between me and him, drawing himself to his full height. Just for a moment I felt like falling to my knees and thanking him just for existence.

"K, we had, like, no choice. You were dying," Zean moaned, looking a touch guilty. He had no idea just how much he should be feeling guilty about.

"Better dead than that," I cried, actual tears spilling out over my cheeks. But then my memory started coming back to me. "Oh my God, my deadline," I cried again, reaching a whole new level of hysteria. I'd got the thing written, and everything.

Zean shook his head. "There's more important things than your deadline, girl. Your mother?"

Oh, no. He was right. Mum. "What were the other messages?" I asked, quickly getting control of myself.

"More from the clinic, a couple from the police, even one from Green. She's under the impression this twat kidnapped her."

"If only he had, I think this could be a lot worse than that," I moaned, gripping hold of an ECG to steady myself from swaying.

Mum was their biggest link, but why now? Why not kidnap her just any time? They'd had a good eight years to do so. "Where's Delia?" I asked, absently staring at the little bruised hole in my arm.

"Eliza took her home. She was given the all clear by the docs—"

"Unlike yourself," the ginger doctor broke in.

"Yeah, well, I don't think Eliza wanted her to have much to do with this, at least not for today anyway. Besides, Delia was so hyped up it was exhausting. What do you mean, worse?" Zean continued.

I shook my head. "I don't have time to expl—"

"Make time." Zean cut me off bluntly, crossing his arms in a move I'd seen him do on countless occasions when we were kids. There would be no moving him from that spot until he got what he wanted. I didn't want to go into it.

"We need to find her," I sighed to myself, holding on tighter to the ECG as my legs started to become rubber below me. "Erm, my mother worked with Nomas when she was younger. She got caught up in the whole witchy thing, and for some reason the, erm, other side is hell-bent on having her be the one the Ti Ilu uses to get through, or something. That's all you're getting at the moment, now we have a harpy bodyguard, a vanished Nomas, and my mother's gone. We. Need. To. Find. Her."

The air was starting to feel heavy again, pressing in on me and slowing my motions like I was wading through porridge. "You think that's where they went?" Loraline stated, chewing her bottom lip. I wasn't sure whether I nodded or shook my head, but they continued anyway.

"We've got no way of finding them. Highly Classified, remember?" Zean added.

They'd taken all that very well. They must have been getting used to the bizarre.

"Maybe we shouldn't," said Loraline. "It's their job to handle it. And look at Khyle. She's not exactly up for a fight. She's not exactly up for standing."

So much for taking it well.

"Loraline, this is my mother. You think I'm going to sit back and let them do God knows what to her?"

"Well, you were happy to have nothing to do with her a couple of weeks ago," she sighed in a tiny voice.

"Well, that was before I remembered the woman she was before they stole that from me, so she's not going to die and, by my life, they're going to pay, whether classified or not, up for a fight or not!" I bellowed, swaying right off my feet just at the effort I'd exerted.

I hit a burning hot brick wall of lean velvety muscle. "Well, sod this," I heard Mark mutter, and then there was a heavy push on my chest like a brick being pressed against my ribs. Liquid warmth leaked in through the weight, easing its way like syrup through the rib-bones over my heart, a magnetic pull jumping through me like a painless electric shock, my body lurching forward. I stumbled a little.

"I told you not to touch her!" said Loraline.

"I was barely connected for five seconds. What precisely are you afraid I'll do to her, woman?"

Only Mark could sound that livid. I steadied myself, blinking quickly. The weight was gone completely; in fact, I felt utterly light. No, not light. High. Totally high like an endocrine rush or something. I was tingling pleasantly, brilliantly, from the neck downwards. I spun around.

"Wait. Aralia. If they've got my Mum so they can bring Ti Ilu through, and Aralia wants to get to him, then, well, we have a way of finding her." I burst my brain coming to life like a torch with a new battery.

"You want to release a governmentally trapped harpy to lead us to the demon of hell on the off-chance that it might lead us to your estranged mother?" Zean laughed. "Well, what a way to spend my weekend! How we gonna break her out?" He gave a mock-diabolical laugh. Loraline rolled her eyes. Mark just looked at him, one eyebrow raised as if he just could not understand Zean at all.

"This is a government-held building. There's no way. Just no way. And besides, she's got that stunning charm, or whatever, on her," Loraline gushed in a hushed voice, pulling us towards her and shooting the eavesdropping doctor a worried look.

I scanned the floor, bending down to pick up the creamy translucent stone from just behind the wheel of the hospital bed I'd been collapsed by. "Not a problem. I've got this. It did it; it should undo it, right? Can't be rocket science," I whispered, searching pair of eyes after pair of eyes, looking for a bit of encouragement. Zean looked nonplussed, Loraline disapproving and sceptical. The only pair of eyes that held onto mine with a fierceness and understanding was the pair I didn't want to. Mark smiled a little.

"Give me the stone. I'll find Aralia. You three go get a car; not mine!" He went to snatch the stone, but I pulled it away. He smirked a little more. I knew my reflexes were awful, but what was more was I'd seen his, first-hand. He was letting me win every now and then to save my ego. That very realization was enough to dent my ego like Zean's car's hood.

"What makes you think you're going alone? This is too important, and I don't trust you enough. I'm coming with you," I hissed, a little over-prickly, so it came out more prim and proper schoolgirl getting her own way. Mark cocked his head to the side, snatching for the stone so quickly I only felt the air as his hand pulled it from my grasp. He tossed it a couple of times in the air, not dropping my gaze.

Arrogant bastard.

"How are you even going to get to her? I know from practice this place has armed guards at every turn, not to mentioned key-card access, plus you're going around fainting." Only Loraline could make a whisper sound like the loudest shout of anger known to mankind.

"Actually, I feel great."

Loraline's eyes fluttered closed, disgusted. "I am sure you do." She sounded revolted, too. I rolled my eyes. I was getting very tired of whatever her problem was.

"And…" I continued as if she hadn't said anything, exchanging a mutually knowing look with Mark, "I don't think you want to know just how we are going to get to Aralia." I couldn't keep the hint of dread from my voice. Mark gave the crystal one last throw into the air, and then, swinging his whole body around in a swirl of colour, lumbered the doctor one so that this two-hundred-pound muscleman fell crumpled like a tissue on the floor.

Mark adjusted his sleeves absently. "Get a car. One that can handle being driven roughly, and preferably through a wall, unlike other pieces of scrap metal I've been forced to navigate recently." He added the last bit specifically to watch the fire rise in Zean's eyes. The look of satisfaction on Mark when Zean went to spit out some comeback was so obvious it was borderline childish. I clamped a hand over Zean's mouth.

"Kill him later. I'll be happy to help."

Chapter Twenty

"Right, so how are we going to find Aralia?" I breathed, trying to make my footsteps on the tiled floor as quiet as possible. Mark was trudging along looking at doors, not even bothering to keep an eye on bumping into anyone. Which was bound to happen eventually; an armed someone. Mark ignored me, stopping dead in his tracks as the first sound of heavy echoing footsteps came from up ahead.

"Finally," he muttered, glancing around.

"Finally! Are you mad? We don't *want* a confrontation," I seethed under my breath, considering hitting him just to knock some sense into that dense… He rolled his eyes, grabbing my arm and flinging me sideways. I stumbled through a door, a quick glance around and the very eye-catching line of urinals telling me where I'd been flung into. Mark came in behind me.

"Get in there." He nodded his head towards one of the cubicles. I wrinkled my nose. Male lavatories… How do they make them smell quite so truly disgusting?

"You are kidding," I groaned. He clearly wasn't, as he pushed me inside just as I heard the swinging of the lavatory door, and deep male voices.

"Hey, mate, what you doing here? Visitors' lavatories are next to the hospital," came a heavy Lancastrian accent.

"Yeah, they're unisex. What do you think I'm doing in here?" Mark bit back as I heard someone walking outside the door, and then the sounds of zippers. I cringed, trying to restrain the urge to knock myself unconscious against the toilet seat. Someone laughed.

"Too many women at that time of the month, huh?" the Lancastrian joked, followed by another guy's laughter. I could hear one of them actually *going* to the toilet. I was going to die of heat exhaustion from excessive blushing. So men really did talk as they lined up against the wall. Who knew?

"Those women; you'd think it was constantly the time of the month. Bloody excuse if you ask me." Mark fitted his tone perfectly to the others as if he was just another lad joking around or something. What? He was paying for that particular remark. I wasn't the least bit a drama queen. Maybe Loraline, but not me.

"Ah, escape," came a new voice that sounded younger than the other.

"No, well, not mine anyway," Mark sighed.

There was a moment of confused silence and then I heard the distinct thuds of fists colliding. One of them gave an already muffled yell and then I heard the crumpled sounds of bodies hitting the floor.

I gasped, wondering whether he was actually planning on murdering everyone we came across, until we somehow miraculously came across Aralia! I flung back the cubical door only to be confronted by one fully naked man and one half-naked as Mark knelt by them, stripping off clothes. I screeched, slamming the door back shut.

"What are you doing?" I cried, feeling my face burn. I could hear outright snorting with laughter outside. A bundle of clothes flew over the cubical door, landing in a pile on the grimy bathroom floor.

"Do you want this to be easy, or do you want to be recognised and arrested within ten minutes?" came Mark's dry voice, as I heard the sounds of unzipping and clothes being thrown carelessly away. I sighed, nose wrinkled, and pulled on a sweaty long-sleeved grey T-shirt and khaki jacket, trying to ignore that musky 'old socks' guy smell as best I could. I was just about to cry out for a belt after finding that the trousers fell right off the moment I pulled them up, when a leather strap was flung so hard over the door that it slapped my shoulder like a whip. "Ow!" I hissed, buckling up and flinging open the door.

Mark glanced up at me, tying a heavy brown leather bootlace, and sucked his cheeks in to stop himself from laughing and the predictable slap it would get him.

"What?" I hissed.

"You look like a kid playing dress-up but found her father's rather than her mother's wardrobe." He got up, pulling a machine-gun over his shoulder and already walking out of the bathroom at a stride. I had to practically run to keep up with him.

"Hey, this was your idea," I scowled, more than just a little embarrassed.

"Try not to walk like that," he moaned, still walking at an inhuman pace.

"Like what?" I choked between gasps for breath.

"Like a girl. Try slouching or something."

"Really? I thought slouching was one art I'd perfected," I muttered.

Mark looked at me, shaking his head a little. "You'd be surprised how feminine you are."

I felt myself blush a little deeper. "Well, why don't you stop walking like an arrogant arse with a pole up his rear end and a fire behind him," I spat defensively. He slowed a little, lips pursed. I could really easily hate him. "How do we know where we're going?" I asked him.

"I just spent twenty minutes using most of my mental and spiritual strength extracting Aralia's life energy from Delia's. I'm *fairly* familiar with her energy pattern; I can sense her."

He sounded a little exasperated, sharply turning a corner and coming face to face with a wide, black iron, double door. He lightly brushed his fingers over the security pad which let off a little whimpering spark, the doors falling open instantly. My eyebrows shot up. I hoped these little tricks of his would take some time for anyone else of his kind coming through or, honestly, I believed we may well be screwed in the whole fight for survival thing.

"If it was such a drag saving her, why did you?"

There was no room inside; just a flight of narrow iron stairs leading straight down, and a flickering of fluorescent light bulbs stuck into the walls.

"Would watching Delia being consumed from the inside out have given you much pleasure, Khyle?"

"Of course not!"

"Then what else do you need to ask? I did what I had to, to stop you from suffering."

I shook my head, almost missing a step. He grabbed my shoulder, sighing as he pulled me back like a clumsy child. I shook him off. "I remember a time when all you wanted was for me to suffer."

"Welcome to the present," Mark whispered in my ear darkly as he pushed past me at the end of the staircase.

We'd walked right into what at first glance resembled a dark alley of massive shop windows, illuminated from the inside out, but as I rushed after the fast-marching Mark I realized it was actually a long narrow walkway of glass-fronted cages, the things trapped inside skulking back from the low lights set at the bottom of the glass.

"Are they hiding from the light?" My pitch had fallen to barely a whisper, afraid to disturb whatever was behind the barriers. I saw Mark's head turn a little, but he didn't fully look over. Instead he aimed the gun he was holding, and lunged it at one of the glasses. I braced myself, waiting for the smash of splintered glass and the ringing of alarm sirens, but instead the gun was held in mid-air, a crackle and pop of electricity keeping it suspended there for a moment before dropping the now melted, destroyed lump of metal to the floor, little streams of smoke rising above it.

"No. No, I think it's quite safe to say it's not the *light* they're avoiding." Mark continued forward while I stood staring wide-eyed at the chunk of metal.

The real question was, what on earth could be trapped in those cages that needed that kind of force to keep it in? Regaining myself, I increased my pace after Mark who'd stopped midway, looking into a cage, absently tossing Ross's quartz crystal up and down in the air. I stopped beside him. There behind the glass was the statue which was Aralia, her face perfectly frozen from the moment Ross's crystal had skimmed her clawed talons.

"What's the matter?"

Mark was looking at her with something other than his usual callous calculating stare. He turned his chin away from me, one eyebrow raised.

"I was there when Aralia underwent her ascension," he sighed.

"Ascension?" I asked tentatively.

"When she was turned. It was after you left. After you awakened… certain feelings within me." His voice was a low bitter snarl, but it didn't frighten me because I somehow knew it wasn't aimed at me. It was aimed at the people who'd done this to her, his people.

"And you felt sorry for her?" I turned to look at Aralia, wondering what she'd done, how she'd failed.

"No. Not pity. It was one of the first times I'd ever heard a woman scream and been able to feel an emotion conditioned out of me: sympathy. I didn't pity her, she didn't pity herself. Duty is duty where I come from. But I would have saved her."

"Why didn't you?"

Mark didn't answer for a moment, every inch of his face cold and tight with tension.

"Because I was imprisoned."

What he really meant was *I was being tortured and captured and humiliated because of you.* The truth was I didn't know whether to feel guilty or not. Nothing about the time I'd spent in his world had been voluntary, and the fact that I just existed was obviously not within my control, but Mark wasn't trying to make me feel guilty. I wasn't sure what he wanted me to feel, or anything he wanted from me for that matter.

"What do we do?" I wanted a change of subject.

Mark looked at the crystal in his hand. He was holding it so tightly I was wondering whether it would turn to powder in his palm.

"Stand back." He held the crystal up, a single, feathery stroke of his fingers turning it to a sand of clear minerals running, tumbling through the gaps between his fingers. There was a quick spark of light and then, just like that, Aralia blinked her eye, turning to Mark. She inclined her head in a small nod. "Go," said Mark. He looked like he'd frozen over from the memories, his face a blank mask.

Aralia inclined her head once more, her wings spreading, filling the cage like pearly, silvery-veined stage curtains.

"Wait," I whispered. Aralia, to my surprise, responded, tilting her back down, her wings falling an inch. "I need to know. Why my Mum? Why now does, eh" – I gasped in a little breath – "the Ti Ilu come through?"

Aralia's eyes weren't evil; they were, they were… surprised, curious.

"You are the daughter, the daughter she spoke of." Her voice was serene and gentle, and I could see the woman she may have been before they'd done this to her. "Protections needed to be lifted from her soul, protections given by this realm, by you. Only then could her soul and body be destroyed in the transversion."

Words rang in my head, echoing, and kicking my heart with each syllable. The spell Anna had made me cast, my lullaby that had trapped us both in Sakhush, had protected us like it was supposed to, just not in the right way: it had kept us both protected in the anti-Lexis. It had kept Mum protected and Anna had made me undo it.

"Khyle, if you want to get there in time—"

"I know. Tell her to go," I breathed, aching so hard with remorse, my voice trembled.

Mark nodded his head at her, and Aralia's wings broke loose, smashing into the glass. Electricity crackled and ran up and down her but she didn't seem to notice, turning perfectly still as though on an invisible revolving plate. She stared at the wall behind her, and in a deafening sparkling current her eyes lit up in a horrific blast of white light, and the sound of rock and cement exploding ricocheted through the hall, the very force of it knocking both me and Mark backwards against the wall. I looked up, shoving my hair away from my face, a cold night's air pushing, brushing against my cheeks. Mark jumped up, kicking rubble away just as a deafening whine and flashing red lights burst into life overhead. The alarm. Mark extended me a hand. The moment my fingers locked with his, he pulled me up so fast I almost stumbled right over again. The electric glass had shattered, Aralia effectively draining it straight from the mains to blow a hole in the wall the size of a small vehicle. Mark pulled us through, stumbling over rubble which was piled up to my knees.

We were on ground level, opening out into the back car park. A skidding screech of wheels broke into the mass of screeching from the captivity area behind us as a huge open-topped military-edition four-wheeler skidded to a halt in front of us, a stark white, nerve-wracked Loraline riding shotgun, both arms braced on the dash, and a beaming Zean up front looking like he'd found the perfect life partner on four wheels.

"What took you two so long? Come on, get a move on. The angelic statue's getting away. Fast," he added, as giddy as a schoolgirl who'd just got her first crush.

Climbing in was like trying to mount a horse. I had to actually take three steps, climbing up over the wheel and then throwing myself forward, falling crumpled onto the rough back seats. Zean hit the accelerator before Mark had properly got in, making him hurtle back about a foot, as bullets started flying and shouts sprang to life. I scrambled up, desperately grabbing the front of his shirt before he could fall overboard, and pulled us both down below the bench seats to avoid ricocheting bullets.

"Thanks," he breathed, his face barely an inch from mine.

"We even?"

A wicked smile crossed his face. "You would like that. Not even close," he teased, hauling himself up into the firing line to get to Zean. "Keep driving," he shouted at a now slightly deflated Zean.

The barbed wire fence was closed, and soldiers were taking their places in front of it, weapons raised. "Are you mad?" Loraline shrieked, twisting her arms over her head and looking away.

I swallowed. If they kept going, we risked being shot straight on or running over a load of innocent men just doing their jobs. If we stopped, we faced maybe a prison sentence and the loss of my mother whom I'd, in a way, already condemned to death. "Keep driving,"

I ordered Zean, channelling my self-hatred into that one statement.

The four-by-four hit the gates full-on, men jumping left and right to get out of the way without firing a single bullet more. There was a moment – a split instant where the gate bent backward, the four-by-four's wheels spinning furiously – that I thought we were going to be flipped backwards like a pancake, and all get crushed, just because Zean hadn't put the pedal to the metal hard enough. Then the gate weakened, broken, and the four-by-four took off, hitting one forty in barely two minutes, the world flying by as Zean attempted to navigate it down the country lanes. I sat back, breathing hard, the cold blasts of wind hitting me smack bang in the face, refreshing beyond belief.

"I think we've lost her," Loraline muttered, straining her thin elegant neck upwards to search the lightening sky.

"No, look there," Zean shouted excitedly, pointing up at the sky at a bird-shaped shadow, too large to be normal, skimming just below the clouds up ahead.

"She's beautiful," Loraline muttered, awed, and lost in some hidden world I didn't have any thought space left to wonder about.

"Alright, up. I'm taking over," Mark ordered sternly.

"What?" Zean exclaimed a little too high-pitched to be considered even remotely manly. "No way, this baby's mine," he almost stuttered, leaning his body forward as if trying to shield the steering wheel from Mark.

"Don't make me hurt you," Mark drawled, eyes narrowed.

I was vaguely aware of the continued bickering but I wasn't listening. I stared up at the early morning sky, the ghosts of pastel colours breaking through the deep blue, and that feel of dead cold and peace and the softness of the dew in the breeze. If we didn't hurry up, any chance of Mum ever feeling those things again, the wonders, these tiny beautiful things our world has just for us, devoid of Sakhush, she'd never feel again. She'd either be stuck for an eternity in a world where the breeze was like acidic flames, or might, would be destroyed, even. Just called into nothingness. Was there an afterlife to go through? Had anyone even asked these questions? The thing was, this whole new truth threw everything we believed or wanted to believe about our world into question.

A thought struck me. They must have known, surely. Was that why Anna had helped me so willingly? Why she had that look of success in her eyes when I had made the agreement? If so, that would have to mean that so much of what had happened from the moment Aralia had latched on to Delia would have set a series of events into sequence, predicted responses just so that they could get the person they had always wanted to have as a Ti Ilu channel through into our realm: my mother. And I had signed her death sentence, the one she'd spent years literally in hell, just to avoid. Or had she? I mean, she'd run, so maybe she hadn't wanted to save this world at all, but had just, via circumstance, ended up saving us and enduring eternal torment. Had she even been in eternal torment? Aralia had known her, which meant that even though I had been separated from her when I had been Sakhush, she was there and the thing could *see* her there. Was that because she was that much more powerful a soul, an energy source, than I had been?

I leant back into the seat, eyes squeezed close as I willed my mind to stop working. I had so many questions to get answered, so many frenzied, panicked questions to get answered, and no way of getting the answers I was so desperate for, not unless we got to wherever they had my mother in time.

Almost an hour later felt like a lifetime watching the little finger-sized shadow skim across the skies which were growing brighter and brighter. "I thought they needed a symbolic boundary to bring him through," Loraline thought aloud, her hair blowing back behind in a sea of ebony strands.

Mark shrugged. "If that's what your professor says," he sighed nonchalantly. He'd finally ripped Zean, who was now sulking in the back seat with me, away from the wheel.

Zean glared at the back of his head. "We're heading in the opposite direction to Dover. We're almost at Bristol," he spat.

Loraline suddenly bolted upright. "Oh my God! Bristol! The Bristol Channel? It's a boundary between Wales and England, right?" she gasped, looking around at me and Zean with wide eyes after giving up trying to get any passionate response from Mark. I shrugged, watching the vast patchworks of emerald and lime hills rolling by, the clear crisp sky meeting them as the Bristol Channel stretched ahead in a white and grey vicious rasping strait. It was so open, so vast, unlike so much of Kent which felt enclosed by trees and city buildings. Here the world just rolled out, empty and wild.

There was morning icy fog rolling in over the hills, making me burrow deeper into the army jacket I was slowly becoming quite fond of because of its thermal inner lining. Loraline's head was twitching back and forth, her neck stretched right back as she strained to see something.

"What?" I croaked, absently.

"Aralia is gone," she cried through her teeth, desperately searching the skies. My own head shot back to look at the rolling white clouds blotting out the baby-blue and pink horizon. She was right. I swallowed, panicking suddenly. Had she landed and we'd missed it?

The four-by-four rolled down a hill obscuring the vastness into tall grasses and picket fences. Zean got to his feet in the back seat, his whole upper torso stretching back to search the skies. "She was there 5.32 two minutes ago!" he muttered, holding his watch up to check. He was obsessive about time. He always knew what the time was, down to the second.

The car suddenly came to a screeching halt, throwing us all forward in our seats, but Zean, who'd been standing, went flying straight up into the air, falling flat onto the road about two feet in front of the car.

"Why the hell did you do that?" Loraline gashed at Mark's bulging eyes as if she could happily knock him one. Zean was groaning but picking himself out of the road.

I leant over the seat to meet Mark's eyes.

"Mark?" I asked, drawing the word out into almost a plea for a response; he'd grown more and more tight and silent by the minute since we'd escaped.

Mark raised an eyebrow, turning his head towards me, saying quietly, just to me, "I thought I saw a rabbit in the road." The sarcasm was burning. Loraline gasped, outraged.

"You cannot be serious." She stressed each word lividly. I searched his eyes, unable to keep the pained look from my face. He was, but he'd only stopped to throw Zean out, that was for sure. He glanced at Loraline, keeping his head tilted towards me, and shrugged.

"You wouldn't want a fluffy bunny to become Welsh rabbit, tree hugger." His tongue was on the edge of his teeth as he taunted Loraline who had now raised her fist. I clamped a hand over it, sighing.

"Mark, there was no rabbit in the road," I moaned, a little disbelieving that he would pull this now, of all times, just for his own personal amusement.

Mark turned to look smugly at Zean, who was standing now looking in the opposite direction. "True, but now there is a chicken," he muttered, smirking to himself. I smirked a little, letting Loraline's hand drop.

"Zean!" I shouted, but he didn't move.

"Zean, what is it? What you looking at?" Loraline shouted, confused.

"Get back in the car, roadkill," Mark shouted dryly.

Zean waved a hand behind him. "Come and look at this," he shouted over his shoulder, taking a step away from us. We hopped out of the car to go and stand where Zean was standing looking up over the hill. I gaped. Mark had been right: there had no doubt been a rabbit in the road, because there were about a hundred scattered, dead still and staring, their ears standing, antenna-like, on end, listening, waiting. And that wasn't all there was. Dotted about in the morning fog, looking down over the hills into the beginning of the rockbeds leading down to the Bristol Channel, were deer, antelopes, wolves, fiery red foxes, squirrels, and anything else that could have lived within a two-hundred-mile radius, perched like statues all facing the same place. Down onto the seabed.

"How amazing," Loraline breathed, staring at the array of almost celestial-looking animals.

I shook my head, eyes wide. Their fur stood on end, their eyes were wide. Animals don't stand still like this. In fact, animals only stood still when they were alert; and terrified. I broke into a run just as the first wolf howl filled the misty morning air, soon joined by other statuesque animals' cries of fear, of pain, of warning; I didn't know. But I thought I knew what they were looking at down there. Actually, I didn't *think* anything; I sensed it in my heart, in my soul, the soul that connected us all by the same energy. It was that energy, a derivation from our Lexis, that was petrified, leaking into its children the warning of the beginning of the end. Unless we stopped it.

I skidded on the slick muddy grass. The hills parted here, becoming rocky green slopes tumbling steeply into the flat muddy, pebbled bays of this part of the Channel, its grey and black water swept into angry tides, crashing up and rumbling in fury to join in with the cries of the animals. One step too fast had mud and rock shooting beneath me, and I fell forward down the incline, skidding roughly to a halt behind an outcrop eight foot above the bay below. I rolled onto my stomach, smelling the salt in the air, almost tasting the spray. Two more bodies flopped down beside me, Zean pushing my raised head down to the ground.

"Get down," he hissed, grabbing both my and Loraline's arms and pulling us back a few feet to stand behind a grass- and moss-covered rock.

"Are they down there?" Loraline gasped at Zean.

"Yeah," he muttered, staring wide-eyed at a patch of ground.

"What?" I knocked him in the ribs. "What did you see?" I'd skidded so hard, and then Zean had reacted so quickly I hadn't had time to get a look at the bay below.

"What are those animals doing?" Loraline asked, staring ahead where the outline of a group of sandy-coloured deer were perched, necks tense and strained upwards to look at what we couldn't see.

"Waiting?" I suggested, clueless. Zean continued to stare.

"Where'd Marcus go?"

"Jeez, Loraline, give me a break with the questions!" I gasped, scrambling out from behind the boulders on my stomach, dead thankful for the combos within, which, though now caked in mud and dew, were still keeping me pleasantly warm. Keeping my head as low as I could, I peeked over at the scene below. The bay was an alcove sheltered by low cliffs like the one I was spying from. It was secluded, no doubt the reason they'd chosen this spot. This part of the Channel was wide enough so that Wales was only a faint ghost on the horizon in the distance.

I could feel the colour draining from my own face as it had Zean's. From here, I literally looked directly down at my mother's sallow, gaunt face, her body quivering where it lay; whether from cold due to the thin black silk draped over her naked body, or the rapture of green and white lightning hovering over her, thin tendrils winding down to her, pressing in through her gaping, gagging mouth, and her wide, blankly-terrified eyes turning them black, as if finally showing her as the true empty shell she'd been reduced to for so long. Anna's white hair was loose and blowing in the wind like the idealisation and embodiment of a witch, with a look of pure joy and jubilance, her clawed hands spread wide and encompassing. There were bowed heads standing robed in a circle around my helpless Mum, one recognisable peroxide blond signalling. Sentel had come along again. I felt my fingers digging into the grassy bank. There was a clump of bodies heaped by the rocky bank, the water lapping up at the pile. A worn sandy blond head signalled Christ, lying face down, limp, on top, and I could see a familiar grey ponytail and biking leathers amongst the mass of shaved heads and military uniforms, which meant Skinner was lying unconscious in there too. Ross was lying away from the mass, still conscious, his glasses gone. Cryon was kneeling by him, absently holding him down with one massive white hand clamped around Ross's comparatively small struggling frame. I felt a hand tug at my knee. I ignored it, transfixed by my mother. She was convulsing upwards, her body shaking in mid-air like she was having a seizure or something. I had to find a way to get down there, to help her.

"Khyle, please," I heard Loraline whisper beggingly behind me.

I crawled back to her.

"What are we going to do?" she asked, yet another annoyingly unhelpful question. I had no idea. I'd wanted to be here to try and save Mum but now I was standing over her with all of the so-called 'professionals' lying heaped together, knocked out and maybe even dead. I was at a loss as to how exactly we were going to do this.

"Call Jackson, Loraline. Tell him Nomas is down, that they need back-up," Zean ordered, his face contorted in thought. Loraline nodded, pulling a slick Apple Touch from the back pocket of her mud-streaked jeans.

"We need to find a way to—"

"—stop the ceremony," I finished for him, exchanging a knowing look. It was almost over. You could just feel it in the air: a crackling pain or foreboding in something, in everything, the wind, the sea. Hell, each strand of grass was bent double away from the rip in reality. The rip in Lexis. I ran a hand through my hair, tempted to pull some out in sheer frustration.

"I've got an idea," Zean suddenly snapped, his lank mousy-brown hair flapping as he jumped up and sped off back up the cliff. To go after him or not to? No, I was staying right where I was. I couldn't leave Mum out of my sight for even a moment. I'd done this to her, after all. And where the *fuck* had Mark gone?

Loraline suddenly burst into a gushing whisper on the end of the phone. I couldn't bear the sound of her worried, desperate whispers so, instead, I crawled back to my vantage point.

I gasped, lifting myself up off the rock. The rapture had gone, the crackling of raw energy dispersed, leaving dead silence behind it. Mum was lying motionless within a circle of kneeling bodies. Everyone. Was she dead? No, please God, no. I lifted myself to my elbows, then my knees, then I was fully standing, fully in view.

"Oh my God, Khyle!" Loraline screeched, grabbing me from

behind to pull me away. I stood stock still, unmoving despite her efforts.

"What's happening?" I asked anxiously, trembling. Loraline looked at me, her face crumpled in confusion, and then she glanced down at the bay below, her face wiped clean of all emotion except one: blank fear.

"We need to go." Her voice was low and flat as she pulled me much harder, almost picking me up off my feet even as I fought with all my strength to keep them planted.

"No!" I gulped back the cry, the word coming out as a gush of breath. Loraline locked eyes with me, her face contorting with sympathy. She shook her head ever so slightly. "No!" I said again, much stronger. Denial had that effect.

There was a sudden roar of an engine in the echoing silence. Loraline's head whipped round, eyes wide. "Oh no. Zean! It's too late," she burst out, panicked.

Too late? No. No. No. There had to be a way. The military four-by-four we'd got here in shot over the hill ahead so fast it was a blur of khaki and metal gliding right towards us, Zean behind the wheel, half-standing up in the driving seat and waving his arms at us to get out of the way. Loraline took control of my limp self, throwing us both left off the cliff just as the four-by-four flew through where we'd been standing and directly down to the bay. It would have made a pretty damned good distraction, I was sure, but the ceremony… Well, the shiny swirly thing was gone, let's put it that way. Me and Loraline hit the muddy rock with a hard crash and flying of pebbles. Loraline groaned, picking herself up. I was too busy wondering what had happened to the much larger crash that we should have heard. I clambered around on all fours. The four-by-four was hovering in mid-air, twirling elegantly on an invisible pivot, a shocked and seriously alarmed Zean staring down from the driver's seat, wide-eyed. The thing was, everyone who should have moved to stop it had remained totally motionless, heads bowed, or their whole body bowed, lying flat to the floor. Who had moved shouldn't have moved.

Mum's body was dead still. Not a muscle had moved, or changed expression in her face or anywhere else, except for one long, thin arm stretched straight up in front of her, her hand clasped in a strained claw, palm side up, to the four-by-four hovering overhead. I hurtled forward but my feet sank ankle-deep into boggy mud, tripping me.

"Zean, get out, just jump, get out now! Quick! Before…" I shouted, waving my hands at him, but it was already happening. Mum's claw-like hand was clenching in on itself, and the obedient four-by-four up above was crumpling like a paper ball, hood to boot, Zean trapped in the middle, looking pained at the car.

"No! No, take my life, leave the car. I love this car," he winced, actually looking close to tears. I rolled my eyes disbelieving, Loraline grabbing my arm to pull me up and exchanging a look of complete exasperation with me.

"Zean. Get. Out!" we both shouted up at his flailing form.

He groaned, but hooked a boot up over the fast shrinking hood, kissing the tips of his fingers, and planting them on the shattered remnants of the windscreen right before the now clump of metal entirely gave in, crumpling perfectly into a ball, Zean losing his foothold and falling straight to the ground. The metal continued to shrink, growing infinitely smaller and smaller, the steel beginning to glow red, a shrieking sound of metal and glass breaking and melding under such an enormous force echoing off and through the hills. Fire burst into the air but soon flickered, going out as a stream of red blurs welled up, blasting through the air and hitting Mum's body square on, building and building until it was so bright I had to look away, my eyes watering like looking into the sun without blinking. Eventually the light just went out, and as I turned, so had the four by four: gone. Just puff. Matter to energy. $E=MC^2$. Just like that. From my Mum.

"We need to go," Loraline gasped, flailing her arms at Zean to get over here. Zean was lying, back on the floor, eyes open, mouth gaping open almost a whole three inches, staring at the spot where the vehicle had just vanished.

"Why? What's happening?" My trembling voice gave away too many fears I wanted to keep buried inside.

"He needs energy," Loraline whispered, looking at me with such pity I felt myself cringe underneath it. I shook my head at her, but before I could fully react there was a bird-screech overhead. A flock of swallows, an overhead squawking black and white cloud, burst up from the horizon, flying straight towards us. A flood of animal cries – wolves howling, foxes, deer – flared to life in a horrific song of animal terror. Loraline was crying, but grabbed my arm, pulling me down to the mud and drawing a circle in it around us.

"Hear my words, protected within, With this circle a shield I spin, I ward you away, far at bay, None to cross this line, no energy intertwine, Mother spirit, hear my plea, so mote it be."

It was the strongest I'd heard Loraline's voice since she'd looked over the cliff. There was a flash of warmth, soothing like a mother's hug, something more inside than physical.

"What did you just do?" I gasped.

"Insurance," she muttered, trembling.

"What about Zean?" I cried.

"Pray he gets enough elsewhere," she croaked.

"Enough what?"

She didn't respond, but my answer was almost instantaneous. Up on the cliffs at least one hundred animals were lying down, howling out in pain, swirls of mist twirling around their bodies like a mother's last touch to her children before… Blasts of light, a swarming sea of rainbows burst into the mist, moving like laser beams straight down off the cliffs to my Mum's jerking, limp form. A vibrant flash like an atomic bomb of iridescent kaleidoscopes exploded into the sky where the flock of swallows had been descending from the clouds to the bay, shifting and dissolving into her. And then there was silence as the world went still. The crying animals, which had lain down and been forced to surrender their lives, had dematerialized into nothingness. Even the sea had calmed, mourning the loss of a mass of our world's beautiful, treasured life-forms. Just gone.

I gasped desperately for air, horrified by what had just happened in a flash lasting barely a minute. A massacre had just occurred, a massacre of innocent, defenceless animals. Mum's body flew upwards, hovering in the air which crackled and sparked as if just the touch of her skin was lethal. In the spine-chilling silence I could hear her bones breaking and reforming as her body distorted, muscles ripping and threading back together in front of our eyes, whole joints lifting up under stretching skin to re-form my mother's body into something new. Blindly and desperately, I jumped up and out of Loraline's circle, rushing towards my mother, screaming "No" at the top of my lungs. If I could just get to her, there had to be something. Someone jumped me, wrapping their arms around me as I kicked and screamed, desperate to get to the gruesome display hovering two feet above us. Zean made shushing noises in my ears, hopelessly trying to soothe me as I lashed out at him, screaming and crying harder than I could have thought possible.

The body lengthened, bones twisting outwards and thickening, her shoulders bulking, the ribs along her torso spreading, stretching out her chest, and before long my mother was gone, and replaced by a horrific skeletal looking male. Mum's hair slipped off the new scalp, floating to the floor like dead leaves, leaving it − because it could only be described as an *it* − bald, its skin a shade of grey, the colour and almost the texture of concrete. The new body was two feet or so taller than my Mum had been, making it way over six foot, and a good twice as broad, but not with muscle; just a gigantic frame so thin that the bones pushed up and out under the painfully taut skin. The body revolved in mid-air, coming vertical to show a long face, jaw, brow and chin almost too prominent, over-exaggerated like a Neanderthal would have been. Two heavily lidded eyes, devoid of eyelashes or eyebrows to border them, flicked open. I'd been expecting blank white or black canvases, lifeless, tainted just with evil or maybe flickering flames where irises should have been, but instead they were quicksilver. They were Mark's, and that was Ventram, the Ti Ilu.

We'd failed.

Chapter Twenty-One

The body, once my mother's, hit the floor with an overly loud thud, the invisible string that had been suspending it in the air cut. It landed perfectly on the balls of its feet, the grass beneath its bare toes going up in little puffs of smoke rising with a soft sizzling sound. I heard Zean swear violently behind me, his arms still holding me back even though I'd long given up struggling. The Ti Ilu turned slowly on the spot, taking in his surroundings, focusing calmly on each and every face in the bay. His gaze, which was like ice, even brushed me, and showed no reflection of knowing who I was or that it was my mother he'd just destroyed. Or rather, whom he'd been destroying for years now.

Anna glanced up. "My honour, sire," she breathed to the patch of ground she knelt on. I found it unsettlingly eerie, to see someone like Anna cautious about meeting another's eye.

Ti Ilu gestured lazily with his hand for her to move, not looking at her but scanning the cliffs and the sea now, pulling in huge lungfuls of air, wide nostrils flaring as he did. I suppose it was probably all different to him, the same way everything had felt wrong in Sakhush; everything might feel wrong for him here. Was it the same for Mark and Loraline?

"Rise, all of you." His voice echoed like the air was running away from the soundwaves, trying to avoid their energy pattern, and he stumbled over the syllables, his words accented in something of a mixture of German and Spanish. It was barely audible; I guessed English was not a first language for them. Zean kept tugging persistently on my arm to move backwards. I pursed my lips, ignoring him. I couldn't move, I just couldn't. I was paralytically frozen to the spot. Anna nodded to Sentel, who brought over a jumble of clothes, helping her naked master pull on the long heavy black overcoat and trousers with such little grace it almost took the intimidation away from him.

"How much time?" he asked Anna politely, gracefully turning the cuffs of the coat up, admiring the wool, holding it up to his nose to see each thread.

"One million, four hundred and sixty-eight thousand, eight hundred and twenty-one micro trimesters," she responded, still kneeling slightly.

"Micro trimesters?" I wondered hoarsely.

"I'm guessing, but if that corresponds to seconds they could be talking about just over seventeen days, which would be right for when they, eh, with Delia," Zean whispered in my ear, still pulling at my arm.

"Late," Ti Ilu sighed, a muscle twitching in his jaw. He reminded me horribly of Mark. Except he was polite, eloquent, and didn't have a fag practically glued to his fingers. Zean pulled me so hard this time I tumbled back a bit. I shot him a look, replanting my feet squarely on the ground.

"Khyle," he begged, and I heard Loraline mimic him softly behind us. I snapped, turning on my heel.

"And what? Leave them all" – I waved a hand at Ross and the mountain of military personnel – "to die?" I hissed.

"What are you planning on doing? He'll annihilate us!" Zean hissed back, equally hysterical.

"And these are? Creatures of this world."

I felt something like pins and needles at the back of my head and saw Zean blanch to a dismal shade of grey. I turned slowly. The Ti Ilu was watching us like a zoo exhibit.

"Yes, sire. In fact, these are the ones who interfered with your first attempt to come through." Anna gave me a wickedly demonic smile. I felt ill.

"No, actually, I fucked up a lot more of your attempts to come through than just the last one. I think the first one was something like twelve years ago," I rambled rather manically, trying to avoid eye contact.

"She killed Sepsu. My son," Anna continued.

A voice said, "Actually, no. That was me."

The Ti Ilu whipped around, his coat billowing out behind him. "Maraknight."

Mark stood just under the cliff, his face drawn and his shoulders tensed. Had he been there the whole time? Had he just stood back and watched?

"It has been many years since we last stood together, my son." Ti Ilu sounded almost warm, actually like a father addressing his son. Mark's eyes closed for a moment, looking beyond annoyed.

"Exile tends to create that form of distance," he spat between his teeth. I had a feeling the next person he had to remind would be losing a previously attached feature of their anatomy.

Ti Ilu smiled. "Yes. I can see it has done you a vast degree of good. Now you are killing high priests-to-be."

Mark snorted. "If Sepsu was your high priest-to-be, father, then it's not much of a surprise your ascension is running late."

Anna took a step forward, but one raised finger from Ti Ilu had her hopping back to her place like a rabbit in headlights.

"And your insolence—"

"My sense of humour." Mark cut him off, a dark, testing smile slowly spreading on his face. He was enjoying himself.

"—has only become more out of control. Tell me, have you forgotten all your teaching of discipline? Of honour? Of your very birthright?" The angrier Ti Ilu got, the more the world around him quivered like heat waves rippling off him. Mark didn't answer him, just stood, the wind whipping up sand around his ankles as he watched and waited for his actions.

"And your purpose here now? You've failed, if it was to thwart me once more."

Mark's eyes were so quick in their glance to me I wasn't sure I'd actually seen it, or at least I wasn't until Ti Ilu held up one finger and my whole body lifted into the air, rocketing me forward and dropping me into the stone-speckled mud, my nose inches from his toes.

I tried to scramble to my feet but my body had different ideas. A feeling like my stomach has been fish hooked yanked at my insides, pulling me vertical to face him. This close, the energy seeping from his every pore and into the air was strong enough to start lifting strands of my hair with static.

"And this is what?" Ti Ilu scanned my hovering form like a doctor over a patient, one long spider-like knobbly finger pointed at my chest. A quick blast of silvery lilac light bounced from my chest to his finger. At the same time, my heart skipped a beat and black spots popped up, dancing in front of my eyes. I shook my head, feeling queasy. Ti Ilu rubbed his finger and thumb together. Seconds ticked by and the silence only got thicker. It seemed by his expression he was outright livid at his fingers. Slowly he redirected his attention to me and breathed, "I know you." He caught my chin so quickly and roughly he may as well have slapped me. "Oh, how you've grown; into a woman, no less. A perfect match," he went on, thin colourless lips twisting up over animal-like teeth to snarl at me. Just under his gaze I felt like the most gruesome abomination that dared to walk Earth.

"Can you put me down? I'm not great with heights."

Of all the things to say. Hysteria was doing nothing for my ego.

"You were the undoing of him. A nasty trick created by Kia to take my son, our reckoning, away. I should suck you dry." He breathed into my face; his breath smelt like lemons.

"You killed my mother, you son of a bitch," I snarled bitterly, wishing I could move my hands enough just to claw his eyes out. "That vessel of yours, that meaningless vessel you've destroyed, *was my Mo-ther!*"

"Your point, please." He barely moved his lips to say it. I gaped at him.

"Let her go, Ventram," came Mark's voice behind me, strained taut. Ti Ilu, or Ventram, or whatever I was supposed to call him, moved his gaze, just his gaze, to Mark.

"An order? From an outcast? A disappointment. I could kill her, Maraknight, and you would come back to us whole again. But, then, *would* you? You could see it as my wrongdoing against you and I would have lost you forever."

His chin shot up, losing patience with both of us. He dropped his finger, letting me fall seven foot down onto the rocks, as some great revelation hit him. I sucked in a deep breath before returning to my feet. I was getting rather tired of being thrown around like a chew toy.

"You do it. Redeem yourself. What a beginning to our conquest: to have you overcome this insignificant obstacle that dominated you so. Kill her, and come back to your destiny."

He made it sound like he was asking Mark to take the car to be washed so that he made a good impression on the neighbours! My death would be that insignificant to his cause. Just like any other death to come. Like my Mum's.

I stumbled up, shoulder to shoulder with Mark, who had turned to face me, his chest rising and falling fast, his gaze running over me, making everywhere it swept over feel like fire had ignited. I felt like hitting my head against the cliff-side. Here he was, considering killing me to get in his father's good books; my mother had just been brutally murdered; we were all in for the chopping board, including a group of secret military agents; and just the feel of him looking at me made my blood pressure peak unnaturally. I clearly needed to be shot. Mark raised his hand very gently, brushing his fingertips, leaving trails of warmth, over my frozen cheek. I heard Loraline shout something at him but it felt like the world had fallen away around us. This felt so surreal. All I could tell myself was that to laugh at this point at the degree of sheer cliche of it all would be absurd, and might perhaps even get me torched alive. And then all I could think was at least I'd be warm. But as I fixed on Mark's eyes mostly I just felt calm; in one of the most incomprehensibly wrong moments of my life, possibly one of the worst to be documented in history if things panned out the wrong way, just being close to him calmed me. I knew I was safe with him. I didn't need Loraline to scream for him to leave me alone or people like Green drumming the gruesome facts into me. Something instinctual, primal, against all logic, told me that killing me, even letting me hurt, would do the exact same to him.

Of course, how any of that was true I had no clue. What did I really know about him? He made me laugh (sometimes not as secretly as I'd like), he had a great car, no sense of interior decorating, and enough knowledge on how to demonically torture someone to write a series of books, which clearly wasn't enough. It was something preordained; his energy matched mine. Just like Ross had once said, this was out of any conscious control I had.

"I've been waiting so long to do this," he breathed, stepping closer to me, shielding me from the blast of salty cold wind. I could feel the energy building in him, evaporating the moisture in the air in little puffs of steam. Another scream from Loraline; one from Zean. Was that Ross? I closed my eyes. *He is not going to hurt me, he is not going to hurt me, please don't kill me…*

There was a blast of heat, like a fire roaring to life, inches from my shoulder. My eyes, which I hadn't realized had fallen closed, snapped open. A ball of black fire the size of a basketball, silver strips orbiting, twisting around it, flew from Mark's outstretched hand straight at an only mildly surprised Ventram. Waves of heat, like an opened oven door billowing it out, cut through the cold air, knocking Ventram's shoulder, and having absolutely no effect. As it met his shoulder the breast pocket of his coat crumbled away, but when it met with skin it simply blinked out. It was like watching a rocket meet a cloud and get knocked right down from the sky. Ventram took a while to react before finally glancing down at his shoulder and touching the frayed edges of the fabric.

"Interesting. I remember you once being powerful."

Mark took in and let out a massive breath, his shoulders relaxing. The insult didn't seem to register, but it didn't matter; he'd made his point.

"Felt damned good though." He examined his hand, flexing it. I got the impression he was disappointed himself at the lack of damage. I laughed. "You thought I was going to kill you, didn't you?" he accused me quietly, still examining his hand intently.

"No… yes… well, it's not like it's never crossed your mind," I defended myself, stumbling a little.

"I could never read Maraknight. So make my existence easy for once. That was a rejection of my offer for redemption?" Ventram's teeth were clenched and he was talking, hissing right through them. There was a shaking level of insanity in the warning look he gave Mark.

Mark cocked his head. "No father. This would be a rejection."

He lifted his hand again. This time, though, Ventram blanched, his skin sucking in on himself until he was no longer a walking skeleton but a mummified walking corpse. Ventram dropped, bent double, and instantaneously every bowed body there sprang to their feet.

Mark didn't wait a moment. He rolled his eyes and grabbed my arm in a familiar painful grip, and answered my stunned, and more than a little worried, expression with, "He's right. I'm out of shape. I needed time to warm up. We need to go." He made as if to run back up the cliffs despite my best efforts, actually dragging me a few feet up with what looked like no effort at all.

"Wait! What about Ross, and Nomas, and Loraline and Zean?" I stammered, watching Ventram already getting back to his feet, Anna helping him navigate his newly acquired body.

Mark cringed. "Losing Loraline would mean far less headaches, and Zean, well—"

"Mark!" I screeched.

Mark laughed just as the first rocket-like energy blast skimmed his shoulder, dissolving his sleeve and searing the skin black. Mark clenched his teeth but it was me who gasped, grabbing his shoulder before I even knew what I was doing. "Oh my God," I stammered, meeting Mark's now very amused gaze and feeling myself go scarlet, dropping his shoulder immediately. Another blast hit within a centimetre of my stomach, the cotton T-shirt burning away little embers, prickling the skin behind it. Mark grabbed my arm, dragging me up the cliffside with so much force it took a lot not to cry out that he'd dislocate my shoulder if he kept going like that. Down below I heard Ventram give an order for someone to come after us and to *dispose* of the rest. I pulled against Mark's arm, trying to get him to slow down as we reached the top of the cliff, but he flung me off, making me hit the ground, scattering wet sand, just as he spun round, grabbing one huge arm as it swung down on him. Cryon flung out his other arm, this one knocking, colliding with Mark's head, forcing him to stagger a little to the left. He swung his leg out, which sank into Cryon's stomach, who doubled over a little, swallowing hard, but otherwise an unmoving statue.

"How could you do this? You were brilliant, my mentor, my idol—" Cryon choked.

Mark screwed his nose up, his arm flying out and striking Cryon's nose. Even in the sudden outbreak of motion I heard a click, followed by a cry of pain.

"Don't be an idiot, Cryon. If I had been your mentor, you would have chosen a better haircut," Mark snarled, a little out of breath, a much smaller sizzling black orb breaking the airspace, eyelevel with him, synthesizing out of an apparent nowhere. It tore through the air towards Cryon, knocking him straight off his feet. Throbbing, I crawled to the cliffside. Sentel had her hands around Loraline's ever-bluer face as she held her up against the rock-face. Zean was dodging a punch from an army-wearing rat of a man. Ross lay forgotten on the sandy shore. My head shot left and right, unsure of where to focus first. Prioritising wasn't as easy as I would have liked in a situation so out of place in reality. I could just make out the bouncing white hair of Anna disappearing around the bend in the bay, and the sound of an engine starting up, leaving us insignificants to be finished off by only three of their lackeys. Something in the very corner of my eye caught my absolute attention: an orange flame had throbbed to life, slow in the strong wet wind, but dancing all the same along a river of slick black oil running and pooled over the heap of bodies by the water's edge. I gasped. Oh no. And they were all out cold. They'd go up in flames in barely minutes. I flung my hand out, closing my eyes and trying to imagine energy around me, centring myself and pulling it all together. I opened my eyes; my palm was empty. I screwed my eyes shut thinking of Ventram and Anna, the way they'd tricked me into giving my mother's life to them totally, unknowingly; how I'd never, ever get to hold her again and have her actually see me just as I was beginning to rebuild hope that one day I would. I felt the heat burst against my open palm, an equally heated feeling of pride swelling simultaneously in my chest. Wouldn't have been able to do that three weeks ago, that was for sure. I hurled it down over the cliff directly at Sentel, watching as the blazing orange and amber ball hit her thick neck , making her lose her grip on Loraline and cry out, singe marks stretching up under her chin and down her chest while she screamed out, clutching the bright *blue* singe marks it had left there.

Behind me I heard Cryon stagger at the sound of her cries. "What did you do?" he raged at me, blocking a blow from Mark and sending him hurtling backwards, sheer rage magnifying his strikes. I dragged myself forward before he could reach me, tipping clumsily straight over the cliff even as I felt the air shudder as Cryon's fist whipped through it over my head. I ran over to Loraline who was collapsed on the floor, her hand pressed against her already black and blue, swollen throat.

"Are you okay?" I gasped breathlessly, not waiting for her hesitant nod before I was already checking around for... Sentel ran at me, a long silvery-white samurai-looking sword brandished straight at me and ready to swing. Loraline jumped up next to me, hand flung out at her side and swinging it through the air. There was a spray of sand and rock from the wall of stone next to us, right before a boulder hurtled – more like an oversized mud and stone bullet – right at Sentel, knocking her out cold and trapping her beneath it.

"Nice one." I gaped at her, a little put out. My pride was back to damaged.

Loraline shrugged, still scowling. "Blondes," she muttered.

I motioned to Ross. "Wake him up and find his glasses," I ordered, already running towards the heap of bodies. The tide had started to come in which helped with the flames fighting to eat up the track of oil, but not with the bodies stacked lower down, air bubbles rising to the surface from men choking to death. I sank to my waist in ice-cold water, grabbing Christ and shaking him as hard I could. I could feel a pulse and I couldn't see any fatal wounds, but they weren't moving.

Back on the beach, Cryon came hurtling down from the cliff above, hitting the ground with so much force he sank into a muddy crater three feet deep. Loraline was nursing Ross who was half sitting, half lying, one hand to his head as Loraline slid on his glasses.

"Oi! Guys! A little help would be good!" I shouted, frantically pulling at Christ's heavy upper body, weighed down by his wet khakis making it that much more difficult to move him with my biceps. The oil had fully lit now, blazing and breaking off into floating pools of sputtering blazing ignition, the motion of the enraged tide actually drawing them out towards us. One floated past me, forcing me to jump back away from the bodies just as one leg caught, going up in a sizzling blaze even as the water tried to eat away at them. Ross leapt up, waving his arms at me to get away. "But they'll die!" I cried, incensed, staring hopelessly at them. The ones lying at the bottom would surely have suffocated by now.

"Khyle, trust me!" Thing was, I *had* trusted Ross since the moment I'd met him. I staggered, wet and heavy, back to shore as Ross grabbed Loraline's hand, his other stretched out, tensed and claw-like, before him. I gaped. If there were devout Christians nearby, Ross would either be burnt at the stake on the six o'clock news or declared the next Messiah. Thankfully, this place was deserted. At the command of his hand and erratically heaving chest the water parted, rising up, towering as solid walls of icy-grey sparks from the flames and oil being engulfed, and sizzling away within them, revealing the stony ocean floor and the mass of entangled bodies there.

I glanced around, but Zean was now sprawled on the floor in a headlock with the rat man, looking as though he was taking out some of his 'two lost vehicles' frustration on him, and Mark was still dealing with Cryon, his nose now bleeding and a two-inch gash on his neck. I ran over to the bodies, but the weight of the water soaked up in their clothes only made it more impossible to move them, and I could see Ross shaking with the effort, the concentration. Loraline had already sunk to her knees on the rocks, gasping for breath, her face as white as marble. "I need help," I muttered to myself, fruitlessly hooking an arm through Christ's and dislodging his torso, but the bodies were so heavily knotted together, limb around limb.

There was a flapping, whirling sound of the wind being stirred up ahead by wings. I strained my neck backwards, watching a shadowy black figure, which had been perched observing the display below from a hill high above us, grow larger and larger, heading straight for where I crouched, struggling so hard tears had started rolling down my already wet cheeks. Aralia's imposing figure landed, folding her bird-like feet beneath her elegantly, wings wrapped around her shoulders as if for warmth, on top of the wall of water, looking down at me.

She almost looked confused as she stared at me, her head making erratic little jerking moves back and forth, her eyes unmoving in their sockets.

"You cannot move them. You are too weak," she said in her musically rising pitch, as if she were wondering why I didn't realize this and hadn't given up yet.

"No. Really? I hadn't guessed that might be an issue!" I spat at her, giving up all sense of delicacy and directly lodging a foot under a head and heaving.

"I could move them," she said, hopping down to perch on top of them now, her eyes wide and staring, too large and bug-like for her chiselled face.

I retreated a little, startled. "Why?" I hissed suspiciously, heaving.

Aralia tilted her chin up, looking out of the corner of her eye, listening to some distant sound only she could hear.

"You released me. I have a very deep sense of honour. Especially to women. But that would be the end. I would owe you nothing more," she sang flatly. I realized she felt nothing for what she was offering; she saw saving these people as a worthless decision which would make no difference to her ultimate mastery. I was once again struck by just how worthless we truly were in their eyes.

"Khyle," came Ross's strained, almost pained, begging from behind me.

"Do it," I demanded of her, disgusted at the revelation that to Aralia, to all the LEs, we were about as good as the cows that were processed to big Macs.

Aralia jerked her head, lifting her body forward, two taloned feet digging right into the bodies, puncturing straight into one man's chest. I let out a scream of protest but she was oblivious, grabbing the wet mess of human bodies and lifting them up into the air, and as she did, dropping them so hard onto shore I heard cracking sounds even from where I stood. Just as she thumped her wings to propel herself up, Ross and Loraline lost their concentration and the walls of ice-cold water started to tumble.

"Oh, no! Khyle, get out of the way!"

"Move!"

"Quick!" came a chorus of shouts from Ross and an exhausted-sounding Loraline, but even as I turned, all that filled my vision were heavy walls of water, spray and foam collapsing almost hungry to take me into them. Frigid, partially frozen water hit me on both sides knocking my legs out from underneath me and the air out of my lungs. It was so much more like being hit by a car than going into the sea.

Pins and needles sprang to life everywhere in response; the empty, throbbing sound of the sea filling my ears as I hit the seabed, flat on my back and looking up at the sparkling ceiling, swallowed under by the strength of the water. The water continued to press down on me and I didn't fight it, watching, entranced, as bubbles exploded from my mouth as I released all the air from my lungs in one quick gush. Peaceful. If there was anything I'd ever thought of as being a semblance of the afterlife it was that feeling of complete abstraction you got when you were underwater, and I was perfectly happy to stay here, wasn't I?

My lungs were already cramping for air, my chest trying to heave, telling me to inhale, but as of yet my brain hadn't got oxygen-deprived enough to stop suppressing the reflex. They thought we were bugs, and in truth they'd just squashed us like bugs. Ventram had wiped out hordes of living beings in under a minute flat and left the rest of us to die without a second glance, any worry, or concern. Could we even match them, him, in strength? No, not physically and not even spiritually. We'd abandoned the teaching of our ancestors for an extreme, along a sliding scale of intertwining knowledge, abandoning spiritualism, faith in creation, and in the meaning of life, for scientific fact, cold and calculating, giving us a whole lot of how and nothing of why. Consequence? We'd emerged ignorant and powerless, and we were all going to die because of it. No, worse than that, we were going to lose everything: our world. There would be no coming back from it. 2012: the destruction or the revelation? Well, it looked to me as if it would turn out a bit of both. So why shouldn't I lie here? Take the easy road out, be the first to go.

I watched a ray of sunlight filter through like a diamond on the water's surface. What would happen to the sun, I wondered, as the pulsating need for oxygen inched through my every sense. Or the birds singing on spring mornings? Or those little wolf pups? Or London buses? Harrods? Marlborough? Those Sex And The City re-runs I watched when I felt totally miserable? Kids wouldn't be able to wake up on frosty Christmas mornings at some horrid hour and beg their parents to let them open their presents. Twenty-first of December, 2012. We only had this Christmas left.

I kicked off the mud, the undercurrents working with me rather than against me, pushing me up at a much faster pace than I would have achieved on my own. My head broke the water and I drew a huge gulp of oxygen; the cold breeze whipped the water from my cheeks and sent shudders down my spine. I would fight, we would fight, regardless of how terrible the odds were, how much they worked against us. We would fight so that everything we took for granted around us, manmade or not, would live on. So that my mother's memory wouldn't be lost, not again.

Chapter Twenty-Two

Little puffs of steam kept forming on Loraline's bedroom window. I watched them form and fade, resting my head against the cool pane. When I was little I used to write messages or draw hearts in the steam and *she'd* just know, inexplicably, where they were, and she'd lean over, her long unruly hair tumbling over her shoulders, breathe over them and write me something back. I couldn't lift my hand to the steamy patch now. All I could do was sit curled up on the leopard-print seat in Loraline's window, marvelling at that particular memory and a billion more.

I was alone in Loraline's bedroom. She'd already gone downstairs by the time I'd woken up. It was seven o'clock, Sunday morning. I'd slept way over twenty-four hours and I still felt like the walking dead. Not particularly physically. Jackson had had us all checked up by the, now, very unfriendly ginger military doctor back at the bay after he'd arrived with what could be easily described as a cavalry of men, a cavalry of men too late. Christ, Skinner, and the other men had been checked out. A couple had some bad burns, and Skinner swore they'd taken the last week and a half of his memory away. Ross said it was more likely the four bottles of Jack Daniels he'd been working his way through on Friday that were to blame. I'd come out of it with some pretty nasty burns of my own, but the worst one was totally invisible to everyone except me. I just couldn't get over the cruel irony: the moment I cared, the moment I loved her was almost the same moment I lost her.

I could hear the clattering of cutlery and a bustle of voices and movement from downstairs echoing up through the cottage walls. Ross, Skinner, Christ, had all been too out of it to find their way home so Jackson had put them up here. Me and Zean? Well, I was dependent on Zean for a ride home and he had suffered a few nasty knocks, and the moment we'd got away from the bay had passed out in the back seat. I meant that figuratively. People didn't snore that loudly once they were unconscious. Jackson had offered to put Mark up too; he'd been in a bloody state, hurt worse than I *could* imagine anyone could hurt him. I'd never so much as seen him with a bruise, but Cryon had apparently been his first-in-command, trained by himself, and it was a fairly *fun* fight. He'd left Cryon alive but in a bloody mass of muscle slumped down in his own crater. Talk about digging your own grave, huh? So it had been me, Loraline, and Jazmine in Loraline's room, Ross, Skinner, and Zean in Jazmine's, and Mark and Christ in the living room. Put basically, I'd been unconscious for most of it, but hearing it down there now, the set-up in Jackson's good-sized but humble house was overcrowded and noisy. How and why Mark was choosing to deal with it, considering his loner personality, was beyond me.

I wasn't exactly a loner, but the idea of going down there was equal to having someone put me, Anna, and Ventram in a room to see who survived the longest without food or water. I'd be expected to talk, or at least not walk around feeling sorry for myself, and at the moment I wanted to do little talking and a lot of moping. It felt like I had so much more to mourn than just my mother, the same way I had felt so totally hopeless, that we were lost, on the seabed. The feeling hadn't really changed; I'd just decided to ignore it. That was probably one of the greatest human gifts, right? Denial, carrying on anyway, forgetting the chances. Look at World War Two: a tiny country against a growing dictatorship and we won; we took Hitler down in a blaze of blue, white and red glory, all because we denied the impossible and we fought against the odds. But those were human circumstances. People can accept a world war; we're used to humans killing humans; but monsters from the blue lagoon? How could humans fight something they didn't believe was possible and, more importantly, how long would it take to convince them? What would it take? Who and what would have to be lost before we put our pig-headed arrogance away and fought against impossible odds?

I could pretty much say without any doubt that I was the only one up here worrying how to convince the human race that monsters were real without invoking outbursts of anarchy, religious assault, and mass psychiatric admissions. They down there were thinking of the now stuff, like how to stop Ventram before it got that far. Was I a pessimist? Or a realist?

There was a tap on Loraline's door, a long crooked nose peeking through awkwardly. Jackson looked surprisingly better for a man who had lost such a dear friend. He looked like he'd slept, his thick white hair Brylcreemed back smoothly, and his shirt and tweed trousers freshly pressed. He was holding an orange and blue mug with *World's Greatest Physics Professor* written on it in bubble writing.

"I was wondering whether a cuppa might help," he said, his eyes warming as he pushed the door open, stepping gingerly over books and semi-diminished candles. "I really must teach Loraline the miracle that we have here on Earth of stuffing things in drawers. I'm a fan of clutter, but I manage to keep the floors clear for sheer ease of movement's sake," he went on, absently holding out a cup of tea and milk.

"Isn't that your mug?" It wasn't a question because I didn't really care for an answer. I just stared at the mug in his hand, my head leant back against the glass, savouring the numbing cold on my skin.

Jackson's old face was glowing with a warm-hearted sympathy that only age and experience could provide. "You can borrow it. Come on, tea helps. You're English. Tea always helps." When I didn't reach out to take the cup, he gently picked my hand up off where it was pressed numbly against the glass and wrapped my pink and white fingers around the warm cup. I took a sip. Tetley's. Nothing herbal, just good old Tetley's. He was right, it was a strange kind of familiar soothing as the warmth seeped into me. The problem was, warm made me feel alive, it brought feeling back to me, and I needed to be numb or I could feel the loss, the anguish, and the guilt that was eating away at my heart.

"I am so sorry, Khyle," he whispered, looking away out of the window.

I felt the first sob choke me. I swallowed it down. "You're sorry? Can you imagine what it's like to have *loved and lost,* only to go through it twice, and the second time it's all your fault?"

Jackson looked me squarely in the eye, his eyebrows raised in sincerity. "Yes I can. I loved your mother very much; she obviously never saw me the same way. But I have loved and lost many people to this war, and the feeling is the same each time regardless of whether you're tricked. Because that's what you were, Khyle; you were tricked, into giving the act permission. You saved Delia's life. There is no fault in any of that."

My lips trembled as I tried and gave in, taking another sip of tea. "No fault?" I choked. "It's not just my mother whose life I chanted away. Ventram is through. I may as well have signed a licence to kill everyone on Earth."

Jackson laughed, and quickly suppressed it, giving me a nervous look over his glasses. "I am sorry. It's just you have the gift of most writers: dramatic exaggeration." I gaped at him as he looked at me like a naive little girl, but in a kind way that was more of a father looking at his naive little girl. I still hated it. "Ventram would have found a way to our dimension one way or another; if not here, then somewhere else in the world, through a different psychic, witch, priest, Buddha, medicine man. It's preordained he'd come through in a lot of ways. We knew we'd never stop it. It's just circumstance that this has affected you, us, so."

I shook my head, forehead still pressed against the glass, unable to look at him any more.

"I wish he had. I wish he'd left my Mum alone. I know it sounds evil, but I would rather have had five hundred people dead, him through, and a life with her, than this."

There was silence, and then I felt Jackson's warm hand pressing down on my shoulder.

"You may be good with words, Khyle, but I'm not. May I show you something?"

I looked up at the deep crow's feet around his eyes and the lines on his forehead, all contorted with sympathy. I followed him, unfolding myself from the window seat and feeling surprisingly light as he led me into the study where I'd first found out, a few hundred lifetimes ago, that he'd known Mum. He gestured to the seat behind his desk as he went to rummage through a closet. On the desk was that old picture of the outside steps of an Oxford University college. I reached out one shaky hand and turned it away, not wanting to see her smiling face, especially now that I could just barely remember a time when those glowing almond eyes had glowed at me.

Jackson emerged and propped up on my lap a two-foot long,

one-foot deep chocolatey-coloured and enormously heavy wood crate. The lid was domed and the whole thing had been carved into a see-through lattice of intertwining leaves, flowers, and bunches of berries. The only part that was solid wood was the base. The lid was latched down with a tiny, rusty, modern padlock. I twisted it in my fingers; it was locked. Jackson handed me a small unopened ivory envelope. My name had been scrawled on the front in child-like, small, separate letters.

"There's more. A few boxes of mostly books – she was a fanatical reader; some other bits, and, of course, that bank account—"

I shot him a look of disgust and he nodded, cringing. "Erm, but this… " – he inclined his head at the box – "she told me she was specifically leaving for you. That, and the letter."

"How did she tell you?"

"I found it when we went to the villa in France. She'd known they were after her, watching her even, while she lived there. So she prepared for the worst; ever the pessimist she was." He laughed tearfully and I joined him.

"I guess that's where I get it from," I said, all snotty-nosed.

"Yes, yes it is," Jackson said in a rush, beaming at me.

I hesitated, and then ripped open the letter, a light silver key falling out first. I slid it into the padlock; it was a perfect fit.

My dear Lilly

If this has been given to you purposely then I'm dead. Not the normal kind of dead, more of a sacrifice. There are worse things than dying, one of which is being left behind. I hope you're old enough when you read this for me to have gone through the important things: the talk, tampons, algebra, but mostly I hope you are old enough to understand that though

I would never leave you by choice, this is my choice. There are only three things I have ever loved alongside you: myself (because I hope you know you have to love yourself first and foremost in life), your father, and magic. Or I call it magic; some might say God, some may give it a name like Jesus or Allah or Mother Nature, but it's what I believe makes summer showers feel good against our skin or lets us love the way I love you, the way you love Oreos! It's what's made us part of our world, and if I had to die so you could experience that, so that you could fight for that in the way I have, then I cannot think of a better way to go.

There is a fight coming, my little girl, and I don't want you to get involved, but you're not even six when I write this, and you're so stubborn I just know you will. I don't know what to give you, if I'm not there, that will save you, except what I've already acquired, my magic. I was a very scientific girl and I do despise that word, but I have also come to respect that we've spent too long trying to separate the two rather than embrace them, and if you can find a way to use what I and many others have learnt in doing just that, and using the scientifically blasphemous M word, then maybe we can find a way to fight back. We are just as strong as they are and we have won before. We have love, creativity, humanity and plenty more overused clichés on our side and we will use them. I love you, and I wish I could leave you more than a page of words but I don't know what to write that will ease the coming years. Never give up and even if I have to leave you, know I loved you. I would never leave you by choice.

Your Mummy

I looked up from the letter feeling strangely sober, the tears gone, the wrenching pain not quite as sharp. I held the letter out to Jackson, who looked at it, confused. "It's yours," he said, bemused.

I smiled up at him. "Jackson, I know intellectuals. You've been dying to know. It's alright; she wouldn't mind you reading it, especially if it would help your grief as well as my own."

Jackson smiled that gentle, shy smile back at me, taking it and pushing his glasses further up his nose. I unlocked the little padlock. The moment I pulled back the lid, a cloud of sage, lavender and cinnamon hit me, reminding me of spring stews and apple pie but I couldn't connect anything concrete with them. The inside was such a treasure trove of different objects of different textures and colours, I leant forward a little, my hand hovering over its depths, unsure where to begin. Jackson lowered the letter, folding it slowly and neatly, making each gesture a little caress and placing it back in the envelope, slipping it into the box as he knelt down beside me to peer inside.

"Lucky dip." He glanced up at me beneath his bushy white and grey eyebrows, a twinkle of humour and a twinkle of sadness there.

The first thing my hand came down on was a thick hand-stitched ruby-coloured leather-bound book, overflowing and spilling out loose papers and torn-out passages from books and magazines. I held it out in front of me, frowning. It was about the size of a diary, about seven inches by five, Celtic knots running along its spine and bordering its front and back in an intricate interconnecting pattern. Silver buckles were placed in each corner, a silver clasp latching it closed. On the front, painted with chipped silver painting on the leather, right in the centre, was a pentagram. Jackson tilted the book in my grip to look at it himself.

"Ah, interesting, this was your mother's Book of Shadows." Noticing the blank look on my face, he clarified. "A Book of Shadows,

Khyle; it's like a diary of personal experiences, spells, erm, potions, charms, sometimes hexes. I never delved too deeply."

"Why's it called a Book of Shadows? Isn't that a bit... corny?" I winced a little, wondering whether my Mum would have laughed, or smacked me for that.

Jackson laughed. "Well, it's nice to know me and you are both on the same wavelength, so to speak. It's just a name, I think, something a little mysterious those of the, eh, Craft—"

"You're not comfortable talking about witchcraft and that, are you?" I smirked.

Jackson took in a deep breath, choosing his words. "I am a scientific man, Khyle, I always have been. There are levels of belief for me, and your mother delved very deeply into a certain side of the scale; this side. The only problem I had with it was when it turned out a little bit too right. That tends to be the problem with metaphysics: sometimes it tells normal physics to go and take a running jump. But then branches of physics within itself tend to tell each of the others to, eh... don't get me started." He cut himself off like he had no doubt taught himself to do most of his life. He reached in and pulled out the next knick-knack while I held the BOS close to my heart. I knew instinctively that nothing else in that box could be more important than the personal messages written in there. Or the spells. Mum had said she wanted me to learn magic and she'd passed this down to me. That had to mean something. And I wasn't sure whether it was my overactive imagination or not, but it almost felt like it was tingling beneath my fingers...

Still keeping the BOS held tightly to my chest, I reached in again, almost tempted to close my eyes. My fingers came down on a very heavy silver charm bracelet of interlocked silver links all holding an array of different things. I saw Jackson's eyes warm out of the corner of mine as he watched me dangle it up in the air, bringing it close to my eyes to get a good look. There was a round filigree silver locket of intertwining vines, a lump of what looked like black jet the size of my fingernail placed inside, a Union Jack, an Eiffel Tower, an obelisk of clear quartz, a silky pink pearl, a mirror about half an inch radius held inside an enamel ring so that it could swing freely between two pivoted little pins, and three symbols I didn't understand. I glanced up at Jackson, who read my mind.

"Ah, well, this" – he pointed to one an inch long which looked a bit like the symbol for the male, but with a half-moon through the circle and a three stuck on the end of the line pointing downwards; honestly, it looked a tad demonic – "is called Monad. It symbolises the first Creator and unity between all living beings." The next was a circle with two crossed lines. "This is very ancient, and one Nomas is very familiar with. It's called the solar cross and it represents the movements of our sun and the impact it has on life. And finally, this." He held the last one right up to his nose, peering down at it. It looked like a musical treble clef gone mad, with a spiral like a snail's shell at one end. "This I gave to your mother as a private joke. It's a Reiki power symbol, Cho-Ku-Rei, which is used to concentrate power and energy."

"What was the joke?"

"She told me a symbol only has capability when the user has faith in it. I told her the only capability a symbol had was to denote meaning. She was right. I watched her bring my tulips back to life with that thing." I burst out laughing, startling Jackson. "Yes, well, you see, that was my response too," he muttered.

I laid it aside, unsure whether I wanted to put it on or not. It was unfinished like so much of my mum's life. There were gaps to fill that might never get there. There was a stack of photos held together by frayed twine. The top one was of me and her. I was so small I only had a wispy mass of light brown curls on my head, and she was wrapping a green and red scarf around my neck, looking radiant. It was a Christmas I was too young to remember. I put them aside, deciding to leave those to when I had some time to myself and didn't have to worry about bursting into tears. A moment later I pulled out the scarf from the photo, red and green and with 'Lilly' written at one end. It was frayed, and smelled like dust and herbs, but I already wanted to wrap it around myself and risk smelling like an Indian spice shop just for how it would make me feel closer to her. There were several lumps of precious gems, including amber, a cat's collar with 'Snowzy' engraved into a silver heart, a thin book on alchemy, which I barely got a look at before Jackson had snatched it from my grip like a three-year-old and was flicking through it, fiddling with the sides of his glasses, and a sharpened length of white wood.

I held it up. It looked maybe like willow, about six inches long, and sanded, sharpened and polished into a perfect dagger. I swallowed, a little horrified. "Self-defence? They didn't have pepper spray back in the eighties?" I asked Jackson, waving it at him.

Jackson glanced up from the book and took it very delicately from my grasp. "That, Khyle, is an athame, a ritual dagger I believe—"

"For, like, sacrifice?" I burst in, utterly horrified.

Jackson rolled his eyes. "Yes, yes, the sacrifice of rosemary sprigs, perhaps. Or is that called something different? Best ask Loraline, either way. Ritualistic sacrifice of animals was not your mother's style, unless, of course, it was in the form of steak and kidney pie in which case she was quite the cannibal."

The thing about Jackson was, he always had such a perpetually serious look on his face it took you a second to realize whether he was actually being funny or had just been funny accidentally. The glint in his eyes now was an indicator that I was in fact allowed to giggle.

Finally, I pulled out a handmade dream-catcher of thread and little beads, but so old it was falling apart a little in places now. Hm, well, a bit of Sellotape and I knew exactly where this was going to hang. I hesitated. "Jackson?" Jackson glanced up from the paperback reluctantly, saw the look on my face, and placed it down, tapping it a little like a pet he was reassuring he wouldn't abandon. "What do you think is after death? I mean, you see all this stuff, you teach all about the origins of the universe, the combinations of physics with religion and philosophy. What do you think has happened to my mother's soul?" The last part was so small, if it hadn't have been for the dead silence in the study not even a mouse would have heard it. I'd never in my life contemplated what happened after death; I'd never had to. I'd considered myself a devout atheist, and when we were dead, that was it, our time was up. I wasn't exactly about to start considering the possibility of pearly gates or fiery vengeance for eating one too many pots of Ben and Jerry's, but after everything I could remember, after everything that had happened in that week, the last days, I had to begin to ask that question of why? If there was so much more than our 2-D picture of the world, then surely that must mean that there was more after our known perspective of life died away?

Jackson was quiet, his eyes squinting and thoughtful. "I am a physics professor. I believe in mathematics as a way to describe the world which revolves around certain solid rules, but I do too believe in there being more than just this. Now, whether that's a Garden of Eden or, as I prefer to believe, a recycling of our own energy—"

"Like turning into a cockroach?" I cut in dryly.

"Yes, cockroaches are always a possibility, but maybe the energy in laughter, or a note of music and then, yes, eventually a cockroach, or even human. If there is no loss, there can be no death. Or at least that is how I sleep at night. It is how I choose to mourn your mother."

It wasn't good enough for me, not at this very moment, not ever.

"But how do we know it's still us, that the… I don't know, our life force, or the energy patterns that make us who we are don't break out into tiny little fractures in a manner, killing off what makes us us! And what about Delia's ghost-thingy, what about what happened to my spirit, to Mum's?"

Jackson didn't say anything; he just moved the box off my lap and wrapped me in the closest thing to a father's hug I'd ever had.

"Khyle, breathe. I wish I could tell you your mother was at peace, that I was sure of it because I had facts and proof, but I can't. I can tell you that I pray she is, that I feel it." I felt his prickly moustache rustle against my chin. I knew his words were only skin deep but they were what I needed.

There was the sound of sock-clad feet on the stairs down the hall followed by Loraline's sleepy pre-coffee, groggy voice. "Khyle? Jackson? We're out of Shreddies and strawberry jam. If you guys want anything at all for breakfast then you'd be—" As she popped her head around the door she stopped, her mouth forming a little O. I pulled back from Jackson. "It's alright, Loraline, I think." Jackson glanced at me questioningly, the hidden meaning of 'do you think you're up for it?' written in the kind fold between his eyebrows made by his worried expression. I nodded, rubbing my nose on my sleeves. Yes, I'm a dignified sort of person.

"How's the coffee situation?" I tried for a light airy tone, but my throat was blocked and sore from all the crying and made my voice sound like it was being pushed through a rusted tube. Loraline leant against the doorframe, her own eyes slightly watery as she watched me. After a moment she held out an arm. Obediently, I got up and let her put it around me, leaning her forehead against mine.

"Overflowing, just for you," she teased.

I paused as she led me away, my fingers lingering on the threshold behind me as I shot a very quick glance over my shoulder. Jackson was holding the photo of me and Mum that Christmas lost in time, his glasses off in one hand as he cried silently. I left before he could look up. He deserved his peace, his moment. I'd known my Mum for a very small period of time; had been able to remember, and been able to love her, even less time. Jackson had that too. He'd known my mother a lot longer, loved her a lot longer, but he hadn't had the... in a way, the twisted gift of the time without her memory. He'd never had a break from having to mourn her. I wondered whether he was crying now because this was an end to her suffering in Sakhush or whether because he believed, like something deep down inside me suspected he did, that this was a continuing sentence to it. What I was afraid of was that Ventram had destroyed my mother's body; he'd killed that part of her, but had her soul, her essence, whatever you wanted to call it, not been *in* her body? So did that mean she'd died, released from Sakhush when her body had been destroyed? Or was she still trapped?

Chapter Twenty-Three

"Nice," I complimented Loraline as I eased as quietly as possible around the door and into what was very clearly Loraline's space within the house. Loraline shrugged, biting the inside of her cheeks to unsuccessfully keep the smug look off her face.

"I try," she sighed, her eyelids fluttering.

I snorted. The room was a kitchen diner taking up at least half of Jackson's bottom floor. Like most of Jackson's house it was a mass of rustic pine, two of the four walls filled with short pine-panelled windows, bunches of fresh herbs, flowers and fruit dangling either side. The kitchen area was black granite worktops on top of flowery curtained drapes disguising the shelving units beneath, a butler's sink, and a dark grey imposing-looking old-fashioned stove indicating the last decade (or century even) ago that the appliances had been replaced in.

Despite its old-fashionedness, it was quite beautifully decorated, reminding me with a pang of the kitchen Mum had had back in the villa in France. The dining table was a seven foot antique of worn light pine, six light-blue- painted iron patio chairs tucked around it. Yellow and blue candles dotted the room in threes on matching squat black iron holders; tulips and wild flowers had been stuck into brown pottery vases, and lined a light-blue-painted dresser in the corner;

and the walls which were not taken up with windows spilling natural light in from the gardens were crowded with handmade shelving units holding mismatched flowered plates, well-used wooden cutlery, a collection of chipped green pottery pots and glass jars of increasing sizes, filled with everything from different shell assortments to brown and wild rice to angelica. It was a mixture of bedlam and disarray but it was bedlam and disarray done classily and done well.

Right now, cereal boxes, a basket of shop-bought croissants, mini blueberry muffins and English muffins, now half empty with only the flaky pastry crumbs scattered on the table top left, were sitting in the middle of the dining table. Opened pots of apricot jam, honey, Philadelphia and butter lay next to a chopping board, rustic seed bread and a half-eaten packet of New York bagels. On the stove, sausages, bacon, pancakes and scrambled egg were also half-demolished and left in the frying pan or cooking tray, growing cold. And to my greatest pleasure, a six-pack of diet Coke and a steaming pot of black coffee were there too. My stomach felt like it hadn't seen food in a century. Ross and Zean were both at the table trying to demolish what was left of the food in record time. Christ was there, too, though all that was in front of him was a cup of coffee, a glass of something soothing, suspiciously coloured like Scotch, and a makeshift ashtray made from a torn-in-half milk carton overflowing with ash and butts. Skinner was sitting beside him, adding to the milk carton, but also trying to eat and drink at the same time.

Then my eyes fell on a stomach-turner: Mark was watching me cautiously across an overloaded plate of three bagels, sausages, bacon and brown sauce. He ate? He ate that much? What was I saying? He was male. If he was going to eat, it only could be that much.

"Morning, sleeping beauty," Skinner beamed, scrambled egg caught in his moustache. Christ also looked up but seemed to grow even sicker at the sight of me, and scowled down at the coffee in his mug. Zean jumped up, licking his fingers, and pulled over a chair.

"Hey, you okay?" he said quietly as I gratefully sank into it, trying to avoid everyone's eyes.

"Peachy," I muttered as Loraline held out a cup of coffee and a Coke. I accepted both. The only question was which I was going to put down me first. Maybe I should just apply the caffeine intravenously.

"Okay, I've got pancakes, eggs, bacon, sausages. I think there may be a hash brown or two." Zean's head shot up from his plate at the mention of hash browns and held out his already overflowing plate. Loraline glared at him, but filled it up obediently, almost like she was enjoying serving the hapless gorillas. "Obviously, what you see on the table. I can also do porridge, Shredded Wheat—"

I cut her off this time. "I'll work off the table, but, eh" – I screwed my nose up at the state of the used knives and forks which had been shared between the men – "a new plate and knife and fork would be appreciated, and, you know, it probably wouldn't kill you to sit down and have something," I added pointedly, shooting the guys a disgusted look.

Zean caught on quickly, jumping up, mouth half full of potato, pulling up another chair and spluttering crumbs everywhere. "Yeah, you sit, Loraline, you ain't our waitress, right? I used to work at Burger King. I'll get you whatever you want." God, he didn't still have a thing for Loraline, surely? Despite the whole lesbian issue he continued to ignore, had he also become oblivious to the not-all-that-human factor?

Loraline laughed, shaking her head. "No, Zean, you sit. I like serving. Once I've done Khyle I'll sit and eat, promise." She really was enjoying herself. Zean smiled even wider as if he'd just fallen that much more, and returned to his plate, gobbling once more. I shook my head as Loraline passed me a plate, and I reached out for a seeded bagel, thinking I'd take things slowly, see how it went down.

"You really like… serving us?" I couldn't keep the feminist disapproval out of my tone. Loraline went a little pink, sitting down herself with a plate of scrambled egg and shrugging.

"She would. It's how she was raised." I glanced at Mark, who was watching Loraline with that cold, calculating look. Loraline busied herself with her scrambled egg, muttering something along the lines of, "I guess I can't deny everything you bastards ground into me." I wondered for a moment whether that's why she despised Mark; he was a major reinforcer of the principles that had made her an outcast back in that world.

I swallowed my mouthful of bagel. "Well, thank God I don't exist there. I would have been burnt at the stake and accused of blasphemy for reasons that have nothing to do being a witch. I'd rip a man's balls off before he expected me to wait on him or consider him my superior." I aimed it straight at a one-raised-eyebrow Mark, who was smirking at me again.

I shrugged at him. Loraline giggled into her scrambled eggs but it was only half-hearted. I wished I knew about what had happened to her; that way I'd stand a chance of making it better, any way I could. She was more of an annoyingly overbearing angel than a demon, after all.

Christ suddenly took a massive inhalation of breath, looking at something behind me. I glanced over my shoulder, and Jackson had just entered the room. "Well, now we're *finally* all together," he grunted, stressing *finally* to the point of plain outright rudeness.

Ross glared at him over his orange juice. "Christ, man, can't it wait for us to eat, at least?"

Christ gave Ross a meaningful look of authority, but it was Mark who threw down his fork with a clatter. "No, he's right, the sooner everyone here understands the threat, the better."

I felt my eyebrows shoot up even as I felt the last ounce of fight in me start to fade. Mark was actually giving positive feedback in this matter now? And here, I thought he despised the human race, me especially, and was looking forward to us perishing in a bright rain of fire.

Apart from the sounds of chewing there was silence. Christ straightened in his chair.

"The threat of Ventram, the threat he holds to our world, our very existence, is now very real. We are not sure of what his next move will be. We can guess. But there are several things we are sure about." If this was a pep talk, Christ needed lessons on the pep part. "One of which is the situation Khyle, Zean, Loraline, and Ma—" Mark leant back in his chair, giving Christ a dry glare. "Yes, well, you too, Mark," Christ continued.

"Situation?" Zean swallowed so hard I saw his Adam's apple bob.

Christ nodded. "Sentel and Cryon; they were given orders to kill you all, orders coming directly from Ventram."

"So? We stopped them. We 're alive; they failed." Zean shrugged.

Christ shook his head, and I swear I saw Loraline wince. Mark also shook his.

"They were given direct orders from their Ti Ilu. They won't stop until you're dead or they're dead. They're both warriors; it's how they're trained. Honour. You, us, with a heartbeat is a disgrace to that honour. Basically, you're on the equivalent of the FBI's most wanted."

"But we're not even a threat. I mean, we're nothing, right? Seems like a bit of a waste of time," I sighed, eyes closed. I really was at the end of my tether.

"It doesn't work like that. The fact that you're easy targets, just means they'll come faster." Mark's voice had grown much softer, regretful. I glanced up at him. His eyes held mine, and for a moment

I just wanted to have him hold me. I shook it off fast, straightening up.

"Is there a way to kill... your kind?"

"Of course there is. We're not indestructible," Loraline gushed fast, trying to encourage me.

"Could have fooled me," I laughed bitterly.

There was a moment of silence after that "Well?" Zean demanded.

Christ and Ross exchanged a look. "Anything that cuts off the heart or brain. So, bullets. You have to get them through first, though. They can dissipate the energy from a flying bullet so that by the time it reaches them it's going about the speed of a feather. Really, it's only the methods in which they're trained that make them so lethal... " Ross trailed off a bit, glancing over at Mark who purposely pretended not to notice, glaring at the wall behind me.

Ross exchanged a much more prolonged look with Christ this time, Christ eventually cutting it off to continue. "Ventram wants to fulfil prophecy, he wants anti-Lexis to conquer our own Lexis, but on a basic level what he really wants is survival of his own race, and the only way he can achieve that is through us."

"Huh?" Zean snorted.

"They feed off us, Zean," I croaked.

Zean spun around in his chair. "Bloody hell, what?" he spluttered. I swallowed.

"They can survive for long periods just on normal food, but ultimately they need to replace their energy source, which is where the human race, or anything alive on this planet, comes in," Jackson cut in, calmly poring himself a cup of coffee, all signs of tears or pain wiped clean, leaving only a cool collectedness.

Zean shook his head. "They're anti-humans, fine, but I don't get how we became dinner in all that." He sounded like he was going to explode, whereas I had now gone numb.

Mark straightened in his chair, looking Zean straight in the face, almost eagerly. "Well, you see, Lexis is very much alive. To say it thinks for itself is maybe pushing the boundaries a little, but it's close. You see, in the beginning of creation your Lexis won out. In our legend our Lexis takes back the dimension taken from it, which it does by the elevation of its offspring. It started with Ti Ilu, who took Lexis straight into itself, a walking god, and it spread until we were more than just human, we'd evolved to a point you haven't. And one of the aspects of this evolution was the taking in of energy, raw energy. It keeps us immortal, because you can only feed off Lexis once, so instead we feed off a different energy source. You."

Something told me that the green pallor Zean had, Mark was enjoying just that little bit too much. "Hence the whole vampire thing," I muttered to Zean, patting his shoulder. Even with my memories, this was a whole lot to take in.

"So Ventram's trying to fulfil your prophecy; he wants to take over our world?" Zean sounded surprisingly together considering his colour.

"How?" I added, stressing the word.

Christ rubbed his forehead.

"Truth be told, we ain't got no clue. We're just a small branch of a much larger operation, you see," Skinner said, rubbing one of his braids thoughtfully.

"So you're saying the professionals who are defending planet Earth and the human race have been around for a good fifty years and, I quote, ain't got no clue," I said dryly, staring wide-eyed at the table.

I heard Mark laugh outright and shot him a livid glare. He swallowed it, holding his hand up defensively. "Your words," he muttered.

Christ looked awkwardly at the table. "Nomas has got a clue. We're arranging the meeting as we speak. It's not just the UK; the organization is spread all over the world. We'll know more soon. But that isn't something for anyone here to worry about. Everything you have seen is classified. If any of this gets to press you are endangering a very fragile state within our economy. There would be anarchy, religious rebellions; it doesn't bear stating what could happen. None of you three will have any more to do with any of this."

Zean jumped up from the table, hands planted firmly down on the wood as he leaned over towards Christ. "You cannot shut us out. Not after everything we've seen. We need to be part of this."

Christ, equally, shot to his feet. "Don't you think, boy, some people sitting at this table have lost enough?" That was like taking a bullet. "And what could any of you do anyway? You'd be dead within an instant," he shouted, his face blood red with anger, fading blond hair falling over his forehead where a vein throbbed under his worn, wrinkled skin.

Zean leant back a bit but wasn't giving up that easily. "Well, actually I'm a pretty bloody impressive mathematician unless all the freelancing I've done for Jackson has gone unnoticed. That gorgeous woman over there" – he pointed to Loraline, who swallowed the last of her scrambled egg down the wrong way – "is not only a witch, but has inside knowledge of the people you're fighting" – Loraline shook her head eyes wide; I tried not to smirk – "and she, well, she actually saved your worthless life unless you hadn't noticed."

Zean sat back down quickly, pleased with his speech. Skinner beamed as if he'd forgotten.

"Yeah, forgotten to say thanks for that, little lady," he said, cheeks pink over his grey-yellow beard as he held out a gloved hand.

I rolled my eyes. "Don't thank me. If it hadn't been for me, you wouldn't have been lying there in the first place, and besides, really it's an eight-foot high walking statue you have to thank."

Skinner nodded blankly, hand still extended. I took it, shaking it even as he bent down to kiss it. I withdrew it as fast as I physically could.

"You will help, Zean, but this is army business and you, like me, have to help in a much more subtle way. You all almost died." Jackson tried to pacify Zean who glared at the table, a glint of something abnormally dark in his eyes.

"Don't you ever talk to them about damned army business, old man," he spat.

"Zean!" I gasped, shocked.

Zean jumped up from the table, almost knocking it over as he said, "This has jack to do with army business. This is human business, and I know you think can deny it at the moment, but it won't be long before this gets out of hand and out in the open. This is all our war, and we all have a right to know and defend ourselves against the truth because in the end it's going to be us who fights." His eyes never left the table, his tone never grew past a calm flat pitch, but when he walked quietly from the room no one said a word. Because he was right. If Nomas couldn't control it before it got too far, we could really be looking at the apocalypse, just not the way we envisioned it.

"Please tell me how we can help," I said. "I don't want to try and cross you, Christ; frankly I don't have the strength at the moment. But my mother died for this, and I don't want to sit back and watch the world fall to pieces. I don't think I actually, physically, can."

Christ held my gaze sombrely, and then nodded slowly. "We'll see. But for now I'm putting you, Zean, and Loraline under protection. We'll have someone watching your house, maybe an escort every now and then," he sighed, dropping all eye contact.

I glanced over at Mark. "I don't need human protection, Khyle. Not from Cryon." He stressed Cryon's name, seeming to be highly amused just by the idea.

"I don't know. You don't look too brilliant from your last encounter with your student," I said sardonically, letting my gaze wander over him. There were two deep gashes in his throat, almost meeting in the middle, one eye was black, his nose broken, and that was just above the shoulders. Mark tilted his head, eyes slanted aggressively. I returned the glare.

"Surely you don't need a reminder of how well trained I am at taking care of myself," he hissed through his teeth.

I rolled my eyes. "Ooh, look, a threat from you. How original. Besides, maybe you're getting rusty, too much time out of the firing line." I didn't know why, but being mean to him almost helped. Mark didn't say anything; he just shrugged, emotionless.

I felt my eyes narrow. That wasn't a good enough response, not now.

"Where did you go? When my mother was being destroyed by Ventram? What, were you scared, afraid you couldn't take him? Couldn't stop it? So thought you'd hide like the exiled, weak coward you really are!" I finally ended in a shout, leaning over him as he sat back, relaxed, looking at me blank-faced.

"I'm sorry, Khyle. I though you wanted your mother dead. The burden you saw her as." He hardly moved his lips but I felt my anger choke me, and stepped back from the table.

"Don't listen to the obnoxious—" Loraline began, but I held a hand up.

"No. He's right. They reduced my Mum to something I saw as pathetic. Once upon a time I did want her dead." I whispered the last bit.

Mark snarled, satisfied he'd read me correctly, as always. "Mm, and they say humanity has no demonic side," he whispered, rising from his seat, his eyes not leaving mine.

"I hate you." I swallowed back the tears so my voice stayed steady, but they rolled down my cheeks. Mark brushed the tears from my cheek. I felt my eyes flutter shut as I turned my head away from his touch.

"There's a fine line between love and hate, Khyle. I should know; I've been walking it the last few centuries."

Mark walked swiftly past the table, but Ross jumped to his feet, grabbing my elbow and pulling me away to one side. "Khyle, look, I know your feelings for him are messed up at the moment. I'm not entirely sure why because the whole thing's rather obvious to me. But whatever; your issues. But we need you to talk to him, now, before he drives off," Ross said in a rush, a little frantic.

I gaped at him. "Excuse me? About what?" I boiled.

Ross hesitated, and then just came out with it. "We need him. In Nomas he was their man. He can really help us, he knows their tactics, he knows how they were trained. Hell, he went up against Cryon and he's still got a pulse, albeit an irregular one." He obviously saw that he wasn't getting anywhere by the look of disgust on my face. "He'll only listen to you—"

"He hates me!" I cut him off, exasperated.

"Well, we both know that's a lie!" Ross snorted.

I rolled my eyes. For the first time I could seriously believe that Ross really was blind and deaf, no matter how strong a psychic he claimed to be, because only a blind-deaf man wouldn't be able to notice the sparks of utter hatred that flew through the air within ten minutes of me and Mark being enclosed in the same space together.

"Look, do it for the sake of humanity," Ross added melodramatically, even he not taking that line seriously. I scoffed, knocking his hand away.

"If that" – I pointed in the direction Mark had disappeared – "is the last sake for humanity then I'm off to Barbados to spend the end of days."

As I walked out of the kitchen and into Jackson's book-cluttered living room, I had every intention of finding Zean and seeing whether he was as ready as I was to get out of here, but Ross's words rang in my head so loudly he could have been speaking in my mind. In fact, I had a sinking feeling he might have been. He was right. Mark had left the front door open and was trying to light a fag outside his car. I wrapped my arms around myself and walked up to him.

"What?" he spat, holding a blunt between his teeth.

"Got another one of those?" I challenged.

"No."

"Liar."

Mark rolled his eyes, holding me out a tin and passing over his Zippo, keeping his hands cupped around the flame so it didn't flicker out in the breeze.

I took a drag, holding his gaze. "Did Ross—?" I began.

"Offer me a position in the rookie military hall of fame. I declined," Mark finished for me, flicking the car open

"Mark, wait, just listen to me. Maybe it's a good idea. I mean, you said it yourself: you were born to fight, made to, and you're brilliant at it. No one can match you."

"You're not good at flattery, Khyle. Your eyes give it all away," he smirked, enjoying it all the same.

I shrugged. "It was fact, not flattery. Mark, they tortured you, they betrayed you as much as you think you betrayed them. What better way to repay them than to turn everything they conditioned you into against them?"

Mark shook his head slowly. "You really should stop making a habit of insulting me and then asking me for favours," he sneered.

I drew in a breath. "Maybe I just always want to insult you and occasionally have to ask for favours, rather than the two going together as some kind of ploy." Mark went to get into the car. I touched his shoulder. "Mark." He looked down at my hand. I withdrew it like his glance could turn it to fire. He turned, slowly captivating me with his stare.

"I have no loyalties to this world," he breathed, his eyes sweeping over me.

"What about me?" My voice was as small as I felt next to him.

Mark moved closer, cutting off the cold of the wind.

"You despise me."

I felt like a rabbit trapped by a wolf. "I don't despise you. Mark. I wish I did. I despise what you've done. I don't know what to feel about you." I couldn't look away from how the silver in his eyes warmed, or how the hard lines his thick black eyebrows were usually drawn into softened.

"That was honest," he muttered seriously.

I shrugged. "Happens occasionally."

He laughed and I managed to smile a little, the tense muscles in my back uncoiling ever so slightly. I leant back against the car, feeling dizzy, and letting the bud fall to the floor.

"Are you okay?" I glanced up. His voice was really soft; everything about him, down to the way his hand was tilting my chin up so that he could look into my eyes, was for the first time purposely, and a bit unnaturally from Mark, tender.

I nodded. "So what do you think?"

Mark looked away, that jaw muscle twitching. I bit my bottom lip to stop from smiling at the gesture.

"Are you sure it's not just so that you have a way of knowing what's going on within Nomas?" he smiled.

I stared up at him, shaking my head ever so slightly. How could it go from one moment wishing he'd just die, just keel over and leave me and my life alone, and the next feeling like my knees would collapse under me so that I had to grip the door of a car to stop from melting like butter, and I wouldn't have left his side for the world.

"We got the rough end of the stick, huh? We'll always hate each other. I mean, we're made from opposites," I whispered, looking away. For the first time I believed what he'd said: my spirit did want his, just to be around his own, whether I was happy about that or not.

Mark shook his head slightly, still close, still searching my face. "Not always hate, Khyle."

I put a hand on his chest, pushing myself out of my trapped position between him and the car. "I'd best go in and see Ross, then," he sighed, slamming the door shut. "It would seem I have a new job."

I nodded, sticking my thumbs into the back pockets of my jeans as I walked back up to Jackson's house beside him, staring at the grassy ground. "Mm, and on the bright side, if you get back into practice you might not get beaten up so badly next time." I shrugged, smiling up teasingly as he began to glare. It took him a long moment to realize I was teasing him, for fun, not malice. He laughed somewhere between surprised and unsure. That seemed to sum up perfectly everything that existed between us.

Epilogue

And at this very moment, watching the world fall apart, I'd really give for one… last… freaking… fag. I leant back from my laptop, reading and re-reading the type glowing on the screen in the oppressing darkness cast by tonight's cloudy sky. I'd effectively just sealed a profitable way to survive a possible apocalypse. If the end came, I'd be the first one with the story even if this particular piece was a little bit more of an emotional vent than an emotive propaganda piece to keep mankind's hopes up. I'd managed to keep my job at *O.O.* after a series of serious beggings and a week of running countless errands for Blain that a personal assistant would have turned their nose up at.

I leant back against the cool metal of the swing, slowly pushing the screen down and losing the majority of my light source. I was sitting in the park where Mark had first taken me. I'd been coming here a lot lately when sleep felt like too much of a daunting process; I snuck out of bed and came down here in the middle of the night. Zean would have killed me if he knew. Ross, who'd been on the last week of surveillance, was either letting it slide, guessing I needed alone time, or was actually asleep in the blue SUV he sat in most of the day and night directly outside Zean's. I closed my eyes against the cold and damp in the air, grateful for the shocks and shivers that were keeping me on an almost constant insomnia kick. I no longer thought I could remember a life before Blackleigh, a life before the bizarre, the scary and the downright gross. But it didn't feel unbelievable any more. In a lot of ways, what had become of my world made a lot more sense to me than the half-life I'd lived before. I finally had a past, even if my future and everyone else's was in dire question.

There was a rustle of dry winter leaves being crushed against the ground. I jumped to my feet, having to grab my laptop, which slipped down my legs as I blindly staggered around blinking in the dark. Absurdly, my first instinct was to see the nightmarish (meant very literally in my case) looming form of Ventram sneaking out of the woods with a chainsaw though he certainly wouldn't need one to wipe me out. But there were just the shadowy gaps between the trees, and the sounds of the occasional owl, and the trickling of running water in the streams a few yards away in the mass of oaks and pines. I felt my shoulders sag, my eyes slipping down, my hand already reaching reflexively to rake through my hair. I paused in mid-motion. At first glance it looked like two dozen hovering topaz crystals were glistening from behind a set of bramble bushes, and then they each blinked out, two sets at a time and at different times.

I walked forward, unfazed and crouching down closer to the ground. I had to press my lips together to stop from muttering out loud, "Grandma, what big eyes you have" as a familiar russet wolf appeared, ears standing straight up on her head, tongue lolling out of her jaw at one side, making her look more like an Alsatian than a wild animal. She padded up to me, crunching the winter remnants under her padded paws, jabbing her muzzle into my chest so hard I almost fell backwards. I caught myself on one outstretched arm and obediently ran my fingers through the coarse fur between her ears. Four bundles of different russet shades of fluff ran out afterward, jumping after each other, teeth digging into their brothers and sisters as they fought to get to their Mum and her midwife.

I giggled, the sound very loud in the quiet night. "Hey little ones, you're so tiny, aren't you?" I crooned, quickly moving my hand away from one as it went to bite me playfully. That swell of love pulsed inside me; how so much love, something so beautiful, could radiate from something so simple, something we take for granted that's given freely in our world. The memory of all those animals crying out in fear and anguish one second, and then just gone the next on the cliffside that awful morning, wiped the smile from my face in an instant and replaced it with a whiff of strong, heady nausea. I leant over a little, feeling dizzy. All five heads sprang up alert, the playing pups scrambling up from the ground and bounding off into the woods. "Hey," I shouted after them, scrambling up as well, and pushing through the brackets of branches, hit by a wave of fear of losing something so precious, even if it was just from my line of sight.

I skidded down the grove where the stream was rushing by, icy and musical. Five sets of fuzzy heads tilted straight back towards the sky, a chorus of five musical howls ripping through the night air. A full silvery crystal ball of a moon appeared from behind a break in the heavy, twisting clouds. I frowned, bemused, but then something caught my eye. There, reflected in the stream, was a wavering reflection of the moon. Hovering right behind it, about half the size but equally as bright-skinned, was an emerald green orb, the night sky behind it rippling like a black curtain. I swallowed, feeling my eyes widen. I'd seen something like that at least a hundred tormented nights before, except it had been reversed, the emerald had been the large one, and our moon had lurked behind in its wake.

My chin shot up to the sky, but there was just our moon, slowly disappearing as a cloud drifted over it. I felt like Alice staring open-mouthed through the looking-glass. Question was, how long would the glass stay before it melted away? The veil was thinning, our world weakening. As I stared down at the thumb-sized green speck I refused to believe that this, 2012, would be the beginning of the end.

It was just the end of the beginning.